Wishbinder

Hayley Ann Solomon

**CALUMET
EDITIONS**
Minneapolis

CALUMET EDITIONS
Minneapolis

SECOND EDITION DECEMBER 2022

WISHBINDER

10 9 8 7 6 5 4 3 2

ISBN: 978-1-960250-60-5

Cover design by Raoul Solomon
Book Design by Gary Lindberg

Contents

Book 2: of Earth

Wishbinder

Hayley Ann Solomon

Book 1: of Elvenswolde

Only a Potion

The Wish Maker removed his spectacles, flinging them with such force they bounced on two manuscripts, landing with an unfortunate dent on the polished marble floor. The duty elf scrambled to pick them up, but the damage was clearly done: a twisted temple and a suspiciously cracked lens. Oops. Not good. But that may have been the light.

Or a streak of yesterday's egg yolk.

Hard to tell.

He placed them warily on the table, stepping back with a kind of respectful half bow, half stumble. *Definitely* with a stupid smile across his face. Which he turned into a cough.

The Wish Maker raised his brows, but refrained from transforming him into a one-eyed newt. Or an ipsichochal virus. Which was good. Decidedly on the good side.

'Thank you, Bickle.'

Ah, a thank you. Even when angry, the Wish Maker had manners. A very nice man, given his greatness. Yet he did not look pleased.

No surprises there—he wasn't.

The memo he glared at could only be regarded as a pathetic piece of scrap. The kind of sorry excuse for a wish that should long have been filtered with the scullery waste, never mind finding its way past the ancient crystal scales. Terribly inferior in both spelling and animus, it was worded with *precisely* the type of poor precision he'd come to expect of make-shift, part-time emergency staff.

As for content, he beheld nothing but bombast and bigotry. *So distasteful for a wish bubble, but, bubble he'd have to make.*

He sighed. Moments like these? He hated his job. He felt dirty. He wiped his fingers on the lining of his robe, contemplating resignation. A satisfying moment.

Then he breathed. Deep, undulating breaths designed to contain his displeasure. He was only partially successful. Anger is inflammable—Wish Maker anger *particularly* so. The parchment began to smoulder.

Bickleberry could see wisps of smoke begin to creep quietly round the note's edges. The Wish Maker absently snapped his fingers, restoring the damaged spectacles to pristine condition. They sat on the edge of his nose with a definite wisp of yolk dangling from the lens. Ah, so that answered *that* question!

Bickle wondered if Ramón would end up setting the turret alight and stifled another chortle. It came out as an unconvincing splutter. Then a choke. Then a horrendously horrific wheeze.

'Now, Bickle, son of Elstar, you can wipe that stupid smirk right off your face! If you think this is amusing, I can find an errand that is less so, for you.'

That did it. Bickle stopped smiling.

Ramón, most noble Wish Maker, waited a moment before nodding.

'I need the truth! All of it! Who *dares* send me these miserable excuses for wishes, and why are they not being stopped on the second floor? If this is some kind of bottling-room prank, I'd advise you to speak fast!'

The Wish Maker glared. Bickle swallowed. His cheeks looked pale and strangely green, perhaps a reflection of the turret's half-light.

He cleared his throat.

'It's not a prank, sir! The sorting room's gone mad, I swear it! If you don't believe me, see for yourself, may it please you, sir. Or ask Scattadew!'

The second floor was very close to the official sorting room, where wishes were bottled, weighed, and quantified.

Officers of the Department of External Dream Regulation assessed almost constantly for urgency and rationality. Unreasonable wishes (by far the majority!) were given ridiculous price tags. In the normal course of events it would take years for a price to be paid. Decades, hundreds, sometimes thousands of earth years before dull wish bottles burst into the brightness of ripened luminescence.

Messenger elves were tasked with transporting ripe bottles carefully to the turret of the queen's tower. That is what Bickle and Xanadel had been doing all afternoon.

They'd been promoted to messengers, because a pair of elves (nasty, uppity creatures, only a year older than they were, but with *such* attitude) had recently been promoted to the first tower. And, holy mackerel, damn dumpling fiddlesticks, it was by Royal warrant!

The elves did not know what to make of their promotion, for on one hand, the new job was quite excessively interesting. On the other, it was incredibly hard work running up and down the thousands of curved marble steps that linked the fourth tower's turret with the larger hall on the second floor below. Elfin slippers were very fine, so Bickle expected quite a few blisters, if not actual bunions, to appear.

Still, it meant that they now wore the queen's livery and dined in her kitchens, which was much better than the open scullery under the watchful eye of Madame Knorr.

You don't want to know about Madame Knorr—a vile woman, too ready with her corrector wand. And of course, the trouble with a corrector wand (apart from the pain) is that it always leaves those fairly obvious purple smudges. They linger for days, leaving one open to embarrassing questions of how one acquired them in the first place.

Madame Knorr's wand had the nastiest manner of pointing out culprits—no chance to yell 'escalantes arius'—very unsporting. (For those unfamiliar with such matters, the escalantes chant is really the most basic of magic, and very effective against trifling matters like toothache, insect bites and temper tantrums. Bickle was not sure about corrector wands but he'd always thought it worth a damn good try.)

He was sick to death of dining on boiled ollingstranga and very happy to escape the clutches of Madame Knorr, but could not help wishing that he'd been sent to the king's tower like Silvajar and Garredung.

Bickle would have loved to sneak a peek at his majesty's residence. It was critical for maintaining Elvenswolde's balanced position with the six other worlds, meaning access was widely restricted.

Not for the first time, he sighed, He *did* retain a modicum of common sense. Setting off the king's alarm and facing the consequent enchantments was not a prospect that appealed.

He might envy Garredung and Silvajar, but he would not put his life in jeopardy. Besides, it was no hardship to be rid of the sight of their sour, pointed faces every day.

'Well?'

Bickle wriggled. Ramón's grip was like a vice. Worse, the Wish Maker had long, elegant nails that were digging into his bare flesh.

Probably unintentional—the Wish Maker was strict, but not cruel. Still, it was undignified and kind of hurt.

'Sir, the bottles are ripening faster than the second floor can weigh the wishes!'

'Why are they being bottled before they are actually weighed?'

Ramón's voice was soft, but the elves were not fooled. Bickleberry remained in a firm grip. He pretended not to notice.

'I don't know, sir, but the weighing room is buzzing with activity. We have a bag of wishes still unopened on the crystal scales. The master weigher refuses to attend to it until the last bags are dealt with, but it's becoming harder to simply ignore.'

'Why?'

'Strange fumes are emanating from the sack. Nice: you know? Lime and lavender and lilac lilies, sir, but then it seems to deepen. Liquorice—'

The wizard's expression changed. He released Bickleberry with a gentle tap. 'Don't tell me! I will hazard a guess: Asphodel, argo, arrowroot, fungus, fenugreek, dill, dirt, dung—'

'Don't continue, sir! We are presently all at the dung stage. Not white unicorn either, by the smell of it!'

Xanadel interrupted. 'Of course not. More like ferret and stoat, though we don't know how they can be so far abroad.' The wizard thought he knew, but said nothing.

'What does it mean, sir?'

'It means, my dear Xanadel, that the master weigher must stop dithering. He must open all bags immediately! If he can't manage, he must call up the second lieutenant. This is no time to quibble over precedence. Dung—no matter how foul—progresses to measles, maggots and meticlaws—you particularly don't want that!' He turned from the window.

'Bickle, go tell the master weigher at once. Tell him it is by order of Ramón the Wish Maker. Here, I will sign a note.'

The elves blinked as the Wish Maker's signature flickered through the air like a curved lightning bolt prefaced by a spiralling capital R. He handed a sheet of ultra-thin crystal—more durable than parchment—to the younger of the elves. The signature was still glowing on the page.

'In the meanwhile,' he said, 'Might I suggest you increase the price of a basic wish by tenfold—I can't be expected to stand here all day turning ugly frogs into princes. So tedious. Not to mention the tiresome business of turning pretty faces spotty, or plain faces pretty. I'm beginning to lose my patience. Now Bickleberry, son of Elfstar, go! No dawdling! I don't have all day, and there is a pewter pot I particularly need to tend.'

Bickle bobbed a bow and quickened his pace down the marble stairwell. A thousand steps! If only he had the courage to slide down the banisters! They were so highly polished, he was certain he could speed up his delivery times. He sighed. He would probably land up in trouble again.

He wished he could stay, to hear Ramón. When he conversed with the elves—which was not often—what he said mattered, somehow.

Now, he could just hear the last of the Wish Maker's words as the great oak door high above creaked slowly closed.

'Xanadel, be warned—'

The door shut and there was nothing more to hear save the clatter of saucepans and the sudden howl of Finchley, the elf watcher. Lord Eltham's corrector wand had just smacked him smartly for taking a midday snooze.

* * *

In the tall tower that overlooked three of Castle Carne's turrets, the dark forests and the winding, cobbled roads beyond, the Wish Maker looked grave.

'Xanadel,' he said, 'be warned—the very heart of Elvenswolde is out of balance. It may be nothing, just a fine adjustment required, but I wonder. I wonder—' The Wish Maker broke off mid-sentence. He strode quickly to a small alcove in the turret where a fire was burning. A pot hovered and mischievously bounced above the polished floor. No chains, of course, just magic.

'Here,' he said. 'Watch this. There is lichen and tarragon in it, mixed with the pewter of the brewing bowl and the faintest twinkle of a Lindolucian lightning star.'

(As if that meant anything to Xanadel!)

His voice hushed a little. Xanadel could see the whiteness of his beard as spoke. It was almost luminous in its brightness, trailing to small wisps at the end.

'If the brew turns purple, add a vial of candlelight. If it lightens to white, call me. Call, for the brilliance may blind. I'm sorry I must leave you without assistance, but my silly apprentice elf has been taken to the sick bay with a sudden case of the stickles. You don't mind, do you?'

The wizard ignored Xanadel's frightened gaze. 'Ah. I thought not. Now remember, candlelight for purple—' But his words were fading even as he was. Xanadel blinked. It seemed that the Wish Maker was lighter, translucent, and more delicately transparent than usual.

He looked a bit like a pencil tracing, all leached of colour. On the next blink, Xanadel was entirely alone in the tower's turret. Alone, that is, but for the creeping feeling of being watched and the nasty, ever-popping, bubbling of a hovering pot.

Xanadel hoped that the brew would turn to purple. He had no idea where the great Ramón had disappeared, so it would be impossible to call him back. Where *was* he, for heaven's sake? People did not vanish for no reason. Not even Wish Makers.

Was he consulting his majesty? Perhaps he was striding the furthest shores of Elvenswolde, where the trees whisper secrets and the waves shiver sands like water bearers. In the East of Elvenswolde, he knew that the seas still frothed with half tides—the soft, echoing secrets of the deep. It would take a Wish Maker to understand, a Wish Maker to decipher the markings left on the shore, the sands random on the beaches, each grain a secret in itself.

Was that where he'd gone? But no, perhaps he'd wandered further, to one of the six worlds beyond Elvenswolde, to the land of the pearl white moon, where the seventh son of a seventh son wandered across the sun-soaked earth, growing to manhood and his powers.

Xanadel blinked. He must stop imagining nonsense. He must be dizzy, in this high tower, feeling creepy. This was no time to be thinking of the myths, the ancient legends passed down from sage to sage, minstrel to minstrel, until it was impossible to tell how much of it was honest Elvin truth and how much fantasy.

On Earth, it was told, man walked unaware of the magic of the grasses and the secrets of the plains. It was there, in the sixth world, that the wishes were appearing, unbalanced and unbottled, outrageous, whimsical, simple, complex, greedy—altogether too greedy— for the delicate balances of Elvenswolde.

Xanadel could feel the weight of some dark shadow upon his chest. But the potion—he was an idiot! He was forgetting the potion! The smoke was now too thick to see; too dark to lean forward and make out any colours in the swirling pewter—he blinked.

His eyes were watering, so he brushed away stupid elfin tears and peered at the pot entrusted to him. He was fearful—so fearful—of white, the dazzling white that might blind him. How was he expected to call for Ramón when his voice was voiceless and his tongue mute against the magic the wizard might have passed through?

Xanadel was both annoyed and scared. He was only a junior messenger, for crying out loud! How could he just be abandoned with some demon pot? One that might forever remove his sight? Dangerous stuff. The Wish Maker must be out of his mind!

The smoke lifted. Xanadel breathed a sigh of relief. All was well. He could cope with purple, and the brew was now a strange mixture of pink flecked with twinkles of lapis lazuli. Ah, now the pinks and the blues were mixing. He reached for the candlelight. There was no need for the wizard's flourish of labelling, for the flame flickered quite clearly in its prison.

To Xanadel, who'd been dealing in common magic since he was out of elfskins, the ingredients were simple and rather obvious. No need to check, like if it had been amberweed or sarspinel, both similar, yet deadly if confused. No, candlelight was easy enough. He uncorked the bottle. The potion was now stabilising—yes, a quite definite purple.

A deep, velvety violet that was pleasing to look at, a purple of promises—Xanadel forgot the candlelight, unstoppered in his palm. He leaned over for a closer look.

He shouldn't, he knew, but the fumes were beginning to furl and unfurl about him like smoke sprites and he was feeling less sensible than usual. Sensible Xanadel. He smiled mistily and bent closer to the bowl.

'Don't touch that!'

Ramón clicked back and the air cleared almost visibly. His fingers spread and the sliver of candlelight emptied itself obediently into the pot. A flash of colour transformed the purple into silver.

'Xanadel, son of Septimus, what did you feel just now?'

'I, sir?'

Goosebumps? Xanadel felt cold prickles on his skin. Each hair seemed to stand out as individual entities. He shivered. Nasty.

The Wish Maker was back and his trance-like state was gone. He felt very much as though a bucket of water had just been thrown over his head. He was surprised at the Wish Maker's interest.

Wish Makers did not usually bother with elves, nor their feelings.

He was relieved that Ramón did not seem angry anymore. Or possibly inclined to send him to a river of troubles to fish for nasty notions, which had once happened to Silvajar. (Or so it was whispered, behind his back.)

'I? I felt pulling, sir. The type of pulling that made me want to look deep into that pot, to part with my innermost thoughts, to—but that is impossible, sir, it's only a potion!'

'Never say "only a potion," Xanadel! Some brews are deadlier than others, some wishes deeper and darker than an innocent like you might imagine. It is not just riches and rainbows I deal in, child. I wish it were. I am not some wizardly Santa. I don't only deal in the stuff of dreams, the light-hearted wishes on stars and tooth fairies.

'By the way, all but three of the ancient tooth fairies have died out, you know—the bulk of the tooth wishes are now bottled on level three, just a story up from the sorting room—much more efficient, with an excellent process for the reintegration of tooth enamel—fascinating, but I mustn't digress.

'No there are wishes, Xanadel, that challenge and disturb. There will always be dark wishes—there needs to be, for balance, but when the balance shifts, I worry about the matter. Who, for example, has paid the price? How have these darker desires ripened in their bottles so quickly?'

Xanadel stared. He had not thought much on the matter.

'Do you know what the price of a wish is, Xanadel?'

Xanadel felt foolish. He'd never thought to ask.

'A lot?'

Ramón rolled his eyes.

'Ummm, bravery?' It was a wild guess, but hey, he had to guess something!

'Sometimes. The commonest wish is granted for saving a fairy's life or for kindness beyond the usual reserve. Most times the wishers do not realize their wishes have been granted. They think it good luck, or fate, or the product of hard labour.'

'Do they ever know?'

'Occasionally, if they happen upon a fairy in one of the old places. The type that is still dappled with half-magic, half-earthlight. At
these times, a fairy might step forward and grant a wish, but always
she will sprinkle a vial of forget-me-dust over her subject, so that her
very existence seems more fantasy than truth.'

'Do those wishes get lodged here, at Castle Carne?'

The Wish Maker nodded. 'Every single wish is lodged with us.
It is the old lore, deeper than granite, wilder than the winds that blow
through Elvenswolde and the lands beyond it.'

The door at the bottom of Ramón's suite of turret rooms opened,
tinkling its melodious alarm.

The Wish Maker raised his brows and waited for footsteps to
draw near. It took a while—a thousand steps is rather a lot for an unfit
elf. Xanadel heard panting and a strange thumping all the way up the
cold, marble stairwell.

The Wish Maker was the first to speak. 'Ah, Bickleberry! You've
returned with a heavy—and rather foul-smelling sack, I see.'

Bickleberry was groaning under his latest load of wishes.

'Set them down, over there, for I have no wish for my immediate
person to reek of meticlaws! Foul stuff. I shall be obliged, I suppose,
to attend to the matter later if I still have strength after this evening's
work!'

Xanadel stepped forward to help Bickleberry. He found that if
he closed his nose and was careful to take only a few gasps of air now
and then, the pungent smell was not as disgusting as it seemed.

Bickle looked green. Both elves valiantly stacked the bottles—
all clearly marked by their distinctive luminous purple tops. They
were oozing something so disgusting the elves were hard pressed not
to drop them. Ramón waved them to be seated.

'Not now. I'll send for some elves on punishment duty to finish
the stacking.

'Do you remember, Xanadel, that I once promised I should speak
to you of your father?'

Xanadel nodded, trembling. Not from the meticlaws (though he
still felt faint) but from sudden anticipation.

He had not, for a long while, dared ask anyone about his father. None seemed to know the tale of it, and those that did were strangely silent, even in their songs.

'You, Xanadel, are the first of your generation. The seed, I believe, of all your father's hopes for you. In you was invested his passion, his hope, his great love of Elvenswolde and of the six worlds beyond.

'After you, there were your brothers and they, too, have been gifted with your father's flair, Fairmeade the harp singer, Ganimede the water sprite, Raven the wing bearer and, of course, the twins, Fillament and Scatadew. Six of you, Xanadel and all as fair and as loyal as one would expect of the line of Septimus.'

Xanadel coloured, for he had not known that Ramón took such an interest.

Bickle flashed him a look with raised brows. Xanadel thought he might laugh. He was just an ordinary elf, after all, no big deal.

'There was a seventh son born that you know little of, birthed in the alignment of the stars known as animus, on the seventh day of the night of the seventh moon. It is of this son, my dear elves, that I wish to speak.'

Bickleberry's eyes were bright with astonishment, but Xanadel swallowed. He felt suddenly all trembly and was terrified Ramón would trail off or disappear, or suddenly change the subject, as was often his custom.

'We are listening,' he prompted eagerly.

One Hundred and Eighty-Two Lines

Barefoot, Septimus ran—faster, faster, until he could feel his pulses literally pushing, tick-ticking like a mechanical clock gone berserk. He ditched the hot pavement to cut across the open paddock of scratchy, yellowed grass. Prickly, but quicker.

Behind him, the shadow of Mt. Arthur peaked high above the sea, twinkling with packed snow. He was not in the mood to notice.

He squinted against the sun, slowing only when he reached the iron gates of Rutherham High. They were open, but that was no big surprise. Neither was the quiet. Damn! He'd missed the bell!! Again!

Septimus fished out his sandals and half-jammed his feet into the open frames. Too late to deal with buckles. He swung his pack from back to shoulder and sighed.

Half a world away, that sigh was monitored.

His every breath was monitored, in fact, by a host of bored wish fairies who every now and then made little markings on their charts and occasionally muttered that they couldn't see the point of such a tedious exercise.

Still, they were not paid to see the point, (as they were very often told, along with being stuck with some annoying little task for their impertinence), so they learnt to shut up. If the earth child Septimus, the seventh son of a seventh son, was so important, they'd jolly well do as they were told.

Right now, they marked up the slamming of his heart against his chest and noted that he was creeping down a cool corridor towards his form class.

Bits of old notices dangled from drawing pins, and the familiar smell of wood mingled with chalk as Septimus opened the second door and tried for a little nonchalance.

Josh sniggered (no surprise!) and Tiffany giggled.

Sep ignored her, setting down his pack and wriggling into the seat.

There was a short silence as he hunted for a pen, and an excellent moment when he thought he might have escaped notice. Nope.

Of course not.

Mr Carlisle's hideous smirk burned into the back of his neck like a brand. He knew that if he turned around, he would see the faint sneer he'd been dreading all through the sprint across the wharf. He held out for a moment, but the class had gone silent in expectation.

Damn! He'd have to get this over with. Nothing for it.

Yes, there it was—the smirk.

'May I see your note, young man? I do trust you actually have one?'

Mr Carlisle spoke politely, but the calm voice and the steady hand that stretched itself towards Septimus did not fool him at all—not in the least.

Why, for the love of lemons, did he have to get stuck in Mr Carlisle's class? How did the stupid git get to be a teacher anyway? His IQ was marginally lower than Tiffany's and his personal hygiene—Sep would rather not dwell on it.

Most of the form teachers were actually quite ok—just not this one.

Archibald Carlisle was not just boring. He was also—using polite language—an antiquated, ignorant, bigoted idiot of the worst type. (There is no polite word for 'idiot,' Sep reflected ruefully.)

Mr Carlisle was superior without being superior. He was one of those people who never quite got over the fact that teachers were no longer permitted use of the strap.

The class held their breath, for Sep's mum was, well... pretty inventive in her excuses.

Mr Carlisle would sometimes simply crush the notes in his palm, but more often than not, he would read extracts aloud. This mortified Septimus: he would rather be quietly punished, than have the class think his mother a raving lunatic.

Sarah Kahikatea was whispered about everywhere. Though it was said she had the art of healing, it was also said she was—mental. Small town gossip hurt.

On certain evenings she could be seen gazing at the stars, murmuring incantations that none could understand but Septimus. He would stand quietly beside her, imagining power surging through his being, at the simple softness of her words.

'I'm not magical, Septimus, but I understand magic. The old ways were lost to your father when he chose me above his heritage. I watched them fade from his eyes, and from his speech, and even from his dreams, but never, ever from his heart.

'All that I know comes from within, from my beliefs and from my occasional flashes of intuition. It stems from my utmost, enduring love for your father. Septimus, your dad, gave up his world for me, but not, I believe, his whole world. Part of it never left him and part of it has been passed from him to you.

'In the land of Galathgraine and Ramalo, Siluse and Ventrimuse, you are not alone. You have six brothers and two cousins, all elf folk of the finest. Your father was very proud. He spoke of them often before his memories faded.'

When Septimus asked her how it was that she could remember, when his father could not, she only shook her head and sighed.

'The million-dollar question, Sep! I can only imagine your father and I were so close that he might, in a moment of extreme unconsciousness, have ceded his knowledge to me. It always seemed to me that as *his* memories dimmed, *my* intuitions deepened, so it is almost as if I too have climbed the turrets of Castle Carne, or ridden the far plains of Plioth.'

Septimus nodded, half understanding, although the thought of his mother riding anything but a stout pony safely connected to a harness, had him secretly smiling. Sometimes though, he had rare flashes of comprehension. Then they smudged. No doubt though, he longed to enter the world Sarah depicted so vividly.

Something deep inside Septimus resented being just an ordinary boy, doing ordinary things like throwing stones in the river and downloading YouTube clips. He wanted to be what his mother *claimed* he was, the seventh son of a seventh son, born of a different, brighter world, where magic was twined with mystery, where kindness was prized above class.

He was not amazingly rich, but then neither were most of the kids. He pretty much had everything he needed though. Not the best fishing rod—Malcolm Nielson probably had that: all fancy flies and stuff that got tangled with the tackle—but he *did* have a fairly ok rod to dangle over the wharf. He had an unlimited text plan for his iPhone 6 plus, but no actual calling time. (Ok, because there was no one to call other than his grandma in Wellington.)

He had an eleven inch MacBook Air (awesome) and though there were clearly no immediate plans for fibre on the slopes of Mt. Arthur, there *was* free Wi-Fi through schoolbang and throughout the CBD. He was perfectly ordinary, really, which frustrated him, for his mother was so sure he was more special than any person in Rutherham. No, amend that: make that the whole, freaking, entire world!

There were times he would believe. Her eyes grew fiercely intense and she regarded him with a passion he knew to be extraordinary. Kevin Kelp's mum did not look at him like that, and Thomas Mitcham's dad was more likely to clip his ear than tell him he was destined for mysterious and glorious things.

He believed Sarah, for he *wanted* to. Fiercely, he wanted to be more than what he was: a fairly alright looking, slightly gangly boy in a standard kiwi backwater town.

He wanted to be Septimus, son of Septimus, destined for enchantment in the Land of Elvenswolde, and the worlds beyond.

But Mr Carlisle was holding out his hand and Elvenswolde, if it even existed—seemed a *heck* of a long way away!

'Ah, Septimus. How very entertaining.' Mr Carlisle read the words carefully before crumpling the sheet in his hand. Septimus felt crimson with embarrassment and the class booed in disappointment.

One of Mrs Kahikatea's notes was surely worth five minutes of Mr Carlisle's droning voice.

But Mr Carlisle had a nasty expression in his eyes. (Nastier than usual, if that is at all possible.) Tiffany cast languishing glances at Septimus. She 'liked' him. He did not know whether to be comforted, amused or exasperated.

'Septimus Kahikatea, I rather think I'm going to have to punish you this time. Lateness is becoming an unfortunate habit. It cannot be tolerated. No, I really do not think it can be tolerated any longer, do you?'

Septimus said nothing, but his heart sank further into his sandals. What had his mother written? Surely not the truth—that they'd stayed up half the night gazing at the stars? With the eclipse of the moon there came, for those who watched, a glimpse—a smidgeon of a glimpse—into the worlds beyond.

Mirror-like and hazy, but the closest earth could come to the merging of Elvenswolde.

They'd stayed up, in a clearing of native trees just on the eastern slopes of Mt. Arthur. Despite an intent—and icy—search of the night sky, their vigil was useless. A light mist had crept in, obscuring the critical moment. Lost went the small, finite opening into that other world!

As they returned to the house, Sarah swallowed tears—which she tried to hide with an unconvincing fit of coughing and a mild shrug of the shoulders. In the dim light of the kitchen, Septimus saw her eyes wet, red-rimmed and sad. She made tea, stirring far too long with her spoon and jamming her hand defiantly across her face. As if Sep wouldn't notice! He felt like crying himself. Instead, he sliced himself some watermelon and dissected out the pips.

Long after dawn lit the new sky, he stared hard, through his curtained window, at an empty patch of cloud. When he'd finally fallen asleep, not even his alarm clock had been loud enough to wake him.

Now he felt humiliated, small and ordinary. Mr Carlisle seemed to feed off those vibes. The top candidate for the world's worst teacher award was muttering something about 'in his day' and phrases like 'cane, never mind strap.' Boring. He always said that. Boring, boring, boring.

'Septimus, wipe my blackboard clean.'

The school had ordered a whiteboard, but it had not yet been installed. Until Mr Lockwitz, the janitor-cum-football coach actually ordered in a working screwdriver to remove the huge, ancient looking relic, the class made do with chalk.

'The whole one?'

The blackboard stretched across the length of the room and had all of yesterday's work on it, still written in orange and green. Usually a little was rubbed off at a time as needed, but today Mr Carlisle seemed to have other ideas, for he held out the dust wiper and seemed to expect Septimus to start at once.

He did, and sneezed, for a cloud filled the air as he wiped and the whole class watched.

Mr Carlisle did not resume his lessons, he just hovered over Septimus as he cleaned the upper left-hand corner and slowly moved across the room to the right. Small traces of yesterday's lesson were still patchy and visible. Septimus moved back to the left and began again, all the time aware of Mr Carlisle behind him and the class's whispers and snickers and, worst of all, the almost-silence.

Septimus felt everyone was looking at him. He felt both annoyed and stupid and very, very angry.

He knew that Mr Carlisle was enjoying himself. He would kind of like to have punched him. Hard in the gut. But he couldn't. He was stuck with being a kid in an adult's world. A relatively small and ordinary looking child, though he did think he was progressing with his growth spurt.

There was no point giving the stupid, idiotic, moronic man the satisfaction of an argument. He clutched the bloody blackboard duster and wiped.

Behind him, he could hear the high-pitched titter of silly Tiffany's infantile giggles. Not helping. And if she thought that was attractive, she had quite a lot to learn! Two more rows.

When at last he was done, he handed the duster over to Mr Carlisle without looking him in the face. He couldn't, for all the rage he felt.

He walked slowly to his seat, but did not quite reach his desk when the low, gravelly voice grated on his ears once more.

'Not so fast, Septimus. Come back here, if you please.'

Septimus sighed, wondering what new humiliation might be in store. Sometimes he thought the frigging strap might have been better, after all.

'I want you to write on that board, Septimus. I want you to write eight hundred and seventy-two times that you must not be late. In your neatest handwriting, otherwise I might be tempted to have you do it all again. You had better get started, and write small, will you? You will need the space.'

Septimus was handed a piece of chalk. It was white, and new.

'If this takes all day, so be it. If you need to stay after school to finish, I will send your mother a note. That will make a refreshing change!'

There were several snickers.

The boy said not a word. He simply began to write.

Contravention of Wing Bearer Bylaw 101

'I must not be late for school. I must not be late for school. I must not be late—' Septimus concentrated hard. He concentrated all his energy on the chalk in his fingers. He did not want to think about Mr Carlisle, watching him closely, or the class, silent with shock. Mr Carlisle was meaner than usual. No one wanted to be next.

He did not want to think of Malcolm grinning or Tiffany sending him glances of wasted sympathy. He just wanted to write the stupid lines and sit down. He wanted it so much that the very chalk seemed to quiver with his energy.

He ignored the sounds of Mr Carlisle resuming his soliloquy on the thorax of an ant. Or was it a bee? He ignored the sounds of Cameron counting, 'One, two, three, four—he's only on four, Malcolm, it will take all day—' he ignored the heat in his heart and the pounding pain in his head.

He just concentrated on the chalk, up, down, neat, curl a little for the c, remember the full stop. Capital letter up, down, neat—the chalk squeaked a little on the board.

Septimus concentrated. He concentrated more than he had ever done in his life, if only to avoid crying and running out of the damn class like a baby. He wished, more powerfully than he had ever wished before, that the stupid job would be done and he could resume his seat.

He wished that he could wipe the smirk off Mr Carlisle's face. He wished that the chalk would stop fighting him when he was trying so hard to be neat—

What was he thinking of? The chalk wasn't fighting him. Chalk could not fight—he must be mad—but the chalk was fighting him. He needed to grip harder else it would fly from his fingers and shatter on the vinyl floor—it did fly from his fingers.

Septimus held his breath. If the new piece of chalk broke, Mr Carlisle would doubtless have something nastier up his sleeve. He would think he had dropped it on purpose—but the chalk didn't drop!

It carried on writing!

'I must not be late—I must not be late—'

It wrote it faster and neater than Septimus would ever have managed. Faster than lightning, really, for it was already on line seven hundred and sixty-three, all neatly numbered and as straight as if Septimus had been using a ruler. Septimus blinked. He could not believe what he was seeing.

Neither could the class, who were no longer thinking about ants. (If they ever were, at all!) They were watching the board in amazement. At number eight hundred and seventy-two the chalk stopped, hovered a little in the air, returned to Septimus's writing, corrected two of the ells which were untidy and not looped enough for cursive, then leaped back, unmoving, into Sep's hand.

The rage drained out of his system. He quietly turned to face the class.

Mr Carlisle was wearing a rather blank expression, almost as though he had forgotten something rather important and was trying his hardest to remember what it was. He did not look nearly so pompous as usual.

Septimus experienced a kind of prickling sixth sense that told him… that told him Mr Carlisle was not himself. He seemed to be—bewitched. But that, of course, was hardly possible. It was true, however, that his supercilious sneer had vanished, slackening his mouth. His sharp eyes were kind of vacant. Still mean (for Mr Carlisle was that sort of a person—mean in small, petty ways and no amount of magic, however potent, can change the very heart of someone's soul).

So yes, he was still mean, but his face no longer held a sneer. He trembled. It was almost as if some greater force had blown across his being and wiped the very smirk from his face. Sep swallowed. Had that not been the very thing he'd been wishing a few moments before? That the stupid lines be written and the smirk wiped off Mr Carlisle's face?

Gracious jiminy-hopping-crickets, it seemed impossible, but so too was chalk flying across a board at the rate of knots. He hadn't imagined *that*, the evidence was still plainly before him.

'Septimus.'

Septimus was puzzled, expecting an explosion of anger, not a kind of prickling sense that Mr Carlisle was struggling with a force greater than himself and losing. He had not yet turned towards the board, but he had stopped speaking mid-sentence, and the whole class held their breath as they watched him expectantly.

It was only a fraction of a second before he did turn round, and Septimus saw that the vacant look was passing, and his old, sarcastic self was returning in short order.

He looked at the board and the words written on it. He looked at the chalk, lifeless on the ledge of the board and at Septimus, who attempted to appear downcast but could not help looking thrilled—simply thrilled—at his incredible discovery.

'Since you are evidently so good at writing, Mr Kahikatea, I will require you to write faster—far faster—and far neater—in your books in future. You obviously have not been applying yourself properly. Now sit down, if you please, you have quite interrupted matters enough for one day.'

There was a murmur from the classroom that Mr Carlisle ignored until Matilda Mattings started whispering to Tiffany. Then Tiffany began whispering to Septimus, and naturally Mr Carlisle's eye fell upon him again.

Septimus cast his own eyes to the polish on the floor. He had far too much to think about to risk incurring Mr Carlisle's annoyance again. He could fervently wish him to the back of beyond, but he was not sure how strong wishes were, or whether they lasted. His last one hadn't, for the words were fast fading from the board and even now they were only a pinkish smudge of dust. If Septimus dared to even look, he would have noticed at once that Mr Carlisle's smirk was fully returned.

Fortunately, he did n*ot* notice, for he was deep in thought quite apart from needing to avoid further trouble. He did not *know* if he had the power of another wish. He hoped he did, for to have wasted an only wish on some stupid punishment lines was really too horrible to bear.

He wanted to run down to the beach and think the matter through, but naturally he couldn't. He could feel Mr Carlisle glaring daggers at him. Worse, Matilda Mattings seemed set on pointing at the board. It was creating a minor sensation. All eyes were upon him, some admiring, some afraid, some patently disbelieving.

He took up his pen and meekly tried to concentrate on his worksheet. For once, he did not feel ordinary. For once, he kind of wished he did.

Mr Carlisle issued a detention to Matilda—who scowled and murmured it was unfair and was promptly given another. She made a face behind her hands, someone snickered, and the class settled down.

All except Max Jones, who stared at Septimus. Not a nice boy, Max. He seemed very inventive in wishing a whole heap of nasty thoughts. None of them ripened, of course, but the very air seemed to feel their ferocity.

The room permeated a nasty, musty kind of smell. Chalk, tedium and bad wishes. The type that made Sep long to throw open a window or run, run, run down the path, across the bridge, past the wharf and away, away onto the slopes of the nearby mountains. He glanced at the clock. It seemed as if he could hear every slow tick, every creaking tock. He braced himself for a very long morning and sighed.

* * *

The baby dragon stretched. He was very comfortable in his egg. He was in no rush to feel the wind at his back, or the salt of the sea on his scaly dragon tongue. Oh no, no hurry at all. He was snug inside his shell and very content, though his stomach had started to rumble of late and his toes now curled within its little blue shelter like an ivy vine.

Occasionally, he felt a crack, which made him cross and out of humour. A crack meant that his cheerful little home was more fragile than he wanted. A crack meant that he would have to soon face the dawn. He had nothing against dawn—indeed, he had never even seen one—but he thought it might not be as snug as his little shell. His shell was, after all, the only home he knew.

He was not convinced, but he rather thought he was a *lazy* dragon, and lazy dragons did not like climbing cliff faces. Neither did they like careering *off* them. Or flapping infant dragon wings and praying that they would somehow work, first go. What if he had trouble getting the hang of things?

He could not be certain, of course, but he thought he might be precariously placed on a ledge somewhere, and that could mean a spot of bother. Not that he worried about dying—why should he, when he had not yet lived? But he *did* think the whole situation might be a bit awkward.

He sneezed and closed his eyes, tucking his toes in, just an incy bit more. Not enough. A claw caught, causing a light vein to appear on the outer shell. He stifled another sneeze, but it came out as a light rendering of flame. Damn! Double dippity damn damn damn! The inner rim of his little egg home was now kind of smoky, a browny cream. And his ear itched. He tucked it in, ignoring another hairline crack.

Never mind, with some really *brilliant* luck, he had at least another day before he needed to start *actually* worrying. Baby dragonettes—whatever the colour of their eggs—needed naps. Lovely, lingering long naps. He closed his eyes contentedly and yawned.

Yes, another little slumber could do him no harm. Very soon, despite the storms, the howling winds and the rolling of his little shelter (which caused him to flip for the fifth time that day) he fell to drag-on-dreaming.

* * *

Max Jones was open-mouthed. Even he, a relatively below average brain type, could see that normality was suspended. Mr Carlisle, igno-rant of all these undercurrents, stared at the board, neither approving nor disapproving. He looked pale, deflated. A bit like a balloon forgot-ten in a cupboard for a week. Septimus noted, for the first time, that the master's hair was thinning—it was somewhere between mousy brown and grey.

He could see where, in a few years' time, he would go bald. Septimus stopped bothering to write. It was impossible, anyway, for eyes kept wandering to him. Pointless pretending not to notice. He wondered what the hell he was going to say when class got out. The whole situation was more bizarre than fantasy. It was then that Tiffany Trewellyn *pretended* to faint and Martha Manning actually *did*. As Mr Carlisle strode towards them, the door opened and blew in a breeze that felt gentle, smelling of the hills of Willowsham and the hollows of the dells.

A wing bearer flew in. (Not that Septimus, watching him, re-alised he was a wing bearer, *per se*, but certainly he was *not* your average kid!) Dressed in green, his rank sparkled on his shoulder in a shower of glittering stars. Not a particularly *high* rank, as it trans-pired, but definitely a fully qualified, newly credentialled wing bearer. He flew about the class with the swift, sprightly curves of exuber-ance that made flying look like precision short-boarding—only from a height. He drew out a pouch of feather-forged forget-me-dust and sprinkled it everywhere, over chairs, over people, over pot plants and over Septimus himself.

No one seemed to see him, nor, apparently, did he *expect* them to. He stuck a rather rude tongue out at Max then looked bloody, plainly *horrified* when Septimus giggled, apparently aware of his ac-tions.

Such catastrophes as human awareness are not expected, *especially* during the application of fast-acting, permeable, highly infallible forget-me-dust. Apart from anything, it is in plain contravention of Act 72, Article 3.1.a of the wing bearer Bylaws with respect to distribution and efficacy of elfin products and their addenda. (He knew, he'd studied the whole Act in boring detail for the wing bearer bar exams.)

Simply speaking, Earth is the counter weight necessary to equilibrium of the universe, the gravitational margin where science replaces sorcery, reason acting in counterpoint to runes and spells. It is an ancient and stringent equation: for the balance to be maintained, earth memory is wiped where magic seeps through the layers of the worlds.

The wing bearer decided to double check. Yip, the earth boy was definitely staring. And damn, damn, and double dipping damn, damn there seemed to be a disconcerting degree of comprehension there. Bother!

Definitely a tentative smile.

How extraordinary! He delved into his bag and fetched out some more dust, which he sprinkled liberally over Septimus's head, ignoring the plumes of talc that coated the desks and his own pristine uniform. A dollop of dust wafted through Sep's hair, clinging to his nostrils. Septimus coughed. He also blinked. Then he closed his eyes against the sweet-smelling powder of dreams.

The wing bearer wiped his brow in relief. A bit short lived.

The boy reeled, lulled by the enchantment that dripped from his lashes, tickling his upper lip. The roomed swirled about him, almost as though he'd just climbed off a very fast merry-go-round. No, make that a rollercoaster. He placed his hand on the desk for support, then struggled to open his eyes. His lids were heavy with charm. The wing bearer hovered in front of his nose looking anxious.

'Hello?'

Septimus thought he should say something momentous, but he could think of nothing more suitable at this moment than a plain 'hi' right back.

'You can speak elfin tongue?'

'No, of course not! Only English, but I've done a year of Spanish which sounds faintly like Italian—'

'But you're speaking in Elf-tongue right now!'

'I am? How peculiar!'

Septimus listened to his words and realised they did, indeed, sound strangely high and somewhat lyrical.

'The forget-me-dust is not working on you.'

'Is that what that disgusting stuff is? Forget-me-dust?'

'Yes, and superior strength—the Wish Maker said it was urgent.'

'What does it do?'

The wing bearer rolled his eyes. 'Duh—Forget-me-dust? It makes you forget. When you guys come round, you won't remember all the magic you've witnessed—it is forbidden on earth to know about these matters.'

'*I* know about them.'

'Do you? How strange.' The wing bearer checked his rank. 'Oh my gosh, my stars are flickering. I can lose a stripe for not being careful enough.'

'You *were* careful. You nearly made me choke on that stuff!'

'Yes, but it didn't do any good, did it?'

'Not much, apart from a moment of giddiness. What is your name?'

'Oh, I cannot say! No! No! Truly! No! We have spoken enough already!'

'We've hardly even started. Do you come from Elvenswolde?'

The wing bearer groaned.

'Oh, no! I'm in so, so, so much trouble! Do you know about Elvenswolde too?'

'Of course! Sarah, my mother, has told me about it.'

'It is strictly against the law for you to know. Contravention of Wing Bearer Bylaw 101. Not to mention Act 72, Article 3.1.a and b. Probably e too, come to think of it. I wish I had never been given this assignment!'

'Why?'

'Because it will be *my* fault when I have to tell the Wish Maker you would not forget! No doubt I shall be sent to the third tower to wash linen. I *hate* that!'

'Do you have to tell him?'

'Of *course* I do! The balance might be overset if I don't. I am a *naughty* elf, but not *bad*, you know.' The wing bearer sounded gloomy.

Septimus grinned. 'Rather like me, then, only I am not an elf. Or only half an elf.'

The wing bearer brightened.

'Half an elf? Are you then? That might explain things. Special circumstances. I am sure there must be a rule about that. Section ten of the Exceptions, perhaps. Or maybe the Foreign Admissables. If forget-me-dust does not work on half-elves, it can't be my fault, can it?'

'Probably not! What are the Wing Bearer Bylaws?'

The little elf tiptoed as he peered at Septimus. (He was short for an elf and elves, generally, are rather slight in frame.)

'You really know very little, don't you? I suppose that's a good thing. I'll report it.'

Septimus sighed. 'Report away, but at least clue me in!'

The wing bearer grinned. 'Well then! The bylaws are a kind of guide, really, for what is permitted and what isn't. Mostly for wing bearers. I may not, for example, use forget-me-dust on elephants, for they are charged with remembering the things, great and small, that take place upon this land of earth.'

'Really? How fascinating! What else is in those bylaws?'

'Oh, the usual, you know—I must not waste forget-me-dust on people or plants that will not remember naturally. You can have no notion how long the list is. Venus flytraps remember, but daffodils don't. Babies under two do not remember, unless they are born under the elfin lights of Galathgraine when the moons are aligned with earth. A lot of study I assure you, and very tedious.'

'What if you make a mistake?'

'It depends how serious it is. Interpretation of the bylaws is a tricky thing. It is better to waste dust than to leave someone remembering, but if you waste too much you have to answer to the Wish Maker, and he may scold you or remove one of your merit stripes or worse, expect you to re-sit the exams.'

'Horrible!'

'Yes, and the worst of it is, you can't use clever potions, charms or amulets to help you, because the exam room is in an enchanted tower. It resists all spells and goodness knows, enough of us have tried!'

Septimus laughed. 'What happens if you fail?'

'We lose our wings and land up having to run horrible errands all around Castle Carne. If we are really bad, we might be sent to another castle altogether, where the Wish Maker could be stricter.'

'I am sure that won't happen to you. Look, will it help if I explained some stuff? My father was Septimus. I think I must have a lot of brothers and cousins in your world. Someone, surely will remember?'

The wing bearer looked a quaint mixture of doubtful and hopeful.

Septimus, by contrast, was abundantly cheerful.

Looking about the class of sleepy people who were all as still as if they had been turned to statues, and twice as deaf, he felt a flood of lightness seep through his being, so that it seemed to him that his shorts were made of gossamer, and his old black T-shirt was a robe of high honour. Only a moment he felt like that, but the moment was one of sheer gladness, for he felt within his being that he was no longer torn between two worlds. Earth and Elvenswolde were one, heart, mind, spirit and truth.

The Balance

Ramón clicked his fingers and gestured for the elves to eat. Twisted eclairs dipped in sugar with pink crystallised sticklethwaites. Not something you could say no to! Bickle grinned and wondered if he could take two?

Just to be safe, he decided on one. The biggest.

Xanadel was too excited to be hungry, but he nibbled on a sticklethwaite just to be polite. Ramón smiled.

'It is something of a myth that your father died on the plains of Lindolucia. In fact, Septimus fought great battles for Elvenswolde and was caught between stars on the way home. He missed the alignment and was compelled to wander earth until Virulus and Tatiana aligned again. In those days, one couldn't simply visualise to move between the worlds. We developed visualisation as a strategy only much later, when we had already lost Septimus, your father.'

'What happened whilst he waited?'

The wizard smiled.

'Love happened.'

Xanadel looked puzzled.

'Love? I thought he was killed!'

Ramón laughed.

'It would take a lot to kill such a man as Septimus! He was one of our greatest warriors, not to mention very well versed in the magical arts!'

'So what happened?'

Xanadel chewed the nails of his left hand. They were short, but were rapidly becoming shorter.

'If you chew your nails down to the cuticles I will have to give you nactocin seed. Nasty stuff. Don't do it!'

Xanadel stopped. He nibbled the eclair, hiding his nails in the edges of chocolate.

'During his travels in that other world, he met an earth woman and fell in love with her.'

So many questions fizzed through the young elf's mind. He said little, but felt sure that the great Wish Maker would understand his feelings.

He did, casting him a warm smile.

'Sarah is her name, Sarah of flaming hair and green eyes that glow as gently as her nature. She is brave like your mother was, and loving, but she is not an elf, or born to the ways of magic like you or I.

'By the laws of Elvenswolde, she could not move between the worlds as your father could, nor would your father permit her to remain behind. Her loving heart would have become shrivelled as a shrunken leaf, left dry 'tween vine and clinging bud, a sad testament to what once was and what might have been.

'His own heart, you know, would have broken both by the weight of this knowledge and by his own inclination.'

Xanadel nodded. He was not sure he could follow all Ramón's poetic prose, but he got the drift. Bickleberry moved close to catch the wizard's low words.

'Septimus of his own free will chose to remain, though Virulus and Tatiana thrice aligned themselves in his lifetime. It was a hard—a dreadfully hard—decision for him. After your mother died, he'd had the spirit of a wanderer. He loved his sons, but they were all busy forging lives of their own. I cannot blame his choice.'

'What happened to him?'

'Gradually, the memory of Elvenswolde faded to nothing more than a pleasant dream, and he became a mortal man, assuming mortal years and living not by elf time, but by earth time, measured by hours and minutes and calculated by the rotations of the world's own sun.

'Not the pink moons of Elvenswolde, but the pearly one of Earth was his nightly comfort. He would stare at that moon, Xanadel, and dream dimly of you and your brothers and that other, once-world, he'd left behind.

'In time, a son was born. Septimus's first in the earth world, but his seventh by the regular reckoning of Elvenswolde, where such things are not to be forgotten. He had no daughters, although I think he always wished for one. Septimus must have been quite a shock!'

The Wish Maker idly produced a few wish bubbles then helped himself to a snack. Not an eclair, this time, but a golden muffin overflowing with what looked like cheese and some sort of elf wart. Bickle was glad he did not try to share.

The Wish Maker swallowed and continued. 'Thus it was that the seventh son of a seventh son, Septimus, son of Septimus, was raised and loved as an earth child, though his blood is as elfin as your own.

'It is good so, for in the deepest legends there are songs sung of such a one, songs so sweet they are rarely sung for fear of rendering the singer immortal, or touched so deeply that she might lose herself forever in the golden beauty of the words.'

'I have heard of such!' Xanadel murmured. 'My grandmother was a sooth singer and they say that if only Scattadew could stop being so flippant, he has the voice to become one too!'

'The voice, yes, but has he the spirit? That we have yet to see, but you are right, Xanadel, your grandmother was a noted sooth singer. She sang of the seventh son—before you were so much as born, and the song was so sweet I still hear faint traces of it when the air is still, and the leaves fresh from the Eastern breezes.'

'Are the songs woven with magic, sir?'

The Wish Maker regarded Bickleberry contemplatively, then shook his head.

'Not magic, Bickleberry, merely Elfin lore entwined in myth. There is none sweeter than the whispers of that seventh son of a seventh son who lives beyond the shores of elfdom and shall one day be the saving of this kingdom and all on yon.'

The wizard popped another few bottles as he spoke and granted some easy wishes with his wand. The messengers watched in silence as each wish ignited, enclosed in tell-tale bubbles of enchantment. They drifted over the window's slate ledge before dissolving into the fabric of the universe, a potent promise of fate.

Bickle wondered, with prickling unease, what happened to the dark wishes? The deeply mean, that sat in bottles and needed to be attended to just as much as the merry? Did they too drift over the tower's edge and sow a sea of distress?

He would rather bite his tongue than ask.

He did not like to think it, nor meet Ramón's eye, for the Wish Maker was staring at him more thoughtfully than was his usual way, and with an intensity that made poor Bickle—for such was he known to his friends—feel he read every single thought, down to the fact that he had forgotten to wash behind his ears. Or had he? He wished he could remember. His ears twitched annoyingly.

But the wizard only granted three more wishes—bigger, this time, with bubbles that seemed to have iridescence floating all through them—before putting his wand away and reaching out for his spectacles.

'Xanadel, the day has come when I give you a jewel of your father's. He died bravely—heroically—on earth, in a faraway land he'd come to love. With his last breath, he ceded you Lindaliss. It has sat in a box in this tower room for many years now and it is time that it once more sees the light.'

The wizard paced across the room and halted in front of a series of drawers that were strange to look at, for some were enormous—almost too enormous for the room—and some were insignificantly small, crammed between each other in untidy array, although all drawers were neatly labelled in the wizard's own hand.

Xanadel tried to read some of the titles but was disappointed to find they were written in unfamiliar script, all flowing and sharply pointed at intervals, with swift black tips and sudden curves that might have been mistaken for spirals were they not so neatly penned.

He had the distinct impression that even in this country of Elvenswolde, the language of the labels was the highest order of magic he had yet seen.

'Ah, there it is! Knew I had it somewhere!' The wizard bent as he drew out a box that was moderate in size but rather plain and old.

It did not look magical, or even particularly special, for it sparkled with none of the glimmer one has come to associate with magical things. The box was made from cardboard—old cardboard at that.

Hardly the famous Elvenswolde silver, or the cunningly wrought miranthristone from the kingdom of Myrrh! The Wish Maker noted Xanadel's reaction but made no comment. Instead, he opened the box and placed the contents on a purple cushion he had conjured for the purpose.

'There! Behold, the amulet of Lindaliss.'

The necklace was the most disappointing looking gem the elves had ever seen. It looked like something between a brick and a mottled pebble. The only shiny thing about it was the chain. This was of purest elfin platinum, deeper, denser, brighter than any of the earth metals. Forged in the fires of Farengarth, the links were plain and strong. Xanadel stared at the simple, unadorned strips of platinum used as binding for the dull jewel within.

Bickle started to make some flippant, disgusted comment, but the wizard stopped him.

'Its brilliance has faded, Xanadel, as your father's elfish powers faded. Where once it was the deepest crimson, the proudest, fiercest shade of red ever forged, it has become burnished and old: an amber, almost, through which flames can be detected, old strengths remembered—sensed, but through a darkness thickly.'

Xanadel stared for a moment and Bickleberry, strangely moved, took his hand.

It took some moments before the young elf spoke.

'It is sad what you say. I feel for the father I have lost, for the man who chose forgetting.'

'Yes. He was so far-flung from Elvenswolde that dreams—dreams only—were his doorframe.'

The Wish Maker looked troubled. Then he smiled.

'No. That is not true. Not entirely. The universe is intertwined, and Elvenswolde lives on in his son, in a manner that only the olden ones could have foretold. Septimus's choice may be the saving of us all.' Ramón smiled mystically.

'Look to the verses of the minstrels, Xanadel, and find comfort there. Your earth brother is the seventh son of a seventh son. It may be coincidence only, but in these darkening times I fear not. Look well at the necklace, my dear, for it is said the seventh son bears one the same. Well, as similar as need be for brothers drawn across the paths of time. When the two are no longer rent asunder, but brought back by birth, by brotherhood and by need, Elvenswolde shall stand once more. Not to fall, not to falter, but to endure and live.'

The amulet (for such it was called in the ancient terms) flashed on its purple cushion. The wizard took it up and placed it in Xanadel's hand. It felt warm, where the little elf had expected it to be cold and leaden to the touch.

'It is a wondrous gift you have given me. I shall treasure this token of my father's. There are so few left.'

'Yes, you have his books, I think, and a few of his notes. That is all, for as his memories faded, so too, did his roots in Elvenswolde and the things that were his. Only the amulet truly remains, and that but a shadow, as you see, of what it once was.'

Xanadel looked as though he might cry. He pushed a stray hair from of his face but Bickle knew he was hiding tears.

The Wish Maker's tone was gentle. Also commanding. 'A shadow, but also a promise.'

Ramón's eyes were surprisingly soft as they rested first on the elf dressed in blue with silver trim—then on his friend Bickleberry. Bickleberry was only a half elf, his mother being born of the woodlands, but in the manner of sprites, he was cheerful if a little mischievous. In the days to come, Xanadel would need such a one as Bickleberry. Friends are the fabric of the universe.

The Wish Maker cleared his throat and his eyes bore into the elves.

'When you are grieving, look for balance. Always, there is that which to sigh over and that wherein to rejoice. Look further into the murky depths of that amulet, Xanadel. Look beyond the faded amber to the fiery light that has never died nor faded to a simple lamplight.

'In spite of their great age, those flames have not become too ancient to flicker with fortune's fervour. It is the way of the heavens and therefore it is also the way of ourselves. Look closely, and you will see a light, so fierce that it burns, in spite of itself.

'Always, when one light dims another brightens in its intensity. It is so with the stars and it is so with every furthest part of the universe, be it magical or logical or simply as wild as the old ways.'

Xanadel, drawn by the wizard's tone, stared deep into his pendant. At first, though he squinted and concentrated more fiercely than ever before in his elfin years, he saw nothing beyond the bleak amber the gem had become. It was painful, for with the fading came the knowledge that his father's memories had faded so, blunted to the dullness of mists. He blinked back wetness as he felt the gaze of the Wish Maker firmly fixed upon his face.

Presently, he saw more vivid sparks of life beneath the dullness of the centre-stone. He felt Ramón willing him to look closer yet. He drew in his breath and allowed his mind to see what his eyes still would not. Not for want of effort, but for want of that seventh sight of Elvenswolde. The sight that relies on more than just heart, more than mere sense. It is a sight that understands. Understands the intrinsic whole and thus sees most completely.

Yes, the more Xanadel unclasped his clenched fist and relaxed into that other, more powerful sense of space, the clearer the flames within the amber became. But how strange! Beyond the crimson that was, and the amber that presently represented a sad, dormant is, he became aware—acutely aware—of a turquoise glow.

Greens and blues that glittered with strength and grace and gave light to the flames nestled within. These were the greens and blues of the earth-world, the seas, the grasses, the plains and the skies. In a strange sense of dislocation, Xanadel understood.

Bickleberry still did not, so he puzzled at the widening of Xanadel's eyes and at the dawning of a comprehension he found incomprehensible. The silly stone still looked just like a broken brick. The wizard drew him in to the circle and cradled the jewel, now warm from the internal fires. He laid it across Bickleberry's open palm.

'Ah, Bickleberry! You look bewildered. What Xanadel understands is that Septimus, son of Septimus, his brother in blood if not in bond, was fortunate. Though he has never known Elvenswolde or his destined role within it, he had a father who loved him truly and Sarah, his mother, who is beautiful as the wind and as ethereal. Always, with anguish there is an equal joy. Remember that when you are sad or fearful.'

'What about joy? Is joy always to be tarnished by sorrow?'

The wizard smiled. 'Sometimes you are too deep for your own good, Xanadel! Yes, Joy is not spared the sorrow of anguish, for without grief across its spectrum, rapture itself cannot be sweet.'

Bickleberry looked dismayed.

'Confused, my little elfkin?'

The Wish Maker laughed. It was a sound that lightened the whole of the room, despite the deepening of the night and the positioning of Siluse and Ventrimuse high on the Southern horizons.

'You love the annual banquet.'

Now that was something Bickleberry found easy to understand!

'Do you think, Bickleberry, you would enjoy it quite so much if you feasted on trifles and sugared plums every night of the year? On—let me see—hot, spiced plover duck and wren roasted in the old ways? With lashings of jocanda herbs and rubbed almandine? On endless platters that were replenished every time you swallowed your last?' Ramón was gaining a rhythm now, actually quite enthusiastic. His eyes twinkled.

'They would taste good, but not so good as after a year in the scullery eating Madame Knorr's collations of onion tripe. I am right, am I not?'

Bickleberry nodded, much struck. The wizard continued.

'After a while, Bickleberry, when your stomach was sated and your plate emptied not for the fifth but for the fiftieth time, you might begin to find yourself wishing for a little of Madam Knorr's meagre portions! You might even begin to think going to bed without dinner an enchanting prospect rather than a cruel punishment! You might, dare I say it, lose the attachment you feel for elfin dew and sugar plums?'

Bickleberry's eyes widened. The wizard touched his brow solemnly.

'There has to be balance and order. The sweet is not so sweet if it has nothing to compare itself to. The sour is not so sour if one has not tasted of the sweet. So it has been, and so it shall always—must always be.'

'But it is not so now!'

Xanadel startled. He had not meant to say this, but the thought just popped into his mind from nowhere. Perhaps it was the sight of a thousand purple-capped bottles jostling for position on the shelf behind him.

They smelt vile now, and were producing meticlaws, whatever that might be. Xanadel had no real wish to find out, but by the looks of the evil slime that was crawling down the glass, he was very soon going to!

The Wish Maker snapped his fingers at the bottles and the slime stopped crawling. Bickleberry had the distinct notion that they were simply suspended in time, and would doubtless crawl again before the morning skies cast their crystal light over Elvenswolde, or the kestrels and skylarks and spirit doves rose in song to meet the dawn.

'I am afraid not, Xanadel! You are correct: It is not so now! You, who are the messenger elves, will be among the first to realize this. The balance is shifting, which is why we have purple bottles popping everywhere, spewing meticlaws and measles, not mermaids or melody or even mellifluous hope that adorns many of the nicer wish bottles in Elvenswolde.

'I wondered first, if the matter was simply a prank, which is why I was so gruff with you earlier. I wouldn't put it past a couple of mischievous messenger elves—but no! I am afraid simple mischief is just wishful thinking on my part.'

Bickle stared at him open mouthed. Ramón was wishing for mischief?

'How happy, I would be, young man, if I found you had switched the price of the dark for the price of the light. What a simple matter that would be to rectify! The purple lids would stop popping and I would not be forced to wish up evil in so large a quantity. I am running short of gall to do it with, even if my inclination allowed.

'But my inclination does not allow, which goes ill with me. I cannot ordain what wishes I grant, but I can be a testament to the shift in tides. I can put a stop, for the moment, to the more terrifying of wishes. I can freeze them, delay them, and shift their order in the great store of wishes awaiting my attention. But they cannot be destroyed, nor can they be put off any longer than my last kind, light, happy-hearted bottle of popping desires.

'These grow less and I worry that the time will come that they run out altogether. When that moment is upon us, I shall be forced to attend exclusively to the wishes of the dark.

'The meticlaws cannot be stopped forever; it can only be balanced and counterbalanced. I am granting, to purchase time, horrible little wishes, mean matters to appease those simmering bottles. The time will come, though, when this is not enough, when more shall be expected of me unless the balance is restored.'

'How does one restore the balance?'

'I do not know, my little elfkin. One has to discover, first, who or what is upsetting the balance of the old lore, who is favouring a shift from light to the very deep of darkness itself.'

'Do you have any ideas?'

'Ideas are dangerous without substance. I shall trust only the truth of my heart which I know to be pure. Not good, precisely, but not bad either. My ills are balanced quite effectively by my strengths.'

'You have no ills, sir!'

Ramón looked amused.

'Bless you, Xanadel! I did not hear you say so when I punished you last week!'

Xanadel blushed, for it is true he had grumbled loudly about the Wish Maker's sense of justice. He had called Ramón unfair and even wished he would be sent away, for a change.

Now he looked with horror at the bottle of oozing meticlaws and thought with shame that this wish might even now be ripening in the bottle. The Wish Maker would be forced to grant it too, if he did not have sufficient nobler wishes to balance the mischief he'd caused. He felt ashamed, but the Wish Maker only smiled.

'I have dealt with that wish, Xanadel. It is why I left you alone with the potions. I had no choice, you see, but to "go away." Don't look so stricken. It was not so very bad a wish, I am sure I have inflicted worse, in my time! Why, I remember when my poor dance master walked about with purple spots about his trousers and all because I wished a corrector wand would strike *his* rear end for a change!

'I have learnt to be more circumspect in my wishes since then. I am not perfect though.'

The elves looked politely disbelieving.

'I am touched with arrogance, with gluttony (especially for cinnaqills and syllabub wrought from pixie creams), with ambition, with a whole host of negative qualities that all mingle to make me the man I am today. Without ambition, greed and a little guile I might never have had the ambition or strength to become a Wish Maker.'

He smiled and his eyes twinkled quite kindly.

'The negatives, I trust, are balanced by good, so that I am a whole person, not a creature entirely of light but neither one whom darkness holds deep in its sway. So it should be, and so it is with you, Bickleberry, and with you too my dear Xanadel.'

'What about Silvajar and Garredung?'

'They too are creatures of balance, though their hues are darker than your own and their manners not as fair. But their very existence equalizes your own, their pettiness is weighed against your kindness, their cunning against your impulsiveness, and your levity against their gloom. So long as it remains so, all will be well with Elvenswolde. If the balance shifts, as I suspect it might be trying to do, then troubles shall descend upon us and poison not only the air of this enchanted place, but also the worlds beyond it.'

Xanadel shivered and drew his cloak about him, but the Wish Maker shook his head sadly. Xanadel's chill was not from the cold, but from the feeling that was slowly creeping into his elfin heart. Ramón snapped his finger for a taper of light and a candle quietly lit itself from the wick. It burnt not so much with luminescence as with warmth: a warmth that pervaded the little turret room and whispered of light.

Night-Magic

That evening, the night-magic seemed more potent.

At Castle Carne, the vast stone towers seemed to quiver in the moonshine. Beyond them stretched the furthest reaches of the sky: black, with wisps of colour fading into darkness.

For two hours it would remain like this, before the twin stars of Siluse and Ventrimuse began their southern travail across the sky.

Tonight it seemed that the very creatures of the forest trembled. The clatter in the kitchens ceased, the night watch at Gildergast, Killyrath and Castle Carne all seemed to whisper, not speak.

The king himself was subdued, his cloak pulled tight against him to ward off the cold. His gaze crept alternately to the sky then to the great atlas cast in front of him, displaying blank pages only he could read. He wished now he had left the tome unopened.

It was late. He sighed and shook away the shadows. He was being watched again, he could feel it. Of a sudden, he felt almost as weary as the weathered hills at Willowsham. The path he'd chosen was twice as treacherous.

Whilst Septimus felt the lightness of being swirl about his person like some glad sprite, darkness was creeping over Elvenswolde. And in that darkness, somewhere in its very heart, stood a man.

Noble by blood, and proud. He did not drape himself in black. There was no need, for twilight seemed to eddy about him like an invisible cloak, so that though his robes were silver, they seemed dark, dark, darkling, darker than the very burrows of the hillsides and blacklier black.

Septimus would have shuddered to know that while he ate toffee apples and little golden pretzels, he carried with him the worst fears of nightmares and stirred up silk-spinning spiders with a webbed stick.

His eyes smiled and he appeared excessively handsome if one ignored the hardness of his features and the dread he seemed to breathe. His hair was as black as his eyes and his teeth were quite enviably white and straight. Though no stranger would wish to cross him, neither would he immediately cringe. On first sight he seemed a nobleman, good looking and arrogant, no more and no less than others before him.

Into a pot he poured meticlaws and wine, bursting the Wish Maker's bubbles as they drifted from the highest windows of Elvenswolde and dissolved into the mists beyond.

He was tousling with the forces, a solitary figure engaged in a slow game of solitaire. It was amusing to see the balances tilted at whim, to see the creatures of dark linger longer over their prey, and the forces of good grow doubtful. He wondered if he could make them impotent entirely and thought, with satisfaction, that he could.

He had learnt with a master, after all. He knew all the little tricks, all the basic subtleties of magic.

He knew them, but was not bound by them. Ramón the Wish Maker, Ramón his teacher, was too soft.

He was too elemental, too reliant on the old lore. All that emphasis placed on balance.

Balance was for those too cautious to grasp at power, too careful to master it. If Ramón wanted to, he could have been a force for light. He could have raised Elvenswolde to the zenith and ruled it with a fist of fire.

He chose not to, he chose to permit of an even path, even when the pain to him was severe. He chose to tolerate jealousies that they might be countered by joys.

He elevated righteousness, but allowed Elvenswolde to be adrift with dark temptations. Foolish, stupid man! He permitted his own undoing in order to preserve the equilibrium of the old lore. He was so scrupulous that he sowed discontent in the very place he reaped happiness.

Now, in the rising, he would be powerless. Sad, foolish, impotent Ramón, to think he could control evil simply by enhancing light.

The balance was shifting, and if the silver cloaked wizard wished, it would never be restored. The seven worlds shuddered with each stir of the copper pot.

The seas rose and the shores broke their banks. Lands quivered and crumbled, worlds—the very worlds—shook like jelly on his fingertips.

The wizard laughed, high in the tower of the king. How he had gained access was his secret, the king's secret. The laughter faded almost as soon as it was breathed, yet the air crackled hours after from its dryness.

And now? Now it was raining in Elvenswolde. Dark skies obscured the light, causing faint shadows to shift across the moors and the far off forests of Freer and Mersham. Several of the elfin castles looked greyer than usual—no sparkling silvers, no crystal dew drops. Even Castle Carne, his majesty's ancestral home, looked bleak.

There was no welcoming rainbow to transform the shadows into dancing light, the lakes looked deeper and darker than usual, and the rain! Oh, it poured down over Elvenswolde, so even the woodland creatures huddled for shelter under the tall trees of Mersham, and the sprites sheltered as best they could under shire bushes and Blackberry vines.

The sculleries were filled with elves all come in from the rain, and Madame Knorr was dishing out tasks faster than the lightning that split the sky. The smell of floor polish and candle wax was everywhere, mingled with the aromas of huge earthen pots cooking more gruel than usual. (Brussel sprout stew, actually. Elvenswolde—even Elvenswolde! has Brussel sprouts, though of a slightly leafier variety, and perhaps a tad greener on the underside.)

Many elves were already sporting large corrector wand smudges and grumbling—one was actually howling—but for the most part, the folk of Elvenswolde were glad to be out of the rain.

The queen called for a hundred stitchers to weave a new generation elfin tapestry. It was to be of threads of gold and silver and magical myrrh, to brighten the walls of Castle Carne and put a use to idle fingers and fractious tongues.

Only the best weavers were selected, so Bickleberry was not among their number. (The last time he had been permitted this honour, ten silk fairies had had to unstitch to the last stitch every last knot he'd made. He'd not been particularly popular, though the queen was kind. Still, it was her fault for giving him such a stupid fairy-chore in the first place!)

Xanadel was also not called to help, though his fingers were nimble and he might have made a good job of sorting (rather than muddling) the silken threads.

As a matter of fact, Xanadel was doing nothing in particular, for the Wish Maker had stopped all wishes for the day and the sorting rooms had forgotten his existence since he'd been elevated to messenger.

No one called him to any kind of activity and he was not complaining! He slipped into one of the small antechambers that led off from the castle and hoped he wouldn't be found.

It was not that he was lazy, only that he had a lot to think about and he felt strangely subdued by the storm, more aware than ever of the forces afield in Elvenswolde.

If Ramón was to be believed (and why shouldn't he be?), the worlds were steadily slipping into disorder.

The darker forces were tipping the scales subtly, but ever so steadily, so that if no stand were taken, the light would slip, unseen, into oblivion. It would happen in a way that no one noticed.

Not, that is, until it was too late. The view from Castle Carne darkened, and though it was still morning, Xanadel could swear he heard the distant howl of a wolf on wing.

Transformations

Septimus was released, at last, by the welcome sound of the school bell. It sounded loud over each tick tock he had been hearing for what seemed like hours. He was in a heightened state of awareness and could hear things much, much more clearly than usual.

He could hear the wind on the tides off the shores of the King Edward Sound and the dim, base call of the lighthouse at Point McKindle. He could hear albatross in flight across the waters and the splash of the diving kuaka. He could hear, with so much clarity, the call of the wilds. From the footsteps of the farm creatures to the tiny, half creeping of a mouse across the school hall's floor, Septimus heard them all.

It was all so strange that he hardly knew how it was happening. He'd tried to concentrate on his breathing and on the steady tick tocking of the school room clock.

As he'd listened, it seemed to him that the rhythm was changing. He listened closer, closing his eyes. It seemed to him that the clock was whispering something, almost like a chant. If he sat perfectly still, his back pressed up hard against his bench, he could almost make it out.

> —*all around, in echoes, in trees,*
> *in woodlands and forests,*
> *in lightning, in breeze*
> *the worlds are awaking,*
> *alive and alive*

—the grasses are singing
brooks bubbling, banks brimming
wet wild birds are bringing
on wing and on whim
intonations of poignancy,
of passion of power—
intonations of perfect—
intimations of him
Him, him, him—
on wing and on whim,
Him, him, sung loud, sung soft,
sung sweet, sung long
Him, the seventh, him the son
Oh seventh son of a seventh son
Come answer now the call from yon

On 'yon,' the clock reverted back to its usual tick and tock, so that Septimus had to convince himself he'd had not been dreaming.

He was not, he knew he was not! That tingle of excitement that crept up his toes and warmed the very insides of his stomach had nothing to do with an ordinary day.

Mr Carlisle might be sneering, his mates might be packing their backpacks—a quick stuffing of pens, pies (half eaten) pencils (no points and no sharpener) and other essentials before they raced out of the door and into the village square, but he—he could feel something was different.

As usual, some of the kids were called back to pick up a wrapper or remember their homework. Terribly ordinary, but Septimus refused to be convinced. Somehow, today was different!

He could feel it in the lightness of his step and in the coolness of the breeze that fluttered across his brow. He hurried out the door, slinging his backpack over his shoulders and ignoring the scowl of Mr Carlisle, who seemed to wish to call him back, but somehow did not find the words.

He did not cross the bridge on his trail back home, as he usually did. Nor did he seek his seventieth Pokémon, Marawak. Marawak, with his lightning rod ability was awesome, awesome, awesome! He needed to restock at the PokéStop near the war memorial, but not today. The waters were calling to him and he knew of a place where he could sit quietly and reflect.

If Sarah wondered where he was, she would find him there. It was a favourite haunt of his. Septimus was almost out of breath as he arrived, for the climb was steep. Flinging down his backpack, he stretched his legs.

Presently, he shifted closer to the water's edge and dangled his feet in the cool, calming waters of the forest lake. He hoped for another sign that his world was somehow opening up to that other, far off world of Elvenswolde.

The water soaked his knees past the hems of his shorts. Below him, two fishermen signalled a catch with steady movements of their hands. Gulls circled overhead and the air smelt quite strongly of fresh, scaled fish.

He wished he had talked to the wing bearer longer, had begged for directions, had convinced him that he was entitled, under the By-laws, to enter the kingdom and claim his place as the seventh son of Septimus, his father.

Instead, like an idiot, he had allowed him to fly off with nothing more than a breezy wink. He could kick himself. Still, he had that tingling feeling that all was not lost. He was still on the cusp of two worlds. At least he hoped so!

He scrabbled in his backpack and found a sandwich. It was rather squashed from being wedged under Christopher Paolini's *Eragon*, but Septimus was not fussy, 'specially since he'd not eaten a thing since breakfast. All around in the trees, in the grass, in the lake, were everyday things. There was the 'keep out' sign on the fence about ten steps away, peeling paint and the 't' scratched out. It always amused Septimus. Then there was the sign on the farm gate 'Closed Monday's' with an apostrophe. People like apostrophes. They seem to be everywhere, even when they are wrong.

There were also the small fantails and the bellbirds that perched on the branches. The twigs were brown from the late winter but just budding whispers of green. Magical in its own way, but not in the mystical ways of Elvenswolde

He rather wished, as he finished his sandwich, that he'd packed another. He was still hungry, and though he had coins in his pocket, he was too lazy to wander all the way back in to town.

It happened so swiftly, so subtly, that Septimus hardly noticed. One minute he was screwing up his wrapper, the next he was unwrapping—it was confusing.

He was certain he had just finished the last crumbs of his squashed sandwich, but there was another in his hand. Only it did not look like another, for it was squashed in the same, disorderly manner and had the identical ooze of tomato creeping out the side. Like the last sandwich, it looked soft and slightly soggy from the warm sun.

Septimus's heart beat faster, but uncertainly. Was this another strange happening, or was he simply going out of his mind? Surely magic was something fine, something special, not a soggy sandwich reproducing itself without so much as a fanfare or sparkle of enchanted light?

A sandwich? Septimus bit into it carefully. It tasted exactly the same as before. Cheese, tomato and no salt, (which he'd forgotten in his hurry.) The bread was brown, but not crunchy or nutty. It was smooth, identical to his last snack. He took another nibble. Lovely, but for the second time that day he wished he'd remembered the salt.

Weird to be eating a sandwich you could swear did not exist. Sep wondered what Sarah would say. He took another bite and choked. The sandwich tasted different.

Horrible, really. Too disgusting—as if someone had unplugged the bottom of a saltcellar and caused the grains to pour instead of sprinkle. Not only over the bread, but over the poor tomato and the soggy sliver of cheese. Septimus grabbed his juice bottle and drank deeply.

Then, a tiny prickling sense of discovery. He'd wished for another sandwich and it had appeared. He had wished for salt and his sandwich had become salty. His wishes, it seemed, were still coming true. Though the ocean looked as blue as usual and the sky as hot and as overcast as always, something was different. Magic was different. Magic was real and happening to him.

Septimus breathed deeply to still his racing heart. He concentrated. Then, slowly, deliberately, he wished for the wing bearer.

Nothing happened. He scanned every high tree and every blade of grass. He waited. Nothing. It was frustrating as hell. He kicked a rock and only succeeded in stubbing his toe. He cursed himself. Maybe he had been granted three wishes and had, in an act of unqualified idiocy, wasted them all.

Only a bumblebee made his appearance and seemed to mock Septimus and the silence as he sat with a stupid, salty sandwich, suspended evenly somewhere between hope and the direst despair.

He could not help thinking he'd wasted his wishes on absolute rubbish, had failed some all-important test. Good God, who could possibly be so careless as to waste magic like that? He could kick himself.

He wished again, this time more intensely. The bee distracted him and he was lucky he did not get stung.

Oh, to see the wing bearer again! He still had so many unanswered questions. He blinked. His vision seemed fuzzy for a moment, then cleared. The bee seemed to enlarge, then flap, his yellow brown stripes merging into a pale lime, slightly less furry—he blinked and squinted into the sunlight. The bee was gone, his annoying buzz replaced by a breezy chuckle with just the faintest echo of a buzz.

'My, my, but it's been a busy, b-b-buzzzzy day for me. Fun though.'

Septimus could hear his heart beat. As a matter of fact, he could feel it, for it pounded in his chest so much he thought it might burst.

'You're back!'

'Yes, but it was a close-run thing gaining all the necessary visas. You need to visualise, Septimus, really you do.'

'What do you mean?'

'You can't go about wishing for things vaguely. It is against the Wish Act, Amendment Five. Causes a great deal of fuss in the bottling room, because the junior elves have no sense at all.'

'What do you mean?' Septimus dropped his salty sandwich onto his backpack. A little of it dropped on Mr Carlisle's homework sheet but the boy neither noticed nor cared.

'If you are vague about a wish it is open to interpretation. If you want salt on a sandwich, for heaven's sake, visualise how much, how you want it to taste, where precisely will the grains land—on the tomato? On the cheese?

'Don't simply wish for salt. Some of the juniors have no idea at all, and some are just plain mischievous. I don't trust Lucinda, daughter of Garvinshilde, for example—give her half a chance and she'd bottle a salt mine for you!'

'What do you mean by "bottle?"'

The wing bearer sighed.

'You really know very little, don't you?'

Septimus shook his head. He tried to keep sarcasm from his tone, but did not succeed particularly. 'It is hard to know anything of the elf world if you have never been there.'

The wing bearer looked thoughtful.

'Yes, I was confused when I first started learning about the six other worlds. Earth is hardest. I shall probably have to begin at the very beginning, but I hope it won't take too long. It's a bit of a nuisance.'

'I am sorry.'

'Not at all, don't mention it. I am sorry if I sound ungracious. It is just that time runs against us—'

'Why? I should think we had all the time in the world.'

'In this world, maybe, but not in Elvenswolde, where the forests grow dark. Don't let me alarm you. I don't mean to. I'll just explain as we go and you can stop me for questions.'

'Great!'

'Mind if I eat the sandwich? I have only had pollen all morning and its beastly stuff!'

'Pollen?'

The wing bearer winked. 'Yes, I was that stupid bumble bee flying about a moment ago. I thought I'd just sneak back and sting Mr Carlisle for you, but then you went and visualised…'

'So?'

'So, what with all the permission slips, visa registrations and so on, I had to come hurrying back. Lucky I've got wings. I thought you were going to swat me.'

Septimus grinned. 'I was. Pity about Mr Carlisle. He could do with a sting!'

'Never mind, I can always try him another day. Bound to get another earth duty sometime. Maybe I'll try a wasp. Hey, about that sandwich—?'

'Eat it, but it tastes disgusting.'

'That's because you did not visualise properly. I, however, shall visualise caramel cream with diced mango in a delicate pastry shell of white cracked candy—I don't know if it will work, because it is really your wish I am modifying—ah! See? Much better, though I need to work on the candy. I think I burnt it. I'd save some for you only you've just eaten and—'

'It's quite alright. Just start talking, will you?'

'Well, if you're quite sure—'

The wing bearer smiled sweetly and gobbled the pastry in two large gulps. 'Now let me see—Wishes. Lecture One. Wishes—all wishes are bottled.

'They have prices attached to them and they are usually too expensive to be attended to. Most earth wishes have a high a price tag. Naturally, there are exceptions. When the correct price has been paid, the bottles start to pop and are dispatched to the Wish Maker for his attention. The Wish Maker has access to high magic—much higher than ours.

'He attends to the wish and they rise up in a stream of fabulous bubbles from his window. A beautiful sight they are, the scene of many an artist's pen, Leonardo, son of Vincarella, for one, but yes, I digress. By the time the wishes are fully ripe, the bubbles pop and the wish is granted.'

'How incredible!'

'Not really, it is the way of Elvenswolde. What is incredible is that your bottles all seem to be ripening. Salt does not usually get past the weighing room, never mind into bottles! You won't mind me saying so, Septimus—your wishes are incredibly trivial!'

'I had no idea they'd come true. If I had, I would have wished Mr Carlisle into a bog!'

'Don't say that!'

'Why not?'

'If a junior wish fairy were to hear—I mean, sometimes they find it difficult to distinguish "do" from "would," never mind the past participle would have! They have to understand and interpret a thousand different languages in a day. Some of the further worlds are worse than English—and English, let me tell you, is only marginally better than Mandarin.

'If they heard you, they might not understand your irony. They would take the silly wish and bottle it! At the rate your wishes are being granted today I wouldn't be surprised if Mr Carlisle were sinking in some bloody quicksand already!'

'I was only joking!'

'Of course you were. You do not have a mean spirit, even the most insignificant of wing bearers can see that.'

Septimus grinned. 'Why do you think my wishes are ripening?'

'I have no idea, only that they are.'

'Do you think—do you think that if I wish myself into Elvenswolde my wish might come true?'

The wing bearer frowned.

'I don't know and I don't recommend it. As far as I know, it is forbidden for people of the earth to enter the lands of Galathgraine and Ramalo and Sarcalet to the south. Maybe somewhere in Elvenswolde—I am not strictly sure. Some say the magic is too deep to be tolerable to humankind. There are many theories on the matter—we had to study them all in 300 level Elfin Anthropology—but that was two years ago and frankly I only scraped a pass by the skin of my teeth.'

Septimus bit his lip to hide a smile.

'Can you find out?'

'I don't see why not. But I'd need an appointment with Ramón the Wish Maker and he is terribly busy at the moment.'

'What if I just wish it?'

'Don't do that!' The wing bearer looked alarmed.

'Why not?'

'What if you get it wrong like the salt in your sandwich? What if you visualised the king's tower, which is more mystical than most, and filled with the dark magic?'

'Dark magic?'

The wing bearer shivered. 'We do not speak of it, but there is a shadow being cast over Elvenswolde. Some say that the shadow gravitates to the king's tower. It is not a place I would like to send you, and not one from which you can easily return.'

Septimus frowned. 'I did not know there were—shadows in Elvenswolde.'

The wing bearer sighed.

'There are shadows everywhere. That is the nature of life itself. But the shade usually gives way to light, and from where I stand in Elvenswolde, this is happening less and less. There are dark times ahead and I fear it.'

Septimus shivered as a cloud momentarily eclipsed the afternoon's warmth.

'I will wait, then.'

The wing bearer smiled.

'Very sensible! And I might even earn a stripe for having convinced you! I do not usually talk of the deeper things. None of us do—that is left to the wizards and the great ones. But we all feel it, this—this shadow. So do not, I pray, waste any more wishes. They are really quite valuable and Ramón is overworked as it is. He is a fierce old man, but we—even the lowliest wing bearers—are really rather fond of him. He is a great man. I am going to disappear now.'

'No! Wait!'

The wing bearer lost his concentration. He looked a little exasperated so Septimus felt a 'sorry' roll smoothly off his tongue.

'I can hear wind in my ears and taste the salt of the sea.'

'There is not a breath of wind. It must be your imagination.'

'The salt?'

'Very likely from your sandwich.'

'No! Wait! I can hear—I hear a scratching.'

'What type of scratching?'

Septimus closed his eyes.

It was as if the world around him was disappearing, but there was nothing save a swirling, misty white to take its place. His ears seemed more acute than usual, almost as if he could feel their very flesh and the pink of their bones as they quivered to hear beyond the audible. Yes, there it was again, the quiet, humble sound of scratching. The wing bearer's voice—more interested now—seemed horizons away as he concentrated on the noise.

It changed, a little, from a scratching to a tapping. Septimus could not be sure, but as he listened, he was certain the tone was duller, more insistent than before. The sound seemed to overtake the mists, so that there was no longer white, but the colour of sound, something Septimus could not describe and had no language for, save in the synchrony of his heart, which seemed, now, to tap to the self-same beat.

'Septimus!'

The wing bearer's voice was shrill, discordant with the swirling sensations. 'What is it? I can't return to Elvenswolde if you bother my visualisation!'

Septimus blinked. He felt himself pulled back to the moment, to the trickle of the forest waters and the normality of the earth day, overcast with just a glimmer of sun. The waves lapped gently at the shores bellow.

'Sorry. It's just—it's just—' Septimus blinked. He could not remember that elusive thing he wanted to say. He looked at the wing bearer and blurted the first thing words that came to mind.

'Well really, it's just that I should like to know your name.'

'Oh!' The wing bearer grinned. 'Well, that's easy and something you don't have to waste a wish on at any rate! How silly of me not to mention it before. I just assumed—well, everyone seems to know my name. I am Arikeet, son of Arikaan. My friends call me Ari.'

'Pleased to meet you.' Septimus offered his hand solemnly, but Ari could not reciprocate, for his hands were wings and he was transforming—rather cheekily—into an over large bumblebee.

'Easier to visualise. Transformations 202,' he murmured. Septimus could not understand a single word. It all sounded just like a great, irritating buzz. He stepped closer to hear, but he made the mistake of blinking. In that single split second, Arikeet vanished. There was no evidence he had ever been, save for some rather delicious pastry crumbs.

Septimus ate them.

The Problem with a Corrector Wand

On the far side of Sarcalet, a baby dragon was nestled inside a large egg. It did not know it yet, but its mother (a very fierce dragon of the line of dragons known as Dargonvilles) had just abandoned it upon a hilltop facing the southern oceans. There were fierce winds blowing and the hill had a sheer cliff face drop on the southerly side. The egg, needless to say, was precariously balanced.

The trouble with it was that it was a delicious shade of fluorescent blue, the particular shade Dargonville dragons had come to disapprove of. As any dragonologist is aware, eggs are traditionally pink with tiny shaded areas of wispy pearl. In extreme instances, they are yellow with shadowy flecks of a crystal known as Ammonite. These eggs are rare but still considered acceptable. The colour seems to indicate an ancestral link to the bygone dragon era of Myranderthuse.

The Myranderthuse were not great fliers, but their fire breathing qualities were quite exceptional. Many older Dargonville dragons feel that it is lucky to have the odd Myranderthuse hatchling belong to the great circle of dragons. For that reason, it is the custom to permit the yellow speckled ammonite eggs to survive.

Blue is another matter entirely! Blue is probably the worst egg to get—especially fluorescent blue, the colour of the skies. A dragon producing one should slink away and destroy it before any other dragon finds out about the embarrassment.

Oh, yes! Even fierce Dargonville dragons could feel rare moments of embarrassment. And producing a blue egg is truly no joke.

If other dragons ever discover it, the mother can be a laughing stock for months. That's if she's lucky.

No one knows why it is so disgraceful (or funny) to produce such an egg, but it is. It simply is. A dragon should rather pretend barrenness than admit to such a mistake.

Imagine Princess Demetria's horror (for the unhatched dragonette perched on the precipice was a royal prince of the house of Dargonville) when she discovered the egg amongst her perfect, smooth coloured, creamy pink eggs. At first, she thought it a practical joke, but when she prodded the blue egg gingerly with her claws, she realised the shell was real.

She told no one of her disgrace, not even her lady's maid the dragon Amelia, who could be relied upon to keep secrets. No, this was too important (and terrible) to trust to Amelia.

For days, the princess dragon hid herself in her cave and pondered what to do. If she was sensible, she would merely have crushed the horrible thing in her great claws, but she was not sensible.

She rolled the blue egg away from her lovely pink eggs and tried to ignore it. It would not be ignored. It seemed to glow, even in the dark, and begged, in a silent, non-speaking kind of way, to be allowed to live.

The princess would harden her heart, but halfway through the day she simply could not resist the temptation to roll the egg back to its position and sit on it. The next day, she would promise herself, she would take the nasty thing and crush it.

Well, the days went by and her royal dragon highness was growing thinner and thinner, for she did not dare leave the egg to hunt for food. She did not worry for the egg so much as for the possibility of another dragon discovering it.

She sat in the darkness of her cave—very comfortable, for it was fitted out in the prevailing neo classical style befitting every princess. It had all manner of modern conveniences including a rose quartz floor and supporting columns of marble, all carefully fashioned from the cave rock itself.

Two of the walls had mirrors made of crystal and the far corner—the darkest corner—had a drinking fountain of mineral water that rose from the springs of Sarcalet itself. On the hottest days, one could be comforted by the cooling sounds of that rushing water, ever present, that carved the far side of the cave into a smooth surface that was as shining as it was beautiful.

A Dargonville dragon, whose eyes were notoriously sharp, could see the smooth outlines easily. It was the princess's favourite place and the one where she now sat, gloomily contemplating the nastiness of her blue egg.

For the tenth time that day she reached out to touch it. She was surprisingly gentle for a dragon of her size. Once, she sneezed and nearly boiled the egg, for her flame was long and blazing hot—but the egg dropped from her claws as she leaned forward, and it rolled harmlessly—annoyingly—onto the floor.

Why, oh why, had it not cracked? She could have eaten the evidence in a single, inspired moment! But no, life was never that simple. The egg had not cracked. It had merely grown fractionally bigger as the baby dragon inside rolled onto its tummy.

Princess Demetria grew more and more panicked as each day passed. Instead of showing off her fine nest of eggs, she cowered in the darkness and hardly thought of the little princes and princesses that were growing ready to hatch in their neat, speckled pink shells. She only thought of the fluorescent egg, the colour of the summer skies, and of how horrible it was, and how much she longed to destroy it but couldn't.

Ah, there was the problem: the Princess Demetria could not destroy her own egg because she was rather fond of it. She loved it and she hated it. There was no separation in her thoughts and her feelings—she felt across the spectrum.

'Why,' she would think, 'are blue eggs so very bad?' They were beautiful, really, in their own way. Or rather, hers was. Such a pretty blue. No speckles. She fondled it for a moment then drew away in horror. She could not believe she was being so silly about this!

She, who was the terror of Sarcalet! Why, it was only last year that she had roasted two wood nymphs with her flames. They had been alive, too. She had eaten any number of troublesome elflings and even a wizard apprentice, too curious for his own good. (Nasty flavour, not to be repeated, especially with the malodorous shoes still intact—should have gutted him first.) Anyway, why was she being so soft-hearted and contrary now? She could not think, but as the day approached for her eggs to hatch she grew more and more distracted.

She pondered travelling the distance of Elvenswolde to consult the great books held in the libraries of Castle Carne. One of them, surely, would explain what to expect of a blue egg, and how a dragon was meant to deal with one.

Were all blue eggs bad, or was it just more blue eggs than not that produced bad dragons? What did a bad dragon mean? Would it be very ugly or very mean or perhaps a puny little weakling? She wished she knew. In the forests of Elvenswolde it was whispered that blue dragons were wicked, but that might after all, simply be the wind talking. Oh, she wished she knew!

Twice, she spread out her wings in the great, cavernous hall preparing them for a long journey. She stretched them from her tail to the tip of her enormous head, so her underside of purple was clearly visible.

Twice, she breathed enormous flames of fire to light her way through the night. (Dragons always fly long distances at night. It is cooler and shadows are less easily detected.)

Each time, she was determined to discover the truth for herself. Each time, she had nearly abandoned her warm, growing clutch of eggs. Then she'd sat down again in black despair. It was no good. She realised this with a sigh that almost extinguished the great flames emanating from her nostrils.

She could not read Elf tongue. If truth were told, she could not read even common dragonesque, for Dargonville dragons are more fierce than literate. Dragons, as a rule, have very little time for the finer arts.

No, she could not read elf tongue and she could not read dragonesque. She was entirely alone and must make her decision quickly.

If the egg did not get destroyed, it would hatch. It must not be allowed to do so, for there were mysteries attached to blue egg dragons: mysteries she did not understand and trembled to find out on the hatching of her own, fluorescent princeling. (Or possibly princessling, she could never be absolutely sure.)

Princess Demetria rolled the egg away from the others. Then she turned toward the water and shifted her enormous tail towards the cave's entrance. She breathed deeply so that her flames lit up the dark, solitary cavern.

A water nymph, drinking secretly from her fountain scuttled away and evaporated into a little star of light that Demetria was too heavy to catch, even if she had wanted to. The dragon princess felt her heart beat as she curled her tail into a tight coil.

She hadn't the courage to pierce the miserable object with her claws but surely her scaly tail, coiled round the shell would curve and crush it? Crush it unmercifully, so that when she once more turned towards the entrance there would be nothing but a mess of yolk and shell and scales to show for her trouble?

She coiled into a very tricky figure of eight position. She was poised, ready, when her dragon-maid, Amelia, lumbered up to the entrance of her lair.

Demetria groaned as the puny creature cleared her throat and rather timidly attempted a roar.

Normally, the great Dargonville dragon would have scorned such a feeble attempt. Now, however, she was terrified that Amelia would notice the egg tucked away in her coils. She flicked her tail quickly so that the egg rolled into the shadows. Amelia's eyesight was notoriously terrible.

'Your highness, you have been very quiet lately—'

'Me?' Demetria roared in her grandest, rumbling dragon's tone. The fact that it sounded unusually hoarse caused her kind-hearted maid to glance at her sharply.

She noticed the high spots on Demetria's cheeks and the wasting scales about her body which seemed less fat than usual, less dragonly regal. She could find no fault however, with the smoke that poured from the princess's nose, or with the blue flames that threatened to lick at her spectacles if she did not step back from the entrance.

'You are certain you are well?'

'Of course I am well, you foolish, dithering dragon! All that is wrong with me is that I am fed up with waiting for my miserable, lazy good-for-nothing eggs to hatch!'

Demetria pointed her long, curled claws at the cluster of perfectly pink eggs and the occasional ammonite that glittered dim in the darkness. She breathed a precautionary fire.

Amelia, peeking at them suspiciously, did not see the blue egg lying hidden in the deeper shadows. She nodded, slightly more satisfied, and suggested that Demetria hunt herself a nice breakfast of wolf meat, for her looks were being neglected by her motherly duties. She would have gladly hunted on Demetria's behalf—only, to suggest such a thing would be to insult her mistress quite beyond what was tolerable.

Demetria's stomach grumbled with hunger and her nostrils flared. She hated the thought of losing any of her beauty. It was true that her scales were looking limp and rather unfleshy. If she lost any more weight she would lose her stature, for beauty was everything to a dragon and the bigger and more brutish one appeared, the more spectacular one was considered to be.

Oh, she longed to hunt herself a tasty morsel of wild wolves and wolfblane sauce, but the wretched matter of the blue egg remained unresolved. Worse, there was now the distinct and increasing danger that it would hatch any day. Two of the pink eggs were showing small, infinitesimal signs of cracking. If that happened with the blue—and Demetria did not see why it should not—the odious little dragonette might be hatched within the week.

Demetria thus ignored her grumbling stomach and all thoughts of wolf meat, medium rare. To herself, she vowed she would do something today or die in the attempt.

To Amelia, however, she merely offered one of her familiar, terrifying snarls and the recommendation—fierce—to mind her own business.

At which Amelia, being a shy, rather retiring sort (as dragons go) bowed her head quietly and withdrew backwards from the darkened cave.

The great dragon watched her unblinkingly as she left, and waited several moments before she was certain she heard the unfurling of wings and the thunderous whoosh of apologetic, extremely tremulous, dragon flight.

Slowly, stealthily, very carefully, Princess Demetria laid her claws on the glowing egg, softly blue in the dim of darkness. Cautiously, she rolled it out towards the light.

* * *

The winds were howling in Elvenswolde when Arikeet returned. It was no use remaining in his bee form—he would have been swept away with the storms. Besides, his magical powers were not strong enough to sustain a disguise in a country that whispered of magic with every rustling leaf.

Talking of leaves—leaves were fluttering to the ground and there was hardly any shelter for a small elf with an empty sack of wishes. Septimus's wish had been the last on his list. Wing bearers were backups for bubbles.

He huddled up against the cold and wished he had brought a gossamer elf tunic, most effective against the northeast winds. Naturally, his wish was instantly bottled in the bottling room, but he had no real expectation of the price being paid (it rarely was for such trivia) so he lifted up the collar of his work-a-day cloak, rubbed his hands vigorously and made a mad dash for one of the castle entrances.

Once past the guard on duty (his old friend Michaela) he wandered hopefully up to the kitchens, but despite the intoxicating smell of roast lamb on a spit with elderberry wine and lichen juices basting, he was granted only a cup of creamy milk from the cook and a crust of warm, freshly baked bread.

He heaped a lump of butter on the crust and avoided cook's eye, for she was forever telling him he was a greedy little elf and prone to plumpness if he did not mend his ways.

He was just (regretfully) on his last swallow and wondering when dinner was likely to be served, when Bickleberry entered from the stone corridor on his left, looking both excited and solemn.

'What's up, Bickle?'

'Can't say. Top secret.'

'I can keep a secret.' Arikeet looked mischievous. 'As a matter of fact, I might be keeping one of my own!'

'Not very well, obviously!'

'Only because you are my best friend.'

'What about Fleetfoot and Xanadel?'

'They are my best friends too! And yes, before you ask, so is Aradight!'

'Aradight doesn't count, he is your twin!'

'*And* best friend! Come on, Bickleberry, what's up?'

But the whispers had to wait, for Silvajar and Garredung were marching past with their noses in the air. Arikeet would not put it past those two busybodies to throw a listening spell into the air. Now that they were working in the king's tower—the tower that seemed to be forever shrouded in gloom—they seemed meaner than ever, and more cunning.

When the castle bells chimed the hour, the elves were forced to scramble from their seats and dash to their places to be signed in. It was damp and wet and everyone was in a cross mood.

Madame Knorr's corrector wand hovered about joyfully. It spotted at least a dozen little elves that had been squabbling and in serious need of correction. Oh, a fine time it had had, bobbing in front of Madame Knorr's face and pointing at culprits here, culprits there. About ten elves had horrible purple smudges across their knuckles, one had a smudge across his palm and one particularly unlucky elf had a hideous purple blob right across his bottom. He tried to hide it by sitting down, but it just seemed to change shape and drift upwards, which made everyone laugh and the poor elf turn pink with embarrassment.

Bickleberry could not help feeling a little sympathetic. He'd had a bottom blob once, and it really was not something he wished to remember. It took ages to fade—much longer than the pain—and even when he'd rushed upstairs to change his leggings, the smudge had simply transferred to his new pants with a magical enthusiasm he found appalling.

Still, he found that if he behaved himself for about five hours or so, the purple faded and did not seem so insistent on being utterly visible. After half a day he could sit down without it drifting upwards. Eventually, of course, it disappeared but because it was on his bottom (a rather difficult angle to see without turning one's head about like a corkscrew) it was impossible to tell whether the wretched thing was gone or not.

He rather thought the whole horrible ordeal lasted about a day. He edged closer to the miserable elf and tried to cheer him up.

'Don't sit, Wendleweed, it makes it worse.'

'What am I to do then? I can't exactly stand during all of the king's speech!'

'The king?'

'Yes, he is going to address us in less than ten minutes! What in the world am I to do? If he notices I will very likely be called upon to explain myself!'

'What were you doing, for heaven's sake?'

'I cast a listening spell on Lord Jenkins. Thought it might be fun to hear him burp in private. Unfortunately he was not burping but flirting with Madame Knorr—hideous, I tell you!—but the listening spell went wrong and I started to laugh…'

'How did it go wrong?'

'Oh, it swivelled by mistake so that it focused on me instead! They heard me laugh and hauled me out by my ears! No sense of humour, I tell you!'

'I should think not! Was it very bad?'

'Dreadful. I sent a million wishes to the weighing room trying to escape, but I don't suppose they were ever even bottled.'

'No, escape from a corrector wand must be one of the most expensive wishes in Elvenswolde!'

Wendleweed looked gloomy.

'I discovered that, alright! I do believe Madame Knorr's wand actually enjoys itself! It hovered over me gleefully and I could swear it did a little dance in the air when it realised I was cornered. I thought I might get one of the velvet chairs, but no! Madame Knorr marched me over to the equilibration laboratory and bent me over a horribly hard lab stool. She didn't spare me, either, stupid witch-elf! It's a wonder my smudge is just a plain purple, not black and blue!'

'Black and blue *is* purple, silly. Just be glad it wasn't Lord Jenkins who dealt with you. I should say after the embarrassment of what he knew you overheard, his corrector wand would have been buzzing.'

'It was, at first. But Madame Knorr dealt with me so thoroughly that his own wand subsided into hardly a hum. At least the wands have to be fair. We have the Wish Maker to thank for that. '

Bickleberry nodded. Wendleweed tried to turn around again to catch a sight of his smudge. 'How long did you say this smudge would last?'

'Only a day if you manage to behave. Sit at the back of the hall and the king might not notice.'

'*He* may not, but Garredung and Silvajar will, and they are part of his majesty's household now.'

'So what? They're still only messenger elves. It is not as though they can punish you themselves!'

'They will never let me hear the end of it!'

'Well, remind them of the river of troubles, then. Ramón once sent them there and I've heard it was worse than ten corrector wands. Ramón does not believe in them.'

'In what?'

'Corrector wands. He thinks they are too simplistic and not very effective in the long term.'

'No, I guess he's right. Can't say I've learned my lesson. I will not stop using listening spells. Much too informative. I will just need to perfect them, that's all.'

Wendleweed giggled and sat down. His smudge rose up before him, so he jumped up again in annoyance.

'I'm going to the back. Have you signed in yet?'

'No, we were just going to now.'

'Hurry! Everyone is being checked. I think this is quite serious. I hope it is something to do with the weather. I can't stand all this rain.

I am certain there is something magic about it. Perhaps the king will know.'

'If he does, will he tell us?'

'I don't see why not. Hush! There is Lord Jenkins and he is frowning! Hurry, sign in or you will be late!'

Bickleberry nodded and sprinted for the queue, which was dwindling down to a few last, breathless latecomers. There would be no seat for him, now, but he didn't mind. The day had been too exciting to sit and at least standing, he could wiggle his weight from side to side and juggle his toes inside their pointed, elfin shoes.

There was meant to be a jaunty curl to the tips of his slippers, but as usual he had forgotten, in his excitement, to apply a good dose of curling polish. His feet now looked particularly long and flat, but he hoped he would not be noticed standing against the hall's back wall.

He signed the noontime register and pushed his way past all the assembled and seated elves to the back. No sign of Xanadel, unfortunately, but he would catch up with him later on the tower stairs. Messenger elves were always running into each other. Bickleberry folded his arms primly (though his toes wriggled secretly and freely) and waited for the arrival of the king.

The Balance Is Broken

It will probably come as no surprise that at the self-same moment that Septimus was hearing the strange, tapping noises and tasting the salts of the sea, Demetria was placing the egg on the summit of her cliff.

It had been a steep climb to the top of Mt. Sarcalet and she was breathless.

Normally, she would have flown, but she did not want to risk being spotted by a dragon on the Southern beaches. No, it was safer (but not easier) to climb. By sheer lumbering, hard work, she finally managed to roll the creature to the edge of the cliff.

She'd again tried the figure of eight position but her tail had not bent far enough. Further, it was true that she was thinner and weaker than usual and seemed to have lost some of her tormenting, crushing spirit.

Without her enormous will, all the scales upon her tail were for nothing. She was fed up with trying to crush the stupid thing. Worse, she was aware that hatching was close. She needed to get back to her perfect, pink eggs.

It was critical that she be there for the hatching, for dragonettes, a little like earth chickens, bond with the first creature their lazy, scaly eyes open and see. A bad mother dragon who leaves her hatchlings at the critical moment might return to find all her fledglings following a lizard (a ridiculous sight, were it not so sad) or a mountain bat. Such things were rare, but not unknown in the dragon world, and a great disgrace and mortification for any mother who has been so careless.

Dragons bred under such conditions have to be immediately parted from their surrogate parent and rigidly retrained, but they are ever after unreliable, and likely at certain seasons of the moon to prefer insects and berry juice to wolf meat, which makes them hopeless hunters and a laughing stock besides.

Demetria pushed the egg onto the very precipice of the cliff and nodded in satisfaction at the rising of the wind. She could waste no more time on the matter, for as soon as the Southerlies kicked in (and they were more fierce now, with the shadow growing over Elvenswolde) the egg was sure to roll off the edge and fall, far flung, to the crashing waves below.

As the princess abandoned her egg, luminous now, and cracking a tiny bit at the tip, she felt more cheerful and light-hearted than she had done in weeks. Mindful of the duties awaiting her, she crawled back to her cave and tried to forget, entirely, the whole, sad incident.

* * *

His majesty looked graver than usual, and older. Wendleweed need not have worried about the tell-tale purple bottom blob that beset him, for the king, for once, was beyond noticing.

His grey beard looked greyer. He looked, in truth, like he was carrying the burden of the kingdom upon his very back. Silvajar and Garredung, standing at attention, looked meaner, more miserable, and thinner.

Bickleberry, who was growing plumper with each day he got to sample the queen's breakfast, grinned. The king's chef must not be so generous!

He shot a glance at Xanadel to see if he would share the joke, but the elf looked sombre. He was touching his amulet and watching the king with an intensity that surprised Bickle, who was more used to him yawning at functions like these than actually listening.

The king softly spoke of strange happenings and dark tidings. He spoke of treachery and imperfections and balance. As he spoke, his voice cracked, as if dry, as if he was struggling to say the things he ought to, struggling to give voice to the strange malady that seemed to be overtaking his land.

'My friends—' his voice cracked and then, to everyone's horror, he dropped to the floor in a dead faint that all but the lowliest of fire sprites could see was bewitched.

There was a scream, and a panic and suddenly all the elves were out of their seats running—Some towards the king, others down the hall, yet more to the closed doors of the tower.

Not the king's tower, which was forbidden, but the queen's. Only the queen's tower was still bathed in sunshine, though it stormed outside and was chill without. At the very peak of that tower, the Wish Maker closed his eyes, refusing to feel the fear that flooded through his veins and vaulted almost through the very fabric of his will.

He ignored the fear, though he knew, as he had known for some time, that the balance of the worlds was now seriously out of kilter.

It was not natural forces that caused this imbalance—he had been careful to study the stars and listen to the whispering of the wood sprites, who knew every leaf of every tree and could predict what winds would come and what wild tides would shake the shores and reach the very roots of their forests.

It was all ordained, the rising and the ebbing, the gales and the quiescence. In every leaf was the tale of balance, of blossom and harvest. But this was no blossoming and no harvesting that Ramón had ever known.

This, he understood, was war. Inevitable, perhaps, for it was the very nature of balance that as he struggled for good there must be an equal struggle, somewhere, for forces of darkness and apathy.

He had known this and tried to control his own impulses, so that the spectrums were not so opposing, not so powerfully antithetical. He had known and failed, for the compulsion to do good was strong, both a blessing and a burden.

Who, he wondered, was that other force, set in opposition to him, bending his mind, reading his will, casting his shadow ever closer over Elvenswolde? The answer, when it came, caused him pain.

He closed his eyes and concentrated on several wish bottles. Two fell off the tower's ledge before they were uncorked. Two precious bottles lost. He steeled himself to concentrate and smiled slowly as the third yielded a master bubble. But before it reached the window's sill, it enlarged, for a moment, then popped.

* * *

Sarah hugged her son closer, joy mingling with loss for she could tell by his eyes that he was no longer hers alone, but a true son of Septimus, come into his own.

Even now, in his shorts and scruffy T-shirt, he had stature; his legs seemed less gangly, more decided, as they wove a path through the tangled weeds to his favourite bench near Ruskin Point. They went there often, she and Septimus. They would take the shoreline walk across the peninsula, he to doodle on a sketchpad, she to take cuttings of wild flowers and herbs.

They would picnic together and as the sun rose to its full height in the skies, they would chat about work, or about school, or about Mr. Carlisle.

Not surprisingly, Sarah disapproved of him and threatened, every so often, to use arrowroot to sour his foolish taste buds. He deserved, she declared, some of his own bitterness.

Septimus would laugh, for arrowroot did not sour up taste buds and was really very harmless, though Sarah believed in it fervently. Sometimes Septimus thought it was *she* who should have been born of Elvenswolde, for she was more whimsical than motherly, and it was far more often *he* who was forced to be the practical one.

Now, as they looked at the sea, it was Septimus who was dreamy and intent, Sarah who was more alert than usual.

'What will you do, Sep?'

'Do?'

'If there is a way back… will you take it?'

Septimus turned to her eagerly.

'Of course I will. Isn't this what you've always hoped for me?'

There was a silence.

Septimus felt less sure of himself, more like a small boy who wanted to throw himself in his mother's arms and have a good, un-ashamed cry. He thought he might have felt that way because Sarah herself looked forlorn, fragile against the stone bench and the brilliant sky behind her.

'Mum…'

She said nothing but held out her arms, half hoping the gesture would cover her confusion and the tears that rushed to her eyes.

'You must go, Sep. You were born to be there. Only promise you will come back!'

'Is there no way… mum, can you not come with me?'

Sarah looked at Septimus sadly. She did not answer, only her hands dropped to her sides in a helpless gesture Septimus found haunting.

'Are you certain?'

'Certain. Look at your father. In loving me, he lost the very memory of Elvenswolde. There is no place for earth people in a land of deep magic.'

'I am half earth myself!'

'There is more of your father in you than there is of me. If El-venswolde has opened to you, then you are worthy.'

'It has not opened! That is the frustrating thing!'

'Have patience, Sep, it will.'

'How can you be so sure?'

Sarah looked smug. Smug and mysterious.

'I may not be born with the deep magic, but I know things. I know you will not rest till you find a way. I know you will not have been shown if there was no meaning. I know… oh, Septimus, I know that this life I am forging for you is not the right one!

'You were born to more, more than I am able to teach you, more than all the Mr. Carlisles of the world can teach you. You are elemen-tal, Septimus, born with a lightness that your friends don't perceive and will never understand. That is why you feel different, Sep, and why people stare at you as though you are strange. Though you wear the same faded shorts as they do and throw the same stones into the same streams and eat the same lunches—'

Septimus, who was having trouble swallowing, and whose glasses would have been fogging up had he worn them—which he didn't, for they were for close up only and he hated the so uncool frames—laughed.

He did not feel like laughing, but it was better than crying and it lightened the worry lines about Sarah's smooth complexion. He watched her push the hair back from her face and chuckled mischievously.

'My lunches are hardly the same as everyone else's, mum! Soggy sandwiches, no salt...' Sarah grinned. She had never been much of a cook and though Septimus senior loved her dearly, he'd more often than not ordered her out of the kitchen to avoid enduring her particular brand of lunch.

What made her food worse was that she would insist on sprinkling some undesirable herb or other, convinced that the properties would guard her family from the ill effects of all sorts of things. These ranged from the real to the truly ridiculous.

Septimus could vaguely stomach chopped nettles for its antiseptic properties, but he drew the line at gorse for danger (keeping out of, that is) and lavender for happiness. No amount of lavender, he'd discovered, could make one happy to have a detention, or to miss out on the Cirque du Soleil when all the other kids were taking the ferry to see it. Besides, it smelled ghastly in muffins, tasted worse in stews and could not be hidden in sandwiches.

No, Sarah was never sensible, or 'normal' as mothers went, but she was wonderful and fun and as spiritual as the night stars that seemed to cluster about her open window. Septimus loved her fiercely. As she smiled, he knew without speaking that she felt the same way.

'I shall come back, I feel it.'

She tousled his head. 'I should hope so! You may be a great warrior in Elvenswolde, but you will always be my little baby, Sep.'

'Ugh!'

Sarah smiled. 'I remember the day you were born. So beautiful and soft, ten perfect fingers...'

Septimus rolled his eyes upwards but played the game they always played. 'And ten perfect little toes... yeah right, mum.'

'Race you back!'

Sarah, always unexpected, grabbed the lunch things and gathered up her skirts. Before Septimus could think about his sandals (which were lying upside down under a rather prickly bush) she had beaten him to the post, which, as it happened, was a sign saying, 'No littering by order of the Rutherham District Council.'

Septimus shook his head. 'I wish you would stop doing that!'

Instantly, the wish was bottled in Elvenswolde and labelled by a confused bottling fairy on the wrong side of Galathgraine, one of the outer districts of Elvenswolde proper. 'Wish she would stop doing what?' Corkindale, the rather junior bottling fairy (no stripe) wondered out loud. Her supervisor ambled over and frowned.

'What was she doing?'

Hardly any of the fairies had noticed, most being on a tea break, or muttering about the smell of meticlaws oozing from some of the bottles.

'You are supposed to be on duty!'

'I know, but I never expected... that is, I expected a bigger wish somehow...'

The supervisor scoffed at such inexperience.

'Let me see. Out of corner of my eye I saw her running down the hill, then she was laughing—'

Septimus would have been horrified to know that Corkindale— silly, silly girl—very nearly bottled a 'do-not-laugh' wish for Sarah.

It was just lucky that another, more sensible fairy had heard his mum cough. She'd suggested, therefore, a bottling of good health. The wish bottle had immediately purpled up and been sent on to the weighing rooms at Castle Carne.

It is a mark of how seriously Septimus's wishes were being taken, that to this day, Sarah Kahikatea has not had a single sniffle, sneeze or hint of a wheeze.

Amberkine

The days dragged on.

Septimus had several detentions. (Deserved, for it was perfectly true he was not paying attention,) and Sarah prepared herself for the day when her son might simply disappear from her world in order to play his part in another.

She baked biscuits filled with… well, Septimus did not like to think what they were filled with, for they had a disgusting greenish goo in the middle that hardly resembled icing… and she made him eat them, which he felt most indignant about.

Sarah was adamant. They were, she was convinced, for clear headedness and stamina.

Septimus could not deny he needed these qualities if he were to enter Elvenswolde by his wits.

One evening, when he was good naturedly scoffing down a number of potions, herbs, lotions and biscuits—Sarah had left him a selection—he was surprised when she appeared carrying a box that looked old, and smelt of rich woods. It was inlaid with delicate copper and twists of sparkling silver that shimmered almost like gold.

Septimus sat up. He could see his mum trembling, almost as though her little trinket box had a life of its own.

'This belonged to your father. Before he entirely lost his memory of Elvenswolde, he asked me to keep it safe for you, his son. He said if ever a day would come when you should need it, I would know. I pressed him to tell me more, but he could not—would not say. There's a jewel in there. From Elvenswolde.'

Sep looked eager, but Sarah looked sad.

'Oh, Sep! When he gave it to me it was such a vivid blue, bluer than the most beautiful of our earth's sapphires, but stranger yet.'

'Why strange?'

'It burned from inside with a fire. The outside was blue, but you could look into the gem and see the oranges and the ambers and the ruby reds of flames burning deep within. It was… it was wonderful!'

Septimus felt a deep sense of foreboding at these words. He needed little telling that the jewel would no longer be as beautiful.

'What happened?'

Sarah sighed wistfully and pushed a hair from her forehead.

'I don't know. I don't understand it. The jewel stopped glowing a long time ago and now it looks as dull as an old glass bottle left to the ravages of time.'

'Let me see.'

Septimus bent over the box. His fingers seemed to tingle as they connected with the shimmering twists of silver. His stomach felt hollow from nerves, but the rich woods smelt comforting and he hesitated only a fraction as he twisted at the copper catches.

He heard the small creak as the old box, rarely opened, unlocked slowly, permitting the light to flood into the folds of dark satin that protected and covered his treasure. Slowly, he pulled aside the soft black and peered in.

His father's gift—the only one he'd ever had—if you discount a tricycle and a penguin hat—lay revealed. It was a necklace, interconnected on a dark rope of some sort. The gem sat in the inside of some fairly rudimentary knots, looking rather like a piece of broken glass – but not sharp. Possibly even a bluish brick, slightly crumbled. Septimus bent over it, hoping to see the fires that Sarah had so wistfully spoken of. There was not a flame to be seen, only particles of dust wedged in a very flawed stone.

'Put it on, Sep. The Amulet of Amberkine. Your dad would have wanted you to.'

Septimus swallowed. He did not wish to seem spoilt, but he was strange enough *not* to want to seem stranger still by appearing at school with a broken bit of glass wound round his neck.

He could almost hear the snickers. Sarah was staring at him anxiously, expectantly. He did not wish to disappoint her. He took the rope and slung it about his neck. (He could always take it off before school. Yes, definitely the thing to do if he did not want to be laughed out of existence!).

For an instant, he could almost have sworn he felt the flame blaze within. A flash, too, startled Sarah. When both looked closely, there was nothing but the dismal bottle-blue and the wedged-in dust.

Very disappointing.

For his mum's sake though, he smiled and murmured politely that he was very pleased to have something of his dad's. Indeed, the box was a treasure in itself. It would be great for his shell collection.

The necklace felt heavy on him, and strange. He wondered if perhaps his inner excitement was playing tricks on him, for he felt a hum—almost a heartbeat—quivering from within the gem. He smiled. Elvenswolde did not seem so very far way, at all. Perhaps he would wear it under his tee.

On Tuesday Septimus was emptying bins. (Mr Carlisle thought detentions should serve a useful purpose—that is, be as unpleasant as possible.) As he dealt with a particularly disgusting one, he experienced a sudden shiver of excitement.

He had been very, very careful with his wishes, lately.

He had not dared to wish Mr Carlisle to the devil or even hope that he had some incurable disease. It was fun thinking curses, but not actually meaning them.

He was tired.

Tired of Mr Carlisle and his petty punishments, tired of cleaning out bins (he'd accidentally wished some of them clean and felt guilty when they'd instantly emptied, becoming bright blue, as if brand new and not ten years old and smelly from a thousand half-eaten sandwiches and dozens of milk cartons thrown away and left to sour in the noonday sun.)

Mr Carlisle had been pleased, which was rare for him, but then he had given Septimus more to do and this time Septimus had felt far too awful about wasting wishes to waste any more, so he'd had to clean harder than ever and waste his entire break and still feel sickened by the smells.

It was very hard being careful about wishes. Septimus had not realised how often he wished for things and silly things too—he wished Tiffany would stare at the blackboard rather than at him (and sure enough the whole of Monday she'd stared unwaveringly at the board until even Mr Carlisle had been exasperated). On Tuesday, Septimus had wished Max on the other side of the world and the boy had vanished—simply vanished—for the entire afternoon.

When he'd reappeared at his seat he had been humming Jaluka's *Scatterlings of Africa* and his lunch was a bowl of soft mieliemiel and pap, much to his disgust and mystification.

Septimus noticed that he was rather vacant, and suspected strongly the workings of forget-me-dust. He grinned, but felt crushed that he had again been so careless with his wishes.

Max relocated to the Northern side of the Limpopo River in Southern Africa was one thing, but wasting possibly the only chance Septimus had of getting into Elvenswolde was quite another.

He was impatient—very impatient—with the waiting.

He remembered what Arikeet had said about visualisation, and spent a long time, after school, imagining Elvenswolde and what it must look like.

Unfortunately, Arikeet had not been very specific about the geography of the place, so it was left solely to Septimus's wild imagining, some of which was very far off the mark and some (had he but known it) had nearly sent him flying off to some of the lesser worlds and even to that dark one, where the wizard of Ramón's torment continued to cast his spells and wreak havoc with the elements of balance.

Oh yes, Septimus had a sudden sense of foreboding. Once, almost like a second sight, he had envisioned a dark room in a round fortress with a silver cloak flying. He had almost smelled meticlaws, though of course no one of his world ever could have done, and he had no knowledge of it himself.

The sensation shocked him. Had he wished, at that moment, he would almost certainly have come face to face with the dark master, not in the dark world, perhaps, but in the tower of the king.

Fortunately, Septimus had not wished. Gracious, why should he have? He could not think of anything worse to wish for. If he wished anything at all, it would have been that the image had not suddenly invaded his thoughts and made him grave.

He remembered the wing bearer's warning that Elvenswolde had not much time and he shivered, wondering if his imagining were in any way real. He hoped not, but dug in his backpack all the same to clutch at his amulet.

It felt warm and wild and comforting and Septimus knew, just at that moment, that he was meant to wear it. He must wear it and head for the sea, for it was the ocean that called him with its wild whispers and its waves of wind-filled sound.

Where had that thought come from?

He stared, for it seemed that the amulet, still clasped in his fingers, was glowing a little. He examined it closely but it was still opaque, that strange, glassy bottle blue that always disappointed him.

But wait! There were flames within, flames curling into crisp little wisps of lettering. He squinted. You had to squint to see it, for staring at the necklace directly did no good at all.

Sep had the strangest feeling that his jewel was glowing, shuddering with life. He stared past it to the grass beyond, allowing his eyes to shift out of focus. Then, terrified to move lest the image vanish like some sad mirage, he slid his gaze back to the gem, but in that same squinty, unfocused way.

It took so long that Septimus seriously thought he was going a little nutty. He was becoming desperate, he was imagining things—

He was not imagining things! There were flames and the flames were unfurling into words! Septimus tried to remain calm. He controlled his breathing. He squinted. He prayed that no one—not even Freddy Watling, who he rather liked—would find him and disturb him. Looking past the stone, beyond him, to the grass, he read the shivers of red flame that blazed from within the deepest, midnight blue:

Oh seventh son of a seventh son,
listen well to worlds half gone,
whisper wishes, oh seventh son,
and let the tides in ribbons run.
Wish in waves, oh elfin mind,
to counter calls from darker kind.
By moons, by dale, by clouded wood,
stand tall where once the wise ones stood.
Stand tall and listen, oh seventh elf,
to whispered worlds, to shattered stealth,
now splintered into half- light shadows
and blades of grass on sleeping meadows,
But hear, oh hear, oh seventh son,
for when you're called the need is long.
Hearken well, oh Septimus,
the song you hear is the call of us—
In Elvenswolde the trees grow tall.
In Elvenswolde we stand, not fall.

The blaze extinguished almost on the last word and no amount of squinting and staring and gazing at grass would make it come back. Septimus cursed that he had no pen to write the message down.

He had no paper, either, to immortalise those strange words that must be so very laden with meaning. He wondered what they meant and was surprised to find that he needed no pen after all.

He could recall the words as clearly as if he had learnt them off by heart for some summer school prize.

They whispered over him, calming him, like a spring breeze filled with the scents of summer. They meant something to him, though he understood so little, so pitifully little. He wondered whether he'd felt that urge to test the tides, or whether it was the amulet's charm that had called him there.

Either way, it was to the sea that he was headed. To the sea, in search of some other world, some secret pathway that would lead him from Rutherham, the familiar haunt of his childhood, to Elvenswolde.

* * *

The queen's tower was still bathed in sunshine, but the king—the King of Elvenswolde itself—was in a swoon such as his subjects had never seen before.

The queen wept and Ramón the Wish Maker looked grave indeed. He had not needed to examine the king to know that the balance of good and evil was swaying, now, in the enemy's favour. Like himself, a Wish Maker, but silver cloaked and dark. Not completely dark, but darker than himself, undoubtedly. He only hoped he was not too late.

He only hoped he had opened Elvenswolde to the base magic, the lower keyed, more resonant magic of myth, fast enough to counter the mark of that other one.

Garbed in silver, yet shadowed so dark, so unbearably, shamefully dark.

Ramón had known of his nature when he taught him, known that the shadows of his mind were ravines he should not traverse. He had known and still taught.

He had thought it necessary, necessary for the balance of life. He had been so conscious of his own gravitation to light, his own pinnacles of brightness. Fearing that his preferences would cause him to act out of kilter with the heavens, he had taught that other, darker incantation of himself.

He had taught Móran, his twin, and now he lived to regret it. Seeing the king's face and ashen countenance, he cursed himself for this arrogance. He had thought himself so good that bad was a necessary ingredient for balance. He had not thought that bad knows no bounds, yields no boundaries, crushes each unspoken barrier.

Good, with its reticence, its circumspection, its respect for rules and rights and reason, is self-limiting. Goodness itself upsets the balance, for it passively permits evil to reign. In the name of fairness and freedom it watches and waits, as evil takes and torments. Oh, hard lessons and late learned!

Ramón could have kicked himself as he watched the king, riddled in pain, not so much of the body as of the soul. The Wish Maker knew well it was the king himself who had welcomed Móran and permitted him through the portals.

It had to have been him, not any lowly messenger of Elvenswolde. Betrayal was by the king himself. It could only have been he, for Ramón had cast the spell of expulsion on his brother. He had taught him, he had loved him and he had learnt to despair.

To protect Elvenswolde—and the balance—he had cast Móran to the furthest world, a world of dark and cold, a world where Ramón had known that deep deeds were being done and poison potions potted.

He had thought to serve both Móran and himself. The balance would be achieved if he committed to light and Móran to dark. But Móran had been cunning, allowing light to filter into his notions, so that Ramón had no option but to tamper with the dark himself. Oh, he had been skilful, very skilful!

The king, torn asunder, blinded by—Ramón did not know what temptations he had been blinded with—had welcomed the twin to his tower.

From the day he had entered there, the spire had never seen the light of the sun, had never been draped in warmth or dappled by dew. It was only the queen's that still smelt of summer and promised of spring. It was to the queen's tower that the king had been carried and it was in Ramón's own chamber that he now lay, ashen and shallow of breath.

'Will he live?'

The queen whispered the only question she dared ask. She knew that there was another, more important query she must not voice. She was loath to think of her husband as a traitor, but she feared he had betrayed them—betrayed Elvenswolde all—by permitting in the darker elements, the wilder things.

Ramón shook his head. 'Your majesty, I cannot tell. The king's malady is not so much of the body as of the spirit, though he is very weak and must rest. He has been fighting, I fear, far more than he ever should have had to.

'I shall prepare some soothing balms for him and a potion for calmness. The potion should keep him still, but increase his breathing from these shallow, hopeless gasps to a deep, more resonant slumber. His breath shall no longer be torn from him.

'Send a messenger—Bickleberry or Wendleweed, perhaps, for Master Hepple—he is the best healer I know. He will bring with him herbs and plants from Willowsham, where the potency is far greater than here by Castle Carne. It will be a day's journey each way or more if this foul weather holds. In the meanwhile, I will attend to the king and you may ask Xanadel if he'd care to help me.'

'What of the king's own attendants?'

Ramón was silent for a moment. Then, speaking in a softer voice, he whispered that it was wiser not to permit the king's servants near his person, now or at any other time. He hesitated, and then added, 'Possibly not even into this tower either, your majesty, though it might prove difficult.'

The queen paled, for though she was not always privy to matters of court, she realised at once what Ramón was hesitant to say.

The king's tower was infected by some powerful magic, some serious state of imbalance that made the balance of her own tower, bathed in sunlight, more imperative than ever.

If by some mischance or calculated act of cunning, the malaise that affected the king should infect her people, the balances would shift to darkness.

Elvenswolde, her dear, beloved Elvenswolde, would never be the same again. She wept for the king, the keeper of her heart, but she wept more for what he had become and what he had permitted, whether through negligence or intent she knew not.

'I will stand firm, Ramón. The king's tower shall be secured and my own guards set at their gates. I grieve for the messengers and the cooks and the attendants and the courtiers, but it must be so. I shall organize fresh supplies to be set at their door every morning and you shall name a man of consequence to rule them, for now, in the king's stead.'

'Very wise, your majesty, for I fear chaos and discontent shall be easy partners in the king's tower. I suggest the Lord Avon for such a responsibility, though he shall not be pleased at the new circumstances. Still, if he is raised to King's chancellor, he might be counted on to keep the peace rather than to fight it.'

The queen nodded.

'Might I also suggest some messenger elves—Garredung and Silvajar perhaps—be enlisted to secure the king's rooms. They are already resident in that tower. We cannot be too careful, and we must protect, at all costs, the great tomes of enchantments and the spells of Elvenswolde, our greatest secrets—against unlawful entry.'

Ramón did not say that he feared that this security had already been breached. The queen had enough to contend with without worrying her further. She nodded, smiled weakly, then called for some parchment to lay forth her decrees.

It was late when Bickleberry and Wendleweed set off, but both were kitted out with moon torches (beautiful lights that drifted above their head like little orbs. They had the added facility of snuffing out on command.)

They were also fully furnished with fairy wings. These were not as wonderful as they sound, for they were standard issue, entry level wings designed for classrooms rather than fairy tales. Believe it or not, they were actually ugly (frog green) and strapped on cumbersomely over the head with ties that Bickleberry found itchy. All the same, for small distances they were handy and flapped gently enough to allow the travellers to merely skim the ground, avoiding nasty mud pools or sharp little rock hills that might cut at their sandalled feet.

The wings were no good for long distances though, for they were slow and required quite a knack to use, rather like roller-blading for the first time, only trickier.

Twice Bickleberry landed up flying backwards and once he got stuck in the branches of a tree. Wendleweed (still sporting a faint purple blob) had to climb up and pull the wings off all by himself. After that, they had mainly walked, for it was foolish to waste time when the queen depended on them so much.

The path smelled wonderful and fresh to Bickleberry, who had not been allowed out of Castle Carne for some time, now, ever since he had got into a spot of trouble over water sprites that lived at the forest's edge.

'Bickleberry, wait up!'

Far, far into the night, the friends, half-running, half-walking, half-resting, half-talking, made their steady way towards Willowsham.

They were watched, but the watchers were still and made no moves, save to call to their master and howl, howl into the night's wind. Bickleberry, not in tune with such matters, shivered but remarked only upon the cold.

The Call

Oh seventh son of a seventh son,
listen well to worlds half gone,
whisper wishes, oh seventh son,
and let the tides in ribbons run.
Wish in waves, oh elfin mind,
to counter calls from darker kind.

Septimus felt he knew the meaning but could not explain it, only that his senses were alert and that the sea was calling to him, more strongly than usual and more plaintively.

High above Rutherham, on the western slopes of Mt. Arthur, he closed his eyes. Out of breath, he desperately tried to visualise as the wing bearer had shown him.

Below, the sea was calm but a breeze was rising, fresh, fresh from the frothy foam beneath him, dappling the sands in white. He felt an aching, then a dark shiver run through his being, a shiver that called not of Elvenswolde, but of something deeper, something much darker and more inexpressible. He felt like he was being pulled asunder.

He felt, for a moment, like he was a plaything, a toy, a mere instrument of forces greater than he understood.

He didn't like the feeling. It was creepy. And he didn't like being alone.

He felt a pain at his forehead, but when he tried to grasp it, his hands were fixed to his side and he could do no more than stare, immobile, at the darkening seas.

Wish in waves, you seventh son,
to counter calls from darker ones

Where had that thought come from? It released him, his hands
pressed at his forehead but the pain had shifted and he felt it, now, behind his back, below his spine, in that one spot where it is impossible
to reach. Wish in waves—he had to, for he was certain that the pain
was not of earth but of Elvenswolde.

The pain was from the darker ones, calling him, striving, striving to reach him from beyond those earthly seas. He had no idea who
the darker ones were, if anything, but he was darn near certain he had
a lousy headache!

He tried to ignore the pain, knowing that he had to, that nothing,
nothing must distract him in this moment, not even his mum, waving
at him from the stone path as she climbed slowly towards him, her
hands filled with flowers. Or maybe a bundle of revolting herbs. With
her, he could never be sure.

He was less afraid than surprised that he had not seen it before,
the running rivers of the tides, reflecting not the waters or the sun's
setting rays, but his thoughts. Some were dark, and here he saw riv-
ulets deeper than the ripple of azure across the sea's great expanse.

Wish in waves—he wished. He wished so hard he thought he
was floating, floating half above the canyon, this point so familiar to
him and Sarah.

But that was seconds only, and though the pain had vanished, so
too had that feeling of flying. He blinked and caught his breath as his
mother, watching closely, ran from his left.

'Septimus! Something has happened! Tell me!'

So Septimus, feeling a little hesitant, tried to describe the last
few moments. It sounded ridiculous in plain English.

But Sarah was a stubborn believer. She patted his shoulder with
understanding and a little of her own sorrow.

'You must be close, Sep. You felt the calls of darker ones. I saw
you, standing there, immobilised. I saw your face in pain. Oh, Sep,
sometimes I would rather you were earth born and not the seventh son
a seventh son after all. Sometimes I can hardly bear it.'

'But you do, mum, and you must help me to bear it too. I feel it now, the weight of it. I hope—I just hope I don't land up disappointing you.'

'Never! You are your father's son. He was strong and he gave me joy. You are strong, and you shall do the same. Now let me think.' Sarah mused. Septimus waited, his eyes still dark from what he had felt.

'Say that verse again? The one you saw through your amulet?
Septimus obediently muttered the words.

'By moons, by dale, by clouded wood,
stand tall where once the wise ones stood.
Stand tall and listen, oh seventh elf,
to whispered worlds and shattered stealth,
now splintered into half-light shadows
And blades of grass on sleeping meadows.'

'It will be night when you leave—that's obvious. I wonder if they mean our moon or their moons? Maybe both, but night definitely. But where, and from what point? Why are prophecies always in riddles, for heaven's sake? What is wrong with plain English or Elf tongue? I think it is the fault of all those sooth singers—they must have too much time on their hands.'

Septimus nodded absently. Sarah was only complaining because she was anxious. She always grumbled when she was worried.

'Who were the wise ones? Some statues, maybe?'

Sarah thought. 'I don't think so. Rutherham is not built on Roman remains.'

'What about in Elvenswolde itself?'

'Could be, but your father never spoke of statues. He used stars to guide him, to capture the single strand in time that overlapped with other worlds.'

'There is no mention of stars in the charm.'

'No, so the path must be different—'

'Different yet the same. The moons—they indicate night.'

'Yes, and a double moon, symbol of Elvenswolde—hey it could be the sea's reflection of our own across the water. Two moons!'

'Yes, stretching it a bit, but ok—so where am I to stand tall? It would help if I weren't so short. And wise ones—We're still no wiser. Ha-ha.'

'Don't be flippant. And you're tall for your age. You're on your growth spurt.'

'So you keep telling me! I'm hardly a giant, mum! Max Jones towers over me.'

'Don't talk to me of that boy. I can't stand him. His dad gives me the creeps and his mum—hmmph.'

'Ok, forget him. So where do I stand tall?'

'Slow down, Sep, I haven't the faintest idea—no, it can't be!'

'What?'

'Sep, it is just an idea but what if the twin stars of Gemini equate to the twins of Siluse and Ventrimuse, the Northern stars of Elvenswolde? It would make sense, with stars as a guide.'

'What then?'

'Siluse and Ventrimuse were known as the wise ones—your father told me the tale while we were first courting. They were evidently great warriors of Elvenswolde who died defending the farthest shores of the realm against dragons. They were renowned for their wisdom and courage and it is said that when they were crushed against the rocks of Sarcalet they transfigured themselves into stars, far higher and far brighter than any dragon could dare to go or be. To this day, their lights cast a night glow on the Elf land. Your father had to wait on their alignment to traverse between the worlds.'

Septimus blinked. 'Ye-es, but even so, even if I look to Castor and Pollux, the twins of Gemini, I would not know where to stand. The stars are above us. Everywhere, not just in one particular spot. You might as well say, "go stand somewhere in the Southern hemisphere."'

'I know, but it's the only kind of idea we have. Tonight. By moon, by dale, by clouded wood—doesn't that remind you of something?'

Septimus shook his head. 'No.'

'What about our forest, Sep, where the woods dip down into the valley, where the forest pines grow so tall I can never reach the best of the cones—come Sep, you know where I mean! Where the sulphur crested cockatoos fly free and I collect that long reed I call willowblane—you know, the one you always make such a fuss about eating?'

Septimus made a face.

'How can I forget, mum? And they're not cockatoos, they're keas, I think. Cockatoos are white and native to Australia. Keas are Green. Alpine parrots, which is why you have to climb so high. But you are right, I suppose, that dip could be considered a dale, and the mists *did* obscure our watching—but there must be hundreds of places just like it!'

'We have to start somewhere, and it makes sense that it should be close. You were ordained for this, remember, in the ancient myths of the magical places. If you just wish, under the stars, in the right place and in the right setting—hey, our surname's Kahikatea. Septimus must have adopted that for a reason. I wonder if that means anything?'

'You mean apart from Kahikatea? As in the native Kahaikatea tree, duh?'

Septimus could not help sounding a little sceptical. Now Sarah was clutching at straws! He was used to his mum going off on a tangent no kid could actually take seriously. He felt a bit depressed. He could just see another weird excuse note being generated for the benefit of Mr Carlisle and a snickering class. He touched the rope about his neck, and somehow felt better.

'Think of the craggy rocks of Sarcalet and the waves crashing against their heights. Think of great rings of dragons and—'

Septimus laughed.

'Mum, your imagination is running wild! I have never seen Sarcalet, never mind a dragon!'

'Neither have I, but think of the danger, of seas pounding against cliffs, think of that lighthouse we saw last winter, Septimus, which looked so marooned and treacherous against the landscape. Think of skies darkened with dragons circling—we may not know what a dragon looks like for sure, but mythology has brought them to us through art, Sep. The images are all very similar. They are large scaly creatures with great talons and wings—Sep, I really think I'm onto something!'

In spite of himself, Septimus laughed. 'I'm sure it will all be wrong! Besides, if you are right, I will be wishing myself into the worst possible place fraught with terrible dragonish danger!'

'Humour me.'

> *But hear, oh hear, oh seventh son*
> *for when you're called the need is long*
> *Hearken well, oh Septimus*
> *The song you hear is the call of us.*

Septimus tried to ignore the whispers that seemed to be exciting his very blood. 'I'm only a kid.'

'You're more than a kid, Sep. You always have been. I felt it when you were just a baby born and you looked at me. Such knowing eyes! I am terrified to let you leave me, do you think I want to permit you to enter a place where I have no control or ability to help when you need help, save only with my love, which surely, surely must cross all boundaries?'

'How can you do it, then, mum?'

The question was almost a whisper.

'I can do it because I believe in you, Sep, and in the base magic which goes deeper even than Elvenswolde. You are not quite mine— you are half of that world. Your time is coming, Septimus, and I will let go because I have to, and because it is what you are born to. There will be dangers, but you will overcome them. You are strong. So are the myths of Elvenswolde that lie deeper than our seas, darker than our night skies. They sing of a seventh son of a seventh son that will be the saving of Elvenswolde. If that is you, then you must, surely, outdistance your enemies and defeat your own terror.'

'Well, I bloody well hope it is me! There are probably a dozen kids who are the seventh sons of seventh sons, now I come to think of it! I will stumble into Elvenswolde like some sort of conquering hero, and feel like an idiot.'

'Don't be ridiculous. How many seventh sons of seventh sons have you come across? And don't forget, it has to be a direct line with no incidental daughters along the way. The statistical chances are infinitesimal. You're it, I'm afraid.'

'But—'

'Shh, no buts. Your dad must have known the path back. Of course he did. That is why he passed the amulet to me. It was almost the last action he took before he lost his lingering memories and became grounded to earth for all time.'

'In all of Elvenswolde, I am sure there is no nicer mum.'

Sarah smiled gently through her tears, then handed him a sandwich. It looked like whole-wheat bread laced with spiders. Ground cinnabar, Septimus was told. The seventh son of a seventh son grinned. One thing was certain; the food could only be better in the next world!

* * *

The dragonette rolled over. 'Bother!' he thought. 'This lovely casement is going to crack and I'm not yet ready!'

He was ready, of course, for his wings were curled about his body in perfect symmetry. His little claws too had grown sharp nails that scratched at the delicate blue above his head. Little patches of sunlight had begun to peek through and annoy his eyes, which he shut more tightly than ever, though it was now impossible to sleep.

The winds were very high, and had the little dragon prince but known it, he was actually closer to death than life. The egg had gradually rolled closer to the edge and was even now in danger of being crushed completely by one of the flying rocks that hurtled in the wind and cascaded down the precipice like a waterfall of falling stones. In the distance, he could faintly hear the muted cries of his brothers and sisters hatching in the comfort of Princess Demetria's cave.

It was just a tiny sound, caught now and again in the wind, but it annoyed the little blue dragon, who hated to be reminded of the fact that his days of laziness were really over. They all sounded like cry-babies and though the dragon was still new to this world, he was perfectly certain he could not abide cry-babies.

He was just beginning to think that maybe, after all, he could stretch his legs just a smidgeon, when his nostrils breathed out an enormous gust of flame and he nearly choked on the smoke. The egg cracked—it had to, it was simply inevitable—and the poor dragon, dazed and confused—had not the time to think of his shell any more.

Now he was caught in a whirling, swirling gust of air that lifted him high, high off the ground and above the cliff tops. He was too small to think of using his wings (which indeed were still stiff from their shell and covered in a moist, oily substance that needed to dry and harden in the sun before they would be of any use) so he kept them folded as he began falling, plunging, dipping, drowning to his death in the icy seas below.

* * *

Septimus, at that precise moment, was gazing at the earth's moon. It was pearly pink and very large and luminous. Sarah, watching him, smiled. He was wearing the amulet and looked as tall as his father and just as handsome. Well, he was a little long and gangly, still youthful, with that wide grin of his and those open, honest eyes, but a man all the same. A young man, on the brink of a very great adventure.

The air crackled with tension. A thousand thoughts whirled through Sarah's head as her hair, waist long, flew about her shoulders, wilder than usual, almost as much a part of the elements as Sarah herself. Her thoughts were multiple and frantic. Would Septimus be warm enough? He had only a jersey in his pack and a whole heap of earth things that were probably no good at all in a land like Elvenswolde. She began an inventory of them in her head. It was best to be prepared—what colour were dragons? Would Sep meet his brothers, his cousins—would she ever see him again—were they wasting their time? Was she being ridiculous?

Above them, the twin stars of Gemini twinkled brightly in the cool breeze. An owl hooted and Sep closed his eyes to concentrate

Not on an owl, but a dragon, and a crashing sea and long, tall trees in the background waving majestically in a wind that howled from the north. He imagined the famous Southerlies of Elvenswolde, whispered in myths and winter legends. They were never spoken of on earth save by the breezes and the gale's gusts that quivered, at times, like leaves shaking from some greater tremor.

He imagined turrets, castles and wing bearer rulebooks. He concentrated on everything he knew, felt and imagined about that land of his father. (He probably got it all wrong, but he did his best.)

He took a deep breath and reflected on himself as a boy and on himself as a young man with a destiny. He was Septimus Kahikatea of Rutherham, his very name—Kahikatea—resonant of the tall trees of this land.

He was also Septimus of Elvenswolde, the seventh son of a seventh son, called by the base magic, half of Earth and half of elf. He thought these things and it seemed to him that as he thought, the magic grew stronger. The glimmer of Sarah's hair seemed to melt into the mists and become part of the pearly moon. Her eyes seemed to become distant lights twinkling at him, star-bright with encouragement, longing and love.

He looked forward, not back, then made the one wish he had been saving, the one wish he had not wasted on Mr Carlisle or sandwiches or taking the bullying look off stupid Max Jones's face.

The wish fairies, tingling and on the alert for such a wish, stood over their bottles with their wands poised. This wish, when bottled, would ripen immediately. It did not matter, they'd been told, how expensive the wish or how difficult. They weren't even to bother with the weigh stations.

Xanadel, waiting, was poised to run up the great marbled staircase, curve after curve, flight after flight without stopping until he reached Ramón. With the king unconscious and the dark forces unleashed, this was the one wish, of all incoming wishes, that would be granted immediately. If it meant that yet another bottle of oozing meticlaws be uncorked, so be it.

In the wish room, the smell was now very dreadful. The wish fairies (those without poised wands) blocked their noses and waited.

When the wish arrived, it was powerful and evocative and incredibly clear, quite unusual for an earth wish. Septimus could hardly hear himself think, such was the raging about his ears as he imagined the sea. He shut his eyes, imagining the circling dragons and the dark enchantment and the rivers of Elvenswolde and the call, the call—

> *But hear, oh hear, oh seventh son*
> *For when you're called the need is long*
> *Hearken well, oh Septimus*
> *The song you hear is the call of us.*

When he opened his eyes, Sarah was gone. He was standing on a cliff and the moon had vanished. It was day, and freezing and the tides were high.

* * *

If a dragon tear could have dropped, it would have. The hatchling was most annoyed at having his life cut so short. He was too innocent to know anything about fairness, but everything in his little being screamed to him that *this* was not fair.

He closed his eyes tightly against the wind and the rain and the impact that he was hurtling towards. He knew, somehow, that it would hurt.

He was caught in a hopeless dive—hopeless—and he would never know what it was to stretch his wings or to breathe the fire of life or to eat the meat of wolves or the morsels of elf stew that dragons so love to steal.

'Aaaaaaaaaah! Aaaaaaah! Aaaaaaaagh!' Thump!

The crash came sooner than he expected.

He had anticipated, with some kind of inborn intuition, the salt of the sea in his nostrils, the freezing of his scales, the thunderous thud of a belly flop.

He felt none of these.

What he felt, in some dazed moments, was pain. It was a warm pain, a pain that was actually quite pleasant if one disregarded the form of it, and the fact that one's wings, still tightly closed, now were dented and out of joint.

Keen ears heard an intake of breath, then an 'ouch!' Then a soft series of boyish moans. Curious, he felt motivated to open his little dragon eye and view his world for the first time.

The Lively Consequences
of a Dragon Hatching

The oceans were raging. It seemed, to a small dragon, as though the very froth was furious. He didn't care. As a matter of fact, he was relieved. He heaved a great sigh of gladness, for though water was crashing about him, splashing high, high across cliffs cragged with moss, wetting him here, wetting him there (the icy splashes were rather invigorating) he felt quite comfy.

He seemed to be safe on something soft on a spiky ledge that jutted out from the sea. Above him loomed the great cliffs of Sarcalet.

He examined the something soft. It was, in fact, the first living thing he'd ever laid eyes upon. Naturally—because it was the dragon way—he assumed that the wingless creature with the long legs and blonde, wispy hair was his mum. Never mind that it had no scales and was staring at him in a very dazed fashion. Never mind that it was not fierce or green or breathing maternal fires of delight. It was warm and sweet and somewhat pale. He loved it.

So glad was he, so full his heart, that he breathed a great gust of happiness. Unfortunately, it took the shape of an enormous—a huge, a really most gigantic flame. It was ten times larger than the one that had cracked his shell and caused all the trouble in the first place.

The person beneath him—who was not, as the dragon seemed to think, his mum—gave a blood-curdling yell and shrieked as his golden earth hair singed. Mortified, the hatchling flapped his wings (quite a feat, for they were still moist from the afterbirth) but only managed to fan the sudden flame.

The boy fell to his knees and dipped his head in the rock pools that were full from the sea's fury. The action extinguished the flames but not, evidently, the pain. He moaned as he glared at the dragon child. He was hideous and probably dangerous.

'Stay! Don't you move a step closer or I'll—I'll—I'll force you over the ledge!'

The dragon blinked sadly. Little puffs of steam emitted from his nostrils. They were paltry wisps—pathetic for a dragon who was a prince among princes.

The rain was streaming down, leaving droplets upon the trees, tall on the horizon and in the woodlands behind them. But here, on the rock, the only droplets were tears, which fell in a great puddle at Septimus's feet.

'Aaahr rewy cornfoy'

The seventh son took a step backwards and came critically close to a fall.

The dragonette leapt towards him, hissing. (Ok, so it sounded like a hiss. It was actually a long stream of affectionate words but Sep wasn't to know that!)

One can't blame the seventh son for being the tiniest bit alarmed. Or for losing his footing when the creature breathed. (Or strictly speaking, steamed.)

Sep ducked and lost his balance.

He would almost certainly not have lived to fulfil any prophecies, poetic or not, had the dragonette not heroically risen into the air (instinct is really a fascinating thing) and reached out a scaly limb.

Septimus had hardly a moment to eye those long, sharp, claws. They were made for ripping at roots.

He had not the time, for he was suspended between earth and air and felt the magic of Elvenswolde creeping into his bones. He was not sure if that was good or bad, but since he had no choice, he stretched out his arm and gripped the hovering dragon with all his strength.

The claws cut, but the dragon bravely flapped until Septimus's balance was restored and his feet were once more on solid earth. Then, exhausted, the creature dropped out of the sky.

'Ouch!'

'Hympjli!'

'You weigh much more than you look!'

'lookit remion grrr.'

'Clumsy oaf. Get off my foot. God, I hope you don't eat feet. I wonder what the heck you're saying. Are you good or bad? I wonder if there's a plaster in my pack.'

Septimus never expected a response as he fished among his things. Sarah had provided several herbs he didn't trust, but no bandage.

He was just giving up, when something really weird—no I mean really weird happened.

He could have sworn he heard the creature think! It was none of those curious, unintelligible noises he'd been making up until now. No, we're talking plain English. The thoughts were transmitted, by some subtle kind of magic, into Septimus's brain.

'I don't eat feet, I'm sure they're smelly. As a matter of fact I haven't had a bite of a thing in my life before. I've just hatched. You should know that, mum. I love you. '

Septimus startled.

'What did you say?'

'grr rrwdso litler feeeee—'

'No! Don't growl. I don't understand dragon. Think it.'

The dragon licked his lips and as Septimus gazed at the moistened pink tongue and the staring white eyes that protruded from a mass of scales, he thought he must have been mad to have imagined the dragon's words.

Mum indeed! Sep grinned. He was just wondering what on earth to do next when he stopped dead in astonishment. The thoughts were creeping into his mind again.

'Mum! Mum! I'm hungry, hungry! Give me food, give me food, let me taste the flesh of wolves!'

Septimus stared.

'Can you think in English?'

The dragon gurgled happily.

'I can think in any language I like. I am a blue dragon, you see. Blue dragons are special!'

'Can you talk in English?'

'Mmmmr grumbel kkkk llleeee.'

'No. Obviously not. But you understand me?'

The dragon grinned and nodded his head. His little teeth (large to Septimus) flashed white in the sudden sunshine.

'I love you. You are my mum.'

'No, I am not!'

'Yes, you are! Lovely mum!'

The dragon came closer and licked Septimus. His tongue was large—very large—for such a tiny dragon, but felt warm and sweet. Unfortunately, the creature happened to sneeze just as he was tenderly basting Septimus with his gentle saliva.

The result was a great rush of hot nostril flame that somehow managed to singe every hair off Septimus's forearm.

'Ouch! Ouch! Oh, ouchy ouch ouch!' Septimus bellowed. (He actually said a few bad words too, but it is not necessary to repeat them. Though his voice was muted in the high wind, the visuals were still working. The dragon could see him hopping in pain.)

'Sorry! Is that some kind of dance? How do you do it?'

'With ease!' Sep retorted sarcastically. The dragonette was oblivious to irony. 'No, this is not a dance you careless, crazy brute! I am in pain! Pain, pain, you understand me?'

The dragon looked sad. His tail curled inward. A great, enormous tear trickled down his left eye. He blinked.

Septimus looked up from his injury.

'Oh, for heaven's sake, don't look so tragic! It's not so very bad. I have herbs. Then I will tend my aching head (where you landed with a thump) and the scratches—oh, they'll heal. With time. Maybe a hundred years. No, don't worry. I will be as right as rain. Don't come hug me—'

Sizzle. Half of Septimus's fringe burned, leaving a distinct and very nasty smell.

The dragon, sorry again, licked Septimus's face.

'No, no—leave me. Go sit there.'

'Yes mum!'

A dejected looking dragon did as he was told.

Septimus sighed. It would not be fair, he thought, to disappoint the creature. If the scaly blue hatchling thought he was mum (rather bizarre) there was no point disillusioning him. Not until he found the actual mother. Who he hoped was kind. And small.

No, mum would be fine. Just fine. Just so long as the creature did not try to hug him again.

'Ooooouuuch!!!!!'

He did.

* * *

Xanadel was breathless from his run up the winding staircase. It had been a solemn moment, watching Ramón concentrate and produce a bubble more exquisite, more delicate, more luminescent and more prism-like than ever he'd seen in his lifetime.

Not even the ancient illustrations of Elven lore had hinted at such a thing. He watched it drift over the tower and float on the breeze, towards Sarcalet as though propelled by a will of its own.

Ramón's words, whispered softly, were haunting.

From the king's tower, a grey shadow was cast in counterpoint. It tugged at the bubble, it pricked and poked and prised at it. But the wish drifted dreamily, as if unaware of danger and its own fragility.

Ramón, usually so serene, clutched at the window ledge as he'd watched its progress, all the time muttering strange incantations.

It was not often that the base magic was evoked: that deeper enchantment that lay dormant in all of the worlds. Only in desperate times, in times evocative of the mythologies and the songs of the sooth singers was base magic ever lifted from the dormant and shifted towards light. It was the magic of unification.

Now, as the shadows over Elvenswolde were darkening, the elf-in folk needed to stand tall. They needed to call to the elders and hear the answers brought to them on the winds.

'Xanadel, you were surprised I chose Wendleweed, not you, for the journey to Willowsham and the great Master Hepple.'

The words were a statement, not a question. Xanadel nodded shyly.

'Fear not, they shall return, I trust, and safely. It is not for them I fear.'

'For whom, then?'

'For you, Xanadel, for it is you I have chosen for the greater task. I cannot undertake it. I am bound to maintain the balance of these towers. If I leave at such a time there is no saying that the king's tower—or rather, the dangers within it—might not seep out, waft through the turrets, stretch beyond the confines of the king's moat and touch the border of the queen's.

'If that happens, the drinking water will not be pure and the en-chantments will creep through our defences. I cannot take that risk. Móran has already evaded banishment. I am cleverer than he is, and swifter, but not if my concentration shifts.'

'What is my task?' Xanadel trembled and felt a sudden tremor in the amulet about his neck. When he checked, it was smooth and dull, the same amber as always.

'Go find your brother, little elfkin. He has been called. Find Septimus Kahikatea, the seventh son of a seventh son. If my bubble has achieved its mark, it will have drifted quite close to the circle of dragons. Close to Sarcalet, where the stars of Siluse and Ventrimuse shimmer brightest in our eastern sky. Bring him to me, Xanadel, in safety and in secrecy.

'Watch for the darker ones. They have lain dormant for a time, but awaken from their slumbers. Stay clear of the dragons, they will eat a lonely elf just as soon as help it. Keep near—but not on—footpaths, if you can, and use the rabbit tunnels only when you have to. Travel on grass, not stone. Stone has resonance and I do not want Móran, the dark one, to be warned of Septimus's progress. If you are captured, call.'

Xanadel's eyes were wide. He looked small beside the wizard, and rather young. He didn't like the sound of 'captured.'

'You may call by wind or by whistle; the rushes and the breezes will show you. I can promise no aid but your own wits. If you call, the answer may come not from me but from the rhythms of the universe, for we are all one. If no help comes at all, then the light is lost.'

Xanadel, who had been beginning to feel excited by the prospect of adventure, paled. 'What will happen when I bring him to you? How will he help us?'

Ramón looked at Xanadel intently. 'It is written in the songs that the seventh son of a seventh son will return to Elvenswolde. More than that I cannot tell you. The magic is not mine; it is the base magic and operates in a different way from my own.

'Still, if I read the signs aright he will have the power—he will restore balance not only here, but in all the worlds beyond us. We are teetering on the edge of darkness, and I seem to be the lone keeper of light. We need another keeper, someone who is young and brave and untouched by the shadows that have already been cast.'

'I am young and brave—'

'Yes, but you have been breathing the wind of Elvenswolde far too long. The air is poisoned with a master's subtle scent—one who is my equal and almost certainly of my flesh.

'A wizard who sees fit to fling potions to the breezes, who charms the seasons, who drugs the deep dells so that our very plants are poisons. You won't have noticed yet—his workings are subtle and cleverly sweet, but every breath you take has his fragrance upon it, every step you make, his footprint. I have balanced this madness with fragrances of my own, potions I had hoped never to need, trusted never to use.

'He has forced my hand. I've used spells best left uncast, words best left unuttered. I comfort myself that this is necessary to the very existence of Elvenswolde but it is bitter comfort. Bitter too, that my strength is sapping away as surely as the tides ebb with the twin moons. His must be too, but we cannot be certain that he will not destroy us first, or that the powers he dabbles in do not increase beyond all balance.

'I am calling forth the seventh son because he has not breathed the air of Elvenswolde. Neither is he bound by the forces that I am. He is not himself magic, but his heritage is deeper than the earth itself. If I reach him before Móran, he will be our greatest help.'

'What if—what if Móran reaches him first?'

Ramón nodded. 'He must not, Xanadel. He must not. That, I am afraid, is the greatest burden of your task.'

Xanadel swallowed. He wished Bickle were with him, for though he was no coward, he did not like the thought of mysterious forces reaching out. Ramón looked tired.

Of a whim (and proving how very daring he actually was!) He reached on tippy toes and hugged the Wish Maker.

Far below, in the valleys beneath the queen's tower, the first daffodils bloomed.

Willowsham: Of Wickles and Stickles

Master Hepple was easy to find. He was the only healer in Willowsham.

If that was not sufficient, a bold, brass sign at the crossroads pointed the path to his home. Bickleberry and Wendleweed were relieved. The journey had been long and wearying. Their feet ached and the stupid fairy wings were all splattered with sneeze dust. This, as Wendleweed grumbled, was due to Bickle's bright idea of flying directly over a field of potion plants.

'You could plainly see they were growing stickles!'

'Could not—looked like annis shoots!'

'Rubbish! The stickles were obvious!'

'Then why did you follow me?'

'Aaah choo!'

Between quarrelling (in a friendly way) the elves agreed they were starving. At midnight, they'd eaten strawberry puff tarts with drippings of jam and cream, but they'd fed the eel pies to the wolves (Better the wolves ate eel than elves!) They'd regretfully stopped chewing Wickles Wondrous Toffee when they'd noticed a pair of dragon eyes watching from a distance. (Usually seeing a pair meant there were hundreds out there—a bit like rats, on earth.)

Somehow, the Wickles had stuck in their throats and tasted slightly less delicious. Also, their chewing seemed to sound louder in the quiet pink of moonbeams.

That'd left them with hard cheese (not Bickle's favourite) and several soft vegetables that they both glumly agreed should have been eaten before the puff tarts. They threw them out to the dragons.

Rain poured down and lightening threatened to rip the skies. The elves found the journey freezing and were rather miserable, despite their sunny natures.

What made things worse was the Wickles. The thing about Wickles toffee (apart from the fact it is wonderful) is that once you get the taste in your mouth, you keep wishing for more. Bickleberry and Wendleweed were still wishing when they finally reached the home of Master Hepple.

It was a very interesting home (at least, Wendleweed thought it was) because it was fashioned from the flowering hills. It had a Gothic front door with a golden knocker, and one window with a pair of cheerful shutters, but the roof and sides were all snowdrops, peonies, buttercups and lendillies, each multi-coloured petal glittering in a fascinating kaleidoscope of colour. No lendilly ever repeated a shade, so the colours were wild, extraordinary and quite beyond the miserable, limited colour spectrum of mankind.

The thing about Master Hepple's house that was so curious—even to elves—was that the flowers could not be cut, broken or squashed. They grew bright and serene and were impervious to stomping, plucking and uprooting. An elf could easily run up the hill, find himself on the roof, jump among the flowers and disturb not a one. How intoxicating to run in lendilillies and peonies. The fragrance would be incredible, so pure, so unblemished, one could be covered in a bouquet and no material damage done! Amazing house. Fabulous building materials.

Bickle wondered if Master Hepple minded footsteps on his roof—he thought he must get many—and wanted to try it at once, but Wendleweed firmly gripped his arm and made him behave. What if Master Hepple was too annoyed to listen to them? There was a royal emergency at stake. They were trusted—trusted—by the Wish Maker to be good.

Fortunately, Master Hepple, recovering from his astonishment at seeing two sneezing, wet and very muddy elves at his doorstep, had the kindness to invite them in. He allowed them to warm themselves by the smouldering fire as he cut huge wedges of freshly baked bread and strips of boar salami that hung from kitchen hooks.

When each elf had a plate, and when one of them had managed to politely swallow and not immediately take another bite (which was very tempting given how hungry they felt) Master Hepple heard about the plight of the king.

Master Hepple frowned thoughtfully and began preparing a first aid bag of bottles and herbs that smelled intriguing.

Each bottle was opened and personally checked for freshness by Master Hepple. The scents drifted towards the elves. It was not long before they started to fiddle with their food and feel light-headed.

Master Hepple looked at them sharply.

'Go outside, will you? I can't have you affected—even in a small way—by potions fit for a king's malady. I will be several moments more. Be patient, I pray you ,and see if you can wash your wings and hang them out to dry. They will be useless caked with sneezes. I shall call you when I am ready. We will travel quickly, my friends. If I read things aright the king has grave need of me.'

Master Hepple pushed his spectacles against his nose and resumed sniffing. Bickleberry stared longingly at the last slice of salami, but all he received was a frown. A particularly fierce fragrance was escaping an ancient looking bottle—tiny—with stars etched into the glass face.

'Go!'

Wendleweed (still struggling in embarrassment with the fading purple blob) stretched up for the two sets of wings hanging neatly from the hall stand and murmured something polite.

Willowsham was set low in a valley so the elves saw hills and mountains all around them, and above them a sky streaked almost with purple. Wild flowers blossomed on the terraces, a little like Master Hepple's house, but in properly tilled meadows. But, where once there had been pinks and oranges and bright, cheerful greens, there were now more muted tones. Russets, mauves and aubergines bobbed in the breezes.

They were pretty blooms, but they were not the petals or shades of light. As the dawn transformed to day, there was a shivering in the mountains, and a wild cry that turned Bickleberry's blood.

* * *

The dragonette was nothing, if not persistent. He followed Sep about like an earth chick and refused to believe a fundamental truth. It was a rather obvious truth to Septimus: he was *not* the dragon's mum!

But would that highly speckled, scaly blue creature with the wide brown eyes (slanted) and nostrils that far too frequently puffed out steam ('oops!') believe him? No, he would not. He just licked Septimus's hand—or nose—or feet—whichever he happened to ignite, and hoped not to annoy. Too much.

Well, Sep was not hard-hearted. He began to feel rather sorry for the creature as it doggedly plodded the pathways trying not to murmur that since he'd only just hatched, he was entitled to a rest.

The end result was that Septimus landed up lugging the creature (and was pierced in the side by one of its very sharp scales). Still, it was better than being accidentally stood on and singed.

The dragon was so excited (and on its best behaviour) that it only managed to burn Sep twice, once above his eyelash and once just under the chin.

Distracting the creature became a matter of some importance. Sarah had not packed salve and Septimus could only vaguely recall that cold water was good for burns. He had already bathed twice in the stuff.

'What shall we call you?'

'Lloitu iigly grrrrr!'

'Think, don't growl. I can't understand dragon tongue!'

The dragon closed his eyes and thought.

'Poor mum! Dragon is so… basic.'

Septimus brushed aside his annoyance. He had bigger things to worry about than a patronising baby calling him mum.

He brushed away what was left of his singed fringe and suddenly grinned.

'Hey, call me Sep. In the world from which I come, it means mum.'

The dragon looked suspicious.

'Really?'

Septimus nodded. 'Yip. Really. Now tell me what I should call you. Do you have a name?'

'Ouch!'

A flame of sheer joy escaped the dragonette's nostril. Unfortunately, it made its way—nothing serious—onto Septimus's bare skin.

'I shall call you Scorcher, you damned animal!'

The dragon tried it on his lips.

'LLLoo terrepp reee grr.'

'No! Think it! Scorcher. Scorch for short.'

'Scorch? There was a muffled choke. 'Scorch? Septimus ignored the mutterings—most in dragon tongue. Words like 'Noooooo… stupid, unoriginal, patronising, puerile, childish…'

'Do you like it?'

The dragon shook his head wildly. The seventh son did not seem to notice.

'Yes. I think it will really suit you. Unoriginal, perhaps—but it is descriptive. Like the storybooks. It kind of suits you. What do you think?'

The dragonette did not look pleased, but who was he to mention he was a Dargonville prince born to better titles than a cliché like Scorcher? He was a polite little fellow at heart and didn't want to hurt Sep's feelings. Much.

He knew nothing of storybooks—how should he—but he could not help thinking 'Scorcher' a trifle undignified. He supposed there might be an ancestral dragon called Scorcher, but he couldn't think of one in living memory.

He wanted to suggest something fearful like Bewarious Flesh-eatarius, like his great godfather the flesh-eater, but the moment was lost.

Septimus was calling him Scorch. Worse, he was climbing very swiftly up a bare rock face. Terribly dangerous. No ropes, stupid earth child. No wings either. If Scorch did not scramble and flap to keep up, he would be left far behind.

Sep's words were growing fainter and the rain was falling hard again. Scorch hurried, flapped, stumbled and snorted flame. Sep stopped. He was still aching from bruises and burns, but he couldn't help admiring the creature's spunk. He seemed as determined to follow him as Sep was to find the wing bearer.

He was panting by the time he reached the summit. Magic seemed to shimmer in the air. On the far horizon, were several castles, but the largest housed the four turrets that he would come to know as Castle Carne.

One turret was shrouded in dark mists, a grey edifice stark in contrast to the tower on the South side. This sparkled crystal, faceted like diamonds in the sunshine. It was so pure it emitted an almost-hum. A sound that was sensation rather than fact, felt but not quite heard.

When Scorch was quiet (which was not often, for Scorch thought a thousand jumbled things at once and Sep heard them all) there was just a faint vibration, the hint of a high note.

It was more something Sep felt in his bones, something that transcended the distance between him and the spires of the horizon, something he could not explain but which gladdened him.

Then he saw dark circles in the sky behind him, and felt his body tense.

He panicked. This was not the vague prickle of disquiet at the shadows in the woods, or the dark tower, or the glint of eyes that seemed to watch.

This was heart-racing fear. Fear from the moment he heard giant wings beating like drumbeats in the air. And smelt something. Rotten fish, but fleshier.

Shadows, purple, grey, green: then the skies cleared save for the rain and the odd flash of lightening splitting the heavens asunder.

'What in the freaking heck was that?'

Septimus breathed the words uneasily. The pungent scent lingered, but for once Scorcher was at a loss for thoughts.

'Ah! Dragons! I'm right, aren't I?'

Scorcher's thoughts were difficult to decipher. He emitted long grunts, almost as though he'd forgotten that he could thought-talk. Septimus couldn't understand a solitary damn word, but sensed the dragon's confusion.

'Should you not be with them, Scorch? Maybe you can find your mum. Your real mum.'

A great flame billowed from a nostril as Scorcher shook his head vigorously and glared.

'Careful, you crazy beast! Very well, stay with me. Not that I have the faintest idea where I'm to go and what I'm to do. I'll probably stumble on their lair, my luck. Hey, tell me they don't eat people!'

Scorch cocked his head to one side.

His eye—very long lashes for such an infant dragon—squinted against the sunlight. He considered Sep thoughtfully.

No, He did not look juicy enough. He was too bony, and his light hair made an unappetizing contrast to the dark fur of wolves.

'I doubt it. More likely to eat *me*!'

'What? What are you talking about?'

But the dragonette, filled with sudden melancholy, cast his eyes on the hills of Willowsham in the far distance and sniffed.

'They're all green!'

'So what? Dragons are green! That's their colour. Oh!'

Septimus stopped as he belatedly realised why a tear was rolling down Scorch's scaly face.

No doubt about it, the dragon was different. He was a beautiful, vibrant, wonderful blue. All wrong for a dragon. Apparently, he would swap good looks for an ugly, mottled olive with deeper, mud-like greens. There was no accounting for taste. Classic peer pressure, but not a moment to mention this.

Sep wiped away the creature's tear.

'Damn! Ouch!!!!' His luck, the teardrop was flame—boiled and hotter than a pot of tea. He sucked his finger.

'It doesn't matter, Scorch. It makes you special.'

'So special I was abandoned on a cliff and left to hatch all alone?'

'You were not alone. You were with me.' (Ok, a little stretch of the truth since the dragon, strictly speaking, had hurtled upon him purely by accident but hey, white lies are sometimes kind.)

Scorcher raised his brow—or it looked like a brow, but was more a ridge of dragon bone. Anyway, he raised it sarcastically.

'Only by accident. You are not my mum, are you?'

'No. I told you that. Really I did.'

The dragon sniffed.

Septimus, alert, managed to avoid getting singed, though the grass smouldered at his feet.

'Well. Goodbye, then.'

The dragonette's tail dropped so low it scraped the ground and uncovered a hornet's nest, long domiciled in an elfin tree stump.

The hornets were not pleased. They could not sting the dragon, for he was covered in scales, so they stung Sep instead.

'Oh my God! Ouch! Ouch! Ouch!'

But Sep was becoming slowly accustomed to pain. The dragon danced about the hornets, shooing them away with his tail. Eventually, they drifted off in a lazy haze, but not before Scorch swiped Sep as well. (Naturally.)

He was now sitting on the grassy bank looking dazed. And lumpy. Angry red bumps graced his skin.

'Grr… mmppo kkll.'

'Think, will you. For the tenth time, I don't understand dragon!' Septimus tried not to shout, but he couldn't help it. His first day in Elvenswolde was very different from Sarah's dreams. Thankfully mum (along with a whole lot of useless junk like willowblane) had also packed anthisan. He applied it vigorously and almost wished himself back home.

He probably would have done, if he'd realised the dark wizard was watching. He had monitored every moment of the bubble floating over Elvenswolde toward Sarcalet. He frowned. Stupid, obvious move. What the hell was the Wish Maker thinking?

He'd only to push his darker powers a little further. Easy. If he just appealed to the little, every day meannesses, the petty quarrels, the small treacheries that were found in each person, in all lands, in all the worlds, he would have strength sufficient to free himself from the king's tower. And imprison Ramón in the queen's.

But he would not do such a thing: no, the towers represented balance. They would have to be destroyed. There should be no counterforce permitted to balance his tyranny. He was not stupid enough to fall into that trap!

As he scanned the horizon for the bubble, he drew charms from the woods. Close, close, he could feel his power hovering over the wish bubble.

Breezily, it billowed away. The wizard shivered, feeling the balance of will stopping him. Not unexpected, just annoying. He closed his eyes and began anew, but the bubble burst and its content, the crucial content of that wish, was obscured from his vision.

Striding the steps of the top tower, his minor annoyance changed to amazed fury. Soft and stupid as he was, Ramón the Wish Maker was powerful—very powerful—he must not again be underestimated.

The wizard slammed a fist into the wall. His knuckles grazed painfully against brick but he waved the blood away with a small incantation. The Wish Maker might be powerful, but the asinine notions of honour and balance were Ramón's Achilles' heel.

He watched silently as tiny, iridescent traces of the burst bubble floated over Sarcalet. Invisible to the naked eye, of course, but not to his. Not when he was applying a powerful charm that bent the site to his will. But alas! Strong though it was, it was not so strong as the base magic.

The wizard Móran gazed through his hourglass, then dropped the charm. It was withered now, and spent. He needed to save his energies.

Messengers poured in. They were his eyes—eyes that waited and watched, in every outpost of Elvenswolde, from Sarcalet to the lowlands of the deep. The eyes had voices—some large, some small, some loud, some soft, depending on the size and nature of the creature. All were filled with his breath, his curious malevolence and the brand of evil that marked them as dark ones.

He listened, and as he listened, he wondered. Had Ramón evoked the base magic? If he had, the stakes were now higher, for neither wizard had the ability to control those deeper forces. But if he had, to what end? And why? He whispered a command to the creatures and they—each and every one—fled.

Circle of Dragons

The dragon circle was rising as dusk approached. The great beasts felt safer in the comfort of shadows.

They loomed high over the landscape, making Septimus's mouth dry with fear, but also with awe, for though they were ugly, they were also very, very impressive. And beautiful. In a strange kind of way.

Their scales were fleshy and fearsome, their claws more like talons than nails. Looking closer, there were areas of boneless skin that looked supple, slighter more sinewy than scales. The colours were all mottled and mud-like. Green, but an autumn green, not the brightness of spring or the fullness of summer apples.

They were all this mottled earth green, save where thick veins lined in red could be seen through thinner parts of their scales. Their eyes were hooded, and too far off for Septimus to judge, but their tongues! Their tongues were as red as poppies and smoke billowed from several nostrils.

In the case of one old dragon, a flame smouldered at his nose, but it was nothing like the quick, bright fires of Scorcher. Septimus wondered why he had ever had an impression of beauty.

Then he noticed their fine curves, their fluid movements, and their graceful tails that seemed to glide through the wind and slice the air with practiced precision.

There was something elegant in their size and in the fact that they remained hovering above their meeting place, not one touching the other, though they were configured within a hairsbreadth. They flapped their wings in low, lazy unison.

They were watching the travellers. It would have been impossible to turn tail and run, now, though Scorcher was filled with baby terror and Septimus's heart was beating louder and longer than it should have.

Septimus had the feeling that if the dragons chose, they could rip him to pieces within a single moment. He muttered to Scorcher to be careful, but there was no need for such a warning. Scorcher was trailing slowly behind him, his eyes cast to the ground, his tail tense, baby blood racing in old, dragon veins.

An air of disapproval hung above the ring. The dragons were not used to being disturbed. What was more, they had just noticed Scorcher's bright blue scales—very pretty in the sunset—but to a dragon, they did not look pretty at all. They looked worrying, very worrying and excessively annoying. As one, the dragons landed, still in their circle formation.

Septimus found himself just a short distance from the heart of the circle.

They looked at him in silence. Then, without warning, there was a great snapping sound, and some roars that rose from the peak of Mt. Sarcalet and seemed to reverberate in Septimus's ears. It was like the steam engines of Kingston and London and all industrial places of yore, where the combination of coal and steam hissed in synergy with the roar of motors and the great crunch of metal in motion.

He felt the same sense of power, only the dragons had minds and they were watching him, hissing, and roaring, talking in one breath. Septimus tried not to look at their teeth and he definitely tried to avoid their eyes.

The dragon eyes were watching and though they did not feel so dreadful as the eyes he had felt in the woods, they were calculating and cunning, rather like those of giant crocodiles.

Septimus introduced himself slowly.

'What are they saying? Do they understand me?'

Scorcher shook his head. 'No, they don't understand English. Or Elf tongue. They speak dragonesque, or a dialect of the ancient language. There are linguistic subtleties—'

'Scorcher! Shut up! What are they saying, for heaven's sake?'

'They are fighting over whether to throw you over the cliffs, fatten up the wolves, or eat you themselves. One—that old, scaly one over there—says they must keep you. Strange things are happening in this land. You could be a messenger.'

Septimus looked hopefully at the hoary one. He yawned, and did not appear to be a very compelling champion. His scales looked so ancient they were dry and peeling in places.

'What else are they saying?'

Scorcher's thoughts became so jumbled, disordered and confused that Septimus could no longer make head or tail of them.

'Scorch?'

'They are saying I am an ugly beast and shall be ripped to pieces as is the custom. They are saying my mother needs to step forward in shame and be cast out of the circle.'

Septimus was very angry. He was so angry he forgot his own fear. 'How dare they? Which is your mother, Scorch? Have they said?'

'No, they are quarrelling—three think it must be Princess Demetria, who has just had hatchlings, but her nurse vouches for her and there are three other new dragon mothers who may be culprits. They are saying they should punish them all.

'Two of the dragons are crying and pleading, one—I think it must be the princess—is fainting. No, it is not the princess—the princess has just stepped forward. She is—oh, Septimus, just look at her! Isn't she lovely?'

Septimus, who had just caught sight of the giant scaly creature who was lumbering up towards the inner circle followed by several hatchlings about Scorcher's size but without his spunk—could not agree.

She was the most hideous creature he had ever beheld. Her tongue was bright red and her white teeth sharp. One incisor was clearly skew and her over-bite was a serious aesthetic defect. She was the same mud colour mottled with green as the other animals, but her flesh looked scrawny, almost as though she had been starving and her eyes had dark circles beneath the puffy green flesh. Her scales were hard and dry, but so tough that Septimus was sure she must be very old, and very, very mean.

She was looking not at the dragons, but straight at Scorcher.

Scorcher's thoughts were by now so muddled it was impossible to make any sense of them. Septimus was confused because instead of sensing Scorcher's fear (which would have been entirely expected under the circumstances) he thought he sensed a bright determination and a great, overwhelming love. All the abject dejection in his being had vanished.

'Mum?'

Septimus translated the thought even as he heard the dragonette revert back to that strange series of vowel-less grunts and roars that he now knew to be a dialect of dragonesque.

The great brute blinked and approached Scorcher slowly. The circle of dragons closed in. One giant dragon roared something incomprehensible. Septimus wished Scorcher would think the translation, but Scorcher was making little grunts of his own and had forgotten, for the moment, that Septimus was powerless to understand.

The next moment, he had more to think about than his friend's reunion with a beast uglier than sin and perfectly capable of crushing his bones to pulp.

He was being hoisted off his feet and dangled high over the cliff tops, so that he could see (or so it seemed to him) all the greatest sights of Elvenswolde, the rivers, the seas, the woodland forests, and the breezes that crept in from the west and cooled the water sprites. Here and there, he caught glimpses of fairies and elves and horsemen on cobble paths, but mostly the land was deserted, quieter than he had imagined, almost like an enchanted lull, the world—the enchanted world of Elvenswolde—in a tremor of waiting.

The dragon spread his great, terrible wings. (Purple underside and slightly spotty.) Septimus felt a jerk, then a lurch, and then all the breath being rushed from his lungs as he experienced, for the first time, the strange sensation of flight.

He was flying! He was flying with his legs dangling like stalks, in the mouth of a mythical creature thought only to be the stuff of dreams and fairy tales. Unfortunately, it hurt, but Septimus was too terrified to yell or even think of yelling. His voice, in any event, would have been lost to the wind and the wild things.

As the dragon changed direction, he smelt the sweet freshness, he caught a glimpse of nymphs and forest creatures and the ends of rainbows. He saw, from on high, what had already been blemished from below. He saw the colours of the wild flowers and the sneeze dust and the neat fields of poppy potions that waved gently in the Elvenswolde mists. Dew filled mists, drenched with goodness, so unlike the harsh rains that had assailed his back on the rocks of Sarcalet.

Even the seas were mild now, and sparkling. Despite his somewhat bleak situation, Septimus smiled. He could not help himself, for in this, this moment of intense danger to himself, he had seen Elvenswolde as it was meant to be, as he had imagined it, as the sooth singers sang it.

The dragon's jaws seemed very terrible indeed, but not so terrible as he when started to open them and Septimus realised he was about to fall—from so high that only enchantment could save him.

Unfortunately, he knew no high magic, nor any comforting words of wisdom. When a tooth pierced him, he experienced a sudden sharp pain in his back, and a trickle of blood oozing through his shirt. He felt a flood of relief. The dragon was tightening his grip. He was not to be dropped, then. This thought was replaced by an uneasy notion. The tooth was drawing blood. Was this nibbling a prelude to actually bring eaten?

His stomach lurched as he saw the world darken, strange fingers reaching out to him, the mists deepening to gloom, the fields darkening with dread, potions withering on their stalks.

The dragon grunted, turned back towards the circle, then opened his jaws. Septimus was flying again, this time in a free fall. It did not last long. He was dropped—yes dropped—onto a pile of rocks that glimmered like so many jewels in a crystal sun.

'Aaaaahhh—'

This time Septimus could not help yelling, for though the rocks were beautiful they were also plentiful and painful. In an incredibly short space of time he'd sustained a pierced back, any number of burns and now, he was certain, two broken legs—not to mention knees that were scratched to ribbons.

His shirt was ripped and he looked a sorry sight, especially as the night flares all around him were not flares at all, but the fire of dragons, flaring from nostrils that seemed huge in the dusk light.

The lamplighter dragons (for such were their titles, as it transpired) formed a circle around the elders and around the jewel like rock upon which Septimus now crouched. He looked about for Scorcher but could not find him.

'Scorcher! Scorcher! Where are you!?' He called out, but there was silence. Then slowly, as if in a dream, the thoughts crept back to him, echoing in his head. 'Sep?'

Septimus closed his eyes and concentrated. The thoughts seemed jumbled and far away. 'Where are you?'

Conscious of the dragons watching him, he used his mind rather than his mouth.

'I am with my mum. My true mum, Sep. I have found her.'

There was joy in those thoughts, but the joy was balanced by a depth of sadness even Septimus could not understand. He was surprised too, that for himself, he felt a sense of loss and loneliness despite his pleasure for the dragonette.

He recognized (with some astonishment) that he'd liked being Scorcher's mum, that he had grown almost accustomed to his clumsiness and the cute way he had of inflicting terrible pain quite by accident.

He would miss Scorcher, and he was lonely, and he still had no way of knowing what he was meant to achieve in this strange, enchanted world. He eyed the dragons with caution. They stared back unblinkingly.

* * *

Xanadel left Castle Carne in a shroud of secret. Ramón created confusion by calling the courtiers to the king's bed, sending solders through the East Gate—the laundry side—with a mysterious bundle of letters and a wing bearer heavily disguised in a mantle of dark cloth that any watcher would recognize at once as the king's.

He was riding a black horse with a mane of pure white, plaited intricately and bearing the unmistakable insignia of royalty. Added to all this, Ramón created an enchanted summer so the people of the queen's tower (those not on duty) streamed out in large, delighted numbers, many with picnic baskets, some with flutes and fanfares.

The baby elves were unswaddled from their tunics and permitted to frolic in the palace gardens, the flowers blossomed a glorious hue of satin white that gleamed with stamens of sheerest gold. Here and there, an elf was scolded and sent inside, but by and large, the whole of Castle Carne seemed to be outdoors.

Ramón the Wish Maker stood, hand outstretched, almost unmoving as the scene unfolded below. The courtiers were closeted in the grand chamber, full of questions but all of these would have to remain unanswered. He would not pace down the long corridor to address them until the most critical task was achieved.

That task was the reason Ramón's arm grew stiff and the queen's people enjoyed their sudden and very unexpected reprieve. He had to get Xanadel out of Castle Carne unnoticed by the watchers.

Móran, fretting from impatience and the incessant complaints of Garredung and Silvajar, narrowed his eyes thoughtfully. Ramón was creating a diversion, he was sure of it. What kind of novice did he think he was? Almost, the action was an insult.

When Silvajar whined about the unfairness of being trapped so long in the king's tower, Móran snapped.

He whirled about in a rush of silver and pointed his long, rather elegant fingers at the offender. Silvajar's face became immobile. His tongue, caught in the very syllable of a gripe, hung slack from his mouth.

Garredung was just about to add his voice to Silvajar's complaints. He gasped in horror, especially as the ruby on the wizard's ring finger flashed in his direction. He sweated and stuttered and pleaded, so that Móran dropped his fingers contemptuously and told him to go find some backbone.

Garredung bowed and tiptoed off, his cocky step transformed to a mere slink. Silvajar remained a statue in the highest tower of the king. Móran cursed himself for becoming distracted.

He needed to think. If this was a diversion, what was he was not supposed to notice? He had hosts of watchers in all the trees, in all the forests, in the very breezes. Surely a whisper, a word, would come to him?

In a moment, of course, there were dozens of whispers and words, but none made Móran any the happier or the wiser. He could see for himself the enchantment Ramón was working. The flowers alone were wrought from precious hirrilium, a plant grown only in the forests of Ilium and as rare as it was beautiful.

The fact that Ramón was wasting this on a tea party—yes, there they were, pouring tea (elf tea which is a shade of indigo—served hot, very sweet, but considered most refreshing) was more than suspicious.

He ignored Silvajar, still an unkempt little statue, and turned his back. He gazed out the window facing the palace gardens and open courtyard.

Through the arched window, he could see the soldiers and their mysterious cloaked messenger. He could see the letters with their seals and the troupe of tumblers tumbling in suits of green and lavender. On the castle lawns there were jugglers and on the other side, when he turned again, there was the moat. The moat was flowing with fruit juice and a rider, dressed in the livery of the queen, was crossing the bridge.

This was not unusual, for messengers were constantly crossing the great drawbridge of Castle Carne, mostly on foot, but often on horseback or with wing packs depending on the weather and the length of the journey. Móran's eyes flicked back to the revels. Something was wrong, something—

Again, he scanned the scene. Everything was out of place. The king lay in a stupor and there was revelry in the gardens. A shadow had fallen over Elvenswolde—his shadow—yet there was light. Soldiers poured out of the laundry turret, queen's messengers were garbed in the livery of the king, hooded, secretive, so unlike the openness of Elvenswolde.

The wizard clicked his fingers and ordered two of the darker ones to follow, to watch. But perhaps he was falling into Ramón's trap.

Ramón wanted him to watch the stealthy ones. He would expect Móran to be attracted to darker deeds, the secrets and conniving. Perhaps he was wrong, perhaps he needed to watch the ordinary rather than the extraordinary—what ordinary had he seen today?

The washer folk, the minstrels, the elves carting herbs and spices to the castle, Madam Knorr and her corrector wand, Bickleberry the elf—he had not seen Bickleberry, he had also not seen the messenger Xanadel, though they were as thick as thieves and known to be particular favourites of the Wish Maker. Yes, hadn't he just promoted them to messengers? Stupid creatures, both of them. Still—

A sixth sense, a prickling of his fingertips, warned him that the answer he was seeking might lie in these insignificant elves.

A Sniffing and a Finding: The Creeping of Discontent

Bickleberry was almost at Master Hepple's by the time Móran noticed his absence. It was not long before sightings of the elf were reported to him and he relaxed. No big threat. He had expected Master Hepple to be called out. Nothing short of his remedies would cure the king, and Ramón, of course, would know that. No, he did not worry particularly about Master Hepple. He liked it when Ramón, like a puppet, did precisely as he expected.

He continued, however, to concentrate on the ordinary. He needed to watch for the little things, the tiny, intricate workings of the day that might matter.

His diligence was rewarded, at last, by the sight of Xanadel—just the elf he had been searching for. Yes, it was certainly him, for he was wearing the queen's livery. He was also carrying a 10/B regulation message bag—a step up from the standard 9/A used in the sorting room. Nothing unusual there. He was whistling under his breath. Out of tune again. No sooth singer, that one!

Móran sneered and was about to scan for some of Ramón's other little pets when he glanced back. His sixth sense was humming.

Yes—yes, that was it. If this day had been set aside for festivities, why was the pet not granted leave of duty? Why was he still trotting out on messages? His eyes narrowed, and as he watched—with more attention, this time—he noticed that the tune was shaky and Xanadel's mouth dry.

'Silvajar!' But of course, there was no answer, as Silvajar was now as useless as a granite slab. He remained unblinking as the wizard cursed and commanded him to speak.

'Oh, you miserable little wretch, wake up, I tell you!'

But Silvajar did not wake up, he only stared unblinkingly at the wizard, not a muscle moving in his pointed elfin face.

'Oh, for heaven's sake! You need a goddamn waking potion! I can't be bothered with that rubbish! Garredung!'

The wizard positively roared, for his temper was fraying. He was not certain he absolutely understood Ramón's designs and the matter made him uneasy.

He need not have roared, for Garredung was cowering outside his door, alternately snivelling and crying and perfectly petrified that it would be he, next, who would be turned into a hideous garden gnome. There was no escape, either, as the entire turret was guarded by foot soldiers. Queen's orders—something very peculiar was happening.

Queen's orders, indeed! Since when did her majesty have jurisdiction over the King's tower? He did not like it, not one little bit!

He entered and bowed low so that his nose practically scraped the floor. He had diligently applied purple curling polish to his shoes. He was very fond of his new uniform. Now, the curl tickled at his nostrils. He did his best not to sneeze. Indeed, his voice, when he spoke, was high and simpering.

'Sir? Your wish, oh most powerful wizard, oh master of my worship, my—'

'Silence, you snivelling creature!'

'Yes.' Garredung gulped.

He tried his best not to look at Silvajar, whose fingers were outstretched in a rather unnatural way and made him feel queasy. He only partially succeeded, for Silvajar's nose was elegantly pointy—very refined—and kept appearing in his peripheral vision. Oh, why had he been so stupid? Why had he not been content with the dear, dear Wish Maker?

He forgot, in his horrified regret, all about the sea of troubles that Ramón had once punished him with. Well, it had been horrible, but not nearly so bad as being turned into an immobile block of indeterminate slate. He grovelled.

'Follow that meddlesome creature Xanadel. Go where he goes. See what he sees. Do what he does. If he meets anyone, if he retreats into the hollows of the old ones, if he does anything he does not normally do in the course of his duties, slow him down, Garredung, and report to me at once.'

'But—but sir—'

'No buts, you spineless imbecile! No buts unless you would like to be—let me see? A toad with warts? A jumping bean? A flying fish in a goblin's frying pan? No?'

Garredung's eyes grew round with fear.

'Enough of this, then. You shall be my puppet, oh, miserable one. You will dance to my tune if I can bother to be bothered. Get up, will you? Go! Shoo!'

'But the tower is closed! The turret is guarded! How, your Excellency, your great highness, your grand and royal majesty—' Garredung gulped and continued, 'Silvajar—'

'Don't speak to me of Silvajar! Silvajar is more use to me as a doorstop than as a servant. I shall wedge him up here, see, to protect me from drafts. Oh, get rid of that long face. If you manage with Xanadel, I might look up the anti-freeze charm or apply a waking potion, if I have enough syllabub in my stores. I have neither the time nor the inclination right now.'

With a flick of the wrist, he was gone. Or rather, Garredung was gone.

He felt himself flying through space, being squashed and squeezed under tunnels so that he could hardly breathe. His nose—too long and not refined at all—got scratched and bent as his body twisted through tight spaces and his feet froze in deep waters beneath the chambers of the tower. Twice he was nearly stuck in the silent, secret grottos, too cold and gloomy to be cheerful, too rotten and smelly to be at all comforting.

Garredung emerged at last into the green grass of Elvenswolde and smelt the fresh air of the pine forests behind him. It was

the first time he had ever really stopped to appreciate them, and
Ramón, who believed in balance, who believed that mean, bad
creatures still had the ability to feel goodness, to appreciate light,
would have smiled.

But Ramón was busy with other matters, and Móran—only
Móran—was watching.

Garredung's moment of epiphany was over.

He felt that familiar sigh of discontent creep over him. It was
made far worse by gnawing fear and loneliness. He was scratched
and wary, but he was determined—determined—to hunt out Xanadel.

He found he was some way away from Castle Carne, and the
wind blew all sorts of scents in its wake, but most of all the sea. He
realised the ocean must be close and decided to keep to the shoreline
if he could. There were strange creatures in the woods, strange eyes
that terrified him.

He was certain they would be watching, waiting to see if he
made a mistake, waiting to report to Móran, the silver wizard, whose
bidding he was bent on doing.

He was not entirely motivated by cowardice (though largely so);
however, there was also a smidgeon of method. He was certain that, if
he were Xanadel, he would have taken the route of the sea.

Where he was to find the silly squirt, he'd not the faintest clue,
but at least he was free. He breathed easier, feeling his jauntiness
return. He was Garredung—king's messenger—he could outsmart a
single-stripe junior elf!

He looked as far as his sharp, button eyes could see (which was
very far) but could detect not a sign of him—not even a track upon
the craggy rocks.

He wondered whether he should have doubled back, rather, and
crept past the perimeter of the castle, forging his way to the other
route, towards Killyrath or Gildergast and Kinning's point. But Kinning was a sleepy hollow on the very edge of Elvenswolde, and Gildergast was hardly much better.

Sure, there were giants there, at times, but not now, in the 'tween
seasons.

No, it was more likely that Xanadel, would head out towards the coast. What if he was to meet someone from the northern shores? Someone who could sail through the dream barrier of Elvenswolde? It had been known to happen. Garredung quickened his step.

He quickened it all the more when his sharp eyes took in the tufts of grass as he rounded the next corner. There was no sign of Xanadel on the rocks, but what of the grass? He could swear he could detect signs of elf feet hurrying! Yes, there were traces here, traces there—nothing on the rocks—by golly, Xanadel—if the tracks, indeed, were his—was hopping!

Hopping and leaping to avoid stone. Garredung wondered why. His own feet did not hesitate to crash down on the rock, causing resonance to touch the very turret of Móran, who watched him closely, but more and more through a haze, for Garredung was fast disappearing beyond his ability to see.

Móran counted on the creatures and returned to his pots. He had much to think about, much to do, to outsmart Ramón. If he were not mistaken, Ramón would act now.

He would have to. The balances were shifting, the meticlaws oozing—the tide was turning. One messenger elf was hardly worth the waste of his concentration. He peered beyond the turret walls and waited.

Garredung, alert, sniffed.

Then he squealed, for his nostrils were still squashed from his horrible ride through the dark tunnels of the tower. The air hurt as it whistled through his long, twisted nose. But on the trail of mischief, Garredung did not care. His mission was to cause trouble for Xanadel and if it meant a minor inconvenience—so be it. He sniffed again.

This time, his efforts were rewarded. A loud, snapping noise signalled the unbending of his nasal cavities, making it easier to breathe. With the sudden rush of air, he at last sniffed out Xanadel.

Ah yes, the elf had a definite scent. An annoying scent, for it was always so fresh and cheerful. Fresh baked bread from the kitchens and orange juice. Fresh squeezed. Puke worthy! His own scent was a more masculine musk, a tantalising brew of crushed dragon tooth and serpent breath. Far, far more mature—

He kicked at the earth and scowled. He would show him! Mr Innocence, Mr Fresh faced, silly-smile Xanadel. What type of a name was Xanadel anyway? Stupid elf. He would track him, disable him then hand him to the silver wizard on a plate. It might even be fun.

Yes, he would follow Xanadel and play with him. He would tease him like one of those earth cats with a mouse. He would shadow him, foil him, and be rewarded, for his trouble, not with the corrector wand (which was usually his unfortunate fate) but with the smile of Móran.

Móran would be so grateful he would likely be rewarded handsomely. In a good mood, the wizard could be quite charming. Perhaps he would make him grand Chancellor of Elvenswolde—no, that was not likely, get real—but a spellbinder, perhaps, or a head messenger elf—or—lost in thought, Garredung tripped over an arrowroot and yelled.

This time it was not just his nose that was squashed flat, but his entire body, which twisted as it landed. His threadbare tunic was now caught up in brambleberries and thistle.

Garredung was a seething, miserable mess. He was so mad he almost missed the low-pitched footsteps on the hillock above him.

Almost, but not quite.

He stopped fiddling with the prickles and listened. Yes, there it was again, a creeping noise, not slithering or snake-like, but pert and elfin. It could have been any number of elves, but at this time, on this plain, he thought not. The castle festivities were still in full force and this was no guard or messenger, hurrying on king's business.

No, he heard stealth and silence and caution and creeping, he heard a heartbeat reverberating in the wind, and most of all, he smelt baked bread. Baked bread and possibly the hint of orange. Xanadel was probably only a copse above him, hidden from view but hurrying.

Garredung flung off his coat (no loss—it was full of prickles, smelt of tunnels and was really too disgusting for a self- respecting king's elf to wear.) He clambered up the rock face quicker than a kookaburra and panted as he caught sight of Xanadel.

Thinking quickly, he withdrew from his tattered cloak a novice wand—not so fine as Móran's, nor so clean as Xanadel's, but serviceable. He pointed it at the vanishing figure and called out loud.

A shower of sparks nearly blinded him, and the power he felt in his hand made him shudder in pain. He realised, with a start, that this was not a novice wand. This was, something powerful, something dark.

He felt elated and terrified. His hand shook, his body shuddered from the aftershock. Then, in the distance, he heard a scream that was Xanadel's. In grim satisfaction, he walked swiftly, elf steps on stone, reverberating all the way to the King's tower and the turret of Móran.

Whilst Xanadel lay dazed on the grass, shock on his face, the creatures of the forest crept closer. They sensed, somehow, that it was safe, that the life force was being sapped slowly from the small elf's body.

Curious and twittery, they were creatures born to balance the light: darker souls, twitching as they stretched out hands and poked a little at Xanadel's bones.

Xanadel, frozen, moaned. He'd forgotten where he was or where he was going. He saw hands and faces—eerie, hollow eyes. Part of him moaned, but not a solitary sound reached his lips.

The amulet about his neck began to flicker, not amber, but turquoise, little flames starting to blaze in the inner depths. He stared unseeing, and the creatures stared back, stretching out their arms, calling in high, whistling voices.

In a trance, Xanadel stood up and stepped towards them.

* * *

The dragons were turned towards the circle. To Septimus, it looked like a circle of fire. The great brutes' underbellies were purple, but mostly, Septimus saw green beneath those flames. Mottled shades of green and black. These were their eyes, flame-reflected and glinting. He could hear belly rumbles and roars.

Ominous.

He was recovering from his fall, still impaled upon the sparkling stones that he knew for a certainty were gems. Half polished, they glittered in the sunshine, an assortment of opals, lapis, emeralds, diamonds, such as had never before been collected on earth, even in the treasury of kings.

There were other jewels too, those whose colours dazzled the eye and whose sparkle blinded the unwary watcher. Septimus blinked and turned from them, though his bottom ached with every small movement.

Not that that was the largest of his problems. The dragons looked more menacing now, in the deepening evening than they had in the lazy afternoon dusk-light. He was pretty sure they were not smiling, and they certainly did not have any degree of Scorcher's cuteness, though he suspected they were just as lethal.

'Scorch?'

He thought the word, because his mouth was really too dry to say anything. To his astonishment, the baby dragon answered, though his thoughts were such a tumbling jumble Septimus could hardly make head or tail of them at all.

'Slow down, Scorcher, I can hardly hear a thing—one idea at a time, ok?'

He thought he heard an answering thought.

'Are they going to eat me, Scorcher?'

'They might. They are still deciding.'

The tone of the thought was sad, but matter-of-fact. Septimus did not feel comforted. In fact, he felt a little angry with Scorcher, who did not seem to be applying himself with any great vigour to his predicament. Still, he supposed the creature was born a dragon, why should he not feel as a dragon?

'Are you going to eat me Scorcher?'

'What?' He could almost hear the squeal of indignation in his head. He put his hands on his eyes to ward it off.

'Are you crazy? Eat you? Why, I've a good mind to abandon you on Mount Zircon—you miserable, appalling person! First you pretend to be my mum, then you insult me—'

'I am not insulting you. You are a dragon! Maybe you have to if that is what they decide! I know you're hungry, for heaven's sake, you've been complaining since you first hatched—'

'But only for wolf's meat. Mum—she's a royal princess, you know, that makes me a prince—ordered some as a last boon before her punishment. It was delicious, Sep, I think I could develop a taste for it—'

'Scorcher! Focus! What is to become of me? Of us? Will they accept you?'

Septimus waited for answering thoughts. They were a long time coming, and an old dragon started salivating in his direction. Septimus knew nothing of dragons, but he looked very hungry indeed. He unfurled his claws and the seventh son had to hurriedly sit back on the jewels.

'I am a blue dragon, remember? I am a disgrace!'

'Still?'

'Of course, still. Nothing's changed, only they're wondering if I might be useful. I am trying to convince them they cannot live without me. Oh, Sep, I've discovered I have wonderful powers. Only think! It is not just human thoughts I can read, but all thoughts!

'There are creatures everywhere; dark creatures, and I can hear them in my head! I am petrified, but the dragons think they cannot afford to waste such a talent. That nasty old one with the wart on his head wants me dead, and a few of the jealous ones—jealous because mum's a princess—want me destroyed, but most think I'll be handy.'

'I should say so!'

'Yes, there is a shadow over Elvenswolde. They are worried. Wart-face says they shouldn't involve themselves in elfin matters and who actually cares? But there is a shifting of balances, and dragons don't like change. At least, I think they don't!'

'Tell them you will lift the shadow off Elvenswolde if they set you free. That, I suspect, is my task. If we do it together we might succeed.'

'You? You are just a scrawny boy! How can you lift the shadow?'

Septimus was offended. 'Now look here, Scorch, a few hours ago you thought I was your mum!'

'A few hours ago I had just hatched!'

'My point exactly! This scrawny boy has a better chance against the shadows than a baby dragonette! I am the seventh son of a seventh son.'

'I am a Dargonville prince!'

'Yes, if they don't drop you from a height or eat you for breakfast!'

There was no answer and Septimus worried. He could not see Scorch from his position on the gem pile. He could only hear his thoughts, and now there was a silence.

'Scorch?'

'I am not crying!'

Septimus smiled, relieved, but also worried.

'Of course you aren't, you are a dragon prince. Now, much as I'd like to continue quarrelling with you, we will have to continue this discussion some other time. Convince them that you will save Elvenswolde and get us out of here!'

'Huh! You don't ask a lot!'

'I know, Scorch, but can you think of anything better? Frankly I don't relish being dragon stew.'

'They have my mother!'

'What? What do you mean?'

But Septimus, peering from the glittering mound, could see what he somehow hadn't noticed before. His heart sank.

Princess Demetria was roaring fire but she was helpless in the wake of three huge dragons (all with nasty sneers and several spots along their tails—very unattractive). They were lashing her to an Eastern Dragon Post meters and meters high, so tall it looked like it would impale the very sky.

The princess was sobbing and roaring (which sounded quite unintelligible to Septimus, but heart wrenching to Scorch) and her tail drooped dolefully. She seemed to be making no real effort to use her powerful muscles to escape.

'She says she has wasted away in the cave. She hasn't the strength to move. She is whispering to me to escape.'

'Can you?'

'Yes, but I'll never leave her!' Scorch sounded indignant.

'After she left you on a cliff to die?'

'She could have crushed me, but she didn't!'

'How kind!'

'We're quarrelling again!'

'Yes, we shouldn't. Just get out of there, will you? Tell them if they release your mother you will save Elvenswolde.'

'I've tried that. They won't. Old Wart-face wants her dead. I think he has a thing about Dargonvilles.'

'Very well, convince them that I have great powers.'

There was a silence—at least, Septimus thought he heard Scorch think something very cheeky, but he could not be certain. Then there was a great roar and some rumbling and one of the dragons in the ring shifted, slightly, so that Septimus could just see Scorch, on a high ledge, a merry shade of blue among all the mottled greens. He was tiny against the huge dragon post, where Princess Demetria was sobbing great dragon tears. Septimus noticed that every huge tear that rolled down her nose turned into a giant pearl.

The baby dragon was making all kinds of strange noises—great roars and sighs and whispers and puffs of wind. The older dragons drew closer, roaring amongst themselves, some nodding, and some sharpening claws against the shadowy rocks.

'Scorch?'

'Wait!'

Septimus waited. He edged his body slowly towards a gold nugget, which looked a lot smoother than the diamond (at least he thought it was a diamond) that was piercing him in the bottom.

Unfortunately, one of the larger dragons turned and breathed a fierce gust of fire from his nostrils, so Septimus had to abandon the attempt. He was rather afraid the dragon might cook him alive, and no gold nugget, however smooth, would be worth such a miserable fate. He did hope though, that Scorch would hurry up.

'Sep!'

'What?'

'They want to see an example of your powers!'

Septimus groaned. He should have guessed there would be a test like this. Now it was not just his own life hanging on a thread, but Princess Demetria's too (not that he cared for her over-much). Scorcher was another matter entirely. Not to mention the entire fate of Elvenswolde.

'Scorch, I hate to disappoint you, but I don't actually have any powers!'

'You must have! You told me to convince them that you did!'

'Convince, I said. Trick, create an illusion, tell a fib—oh, Scorch, we're doomed!'

'We're doomed if you give up so easily! I am only a hatchling and I already know that it is better to try than do nothing at all. Take you, for instance. If I hadn't kept on at you, you would never have become my mum!'

'I am not your mum!'

Septimus heard silence. He worried.

'Scorch? Scorch? Answer me!'

But Scorch had begun the long climb towards him. Beady black eyes watched, but the dragons grudgingly stepped back as he approached. Scorch, as clumsy as ever, twice tripped over the toes of two intermediate dragons. As he puffed his way up the treasure mound, he was blissfully unaware of the trouble he caused in his wake.

That trouble was a dragon duel, each intermediate dragon thinking it was the other that had invaded his space. Dragons are very sensitive that way.

Anyway, Septimus could just make out Scorcher's little blue body heading towards him. He looked a long way down.

'Use your wings!'

'Oh! I forgot I could fly!'

Scorcher flapped his wings unsteadily. For a moment he looked a little wobbly, then, recovering, he flew beautifully—absolutely beautifully—up towards the apex of the treasure mound. Septimus was quite proud of that little hatchling. That is, until Scorch decided to shut his wings.

He did this as quickly as he'd opened them, dropping onto the amethysts and rubies with such an enormous jolt that the entire pile started an avalanche. Septimus yelled, but it was too late. Diamonds the size of birds' eggs were hurtling towards him and pelting his face and his arms. His bottom slipped off its crusty edge of jewels and began to slide.

'Help—'

He was helped by one of the dragons. Not Wart-face—but his breath was bad—very bad. Smelling it, Septimus yearned for Rutherham. For home.

It was lucky it was an almost wish, for at that precise moment Mr Carlisle looked up from the science test. He focused his eyes on Septimus's empty seat. It was almost as if he were expecting him, and he'd such a nasty sneer on his face that it was just as well the wish fairy, standing over the bottled wish, did not actually get a chance to cork it.

At precisely the right moment, Septimus remembered not to waste his wishes.

Instead, he yelled.

The dragon that'd stopped his fall placed him gently (as gently as dragons can) onto the jewels. Septimus only suffered two more tumbles and some severe bruising before coming to a halt close to the anxious Scorcher. He extricated himself from the bright blue wings with some serious muttering.

'Sorry!' The dragon managed to look cute and contrite at the same time.

Septimus smiled in spite of himself.

'Never mind. I've just remembered I might have some wishes. It's a small chance, but our only chance. I don't want to try anything too hard, and only one wish. I will need to concentrate hard to visualise. What do they want me to do?'

'Oh, anything. You know—prove you have the power to battle the darker things that are creeping over Elvenswolde and the furthest reaches of Sarcalet.'

'How simple!'

Septimus's tone was dripping with sarcasm. It was wasted.

'What do they want? More jewels?'

'Dragons can never have too many jewels. Even a tiny dragon-ette like me knows that. Jewels will do, I suppose!'

'There can be no supposes about this, Scorch. Are you sure?'

Scorch shook his head, causing a great gust of hot smoke to float past Septimus's face.

'We're dragons, remember! Dragons never agree! If I ask them what they want they'll fight about it amongst themselves. It could take days, weeks, months before they reach an agreement. Maybe years. Dragons live for thousands of years, you know. They have all the time in the world.'

There was a touch of pride in Scorch's voice that Septimus found annoying, especially in light of their present dangers, and the darkening skies.

Soon, even if they were freed (which at this rate was unlikely) they would only have the stars to guide their way. The stars, and Elvenswolde's twin moons, strange to Septimus.

Sep scrambled to his feet, his blonde hair a terrible tangle about his shoulders. He narrowly avoiding Scorcher's helping claws. He tried not to sound impatient, but he did.

'They may have all the time in the world, but we don't! For one, Princess Demetria will catch her death of cold up there if she is not untied soon.'

Scorcher looked alarmed.

Septimus stared at him thoughtfully.

'We are going to have to scare them.'

'Mmmhh ddd ggkd xllls mmmk lll!'

'Think, will you! I can't understand your growls.'

'Oh, sorry. I just said, dragons don't scare!'

'Nonsense, they must do. Think, Scorch. What will scare even Wart-face? There must be something! And I have to be able to visual-ise it. Think, think! I have a notion our time is running out.'

Just as he said this, his words were born out by the approach of a scaly, toothy dragon. He was squatter than Wart-face, but up close he looked just as mean. He regarded Septimus gravely then picked him up as if he weighed no more than a feather.

Scorcher was thinking again, thinking furiously, but Septimus could hardly hear a word. Just as well, for the dragonette was telling him that he was to be crushed in the ancient way, using the old dragon methods.

Apparently, it was going to be horrible.

Scorcher was beside himself, thinking and roaring and hissing all at once, so nothing at all made any sense. Worse, his hysteria caused huge puffs of smoke to billow into Septimus's eyes as if his present fate was not undesirable enough.

Then, as the great, squat looking dragon squeezed his arms, squeezed his chest, crushed his stomach so he could barely yelp in pain never mind breathe, a desperate idea entered his head. The thing about it was that he could visualise the matter so clearly, so perfectly, so lucidly—he closed his eyes and wished.

Granite Green, Sight Unseen: Forests of the Gemra

Further, far further to climb, though the murmur of doubt
    haunts him,
and he longs to linger over each willow swept twine
or to cling with cold fingers to wattles or weeds.
Wind wept,
they grow bold upon bark-burnt banks
here leaning, here lithe.
Gold, green-folds gleaming, summer weaning.
They are old, old gold holding—they cling to the earth to the
    roots and the reeds.
Was he meant to remain, to stay with the birch and
the bark?
To refrain from the climbing, to surrender the rock for the sun
    soft grasses?
He thinks not,
though his limbs misgive him, and his heart sighs from this
    task—unasked yet asking.
Demand—not demanding
Time scares him as darkness dares, dare darkness daring.
Night enfolds but not traps,
for the net, though wrapped black, bleak dark and blackly,
is holed in all places with scatters of light
Caves, mild mold mildewed and curved,

tame the reckless ravages of rock.
Rock, rock- hard, rock rending, is not an end
or unending.
It is a beginning: a may, not a might.
He clambers on, seeking pinnacles. He climbs, not to fall, but
to find.
It is in the finding that he knows that
rock hard, bleak dark and green gleaming are all one whole.
If he gives himself to the universe,
he is part of it, he makes it, he is it.
Darkness, then, is light itself.

The creatures of the forest, faceless in the shadows, lured Xanadel up, up, towards them. He obeyed their call, though his body was wracked with a strange trembling and part of him was shouting a feeble, disjointed 'no!'

Móran, in the tower, smiled.

He could not see the forest, or the dangers that lurked within, but he knew they were manifoldly there, for he had sown every germ of deceit, every web of discontent, every malodorous plant that threaded and twined its way through the pines like infested ivy.

He knew the tangle of hands and the tight-lipped voices of the gemra, a breed of hobgoblin he had nurtured as a wizard's project then thrown, forgotten, sight unseen, into the far-flung forests of Elvenswolde.

He knew they would spread and breed and they had. He had little control over them, for they were wild, but dark too, dark of spirit and so still mirrored something of himself in their green-granite eyes.

Sharp eyes, eyes that sparkled with mischief and meanness, eyes and hands that drew Xanadel further into their forest, into the places of their people where the twin moons of Elvenswolde were a figment of the past, and by day the sun's rays glimmered mutely between branches, half hidden, half held.

Xanadel shivered, that part of him still whole shrinking from what he was becoming, the path he was treading, the steps he was taking.

He was walking away from light into the very heart of darkness itself. Already, he felt that stirring in his being, the darkness dormant within him stretched out toffee-thin, but lengthening with each step he took. He was forgetting who he was—Xanadel, son of Septimus, the first in the ancient line of light.

He was forgetting, touched by Móran even in the places beyond his reach. Touched by Móran through his wand and his wishes and his will—Xanadel faltered, remembering will. Ramón had said something about will—His hand brushed lightly over the amulet that was now flickering brighter than ever. It felt warm to his touch, warm despite the chill that was creeping into his being. Instinctively, unwittingly, he glanced at it.

At the very moment he glanced at the amulet, Garredung was dithering about entering the forest. He had seen, of course, Xanadel's dramatic entrance, his clamour up cliffs, his steady, enchanted march towards doom itself.

Rather than feeling triumphant, he felt deflated and forlorn. Perhaps it was the act of wielding Móran's power through the use of his wand, perhaps it was the winds themselves, so changeable, so whistling, so hissing, even to his ears. Whatever it was, he did not feel himself.

He felt afraid, more afraid than ever before, and lonely. The cold chill crept into his being and very nigh froze at his heart. It might have done, for Móran had no further use for Garredung, now that his work was done. The work of the wand—placed in the hands of a novice, but used to such treacherous effect.

No, he had no further use for Garredung, save, perhaps, as a minor hindrance to Xanadel. Whether he lived, or longed, or simply lingered in the forest ferns was not Móran's most pressing concern. He stopped watching and turned his eyes west to the horizon, where another tale unfolded.

Garredung staggered. He could feel a weight fall from his shoulders, though he had been bearing nothing but his tattered tunic and the wand, now a burnt-out stick in his elfin hand. He felt rather peculiar, really, almost as if in a dream, for though he knew he was to follow Xanadel into the forest, he could not remember why.

At Castle Carne, Ramón the Wish Maker, sickened by meticlaws (he'd had to release five barrels in order to achieve one sweet wish,) breathed a sigh. Yes, he thought he had done it. He had not prevented the use of Móran's wand, but he had mitigated the damage.

The wand, emitting its dark powers, its malicious, tormenting torrent of poisons, had released, by sheer force, those held within Garredung's own being. All the petty meannesses, the evil, cloying wickedness, had flown from heart to hand to wand, then far beyond.

Some of it touched Xanadel, causing his current distress, but some had been flung to the winds and the furthest reaches of the forest, were they hid with the wolves and the wild things, clinging to thorns and blossoming weeds when touched by water.

Garredung, empty of his nature, of his needy, grasping, greedy soul, was left only with the shaky remainder and a pale fragment of light. It would grow stronger, untrammelled by the choking vines of hate.

Ramón, in his cherishing of balances, had known, of course, that it was there. In every creature there is both a good, a bad, a light, a dark, a preponderance of one, a smidgeon of the other, but always something that creates balance in Elvenswolde and the worlds beyond.

Now, the good in Garredung, weak and very small and hardly much help at all, stepped towards the forest of darkness. There was fear, but from being so long a confident, fearless bully, there was also, now, a saving bravery.

Garredung climbed those cliffs, lithe and lean, and fitter than Xanadel. He sneaked quietly in through the vines and the twining ivy like the gemra, light-footed and stealthy. It was his way, and though his soul had been emptied, the very artistry of his being remained unchanged.

He crept towards the voices, the whispering winds, and the call of Xanadel in the centre. Xanadel, touching the amulet, now blazing a fire of turquoise, took a deep breath and opened his eyes. The crippling enchantment of the wand was almost gone, but he needed elf sound and there were no elves in that forest, nothing but hobgoblins and wasted wants. It was almost as if Móran had planned such a wilderness for such a day.

Of course, he had only carelessly loosed some evil and allowed it all to sprout. And it had, the gemra were quick footed, quick-witted and everywhere, in the trees, in the grasses, in the lakes and in the weeds. They watched him.

He was rooted to the spot, horrified by this place, but aware that he must move, move, lest he be locked here forever, twixt day and twixt night, in this half-light of the strange creatures. He needed to move on, to find his brother, the seventh of his line.

'I need fire to find fire.' He had no idea where that thought came from, save that his amulet was flashing flames of brilliant turquoise. Gone was the dull glass, replaced in its entirety by a quite incredible gem. Delight echoed a little even in that forest, for Ramón's striving for balance was nothing, if not thorough.

For every darkness there is a corresponding light, for every despair a pleasure, for every pain a joy, no matter how small or how discreet. In that forest, it was very small, very hidden, but starting to reflect as the amulet flickered and reflected.

Even Garredung, burdened with near emptiness, felt it.

It warmed him so that, unbidden, he called a greeting to the astonished Xanadel. It sounded almost friendly. Perhaps loneliness had taught the value of companionship, or strangeness the joy of the familiar. Whatever the case, the last remnants of Xanadel's spell was broken with elf sound. In the tower of the king, Móran grew faint from rage.

* * *

The wish came easily and quickly to Septimus. He held on to it, making sure his visualisation was absolutely perfect. He imagined, with all his skill, a nest. A soft, downy nest. It was much larger than an eagle's, but far softer, feathered from the plumes of phoenixes and constructed from scales (the soft ones, from a dragon's underbelly) and straw.

In the nest, he pictured, very clearly, a series of eggs. They were pleasant, nestling together in innocent harmony. Septimus concentrated intently, first on their shape, then, more carefully, on their colour. They were not white or brown like hens' eggs. Neither were they pink with tiny shaded areas of wispy pearl.

All of them were blue. A bright, whimsical blue calculated to shock any self-respecting dragon right out of his scales.

Septimus remembered reading once (in an ancient tome dredged up by Sarah at Lambton Market) that dragons hated blue eggs. He certainly knew they hated poor Scorch, and not because he was cute and cuddly (or maybe that too!) but simply because he was such a brilliant mix of the sky and the sea on a clear day, maybe with just a touch of magical luminescence that made him impossible to miss.

He wouldn't even have remembered what he privately thought of as 'yet another piece of mum's useless information' (Sarah was an expert in the useless info department) but for the shabby way poor Scorch was being treated.

From what he recollected (and it had been a very cruddy and possibly entirely fictional account of dragonology) dragons not only loathed blue eggs, they feared them.

They believed the hatchlings had strange and unbecoming powers. This unnerved the adult brutes who found it disturbing to have unpredictable younglings in their midst.

The powers were apparently variable and often went unnoticed for years.

Sometimes, as with Scorch, it was immediately apparent, like his heightened language telepathy, but sometimes the power could build and present itself unexpectedly over time. Aqua dragons had been known to blind, some to cast spells in the old way.

Terror of the unknown was what had caused the circle of dragons to outlaw blue eggs.

They mocked them and teased and destroyed them so that no one—not elf or man—could ever accuse them of cowardice.

Now, Septimus allowed the wish to wave through his being.

He closed his eyes tightly and visualised those eggs so clearly it was almost as if he'd seen them before, though naturally he hadn't.

Still, something in Septimus knew.

Like Xanadel, he would have been surprised to know that something at his neck flickered too. It was a sudden light, a glow, and a red fire warming the innermost heart of his amulet.

From the moment that flickering occurred, Septimus's visualisation warmed through his being and grew stronger. He strengthened the shells in his mind, adding indestructibility as a compound. He did this so fluidly that it seemed, to the waiting wish fairies, like one single, simple wish.

Then, with clarity, he pictured warmth, a soft glow above and beneath them, like a halo glittering among the evening stars. He wanted to picture more, but he was losing the vision, stretching his ability to the limit, wavering, a little.

The dragons approached and little Scorcher screamed. Not a thought scream, but the shrill, high pitched lament of a dragon prince. His fear, if not his words, was unmistakable.

Winged Wolves of Astra

Septimus blinked, the vision blurry. In a steadying movement he raised his hand as best he could against the crushing beast and accidentally touched the amulet.

This time, he felt the warmth suffuse his being and the steadiness that balanced his vision. He waited not a second more, but concentrated the vision into a full-blown elfin wish.

There was a hissing, and a sizzling. The dragons moved forward, but roared as their feet scorched on the mountain of gems. Steam, steam everywhere—Septimus thought it was from the dragons' nostrils—but he was wrong.

It was steam from the nest he had just created. As he watched, the eggs appeared. One by one, at first, then in twos and threes, all nestled as snugly as Septimus imagined, glistening here and there with Ammonite, but mostly blue, a bright, cheerful blue that caused the circle of dragons to howl when they saw them. Best of all, the squat one loosened his grip, his attention as riveted as the rest.

Septimus wriggled from his grasp and ducked under his hoary, bony wingspan.

Scorcher, as amazed as the dragons, stopped his hysterical dragon lament.

'I thought you said you had no powers.'

Septimus drew a deep breath and ignored the pain in his ribs.

'I don't—at least none that I am certain of. Look here, Scorch, I am going to stand up and make a speech. Translate for me in the largest voice you have and don't look surprised or doubtful about what I say.'

Scorcher grinned. For a dragon, he was really rather cute. A feisty cute.

Septimus would have grinned back, only the circle was staring at him silently and he was not absolutely certain the blue eggs were enough to secure himself from a death by crushing in the old ways. (He was not certain what the old ways entailed, but pretty positive he wouldn't like it.)

Indeed, he could have sworn there was not a dragon about who would not have destroyed him at the first opportunity. He needed to tap their combined curiosity and fear.

The seventh son drew himself up to his full height. Next to the dragons this was still rather minute and it was hard to balance on Mt. Zircon, the mountain of jewels.

When he spoke, his voice resonated clearly through the air, the trace of an echo giving it both power and an eerie depth that was not unpleasing to him. He was delighted to note the dragons all backed off a little, to listen.

'Dragons, I salute you! I am Septimus, son of Septimus, the seventh son of a seventh son, born half elf, half earth. I pray you, do not destroy me for I come in peace and mean you no harm.'

At this, there was a decided snarling among the older folk, and an agitated murmur from the younger dragons, even the duelling dragons, who were both now sporting burns across their wing tips and suffering from a severe form of smoke inhalation known, in dragonesque, as 'Lerytthhhrindo.'

Still, they choked out something that Scorcher seemed to find encouraging, for he smiled at them and nodded, whilst the older dragons glared.

Princess Demetria, still tied in an uncomfortable position and looking miserably down on the proceedings, nodded too.

No one paid her the slightest attention. Not even Scorcher, who was listening carefully to Septimus and who was determined to translate correctly, no matter how young and how newborn he might be.

Not only his survival depended on it, but also Septimus's good opinion. Despite having crash-landed on the boy, bruising him, burning him and even crushing him, he was very fond of him.

'You wanted proof of my powers and I have shown them to you. Behold, there are nine blue eggs all nestling in a bed of the softest, featherweight straw. They are magical, warm with an inner glow, heated on top and from bottom with a sparkling halo of my making. That halo will keep them warm till their hatching.'

At the very mention of hatching, Wart-face roared in rage and swooped down from the evening skies. It was very dark, now, and Septimus could only see because of the light from the dragon flame that encircled them. Wart-face grabbed an egg with huge talons and dashed it against the rock with a snarl that echoed further than the winds, almost, but not quite, to the very towers of Castle Carne, where the king lay in a stupor, and Ramón waited.

Yes, the roar echoed so loudly there was hardly a creature undisturbed by its call, and several darker ones that reported it to Móran by way of wing and water, later in the evening. Almost, but not quite, did it reach the furthest rim of Elvenswolde. The echo of that roar stopped short of the eastern winds, but only by a hairsbreadth.

Septimus shivered and Scorcher cringed beneath his pretty blue wings. Wart-face paid no mind, but gripped the largest of the eggs in his crushing claws and squeezed it in his grip. The egg remained unyielding.

He flew with it to a great height, so that only his purple underbelly could be glimpsed in the blackening skies. He dropped the egg with full force and though it rolled and bounced against the jagged edges of the jewels, it did not crack. Septimus, who had been holding his breath, released it.

His wish, it seemed, had been perfectly fulfilled.

'Ladies and gentlemen dragons, these eggs are unbreakable. This dragon,' (He did not call him Wart-face—thought this might be rude—so he pointed instead, to the purple underbelly flapping high above him), 'this dragon has tonight been so kind as to prove this. The eggs will only break if and when they are ready to hatch.'

'Hatch—hatch—' There was a great echo of alarm among the dragons. Septimus could not understand a thing—for all he knew they were electing to crush him—but Scorcher was translating beautifully and apparently they were being thrown into a panic, even the older, surlier specimens.

'When they hatch, they will have incredible powers, the baby dragonettes. So incredible you hardly dare dream of them, vast, much more vast than poor Scorcher here, who only has one miserable power and is no threat to you at all.'

'Pkkkrjhhewwwr! Hey' Scorch looked indignant. He glared at Septimus and nearly stopped translating, but Princess Demetria moaned so mournfully that Scorch started to rapidly repeat every word Septimus uttered.

The dragons paled at his words. Yes, their green pallor actually faded a little, though Septimus could hardly tell this from the starlight. Still, by their sudden fidgeting and flapping he guessed they were listening with the kind of rapt attention usually reserved for wizards or visiting dragon dignitaries.

'You will note the little warming halos above and below every single egg. These halos ensure that the eggs are kept at the perfect temperature whether or not a dragon mother is sitting on them.'

There were gasps at this, for even unintelligent dragons (and most are pretty stupid) could understand the implications of this announcement. If the blue eggs could lie upon their nest and retain their heat without a dragon mother warming them, they would eventually hatch. They were bound to hatch.

Imagine! Nine magical dragonettes! Ten with little Scorcher, though he did not seem so terrible—yet. But ten blue dragons would upset the balance dreadfully. Who knew? They could take over the kingdom of dragons with their power, they could rule Sarcalet and even Lindolucia beyond—oh, the consequences did not bear thinking of.

One of the dragons leant forward and breathed fire on the egg. Huge gusts of smoke billowed from his nostrils so that he started coughing from the steam. An ordinary egg would have cooked at once. It would have overcooked, in fact, so that bits of dragon albumen frothed over the side in bluish green globules. No dragonette could withstand such heat. But this egg? The halo only shone brighter and the shell seemed, if anything, smoother.

The dragons blinked. 'I told you they were indestructible!' Septimus smiled as Scorcher translated quickly.

'Now listen, we have not much time. Do you want these blue eggs to hatch?'

There was a thunderous roar, which Septimus took for 'no' without waiting for the translation.

'Good. Well, then, there is only one way they can be prevented from hatching. Release Princess Demetria. She is the mother of a blue dragon and her eyes are wet with tears. Those tears have cooled her lashes, her lids and her inner being. They have calmed her soul and cleansed her spirit. Release her, place the pearls of her tears in the nest and permit her to gaze upon those eggs.

'So long as she is watching them, she will serve to keep the balance. She will countermand the halo effect and keep their temperatures from rising. They shall be warm, but not warm enough to hatch. If her gaze should slip, they will begin slowly to heat. If they heat long enough, they will hatch. You will have a small colony of blue dragons all with very different—and very magical—powers. Some, I warn you, might not be so sweet as Scorcher here!

'Look after her well, your princess, because it is only she who stands in the way of a hatching. Feed her and love her and find a pillow for her great underbelly to rest.

She must be very relaxed if she is to concentrate on those squirming blue dragonettes, all restless and straining to hear the very first cracking sounds of their shell-like prison. It is Princess Demetria—and Demetria alone—who can prevent this happening.'

As Scorcher translated, he looked at his mum with a fierce pride Septimus found quite incomprehensible given the princess's recent attempts at his murder. Still, there was no accounting for taste and it could not be denied that the great, snivelling dragon had stopped dripping enormous pearl tears on Mt. Zircon.

Pinioned up high, she was gazing adoringly at Scorch's bright blue face as if every word he uttered was wisdom from heaven itself. The other dragons, distinctly uneasy, resumed fighting amongst themselves, with a great series of roars. Septimus resigned himself to a wait because he could not make head or tail of the babble.

Finally, he could see the silhouettes of several lamplighter dragons biting into the rope and releasing the princess, who would have fainted from relief, had a dragon not felicitously set a pillow beneath her, so that she sank gracefully to her knees instead.

Septimus noticed with a grin that she was very soon puffing herself off and eyeing the eggs with a calm interest that the other dragons found most satisfying. Very soon, wolf meat was being brought up to her makeshift pillow-throne (for she was now acting, once more, like her regal self) and the debate turned to the more urgent matter confronting Septimus.

Scorcher transmitted his thoughts quickly. 'They believe in your powers. Two want to rip you to shreds, but most of the circle has come round. They want to know how long Princess Demetria has to watch the eggs?'

'As long as it takes for me to return.'

'But Sep, that could be weeks! How uncomfortable for mum!'

'Nonsense! She will be waited on hand and foot!'

'Yes, but they won't let her rest! They won't let her take her eyes off those eggs!'

'A small punishment for trying to kill you, Scorch! Besides, dragons don't need much sleep, and you know it!'

'Yes, but—'

'Think of the alternative! It is better, surely, than being pinioned to a dragon post! Better, I am sure, than being roasted alive! Just see how they are attending to her!'

Scorch, still a little hungry, had to agree. He would have swapped places with his mum any day judging by the feast that was miraculously materializing around her cushion throne. The smell of wolf meat wafted to his nostrils causing his mouth to water.

Septimus moved just in time as great drops of saliva—very un-attractive—fell like a puddle on Mt. Zircon. Several jewels instantly lost their lustre.

'I suppose. But what if her attention slips and the eggs hatch? They will kill her, torture her, tear her limb from limb—'

'It won't happen.'

'How can you be certain?'

Septimus chuckled. 'Because I am not clever enough to visual-ise the anatomy of a dragonette. Far too complex for me to visualise accurately. Imagine conjuring nine of you! Nine in one blended wish! Impossible!'

'But—'

'Those eggs have no more internal substance than juggling balls. They were the only things I could visualise pretty accurately. I just elongated them a little, a small tweak here and there—I once had an ambition to be in the Cirque Du Soleil—'

Scorcher blinked.

'No, never mind, you wouldn't know what I mean. Anyway, I know how juggling balls are weighted, how they feel. The halos are simply a nice, decorative touch.'

Scorcher, bereft, for an instant, of mind-thought, could only gasp in admiration. Tricking an entire circle of dragons, no matter how stu-pid, took bravery beyond bearing, wit beyond wonder. Which all went to prove what the little dragonette had been saying all along—it was a pity, a great pity, that Septimus was not his mum.

* * *

Master Hepple, true to his word, was swift. When Bickleberry and Wendleweed (whose rear-end purple smudge was now, happily, a thing of the past) returned to the hill-house, he was strapping his suit-case closed with a business-like nod.

He removed his fairy wings from the hat stand and bade the two friends fetch theirs, still drying outside.

Both elves were subdued, having felt, in the few moments they'd spent in Willowsham, the shadow that was cast subtly over the landscape and across the horizon, further than they could see.

Not even the purple toffee apples Master Hepple snatched from the table as an after-thought seemed to cheer them. Wendleweed wrapped them in wax paper almost absently, as though his mind was elsewhere.

Master Hepple too seemed preoccupied, though he carefully checked the straps of each elf's wings and tightened Bickleberry's, which were far too loose and probably accounted for his earlier episode of backwards-flying.

He cautioned them not to loosen the ties no matter how itchy they might get, for wings were temperamental things and if one side unwound, the other side could disentangle and loosen too, causing havoc.

Poor Bickleberry! He had an itch right at the back of his back, under his wings, but there was no time to do anything about it at all. He wished Master Hepple had not mentioned about scratching, because everyone knows that as soon as you talk about it, you want to. He sighed, trailing Master Hepple out the house. The apothecary-healer locked up carefully (there was no saying, any more, with hobgoblins round and about) before strapping on his own, more elegant, wings.

Then, it was hurry, hurry, hurry, all the way back whence they had come, and also through some shorter routes that took the elves to areas of Elvenswolde they hadn't known existed. They were anxious most of the journey, terribly worried that the king would die or sink further into the strange malady that was troubling him.

This said, elves were elves and these two had sunny natures. No anxiety could completely stop them loving the great water slides that gushed from the north to the south, from the highlands right through to the lowlands, courtesy of the water sprites.

They had been sprinkled with waterproofing (a short acting spell that was designed to protect their wings) but their tunics were still drenched in water from the flowing falls.

Bickleberry was disappointed to learn that the waterways—especially the slides—were forbidden, in the main, to elves.

'Very unfair,' he commented, but Master Hepple, (who knew all too well what elves could get up to) did not agree. After the water slides there was an hour of flying—during which Bickleberry managed to loosen his straps and have a quick, surreptitious scratch—then a sudden landing, on soft moss.

The elves were amazed, after a quick search, to find an underground tunnel route, fashioned by earth sprites, just beside Master Hepple's feet. There was a heavy marble stone to be lifted—green as the surrounding moss and grasses, hidden so skilfully the elves would not have seen it had they not been shown.

Master Hepple muttered he must remember to sprinkle forget-me-dust on their faces when they reached the castle. It was no good naughty elves knowing of the old places and of the ancient dwelling routes of earth sprites.

The tunnels were long, and deep, and smelt slightly damp, of oiled wood and summer soil. It was a strange combination, made stranger still by the odd lantern hanging from a tree root, burning steadily, though there was no attendant to fan its flames or check its fuel.

The lanterns were pretty, but solid enough to be functional and certainly cast the only light possible in those deep places of Elvenswolde. Odd how cosy it was when one might have expected dark and shivering cold.

They went on and on, often requiring single file and the careful negotiation of vertical ladders, gleaming gold. They were wrought in the ancient metal of ilianite, much scarcer than gold, but a favourite among earth sprites who found the warm, glowing colour comforting and the strength critical.

It was hard work descending the ladders, for though there were bars to hold, one was conscious of the great depths. One had to hold on incredibly tightly and use much strength just to keep a foot-hold. Also, of course, this had to be done backwards, facing the outer tunnel wall. The going was slow despite the appearance of the odd earth sprite from smaller, inter-leading cavities. Very helpful they were, and well mannered.

Their voices were deep and gravelly, but solemnly polite, as though it were no intrusion at all to suddenly have messenger elves cluttering up their byways.

Even with the slow tedium of the route, Master Hepple was confident that they were saving a great deal of time taking the more direct path to Castle Carne.

They were approaching from the less used Meridian side, which bypassed the king's tower and also the eastern moat. This made it less likely that the vigilant eyes of Móran would witness their arrival through the town streets.

The wizard would be expecting them, but the less he knew of their precise comings and goings, the better it would be.

They were relieved to start climbing, again, for it signalled the end of this leg of the journey, and though they did not complain, their limbs were tired and they were feeling rather hungry. (As elves do!)

When they finally made it to the exit, Wendleweed stretched and took great gusts of fresh Elvenswolde air, glad to be so unrestricted. Bickle wanted to kick off his pointy elfin shoes (their curl was quite gone and they needed a jolly good polish!) but restrained himself as he caught Master Hepple's raised brow. Both elves wondered if they might broach the matter of the toffee apples, but the healer was peering from his spectacles and frowning.

The three travellers were exposed, again, to the elements. A darkening cloud was forming, but it was not this that seemed to bother the great master. As a matter of fact, he was staring in another direction entirely, squinting into the middle distance. He looked grave, and bade the elves be silent. As he pulled the travellers to a touchstone, he slid a hushed finger of warning to his lips.

He need not have worried: Bickleberry and Wendleweed would not have made a noise for the world. The fabled earth wolves of Astra that ravaged the darker parts of Elvenswolde—those already under shadow—approached as if from nowhere, their teeth white against their dark fur, their tongues lolling idly from side to side.

One of them sniffed, and the pack stiffened, their hairs on end. It did not need Master Hepple's grimace to know that the company's scent had been captured on the tell-tale wind.

They drew closer, random at first, then more certain. Closer, towards the touchstone where the elves crouched, trembling. In the far distance, dragons howled. Bickleberry could see the dark outline of several circling, far away. He shivered; less scared of those lumbering creatures than the dark - furred demons that faced them now.

The wolves were permitted to roam Elvenswolde unguarded. It was a much-debated matter, but in the end decreed by Ramón himself: balance in all things. The Astran wolves ran free in tight packs that killed where they could. Móran, of course, had made them his own, bending them to his will, binding them to his call, so that though they were creatures of the wild, they were also creatures of the dark.

The winged wolves of Ilra and the dark, earth wolves of Astra made possible the existence of the wood sprites and the mermaids, the phoenix and the white unicorn, the gentler, more beautiful life forms of Elvenswolde. The contrast made them all the sweeter, but at such price!

Bickleberry had a sudden impulse to rush out with a stick, but Wendleweed grabbed at his belt. So long as they could feel the touchstone, they would be safe. Master Hepple had said it was so. They had to trust.

Wendleweed clung to the long, angular stone, cracked like marble, silky smooth to the touch. Bickleberry, half-annoyed at his friend's interference, did the same.

The wolves watched hungrily and waited. They did not move except when Bickleberry scratched his itchy back and forgot, for a second, to hold the stone. Then their speed seemed to be a mere twitch, for as soon as Bickleberry's hand returned, they were still. Still and waiting.

How long the adventurers sat there, Master Hepple with his suitcase of potions, the elves with their heavy wing packs, none could say. It seemed like an age. Worse, more wolves appeared on the horizon and were soon sitting, tongues panting, grim eyes watchful, when dusk began to fall.

By now, the elves' hands were stiff from holding the touchstone and Bickleberry was itchier than ever. He moved, slightly, and the unthinkable happened: his wing pack did precisely what Master Hepple had warned about. It loosened and a wing emerged, flapping in the evening breeze. Bickleberry immediately grabbed at the pack, forgetting to maintain his hold on the touchstone.

In that precise instant, the wolves sprang and the second wing released. Bickle found himself hovering over the wolves as they bayed at him, and leapt, and ripped at a piece of his fine new livery.

Master Hepple wavered, for his first duty was to the king. Bickle's wings seemed to have a mind of their own and were carrying him further from their path, toward the forest of enchantment.

A dark domain, Móran's domain. Master Hepple felt a deep sense of foreboding and made a decision that might ever after haunt him.

'Leave him, Wendleweed. We have no time to follow. The wolves are distracted; they are chasing after Bickleberry's scent. Come, you and I must turn from here and complete our task, we need to get to the king.'

'What? And leave Bickleberry with those—those—creatures?'

'There is nothing more we can do for him. If he is headed to the wild place, the wolves will be the least of his worries. I am sorry, elf, but our loyalties must be to Ramón and the king.'

'They are. I was to fetch you and keep Bickle of trouble!'

'You should not have let him release his straps.'

Wendleweed gasped.

'No, that is unfair of me. Forget I said that. It isn't true and you can't be held responsible for every foolish elf. Even I cannot! I should have—but come, it is with heavy hearts that we must—'

'Not we, you! You must continue, I quite see that!' Wendleweed swallowed. 'But I? I must go after Bickle and try—I don't know—I can't be expected to desert him, I can't! I would not be able to live with myself. I have fetched you for the king. The rest of the route you know better than I, you have no need of me.'

Master Hepple sighed. 'Very well, little elf. You are noble and Elvenswolde is the brighter for you. In these dark days, that counts for something.'

He had not finished before Wendleweed had his wing pack out and had risen high above the touchstone. The wolves, noticing this development, divided and returned to bay after him. Wendleweed did not look down, only across, to the patch at the beginning of the forest where Bickleberry had disappeared. He took a deep breath and accelerated speed, not for a moment stopping to think about whether he could or not, whether his wings would stand it or not, whether he was being sensible or not. He just wanted, with all his being, to find his friend.

Had he but known it, he had just strengthened Ramón's powers. There is no goodness more pure than the act of friendship itself.

Breathing the Balance

Night was upon the dragons of Sarcalet. An aura of excitement hung in the air like elf light. Septimus thought he had turned the corner, though there were still some who eyed him distastefully and who smirked when the hoariest of the pack—not a Dargonville but a Beurgandeaux (horrible beasts, ancestry back to the Germanic lizards, all teeth)—threatened death to Demetria if Septimus should fail.

Demetria trembled at this remark. Her scales, still thin from starvation, shook upon her ribcage. She eyed the 'eggs' with awe—for even she believed Septimus's garbled tale of her powers.

Septimus, feeling the winds of freedom blowing across his face, smiled and pulled himself to his full height.

'If I fail, it shall not be for want of trying. Take care, I pray you, of the eggs and of little Scorcher, here, who is a braver dragon than you know and deserving, not of scorn, but of the highest of dragon honours.'

Scorcher, who had been translating with a rapidity Septimus found impressive, now stopped mid-sentence.

'What do you mean, they must take care of me? I am coming with you!'

Septimus shook his head. He stepped back neatly as the dragon accidentally breathed a great gust of fire in his face, very nearly singeing the last remaining hair on his eyebrow. For once, he did not scold.

'This is no adventure for a dragonette, Scorch. You've just found your mum and your people. Stay with them, for I fear the forces that call me, the powers that have summoned me from earth itself will not always be kind. As a dragon, you are safer with dragons than with elves. I don't know how I know this, but I feel it.' The amulet about Septimus's neck flashed fire, causing the dragonette to blink.

'Hey, Sep, that necklace—it breathes like a dragon!'

But the amulet was bottle blue, again, so Septimus only smiled and shook his head.

'It's a piece of glass, but it belonged to my father. It is fitting that I should wear it at such a time. Now listen! Time is against me, though the stars are so bright they shall light my way.

'I haven't the faintest idea which direction to take, though my heart tells me straight, past the cliffs from which we came, along the edge of the sea. I'll just have to follow my senses until Arikeet arrives to guide my way. I am sure it will be so—at least, I hope so.'

Scorch's tail drooped. He assumed his most pathetic dragon stare. It was so effective that even old Wart-face felt his heart moved by the hatchling. Princess Demetria saw the tear well up in Scorch's eye then release, slowly, across the bridge of his dragon nose.

In so doing, it extinguished the last vestiges of flame and caused a sizzle of smoke to slightly—just slightly—scorch Septimus once more, but this time only the wrinkle above his left cheekbone—a decided improvement on earlier.

Demetria was so moved by this single tear that she nearly rose from her regal position. Yes, she finally felt a stirring of maternal feeling, the beginnings of the pride she should have felt in Scorch, right from the start.

She would have clasped him to her great dragon breast, but the other dragons, mindful of the nasty eggs trembling with readiness to hatch, howled at her to keep her mind on her task.

This she did, but only when assured by Scorcher that he could manage very well without her motherly ministrations, something that seemed to alarm him more than anything else.

'Let me come with you, Sep!'

'No! You might as well stop with those dragon tears, they won't do you any good.'

'The other dragons will tease me! Eat me! Crush me!'

'Nonsense! So long as they have the eggs to worry about, they will treat you royally as you deserve.'

'Let me have a chance to prove myself! I could be useful!'

Septimus, thinking rather fondly of all his aches, burns and scratches, smiled. 'I'm sure you could, but you are a mere hatchling. When I have found what I have come for, when I have fulfilled the prophecies and my destiny, I'll come back. We'll have heaps of adventures then.'

Septimus did not wait to see if Scorcher agreed.

He bowed to the watchful circle, all dark silhouettes against the evening's shadow. Quiet, now, but for the odd roar and hiss of smoke. Then he turned his back and headed towards the sound of the sea and the crashing, salty waves that called him.

* * *

Master Hepple found his way to Castle Carne far quicker now that he was unhampered by his companions. Though his heart was heavy, the gravity of his task forced him to put aside his feelings and hasten up the auxiliary castle stairs with all speed.

He could not be certain whether he had been noticed or not, but as he cast off his cloak and handed it to a waiting foot-elf, he reflected that Móran would soon be in possession of the fact of his arrival.

Ramón, dishevelled and smelling vilely from meticlaws, emerged from his turret (something he had not done in days) and escorted Master Hepple across the great hall to the receiving room, where the queen paced the floors anxiously.

'Your majesty.' The healer bowed low, but the queen took his hand and bade him rise.

'Master Hepple, I am so thankful you have come! The king remains unchanged, I fear, though his eyes flicker a little, as though he would wake and say something.'

Master Hepple nodded and asked that he may be permitted to examine the king, and administer such herbs as might be healing.

The queen looked vastly relieved, though the Wish Maker himself looked grave.

Courteously, Master Hepple accompanied her majesty to the inner sanctuary, where the king, dazed and unconscious, lay quietly upon a bed of satin with sheets that shimmered as if by fairy light and were wrought in the finest threads of silver. There was a faint, high hum about the room, tingling from the walls, where the newest tapestry, embroidered with the high magic, took its place amidst the remaining, more ancient pieces.

If Master Hepple had looked closer, he would have seen that ancient runes were stitched skilfully both into the bed linen and the wall designs, but he did not. Such matters were for Ramon, and doubtless the Wish Maker knew precisely what he was doing.

He, however, held the gift of healing and potions. When everyone had left the king's chamber, he examined his majesty with kind concern, knowing, as the queen did not, the depths of the malady that overcame him.

The king had chosen a path of betrayal and the guilt lay so heavily upon his shoulders that he rested in fitful slumbers rather than reason in wakeful knowledge.

Master Hepple divined this truth by the furrowed look on the king's brow, and the unrested demeanour he presented, despite his present condition of unconsciousness. With a sad sigh, he withdrew from his suitcase a potion bottle that was much smaller than some of the others he carried, but rather more powerful.

He opened the stopper and whisked the potion—petals of purity, an ancient essence of truth—under his majesty's nose. Almost instantly, the king awoke, though his eyes seemed focused on a point further than Master Hepple, and when he spoke, it was with confusion rather than conviction.

The healer gently placed some cushions beneath the king's back and drew forth a drink. Not a potion this time, but a restorative of sorts, lemon and icy cold. The king's lips were dry, but he drank after the whisper of a coaxing and afterwards seemed very much more himself, though his brow remained furrowed in a sad, unnecessary type of pain.

Master Hepple was gentle.

'Your majesty, I understand your trouble. To release it from your system you have to speak, speak to me, and then to your kingdom. You cannot be cleansed from your malady unless you do this, and undertake the task truthfully and in good faith.'

For a long while, it seemed that the king had either not heard, or not understood, for he remained very silent indeed, though he sipped, from time to time, on the restorative.

Master Hepple said nothing. He was a patient man and the healing could not be rushed.

After what seemed an eternity but really by elf time was no more than a few considered minutes, the king breathed deeply and began his tale.

'Master Hepple, I am not fit to rule this realm. You, who know the truth, who hold all the answers in your hand, can wrest them from me with that bottle.'

The healer's eyebrows rose.

'Yes, I recognise eralblis variens, essence of truth, when I see it. I was shown the Fillament a long time ago, in another age, and for a more noble reason. I feel the drops working on my soul. You gave me such a little, but the truth has never been far from my consciousness. Every moment of my immobility it has been with me, poisoning me. Guilt is a terrible thing, Master Hepple, made more terrible by the truth.'

The healer said not a word, but gently smoothed a wrinkle in the crisp top sheet.

'You, who know the truth, know that I am unfit to rule. What ails me is a melancholy of the soul, not a malady of the flesh. I would rather sleep, now, than remain awake to see the product of my vanities.'

'Your majesty, this is not a time for sleep! Sleep is for the free of spirit, for those of us endowed with the lightness of being. You are not, and until you are again, you must rise up from your bed and fight! Fight with your heart what you have begun to fight with your mind!'

'I never meant to, Master Hepple. I meant only to satisfy my curiosity, to see, a little, into the destinies of Elvenswolde, the land of my birth and my blood.'

'That may be, but to satisfy your curiosities you engaged, in secret, the services of Móran the silver one, the wizard of whom you had been warned, of whom you had been begged to be wary.'

Master Hepple did not bother to keep the disapproval from his voice. The king needed, for his healing, to face up to his weaknesses.

'I thought the Wish Maker over cautious. I thought his fears were transmuted to mine. I could not understand his reservations, nor see the wild winds I stirred when I sought enlightenment.'

'You were warned though.'

'Yes, I was warned, but by the Wish Maker, the brother—the blood brother—of Móran himself. I suspected nothing more than the age-old rivalry of siblings.'

'There you were correct, but it was not Ramón's jealousies you should have been wary of, but his namesake's.'

'His namesake?'

'Have you not noticed? Ramón spelt the old way, spoken backwards to invoke the darker powers, is Móran.'

There was a silence.

'I see you tremble at the truth. I marvel you did not see it yourself and have more care.'

The king lay back on his pillows, paler than the satin sheets that surrounded him, though deep shadows circled his eyes.

'I have been a fool, Master Hepple. I chose the dark way because I doubted light.'

'Indeed. You permitted Móran first into your counsel, then into your heart and finally into your tower. That last act empowered him, breaking the spell of banishment, transmuting the exile, granting him the strength to cast into shadow what Ramón has always cast into light.'

'Except for the forests and the wolves—'

'You know his theories of balance. There have to be places and creatures of dark for there to be places and creatures of light. That is why he has always accepted the existence of Móran, why he chose banishment, not death, why he took such pains to teach him, to steep him in the ways of enchantment.

'He could not act for light if there was not someone, somewhere, speaking for dark. The earth has enough places and uses for Móran—the balance of earth and the other worlds has permitted Elvenswolde to be as wondrous and as light driven as it is.'

'No longer.'

The king whispered this, his hands on his face.

'No longer, your highness, since you invited Móran in with your own lips and your own mantle of majesty.'

'I have been a fool. I opened the great atlas of Elvenswolde and I saw the country dark with shadows, wracked with the very vines and pods of measles, maggots, meticlaws—from Sarcalet across the borders of Lindolucia and Willowsham—Master Hepple, you can have no notion of what I have done.'

Master Hepple had a very good notion, but he only asked quietly, 'What did he promise you?'

'The gift of sight, the ability to foresee the future, to read the stars, to hazard great storms and foresee where lightening will fork, splitting the sky and the worlds apart, marking on a map the making of Elvenswolde and the divisions of the six worlds beyond.'

'Heady stuff.'

'Móran is very compelling. His tongue is as silver as his cloak.'

'And a heart as black as a brewing pot.'

'What made you see the truth? You were going to address the court.'

'I happened on Móran whilst I was sleeping. Dream-filled, I wandered into his mind, perhaps by accident, perhaps by design. I think he thought to control me, to speak to the people with my body and my vision and my voice.'

'Yes?'

'Something went wrong. Something pulled me away from his temptations at the precise moment he needed my quiescence.'

'I think we can safely say that was the Wish Maker, who has risked life and limb to save you. He invoked the base magic and the old legends. He has conjured Septimus, son of Septimus, the child of legend, he has woven great webs of enchantment—'

'I am grateful. What I saw in that sleep's dream appalled me. I could no longer lend countenance to the wizard, though I had sworn to permit him the freedom of the realm. I broke my oath to address the council.'

'That is why you were drained of energy and strength. That is why you have been so ill and paid so great a price.'

'The people of Elvenswolde are paying a greater price.'

'No, the people of Elvenswolde are fighting and so must you. Get well, your majesty, and lead the march against Móran and his creatures. Fight the seeds of destruction he has sown within you. Do it with your own inner strength and courage. I can help with my potions but I cannot cure. Only conviction and courage and strength of will can do that. If you wish to drive away shadows, invoke the light. Not all the light, that is too high a price to pay.

Leave some balance, some valleys to highlight the pinnacle of your elfin mountains. But find the strength, majesty, and let your will be steel, lest our waters are poisoned and our air made rank with enchantment.'

The king, hearing these words, rose from his bed slowly, without another word. He drained the last drop of the restorative and was rueful to see that the essence vial was still mostly full. He had not needed much, he saw, to reveal the aching uncertainties of his heart. He had been vain; he had wanted to know, to see the future, to bend it to his will. Now was the moment to make amends.

'Take me,' he said, 'to the queen.'

* * *

Xanadel smiled uncertainly at Garredung. He was defenceless and unsure of the elf's loyalties. He seemed less nasty, somehow, but that might have been because of the sad realignment of his nose, or mere wishful thinking.

'What are you doing here? What am I doing here? I was walking—'

'You were enchanted. I was to follow you and dog your steps and stop you from your task.'

'Was to have?'

Xanadel looked troubled and the gemra, still uncertain, but exuding menace, stepped closer.

Garredung shook them off and they hung back, confused. They recognised the remnants of darkness in Garredung, so they did not sink their claws into his being and taste his mind with their soft tongues. They hung back, uncertain, frightened, even, as the light of the amulet glowed stronger about Xanadel's neck.

Xanadel, released from his spell, was not sure how long they had been there, in this forest, or to what end, but night was now deep upon them and the stars twinkled brightly above the outlines of the branches.

The gemra were less uncertain of Septimus and would have advanced readily towards him, but Garredung fended them off with a flick of the burnt wand. It was laden with dark energy, soggy from use but still humming with power. Like repels like. It repelled the creatures as a polar magnet repels a like polar force.

The gemra struggled, as if against an invisible wall. Garredung cast a sullen glance at Xanadel: he may have been emptied of malice, but his nature was nevertheless grim.

'You had better go. I'll keep them at bay.'

He did not offer to join Xanadel, but continued to hold the wand, burnt, but emitting a strange, evocative power. Its force rendered the shrieking gemra impotent.

Xanadel could not understand why Garredung was helping him. He thanked him suspiciously, but was diverted by a sudden opening of the branches, a twittering of birds and some nasty calls—not owls—and the sudden emergence of a dark shadow. It seemed to be hurtling towards them, crashing among twigs, breaking branches—it was shrieking—

Bickle landed with a smash on the wrong side of the magnetic wall. There was a great flutter of wings and a further screech. Elfin, not sinister. Xanadel had no time to breathe, or feel relieved, or stop the pace of his accelerated heartbeat. The gemra, sensing light, set upon his friend. In the terrible darkness, it was impossible to see the struggle.

There was a scream—a gut-wrenching, tearing scream and a rip of feathered wings. Xanadel rushed forward, away from the protection of the wand. Instantly, he was surrounded by the creatures of the dark, ugly twisted things, some winged, some wild. All of them malevolent, with eyes that shone fiercely and seemed to seek out his very soul.

They touched him, they grabbed at him, worse, they licked him, with tongues that were terrible, gnarled and warm and strangely soft. He felt himself shiver, his will spent, his mind melting to a puddle of warm jelly.

He could hear Bickleberry screaming, putting up far more of a fight than himself. He wanted to kick the creatures away, but they were curling over him, thronging to him, flinching only when his head shifted and the amulet about his neck glittered its strange, empowering blue.

Garredung sighed in a certain satisfaction, that creeping sense of discontent filling his lungs again, and his heart. He had been a creature of dark too long himself to now be bathed entirely in light.

He derived a certain pleasure from seeing Xanadel so beset, and the miserable elf Bickle, who was struggling in earnest, and with a bravery Garredung felt a pang at seeing. He felt a pang because he was envious, knowing that he was the lesser elf. Perhaps he had always known it, denying the truth in the dressing of a bully.

In a moment of rare elfin honesty he felt small, and petty, and afraid. He hated seeing Bickle braver than he, or Xanadel exuding the type of stoic heroism he'd always wished for himself.

His hand dropped to his waist, the wand so effective against the forest creatures, once more dormant. Xanadel's jewel was positively on fire, and the gemra were beginning to scatter, squealing in pain as their tongues touched the shimmering cut of cabochon, or their fingers curled at the fire that seemed to flash like some summer lightning. There were more advancing each moment, and as one fell back, another took his place.

Xanadel, exhausted, dropped to the forest floor just as Bickleberry threw himself over his form and withdrew the simple silver sword most elves carried sheathed beneath their cloaks. Ornamental, mostly, while Swords 213 was part of any apprentice syllabus. This particular weapon was nothing special. The hilt had the usual house emblem etched in plated irrilium, but the blade was wrought from simple steel—nothing magical—standard order of the blacksmith elves. Bickle wondered how effective it would be but had no time to debate the matter, for two of the creatures were regaining their courage and counterattacking, regardless of the strange light in the depths of the jewel.

The sword seemed dark in the shadows, and was heavy. Bickle was squeamish. It was one thing saying 'en guarde' politely in a classroom situation, another thing entirely to slice another creature in two. Still, he had to find courage. If he did not, Xanadel would be dead. He felt the lick of a tongue, stealthy, in the trees beside him. Something thin and bony clawed at his arm—his left arm, defenceless. He raised the right and found the inner strength to do what he had to do.

Killing is a horrible business. No one talks about the blood and grime and squeals and sighs of regret as a life passes. No one in class prepares one for the sorrow, the inner horror, the regret. It is not a heroic business, Bickle found, but one he had to undertake. His sword was dark, now, not from shadow, but from blood. He had hardly time to flinch or feel disgusted, for he needed to do the same thing again—and then again, though it afforded such little pleasure. He had to take advantage of this lull when the gemra were still confused and crazed, unused to these strange, stalwart victims with their swords and flickering light.

Bickleberry sliced two almost in half, ignoring their screams. He found he had to harden his heart for the strokes cut as deeply at his conscience as it bit into gemra flesh. As he shook his blade—no time to clean and the next creature was upon him—he shouted to Xanadel.

'Remember your sword!'

'For freaking heaven's sake, Xanadel, unsheathe your sword!'

The elf seemed dazed. True, he withdrew his weapon, but it was a sorry, bewildered, half-hearted attempt that would have scored an instant 'fail' in swords 213. He did not seem to have the inner strength to drive into the enemy as Bickle did.

Without magic in the sword, the gemra were unafraid. They stepped unblinkingly over their dead and smiled little smiles of relish.

'Vigour, Xanadel! Vigour!'

But Bickle might have spared his breath. Only the necklace saved the elf from oblivion, for more than once it sparked such flashes of light that the gemra were forced to retreat, though only for seconds and even then, the deep, unspeakable listlessness they inflicted on Xanadel was enough to succour them, and grant them glory.

Bright eyes glinted in the half-light, and the twin moons of Elvenswolde, hanging like pale orbs above them, seemed dimmer than usual, confused by the forest's depths. Xanadel faltered—his necklace the only bright light in the sudden pitch of darkness.

This was a double-edged sword, for the gemra were repelled by light, but the light itself drew all of their attention to Xanadel. There would be no respite for the elf.

Garredung stood on the outer edges of the fray, wand burnt and listless at his side. Part of him gloated, but a tiny piece of him was sad, sad that any elf of Elvenswolde should come to such an end. He was sorry too—sorry that he was not friend enough to help.

Garredung knew little of friendship or love or trust. He hobnobbed with Silvajar, but only because they were both small of heart and mean. He knew it, and something in the forest made him understand it all the more. It was as if the very leaves were laughing. Laughing at Garredung, who had no heart and could be no friend. He was ashamed, but the wand had become as heavy as lead, almost as if it had a will of its own.

Part of him wanted to use it again, to channel the enchantments of Móran, to propel the power he'd felt away from the woods and the wild things, towards the sea and the stars and the pinnacles of light that pricked at his conscience and that secret, small place in his being still untouched by shadows.

Xanadel was overcome.

Not even the amulet could save him, for there were more gemra than elves and though Bickle's sword was bloody, it was not bloody enough. His own dropped unused upon the long blades of grass that cut him like nettles and thrust at him like the autumn thistles of Sep-timus's earth world.

He had not the heart to use the blade, nor the darkness of spirit to poke at the gemra's eyes. The gemra sucked strength from their stares. Their eyes—their curved, slightly elongated eyes—were Móran's windows on the world, his vision from the tower.

'His bloody goodness is going to kill him!'

Bickle saw it in dawning shock and so too did Garredung.

He saw the strength drawn from Xanadel and the many chances he had of using his amulet as a weapon or his sword or his hands. He used none of these, too careful not to kill, too kind to hurt, though he was in ever more agony himself.

Tears were streaming from his face and Bickle was swinging furiously with his sword, but the gemra kept coming. When they could come no more, when Xanadel could take no more, Garredung found the strength.

In that growing part of his heart, he found the strength to defend the light, to raise the charred wand that warred against him and to rebuild the magnetic wall that protected them.

Xanadel drew a breath, brought back from the brink.

It was then that Wendleweed entered the night forest. He had been calling, calling Bickleberry, but his cries had been returned to him like echoes on an ethereal wind.

He was lost, almost hopeless, a beacon for wolves, when he heard the scuffle and the clash of sword on skin and the shrill cries of the dark. Without hesitation, he had flown toward the sounds, towards the innermost dark of that dank forest. What he saw there shocked him, but before he could enter the fray, a gemra grabbed at him from a tree and pinioned him to the bark. The tree had branches that over-hung the forest floor like giant tentacles. They scratched at him and ripped his wings apart.

He gasped in shock and that gasp was mirrored by Xanadel and echoed by Bickleberry and breathed by Garredung himself, who was learning the light and embracing friendship quicker than Ramón the Wish Maker could have hoped possible.

Ramón, who always believed in balance, in the possibility for good within bad, for light within dark, for kindness within greed. Garredung's small seeds of goodness were blossoming in a place where evil flourished. Perverse, but fitting for the balance of Elvenswolde and the six worlds beyond.

'Kill that gemra!'

Garredung concentrated on holding the wand in place, the magnetic wall that kept back the balance of those forest folk. He ignored the evil smell of meticlaws oozing from their frustrated limbs.

'I can't kill him—I'll release the wand! Bickle, you will have to do it!'

But Bickleberry was wounded, and though he tried, he could no longer lift his blade and slice at the creatures that clung to the forest and desired, with dark hearts, a streaming in of shadows.

Wendleweed looked terrified, but he called to Garredung not to drop the wand, not to risk endangering Xanadel in order to spare himself.

At this—yet another display of friendship, Xanadel was released from his stuporous inertia. He summoned, within himself, not the forces of light, but the very depths of dark, those innermost secrets that he permitted not even himself to share, though they slumbered within his soul. He summoned that small pocket of vengeance and hate, that tiny whisper of rage and treachery.

He found within himself the balance. He breathed it. The quiet dark needed to inflict pain, possibly death on another living thing. Not triumphant, not pleased, but firm. With resolve, he drew himself tall and slashed at the gemra with his clean, unmarked sword. Wailing, the creature sank to the ground, steaming and sizzling and transforming, eventually, to a dark, shapeless wisp of smoke.

Then, all that was left were Xanadel, Bickleberry, Wendleweed and Garredung in a forest of lifting gloom. The gemra—each and every one—had fled.

Of Potions and Poisons

Dawn was drifting over Elvenswolde when Septimus reached the path that divides ocean from sea, reef from land. He was worried, for it had been hours since his leave-taking from the dragons, and despite a careful watch, there was still no sign of Arikeet—who he had been certain would guide him—or any sign that he was on the right track, or heading in the direction he should have been.

Now and again, he startled, for he heard a crack of a branch or a twist of a root upon the sandbank. It was almost as though he was being followed, though he could see nothing more than the track behind him when he turned.

The entire world seemed suspended in time. Though he was tired—very tired—he quickened his pace, wondering where his journey would end and whether his arrival in Elvenswolde would mean something, or nothing at all.

He had begun to understand what Arikeet had told him of shadows, for the land, though undoubtedly magical (there was something about it that caused him to tingle) was also very subdued, darker and more melancholy than Sarah's bright tales had led him to expect. Sarah, who had learnt all she knew from Septimus, his father.

A branch broke behind him and he felt his heart quiver, but when he gazed back, there was only the track, and the cold seas and the high winds. Not a creature stirred, or a fairy, or a nymph, or a wood sprite. He was puzzled, for he had been led to imagine a thousand such creatures out and about, chattering in soft, melodious voices or in high pitched squeaks. (In the case of earth sprites, it would have been deep, gravelly tones, but he was not to know that.)

A sense of foreboding touched him, and he could not shake the feeling that he was being watched. Of course, he was.

In the tower of the king, Septimus had just stepped into Móran's direct vision. The resonance of his boots upon the stones had alerted the angry wizard long since. He was furious with Garredung, outraged at the manner in which the gemra had fled, but grimly determined, to stop the seventh son before the base magic could begin its slow course through the realm.

Ramón had invoked magic deeper than his own, deeper than Elvenswolde itself. In his simple shorts and T-shirt, unencumbered by wands or potions, the seventh son of a seventh son, half earth, half elf, best represented this.

A child on the brink of adulthood, but one of the deeper order, one that lay dormant until the balances were out of synchrony, when universes could blossom or be crushed by greed or tyranny.

Then, and only if invoked, the base magic could assume control, eroding the enchantments, undermining the magic, wreaking havoc with charms and signets and signs long conceived. It could act as a neutraliser of both sides of dark and light.

Móran had not thought Ramón would evoke such power for in so doing, he was also revoking his own. He was sublimating his ability to enchant in the hope that the base magic would restore what had been lost.

Oh, foolishness! As Ramón grew weak he, Móran, would grow strong. As his brother's gaze faltered, and his counter enchantments wore thin, the shadows would deepen across the land and the wolves would return from the wild. Creatures—Móran's creatures—would dominate—subject only to his whims, his fancies, and his regime.

Only the base magic could determine anything else. He knew little of this, and closed that portion of his mind that was afraid. He would not be afraid of myths and legends and ancient elfin lore! He would use the base magic, twist it as he had twisted the dark. He would mould it and shape it.

He would capture the child and find his weakness. Working on weakness was his private pleasure. He would derive such pleasure from reaching the child—not to kill but to keep—to keep from Ramón and from those who sought the dark's destruction.

The time had come, he thought, to break free of the tower. It had pleased him to allow Ramón to think him contained. It had pleased him to pace the round chambers of the king and plot his freedom. If ever there was a time for freedom, it was now.

He snapped his fingers for Silvajar, but received no response. Forgetting, in his annoyance, that the messenger was now utterly deaf as a doorstop, he threatened a series of very nasty spells if the elf did not appear on the instant.

Silvajar, immobilized, could do nothing. Nothing at all, though he despaired.

Irritated, the silver wizard cast his first punishment spell—one of a habitual series—that the stupid elf should turn to serpent, crawling on his belly until it was the wizard's own whim he be returned to elfin form.

Móran's mind was on greater things than the errant elf. Still, there was no reason Silvajar should not escape discipline. Doubtless he was playing truant in the tower gardens. It amused him to think the fairies would be screaming and the little wood sprites jumping in alarm, deadly afraid.

The idea intrigued him so much that he added a little venom to Silvajar's spell as he opened up the tome of tomes.

It would take enormous concentration to break free of the enchantments Ramón had cast about the tower. Two of the guards had already tried. One had fallen into a deathly stupor; the other had broken his shoulder charging at an invisible barrier that was solid as stone itself.

Still, he, Móran, knew the secret ways, the spell-rich passages that led to freedom. He'd sent Garredung successfully through the barricade and he would do the same for himself.

He paged through the tome of tomes, reminding himself, here and there, of this ingredient and that that would be required. He never admitted it, but his skill did not come naturally to him as Ramón's did.

He could not intuitively cast spells (except juvenile levels, like bewitching and possibly some more advanced climatology.) No, he relied heavily on recipes and ingredients—cookbook magic if you will, but nevertheless powerfully effective. The only problem with this approach was that the items required often needed preparation and the collection phase was tedious, to say the least.

Over the years he had developed an excessively well stocked larder so that if it was simply a matter of dried lightning rods or silver wings he was pretty well prepared, but other items—the fresher variety—had to come to him via the woods and the winds and the wolves.

Essences from the winds—lavender and teardrops, fear (distilled) and fright, the more acute version. The wolves would bring all the livestock—bats and rats, but more importantly, the secret things, the strange, quivering creatures that lived on the far plains, sometimes in the fifth and sixth realms beyond.

The woods brought the roots and the herbs, the arrowroot and bulbs of meticlaws, the truffle of elgins, the scourges, the red- ripe lichens, all omens of sorrow.

Now, as he gazed thoughtfully at his chapter on escapology, he scolded himself for not checking on the trance weed stocks. He needed nine strands at least, if he did not want his nose twisted out of all proportion, as Garredung's had been. He marked the page, then screamed—screamed—as he felt pain—a stinging, searing quicksilver pain—at his ankles and at his feet.

The tome dropped from his hand with a thunderous crash that sent sparks of glowing stars and darkening moons right through the very turret itself. Castle Carne lit up in a mystical spray of charms.

Thousands of elves and fairies scurried hither and thither, unsure of the meaning of this display, especially as it came from the king's tower, the tower that had been enshrouded in gloom and bad weather for days.

The guards on watch flinched as several dark moons landed close to their boots, the echoes resonating in sharp pains up their shins and toes. Stars seemed more harmless, but even so, they blinded if one gazed too closely, and many a fairy had swollen eyes for days thereafter.

In the castle, Móran was reaching, in panic, for his wand. His legs were swollen with some ugly charm of his making. He called, again, for Silvajar, but Silvajar did not come.

Silvajar, it should be said, was a stone no more. As Móran swirled his silver cloaks in pain and impotent rage, a black—a deeply black— snake slithered across the floor and down the one thousand, seven hundred and seventy-seven steps of the king's tower. The scales on his stomach were purple and silver, the precise colour of the king's livery.

The snake slithered on its belly and did, indeed, frighten the fairies and the elves as Móran had wished.

He forked his tongue in curious joy as he savoured the first fruits of his freedom, the delicious delight of writhing and squirming where once he had been fixed as rock, a marble edifice with no known means to sample the small pleasures of the day.

His tail twitched as he felt the power of Móran suffuse his being once more and tame him. He hated the sudden darkness that clouded his mind, but he was compelled by it. Slowly—much more slowly—he slithered across the plains and down, down to the beach and waiting sea.

* * *

Septimus knelt on the sands, breathing heavily and watching, for the first time, dawn over the land of his father, the mysterious world of Elvenswolde. He too had watched, in wonder, as the dark moons and the shimmering stars had cascaded from the king's turret colliding, like a veritable waterfall of light, with the day's dawn.

He had known then that he was close, close to the reason for which he had come and to the task that he'd been set. He felt it in his bones, and exulted in the moment. He felt the utter certainty that his moment was upon him, that rebirth was hanging in the balance like a delicate icicle in a snow storm.

He must neither warm it with his breath nor freeze it with his mind. He must nurture and preserve the balance of this land and give himself up to the high magic.He felt a singing about his ears and on the wind, high pitched and pure. At last he sensed the presence of fairies and the elves, all scattered about hither and thither as a result of the charms.

Once or twice he thought he spied something, but it was no more than the sudden flutter of a wing, well hid, or the tinkle of a fairy bell in a meadow far away. The trees, to the right, were tall. He stared hard, but could see little to disturb.

He felt in his pocket for some chocolate. Melted, but good. The sugar stripped him of the dull tiredness. It was a sweet moment— Septimus, the chocolate and the calm seas lapping gently at the shore. They were no longer raging.

He walked steadily towards Castle Carne, his thoughts a calm jumble of the old and the new. Sarah, home, Elvenswolde, his father, Scorch, the unknown magic—his long legs stretched in their sandals, sand between his toes. He felt alone and yet among friends. It was a strange sensation, but one he rather liked. He was tingling with expectation. Somewhere, at the back of his mind, there was also dread.

Idly, he noticed the faint line in the sand. It was like a thread of cotton, thin, hardly visible, but unearthing just enough of the golden grains to be noticeable. It undulated in long, lithe patterns that seemed to have some purpose.

As Septimus watched, it seemed to move in a line directly parallel with his shadow. Septimus stepped sideways and noticed that the streak, still some way distant, changed course as well. The boy zigzagged, a little, tracking back towards the cliffs on the right, and the strand of thread—black, he could see it now—seemed to do the same.

His heart beat faster, for he knew that the moment was upon him. As he reached into his pack for a knife, he realised that he would need his wits. The line approaching him was sleek, and grew less slender as it drew near.

As his hand gripped the knife's handle, the black line took a more vibrant shape, the shifting sands revealing their quiet secret. A snake, with small eyes and an unwavering stare, was approaching him from the direction of Castle Carne.

This he could now see in much more perspective: the turrets and the towers as he had imagined, only higher and more detailed in form. A cloud seemed to swirl about the castle, enveloping it in a type of gauzy gloom that altered its visibility from the north, from Sarcalet and the dragon circle whence he'd come.

Dawn was now lending its elfin light, but even so, the famous castle of the king seemed trapped under a veil, a quiet edifice almost certainly under shadow. Septimus had not a moment to take all this in: the snake was approaching faster than he liked and he had no doubt that the creature did not represent his majesty's welcoming committee.

Every muscle in his body wanted to turn tail and run, but he forced himself to be still.

Cautiously, he raised his arm to throw his blade. As he did, the movement was mirrored in the long, languorous gesture of the creature, which seemed to mock him even as his body positioned himself for a strike.

Silvajar—for naturally, the serpent was he—raised his body from the golden sands and felt the venom infuse his being and nestle gently on his tongue. He had an overwhelming urge to expel it, for such is the nature of serpents and such is the fate of their prey.

He quivered, ready to bite as he had already bitten, to poison as he had already poisoned, but a flicker of red flame stopped him, mesmerising him, forcing him to find within himself the balance, that small goodness that remained buried under years of neglect and mistrust.

Septimus felt, rather than saw, the glow of his amulet. The bottle blue had more clarity, now, than the purest of earth sapphires. Certainly, it sparkled more brightly than the jewels of his world, though the seventh son could not see it, so fixed was he on the eyes of the serpent. It seemed to know him, to acknowledge his being. It seemed to say, in its beady gaze, 'I too am a living creature, as you are.'

Septimus did a foolish thing. He dropped the knife. He could not, in cold blood, kill this creature.

Silvajar was looking beyond the blue to the greater depths of molten fire that blazed, now, like red gold flames, copper and crimson, scarlet and bronze, all a flicker to taunt him, to search his soul, to find his very depths.

The venom willed itself to be released, but Silvajar's mouth clamped shut. As he watched the flames, he remembered friendship and small kindnesses and the little joys of sharing. He remembered long gone days when he was untainted by greed and the little jealousies that grew in him like untamed weeds in a garden of discontent.

His small, black mind flashed to tiny pleasures, long buried. Like a kaleidoscope, his thoughts tumbled to forgotten places, lingering over love and longing and those small impulses of forgotten helpfulness.

He remembered, for some reason, releasing an elf from a rather mean torment of Garredung's devising. He flashed back, rather distantly, to the time he'd misdirected a corrector wand. Mischievous, perhaps, but the victim's gratitude had warmed a hidden place in his heart.

Silvajar was not wicked, like Móran. He was mean, and that meanness was born of many things, some chance, some choosing. Perhaps if the balances had been attended to more carefully, his heart would not have been so out of kilter with his mind. As it was, the amulet raised to prominence that part of him that was untainted and used that part which was.

It used his fury and his venom. He channelled it towards Móran, who thought no more of Silvajar than he would of a toad. Móran, whom he'd served, obeyed, in some small measure, respected.

The same Móran who'd unflinchingly turned him to stone and given so little weight to the act that he'd actually forgotten. Móran, who turned elves to creatures of the wild and who blackened the hearts of snakes.

Yes, the amulet used the tainted. It deflected poison away from its purpose and cajoled it elsewhere. The venom was still dark, still deep, still akin to the forces of evil that seethed in slow swirls about

Elvenswolde, like tentacles. There was little the amulet could do about such a force, save turn it on itself.

It did, however, draw out and emphasize the kindness in Silvajar, the hidden whispers in his soul that he was embarrassed about. Yes, it drew out Silvajar's softness for sea sprites, and his yearning for the touch of a baby on his skin, elf or earth. It reminded Silvajar of cuddles, as an elfling, of sharing Wickles, of forgiving, and of saving a place for Garredung when he was late.

Small things, little things, but all as important as the day itself, and all counted upon by the Wish Maker, who valued their existence higher than even the bravery of knights, or the smiles of the favoured ones.

The snake eyed Septimus, considering. The balance, when weighed, was not enough. Though the amulet flared bright across the boy's neck, causing the serpent to squint, the base power was insufficient. Not enough to fight the dark, the will of Móran, the plain cravings of a simple snake upon the sand.

Remesis Rising

The sky darkened to blue as Silvajar moved to attack, his small head swaying in the freedom of evil. His goodness was outweighed. Outweighed by the ill will that fermented in his being like the worst of Móran's blood-bled potions.

There was a hiss and a roar, then a huge sizzle of flames and a darkening of sky. A dragon—a blue dragon—swooped from the heavens and in a dramatic arch of its tail set Septimus's backpack alight.

The snake, long and lean, was carelessly plucked from the beach like seaweed, black and flecked with sand.

It flickered helplessly in the air, coiling and uncoiling but to no avail. An energetic dragonette, in the throes of triumph itself, refused to release its hold. Instead, it hovered above Septimus, flapping its scaly wings and looking, for all, the world, like a veritable prince among his people.

Septimus could have kissed him. True, there was the small matter of his burning pack (which he found necessary to stamp out with sudden vigour) but all the same, he felt very well disposed towards the dragonette, who was displaying some remarkable courage, not to mention an excellent talent for showing up at the right moment.

'Oops, sorry.' The dragon eyed the charred pack guiltily.

'Scorcher!' (For yes, it was he!)

'What in the world—how on earth?'

Septimus, for once, was speechless.

The blue hatchling, if he could have grinned, would have. But his dragon mouth was clamped tightly shut, well out of reach of Silvajar's infuriated snake head.

In rage, Silvajar spat the venom that had been building within him. He spat it so far that it passed way beyond Septimus's head and landed in an ugly, spreading, purple pool, on the shores of Elvenswolde itself. For a moment, time seemed suspended as the waves crept in, turning the purple to salt and the salt to sea, until there was no more evidence of the venom than the great ocean itself, mightier than wishes, more powerful than enchantment.

'Sorry, Sep! I've burned that—that—earth thing.'

'Never mind, forget about the pack. It can be mended. Scorch, what are you doing here?'

'I followed you! You've left tracks everywhere! Even a dragonette like me could keep up, especially as the stones resonate. Do you not know to keep off stones?'

'No, how should I?'

'See? You need a dragon with you at all times!'

'Yes, but Scorch—'

'No buts, Sep! I would have kept out of your way—I promise I would have—only my wings got caught in the trees and I accidentally started a forest fire so I needed to get out of the shadows to fetch some water because every time I breathed I made it worse—'

'Stop!'

Septimus almost chuckled, unafraid now that his deadly enemy looked like no more than a piece of dark spaghetti or perhaps a dirty clothesline blowing in the eastern wind.

'Stop! I am losing track! Start again.'

'Very well—'

Scorch opened his mouth to speak, nearly causing Silvajar to make a hasty and miraculous escape.

'Don't talk. Think, think, will you!' Septimus practically bellowed the words so Scorch remembered in time and snapped his mouth shut again, much to Silvajar's acute discomfort and misery.

'Sorry! As I said, I started a forest fire—clumsy, me—so I thought I'd better put it out. I flew to the water's edge to siphon some water into my mouth—I can blow steam, you know, so I thought maybe I could just store the water and blow it over any smouldering roots—'

'What about the fire itself?'

'Oh, that was extinguished by the waterfall of enchantment that cascaded from Castle Carne. Most seemed to land on the fire, and fire and fire don't mix. Not enchanted fire anyway, especially those dark moon things. No, I just wanted to wet some of the forest floor and sneak another glimpse of you—'

'Have you been sneaking glimpses?'

Scorcher definitely would have grinned had the snake not squirmed and Septimus not yelled at precisely the same moment.

'Oops! Sorry, I keep forgetting. Yes, I have been sneaking glimpses all night—'

'So that is what I kept hearing. You frightened the living daylights out of me!'

'Only protecting you! You never know when you might need a dragon—'

Septimus's indignation turned to laughter.

'Thanks, Scorch! Er—do you intend to fly all day with that thing in your mouth?'

'What thing? Oh, him! Should I eat him? Snakes, I believe, have a nasty, bitter after taste—not at all like wolf meat which is really quite delicious, you know—but I will give him a go if you want me to!'

'No!' Septimus did not know why, but the idea shocked him.

It was fortunate that Silvajar did not have the gift of mind talk else he would very likely have fainted in fright. As it was, now that the venom was removed from his system, he was feeling small and vulnerable and rather lost. Also, though he could not put his finger (not that he had one, at present!) on the feeling, he was experiencing a high degree of remorse and shame. Yes, Silvajar was positively embarrassed by his behaviour.

He had attacked for no good reason and having attacked, the boy—the boy of all the myths, the golden-haired child from across the worlds, he the seventh, he the son—the chant repeated itself in Silvajar's mind like a mantra—that child had thrown away his weapon, had chosen not to use it, had submitted to dark rather than weaken the light.

He, pathetic creature, had acted from instinct and habit, had obeyed the dark when drawn to light. How perfectly miserable, how spineless, he deserved to be a snake, to slither on his belly, to spit venom ever more into the sea and watch it wash away on the tides. He deserved to have no evidence of his being, for he was no being, no person, no soul.

He was just a snake.

'What shall I do with him, then?'

'Can you fly him to the depths of that forest and drop him in? Hopefully he'll not find his way out of the undergrowth.'

The dragon was cheerful.

'Sure can! I'll pop him in the deepest and darkest of the thickets. Where poisons grow and potions curl about tree stumps. Very suitable. Wait for me, will you? It would be too bad of you to go on alone!'

Septimus smiled. 'I think you've earned your right to accompany me! But hurry, Scorch! The dark is near, I can feel it. It may be that I'll have to face it before you return, or before Arikeet finds me. Hurry, will you?'

The dragon flicked his tail in answer. Then, in a great swirl of wings that drove the sands up into Sep's face—nearly choking and almost blinding him—he was gone.

The fabled seventh son, coughing, sneezing and rubbing his eyes tearfully, gazed after the dragon with a fondness quite remarkable given his current condition. The backpack, a tattered ruin, lay scattering it contents on the shadowed sands of the beach.

* * *

Móran's wand—his staff of power—was not working. The wizard had used it to embrace the snake, to ensure that Silvajar the traitor would nevertheless do his bidding. He had ignored his own pain and swelling leg to invest the serpent with his powers and the darkness of his mind.

Now those powers were spent, and the serpent had vanished from his view, leaving the boy, he the seventh, he the son, alone on the golden sands of Elvenswolde, beneath the pillars of Ventrimuse, where once the wise ones stood. The wizard had it marked on a mind map and could see, with a calmness born of fate, that the child had wandered beneath those invisible portals as surely as he had been drawn there by the base magic itself.

Now the pain set in. The screaming, maddening pain of the snake bite and the potions he had carelessly thrust into his bewitching spell. Not life threatening or deadly, but painful and debilitating at a time he needed strength. He called to the creatures of the forest, but they had fled, an omen that set the silver wizard's spine tingling and his mind into a shock of activity.

He could do nothing incarcerated in this tower. Escape—the type of escape he had always planned for himself—was impossible given his rapidly swelling leg. He needed an antidote and he needed a way to finish this thing he had started. Brother to brother, he needed to face Ramón and challenge the forces that kept them there, suspended between the worlds, two opposite forces born of the same parents, mingled with the same, elfin blood.

He called to Ramón. The Wish Maker in the queen's tower, watching every spell, deflecting every strange, unearthly scent that drifted on the breeze, heard. He heard his brother's call, but was silent.

He heard his brother's pain and though it felt like his own pain, so intently could he sense it, he remained still upon his wizard's seat. He moved not at all, though wish bubbles—faint—floated from his window and meticlaws, maggots and measles, uncorked, oozed across his floor.

Móran called again, this time in a silky tongue that lashed at Ramón like a thread of yearning, tugging at his dormant love, at his hopes, at his very dreams. There had been a time, once, when the only bond between them had been brotherhood, the only tie that bound them that of tenderness. That time, long gone, called to Ramón as no other cry, no other torment, no other fear.

Móran, reading his soul as he read his secrets, called again.

This time, Ramón did move. This time he was drawn to the window, to gaze across the courtyard, across the sweeping moat and the queen's own guards, upward and skywards towards the turret of the king.

Móran, calling, drew him there with his eyes, though his flesh burned with poison and his leg ached with the venom of enchantment.

Ramón, seeing him, knowing the vileness of his intentions, wavered. He loved, as brothers were meant to love, though it sent the balance shattering into a thousand waves of discord.

He felt sick with pain, riddled with an unspeakable torment. He, who lived for light, who had been knighted the Wish Maker, who honoured happiness, now looked into the shadows of discontent, the very pools of darkness that were his brother's eyes. He absorbed the pain, and as he absorbed it, Móran became free of his.

As Ramón wept, the dark wizard—the brother of silver—began to laugh. When Ramón's sadness was so deep it was embedded in his heart itself, Móran felt healed.

His leg, once foul with stinking flesh, now felt free.

Ramón, heart heavy, watched as Móran, his nemesis, grew in grandeur. It seemed that the very sweep of his shoulders seemed to alter, and the curl about his mouth—handsome, but deadly sweet—seemed more distinct. He smiled but his countenance held no joy. He laughed, but Ramón, in an agony of his own, could hear no mirth.

'Well met, brother.'

Across the towers, the words resonated in Ramón's ears. He did not answer, for he knew, without looking, that Móran was free.

Scorcher flew swiftly through the forest. Though he was just a hatchling, his blue colour imbued him with more powers than he knew, more gifts than he could conceive, more cunning than the hoariest of ancient dragons. He knew instinctively what resonated with magic and what was dull, what whispered enchantment and what grew innocently upon the banks.

He circled about, taking care not to touch branches blowing with enchantments, some dark, some daring, some teasing tendrils of twigs that danced to a darker music than his own.

Of course, Scorcher being Scorch, he broke off a great many boughs with his clumsy wings and his cumbersome way of flapping in flight, but he was an excessively lucky little dragon (again, perhaps because he was blue—though this theory remains unproven despite some investigation by Lord Elgin, a foremost authority on modern dragon lore.)

Be that as it may, none of the enchantments—though they were thick in the forest—seemed to upset Scorcher. When he finally dropped Silvajar on the leafy floor, Scorch tripped over an aspodel and was sent sprawling across the root lined forest, sustaining no more injury than an aching tail (dragons find tails particularly sensitive to bumps) and a horrible fear the snake would bite his bottom.

None of these calamities occurred. The tail stopped aching almost immediately (It landed in a tangle of heather—very soothing for all creatures with scales) and the snake, far from biting, stared sorrowfully at him from unblinking eyes and hissed.

Well, generally speaking, hissing would be enough to give any dragon a serious fright, especially when it hissed with a nasty, flickering, forked tongue—but Scorcher, of course, was no ordinary dragon. It might be easy to forget, but he had the knack of thought telepathy—the extraordinarily strange (but decidedly handy) gift of understanding.

The snake—freed, at last, from the uncomfortable grip of Scorcher's jaws—hissed frantically, terrified that the hatchling would desert him in this forest of blackness. Terrified that he, who once was Silvajar, would be condemned to this dreadful life. Doomed to a life of the belly, forever tormenting creatures less agile than he.

Yes, Silvajar was repenting bitterly of his cowardice and his meanness. He'd witnessed, first hand, the nobility of the seventh son, the kindness that had caused him neither to kill nor to harm, a creature of the dark.

Caught between death and dragon teeth, he had learnt, contrarily, of light. He was embarrassed by his bullying—ashamed of his legacy of deceit and petty unkindness. He wished, though he was now but a snake, to make amends.

All this was hissed so violently and with so much passion that Scorcher might not have understood (in fact, chances were, he might have died of fright), were it not for the fact that the snake repeated himself several times and with so much pleading that his fangs were raw from the effort.

Now the prince of Dargonvilles might have been slightly clumsy, but he was not at all a stupid dragon. He would not have believed a hissing serpent (however repentant) for one moment. He certainly would not have believed this one, nasty slimy reptile that he was, but for one, small matter.

The snake was changing, before his eyes, into an elf.

At first, Scorcher thought he was imagining things, but as he watched, he became more and more certain that he was not.

As Móran's concentration shifted from the snake to Ramón, the spell weakened. With every contrite utterance of Silvajar, the dark released its hold. At the very moment Silvajar hissed—positively hissed—that he wished to make amends, his form—his own, dear elfin form—returned to him in a pop. It was a hollow kind of pop, like some old can, out of shape and bouncing back after a tight squeeze.

Silvajar did not know who was more astonished—he, or Scorcher. He made a low bow, however, and repeated his plea both in English (learnt from earth matters 301) and in elf. His dragonesque was too rusty to even make the attempt.

Scorcher was just pondering whether to believe the horrible little creature (no, he could not like him!) or to abandon him to the wilds of the wood, when Silvajar gave a little shriek of joy and hurtled deeper into the forest, after a flash of purple that the dragon had seen, but hoped to ignore.

No chance of that!

Garredung, perfectly filthy, was impossible to ignore when he held Silvajar in such a tight clasp the dragon had to reluctantly intervene to allow the poor fellow to breathe.

Yes, the elves were united, at last, in that same, dark place where Xanadel had been lured. Not far behind, in various states of injury, were Bickleberry and Wendleweed.

Silvajar's reunion with Garredung was a peculiar sight. Xanadel, regarding the pair with a mixture of amusement and astonishment, could only shake his head and mutter that he had seen strange things, but none so strange as the sight of Garredung and Silvajar actually looking happy.

The amulet about his neck flickered bright blue flame, so blue it reflected the sea and the sky and made the place—Móran's place—a land of darkness no more.

Scorcher was impatient to return to Septimus, but the elves were loath to see him go, especially as they were lost. They were also terrified out of their wits that the gemra would reappear to seize them. Though Scorcher did not look very terrifying, there was no doubt that a dragon—a relatively friendly dragon—was just the advantage they needed if the loathsome creatures were to return.

That Scorcher was benign was established almost at once, for though he remained slightly aloof from Silvajar, he took instantly to Garredung, Xanadel and Wendleweed.

Bickleberry he licked—gently—for the elf had sustained a very nasty flesh wound and was sporting some makeshift bandages of forest leaves.

In this dank, dark forest there had been none of the usual healing herbs, but Wendleweed had carried with him a small vial of elf light, and Garredung had searched the forest floor for tinnitus radioli, a noxious smelling plant that emitted a surprisingly healing balm.

These had been applied with strawberry leaves, rare but resilient even in the darker places. Bickleberry was recovering, but hardly capable of the long trudge to Castle Carne.

Garredung was wondering whether the wand would be of any use in meta-transportation, a higher form of translocation used by tree sprites and gnomes, but none of the elves were keen. Móran's wand had done more than enough already, and they were unsure how much of the dark power might leak from it. Heaven knew, it looked so charred it was hardly likely to function properly anyway.

Scorcher, his tail swishing thoughtfully, did not know what to do. On the one hand, he could not—should not—leave Septimus. On the other hand, the elves were depending on him for help.

It felt rather good being depended upon: baby dragons usually waited years for such an occurrence to occur. Scorcher puffed out his bright blue wings and inhaled loudly. This, naturally, was not so much of a problem as when he exhaled—

'Scorcher!'

Four voices were raised in alarm as the dragonette single-handedly divested half the forest of its trees. It took quite a few moments to stamp out the fires, but Móran's charred wand came in handy after all. For such a minor matter it seemed safe to use, and indeed, it did put out the flames with astonishing speed.

'Sorry!'

The elves eyed the dragon severely so that his tail crept down to the floor and his mischievous eyes looked as contrite as any dragonette's could.

'Be careful, will you!'

Scorcher nodded.

Garredung and Silvajar conferred amongst themselves. They were used to the dark places, having been sent on enough messages to last them a lifetime. It would be no trouble for them to wait in the forest, though their hearts thirsted for adventure and their minds, slowly healing, longed for a place in the annals of elfin history.

An honourable place, this time, a place where they could be listed ever after with Arikaan the elder and Lorien, Sintolas or even Ravenslock, all great keepers and guardians of Elvenswolde.

It was not to be. There was no place for Garredung and Silvajar in this, the most heroic chapter of elfin history. At least, not now, when Scorcher's destiny was to return to Septimus and theirs to the long, dark trail northwards, toward Castle Carne—back, back, whence they came, to Móran and the mystical tower of the king.

They had no business with light, though their hearts now tugged towards it and their smiles, like tremulous sunshine, begged to bask in its glow. No, as creatures of the dark—former creatures—they had a longer, harder road to traverse.

The road of patience and travail. It was for them to find the hidden undergrowth and the tucked - in tunnels. It was for them to lead, by example, through the darker places.

For them to offer Bickleberry succour and Wendleweed hope. The elves would have to find faith and follow, else all that had been gained would be lost.

Already, Garredung could hear the wild wolves baying for blood. He, who was shifty and sly, could set false trails and tracks. Silvajar, who was clever, could weave webs of tortuous tanglement. They could not vanquish the dark, but they could impede it.

Bickleberry's shoulder was healing from ministrations that were half-magical, half-mythical and a small, unquantifiable portion of common sense. He was demanding his wing pack. This was a ridiculous suggestion, given his condition, but one that made poor Wendleweed (very worried) sigh in relief.

'Don't be a silly gudgeon, Bickle! You can't fly when you're half-faint from weakness! Think what trouble that stupid wing pack has already caused you! Besides, it's completely destroyed now.

'No, we will walk with Garredung and Silvajar, and they shall show us the silent ways and the secret paths. They will lead us, with their skill and cunning, out of this dark maze and back to the Castle of the king. I feel sure the Wish Maker would want that, and Master Hepple too. They are relying on us to be sensible, Bickle!'

Bickle scowled. He hated 'sensible' but had to admit the thought of navigating his way out of the forest with a troublesome wing pack and a fairly serious shoulder injury was not appealing.

A few days ago he would have found it even more unappealing to team with Garredung and Silvajar, but they both seemed quite a bit nicer, now, now that their balance had been restored. Reluctantly, he agreed, though he still grumbled. Silvajar, slightly miffed at this ingratitude, poked out his long, elfin tongue.

Just that once—which, when all is said and done, was a great improvement on his past behaviour.

It was time for Scorcher to leave. Xanadel rather shyly asked if he might return with him. 'I am to find Septimus, you see, and bring him into the presence of our Wish Maker.'

Scorcher, who was the type of dragon who took instant likes and dislikes, had liked Xanadel from the start. He was intrigued, too, by the amulet, which reminded him so vividly of Sep's, though of course the colours were very different and the magic quite distinct.

Call it instinct, but he extra, extra liked Xanadel! He grinned his dragon grin (very cute, for hatchling milk teeth are a bit like our own—small and white and flatter than an adult's. Also, adult dragons tend to be somewhat smellier, for though they eat a lot of wolf meat, they very seldom take the sort of trouble over dental hygiene that they should. Scorcher did not yet have this unfortunate problem, so his smile was unmarred by such considerations.)

'Gttt lllle eeemmmro rrrreaoa!'

'Pardon?'

'Gttt lllle eeemmmro rrrreaoa!'

'I can't understand him! What is he saying?'

Wendleweed looked as puzzled as Xanadel, but fortunately Scorcher remembered that elves were not gifted as he was. They simply did not comprehend well elocuted dragonesque.

He lay flat on his haunches, hoping Xanadel would realize what he meant. He did.

The elf swallowed his misgiving. It was wonderful having the opportunity to fly a dragon (and a great honour, he was very sensible of it) but he was rather alarmed by little Scorcher's clumsiness. Still, if he wanted to reach Septimus quickly, as he needed to, there was no other option.

Tentatively, he mounted the dragon and apologised for using his bony wing joints as handles.

Scorcher didn't mind—hardly felt him, in fact. Soon they were flying.

Xanadel politely shouted that Scorcher's colour was incredible. It was the wrong thing to say. His tail (which had been upright, in full flight position) drooped immediately and his shoulders hunched back in a most un-aerodynamic like manner.

Xanadel gulped as they lost attitude.

'What's the matter?'

'Can't you see I am blue?'

Xanadel could not understand the grunts, but he could sense distress.

'You're beautiful, little dragon.' He patted a scaly rim.

Scorch sniffed, but there was no doubt that his tail regained its airborne position and his ears pricked a little. Now it was just a matter of his shoulders—

'Come on, Scorch, hurry! My brother might need me!'

'Grrewwww?'

The dragon thought mid-air. Septimus was the elf's brother? It explained a lot. It explained their likeness—both were tall for elves, with golden hair and smiling eyes, both wore amulets (Scorch could detect the work of a master craftsman) and both attracted him.

He had not long been hatched, but he knew enough to know that dragons aren't usually drawn to creatures of another kind.

Lord alone knew, he did not like Silvajar much, but Xanadel and Septimus were different. They were special, his brothers in bond if not blood. If Sep was like his mum, this one must be like his—uncle! He grinned. Shoulders straightened in great spikes of scaly horns. He accelerated in the air like a dragon of old, puffing steam (great gusts that floated high up over the elm trees and the dark Hirridium Elminoso that flanked the outer rims of the forest.)

He roared, a great giant roar that was like thunder, so that Xanadel had to close his ears and the other elves, watching from the distance, wondered why they had not been more terrified of the little fellow.

With a huge, whooshing of wings and several flapping motions that made Xanadel almost sick with a combination of fright and sky sickness, Scorcher rose higher, high into that sky, like nemesis rising.

Whisper Wishes, Oh Seventh Son

Septimus, alone on the beach, looked up at the castle that called to him, the castle of his father and of Arikeet and of all his lineage. He wondered where they were and what might be expected of him on this day.

The winds were high again, and the curious almost-hum he'd heard once before grew louder, causing his eardrums to throb.

It was harder and harder to tolerate the sequence of magic that seemed embedded in the curious, lilting note.

He walked steadily, wondering what was keeping Scorcher and whether the dreadful serpent creature had managed to bite him, after all. Damn! He should have killed him. Stupid thing to do, sparing the life of a snake.

Mindful of Scorch's warning, he avoided all stones, keeping entirely to the beach though the sands grew cold.

Elvenswolde's sun was colder than Sarah imagined. He had the strangest feeling that as he walked towards Castle Carne, the winds grew icier yet.

He kept going, certain that Scorcher would find him. He almost longed for the dragon to breathe slow, deep breaths over him to unfreeze his limbs with fire. On second thoughts, the burns still hurt like blazes. Maybe not.

He walked into the shadows that had fallen across the beach like a velvet blanket. The silhouette of a conch shell caught his eye. It glowed with an inner light and held captive the sound of the sea.

He listened and could have sworn he heard the sounds of home, for all worlds are interconnected—shells seem to whisper ever of this truth.

When he looked up, he was alone no more.

He was staring, point blank, into the eyes of the silver wizard.

'Well met, my—child.'

Móran's voice was like a whisper, so soft that Septimus almost had to stop breathing to hear his greeting.

The breeze struck at his legs and flapped at his T-shirt. Against the counterpoint of a wildly beating heart he noticed, in some surprise, that the wizard's garments were untouched by wind. They trailed softly in the sands like a cloak of office.

The amulet was burning around his neck, but he did not know why, or whether the wizard was friend or enemy. His silver robes sparkled in the cold sunshine, glittering like hard, bright diamonds. He looked younger than Septimus would have imagined, but more aloof.

Did one bow, or did one just push past and walk on? Septimus was not partial to strangers, especially this one. He was good looking (if you noticed such things) but definitely creepy.

After a fraction's hesitation, he chose the path of politeness, though a frisson of fear flickered through his slightly skinny frame and he found it hard to meet the wizard's eye.

'Good afternoon, sir.'

The wizard nodded. 'Charming manners, charming. Shall we step out of the cold?'

Septimus could not think of a thing he would like to do more. There were goose bumps all the way up his arm and though he told himself it was from the icy chill, he wasn't entirely certain it was the weather causing this strange reaction.

'I am waiting on a friend.'

'Ah, yes. The excellent Xanadel. Remiss of me not to expect it.' The wizard smiled, but the gesture did not reach his eyes. Septimus felt repelled. He neglected to mention that it was not Xanadel (whoever he might be) that he awaited, but a dragon.

The wizard smoothed out his robes—they were magnificent. Septimus found himself staring at the intricately stitched emblems and half moons that bordered one of the lengths of silk.

'Ah, yes, exquisite is it not? Stitched by ninety-seven fairies all bound, now, by a thousand years of sleep.

Look well, my friend. Pretty, is it not? Yes, stare as you look, for staring will warm your very soul—can you not feel your fingers unthaw? See, the chill is going, flying, flying from your earthen form. Half elf, half earth—very good. Yes, keep staring. See how the light shimmers as the intricate little enchantments catch the sun.'

Septimus nodded, though he felt his head pulled into a nod, almost as though he were a puppet on a strange, silken thread.

'It is warming you—warming—Give me that necklace, Septimus son of Septimus, half elf, half earth, born of the base magic—'

Septimus hesitated. The amulet was flashing so brilliantly even the wizard's eyes were blinded. The sapphire jewel was blazing brighter than it had ever been, brighter than the moment of its forging. Slowly, he touched it, then once again, he hesitated.

The wizard averted his gaze from the stone and engaged Septimus's eyes instead. 'Oh, seventh son of a seventh son, listen well to worlds half gone. Whisper wishes, oh, seventh son and let the tides in rivers run—'

The words washed over Septimus like a current of dreams, strangely familiar. They were comforting, like something accustomed, something he could know and understand. He placed his hand at his throat, unsure why he was doing this, or what was required of him.

The silver robe twinkled, again, in the elf light. The wizard shifted, so the shimmer caught at Septimus's mind and heart.

'Come, seventh son, come, creature of the wild, child of earth, son of light. Lend me that necklace. Lend, that I might fight the shadows that are falling, and the night that hearkens upon us.'

The words were quiet as a whisper, but Septimus heard them with clarity. Indeed, they hung on the air like the softest of stars, haunting his very being. He ached for the beauty of those words, and for their compulsion.

His hand crept to his neck again, to unclasp the jewel of his father. Though he was cold—shivering as he had never shivered before—he was drawn to the wizard, with his cool smile and his words of gentle warming.

'The necklace—the amulet of Amberkine—give it—grant it— feel warmth flood your being as you give—give—giving—give now, give well, give warmth—'

Septimus felt the jewel in his hand. It did more than flicker, now, it blazed so that the silver wizard flinched as his hand extended, palm upturned.

He advanced slowly—very slowly—towards Septimus, so as not to startle him, always, always remembering to keep the sash of his satin robes twinkling as he talked.

He was murmuring now, words of warmth, though Septimus remained shivering uncontrollably and the winds, once high, now howled.

'Come, hand me the stone.' The words were more commanding, and sibilant. Septimus's heart beat a fraction faster and his hand hesitated, though his mind did not. With a small bow—was it of deference?—He stepped towards the wizard to hand him the stone.

Lightning forked the sky. Septimus trembled so much he shook, dropping the gem harmlessly on the shadowed sands. The wizard stooped, and as he did, a haze of blue struck at him, struck fiercely.

The silver cloaks, so immaculately arranged, now flew hither and thither, breaking several thousand-year enchantments and, in the interim, the spell that was tying Septimus to his will.

'Oops, sorry!' Scorch roared. 'Slight trouble with landing—Grrr nmmohh quiil!'

He circled the wizard in a giddy swoop. He was so horribly unbalanced that Xanadel (clinging on for life) was sky-sick. Severely so. He grabbed some bony ligaments and prayed to the God Thor and the Elfin goddess Tetra-heeta.

Just as well, for the dragon's clumsiness was nothing short of awe inspiring. On his second circuit, he managed to strike the wizard in the jaw.

Scorch did not precisely attack, but his wings (very muscular now that they'd been fully aired) seemed to accidentally smash the wizard full in his long, angular face. Móran extended his hands, shrieking with rage and the shriek—a much higher tone than he'd used with Septimus—roused the boy, finally, from his trance-like state.

He could see now that the wizard was not the Wish Maker of Arikeet's description. He was handsome, but his mouth was thin and his eyes—those steely, twilight eyes—were cold. A deepening red gash appeared on the jawline where the dragon had struck. He did not look pleased. Septimus, eying him with the eyes of sudden clarity, knew that he was dangerous.

He was desperately ashamed. The jewel was gone. Some kind of a seventh son of a seventh son he was! What could he have been think-ing? He shivered, cold biting worse than the winter solstice moon.

But Scorch—trust Scorch—in his happy dragon element, breathed crimson flames upon his back. Finding this fun, he blew again: golds and purples and pinks, so that each fiery wave brought with it warmth. (Xanadel, still clinging on, felt nothing but green.)

'Let me down, will you!'

'Oh, sorry!' said Scorcher.

Sorry was becoming his favourite word.

Xanadel was set down, looking pale and rather grim. He'd not yet had the chance to make Septimus's acquaintance, for the dark wizard, eying him evilly, thrust out his hand in greeting.

Xanadel felt shocked. A hot pain tore at him like a blade, but he remained still, refusing to allow the poison—for such it must be—to enter into his mind.

Móran, not bothering to smile, dropped his hand and eyed the sands with calculation.

He was two steps from the amulet, half buried in the shores, but two steps were not enough. By his calculation, the ridiculous drag-on-child was closer. The earth boy, if he kept his wits, not much more.

If he showed any interest in the item, he would be foiled.

How annoying—to be so near and yet so very far from his am-bition. The base magic could be invoked—but not adjured—until the two amulets—that of Amberkine and that of Lindaliss—were joined. If he could thrust one, at least, into the raging oceans of Elvenswolde, he'd be satisfied.

The half-wit, bumbling, son of a freaking lackwit-dragon struck at him again, this time ripping at his gown, so that sparks of tythran-dorol and whistleweed pricked at his shirt, causing his face to itch. He sneezed, for like any self-respecting warlock, he suffered from hay fever, and was generally very careful with the application of substances like tythrandorol.

Móran was simply beyond fury. He pointed his fingers at the dragon, but Scorch dodged by streaking into the sky. High, higher than he had ever flown before. The view was marvellous.

The wizard—now malicious beyond words—flung an enchantment into the sky, but Scorcher missed it by swooping down, down onto the sands then uppity up again, so that Móran's eyes had to focus and refocus, his head bobbing up and down like an undignified cork, hardly the demeanour he habitually assumed.

By this time, a large audience appeared from nowhere. There were sea sprites and nymphs, a couple of elves and several tree-dwelling fairies. Most were terrified of dragons but more terrified still of the dark wizard.

There were tales aplenty of Móran of the silver cloak, long since banished from Elvenswolde but returned—returned by whim and by wile.

Already, he was causing darkness over the cities and spires, turrets and treetops, the heart of Elvenswolde itself.

They quivered in fright but still waited, watching history unfold. They would be the witnesses for the ballad bearers and the sooth singers.

Curiously, they watched as a cheeky dragonette played havoc with the world's balances. He seemed not to know or care for the danger—perhaps because he was a hatchling, he had little idea of the power of Móran's spells.

Perhaps because he was a hatchling, he was uncommonly brave. Either way, he was having a merry time of it. He blew up such a sandstorm that Septimus, who was bent on retrieving the missing amulet, lost sight of the jewel. He felt defeated and near tears.

'Stop it, Scorch! Stop!'

But it was not just he who had lost sight of it—Móran had too.

The wizard fell to hands and knees, searching the area in which it had fallen like a man possessed. He seemed strangely stripped of dignity, his incantations useless against an object of such base resonance.

He no longer bothered with the dragon (who gave him quite a few 'accidental' swipes across his bottom, much to the hushed laughter of the growing audience).

No, he schooled himself to ignore minor annoyances. Dragons could be stewed and elves placed in pots. What he needed—desperately—was the amulet.

It was wasted on the neck of the earth child, too young to use it, too stupid to recognise it for its proper function. The wizard writhed in rage, impotent with fear and fury.

He had to have it; he had to have the amulet of Amberkine, with its ancient cabochon sapphire and the raging freedom of flame.

Septimus, frantic to prevent him, pushed his way forward and yelled to Scorcher to stop blowing up the sandstorm. He thrust his fingers into the beach and sifted grains in panic, his neck bare, pale and quite forlorn. He could have kicked himself for losing the jewel. Tears stung at his eyes but he only dug the harder, frantic—frantic—

The wizard next to him felt his fright.

He stopped what he was doing and looked speculatively at Septimus, who was closer to the dark than he had ever been before. Septimus could have killed, at that moment. Killed to have the amulet safe about his neck—

Móran pulled himself together. He could use that panic—he was a master at such things.

He focused his mind not on the sand, but on Septimus, and Septimus, feeling the cold creep about him once more, felt frozen in time, frozen in the anxiety—empty. His mouth tasted the dark tang of Móran's despair. He had failed.

Before he had begun, he had failed the light, the quest of El-venswolde, and the legacy of his father. He had simply lost it, on the shores of Elvenswolde where the trees grow tall.

The wizard ceased his digging, concentrating utterly on Septimus's mind. When he was sure he could seize it, control it, command it, if need be, he clicked his fingers and watched as all about him sand began to fall.

It was not the sand of summer, but of a storm, swirling about the heads and into the eyes of all the onlookers, elf, fairy and sprite alike. It brushed at his own hooded eyes, but he was beyond thinking of such things or caring.

All he cared about was burying the amulet. Burying it deeper than the seas itself. He would have cast it to the oceans—now he was ceding it to the earth.

Septimus screamed, sensing this, but his scream was lost on the wind and even Scorcher, swooping and diving, could not distract the wizard's attention—though he did manage to burn a hole in his sash and cause green smoke to billow from robes of shimmering silver.

'Stop him!' It was a call of anguish, this time from Xanadel, who knew, as only a brother could, that Septimus was suffering. He stepped out to fend off the wizard's gaze, to distract him from his control of Septimus's mind and the whim of the winds.

Oh, what fickle winds were these that blew so gently for the fairy folk and yet, when called, answered to the dark one's voice? Such storm-racked sands, such cutting cold!

There was hardly a creature in Elvenswolde that did not now feel the pull of the shadows and the deepening of the dark. Móran's face, crushed into concentration, hardly heard the brother's call.

Ramón did, and Arikeet. High, in the queen's tower, they heard it. Ramón, stirring a pot bigger than Arikeet had ever seen, poured an ounce of death root and a herb so strange even he wore gloves.

'Leave him!' Xanadel's yearning was palpable in the winds. The feeling invested in his words was so deep, it cut even the wizard—the dark wizard—to the quick.

He looked up, and the sand storm ceased. Septimus, dazed, blinked several times. An object close to him glittered, but he did not see it, so intent was he on the drama unfolding.

The wizard gazed at Xanadel, who slid surprisingly nimbly from Scorcher, then stared defiantly at the silver lord. Móran drew him forward, so that the small elf, half his size, was looking up, up and upward, to meet the gaze of those curiously harsh features in that strangely handsome face.

'Well met, Xanadel. You have come, I see, in a meeting of earth and elf, half brothers across the worlds, to grant me my greatest desires.'

Xanadel said nothing. It was no use contradicting the dark one, the words just stuck to the roof of one's mouth. Behind him, Scorcher was creating a bonfire, but no one was paying him any attention at all.

'I had hoped for the amulet of Amberkine, but I see, after all, I shall do very well with the lesser gem of Lindaliss. Grant it to me, I beg, that your brother be freed of his torment. Grant it, lest the sands bury the very beaches of Elvenswolde in their eagerness to do my bidding.'

Xanadel wavered. He felt Sep's pain as surely as if it were his own.

He wanted to pull the necklace from his throat and defiantly thrust it into the sea. Out of the reach of this wizard of dark. He felt the platinum chains pulling, as if they had a life of their own.

Despite his robes, Móran was not a Wish Maker. He was everything that Ramón was not, the opposite, the antithesis. Not the Wish Maker, but the maker of fear.

Yes, he was afraid, very afraid.

'Give it to me, Xanadel.'

Xanadel, even then, would have resisted, but for the bewildered look in Septimus's silver-blue eyes.

He could not bear such a look, so much anguish.

'Free my brother first.'

'He shall be free of his pain when my hands are on Lindaliss.'

'Swear it.'

The wizard quirked his brows but he was too close to victory to care much about oaths. The seventh son lost all of his significance if he was only the bearer of Amberkine and no more. The invocation of base magic required unity

Amberkine and Lindaliss—pretty playthings in themselves, but without each other, worthless. He would take Lindaliss though.

Lindaliss, his insurance against Amberkine.

He nodded his head and swore one of the great oaths of Elvenswolde, one that caused the earth to tremble and the elf world itself to glow a sudden pink, as if blinking from out some springtime dream.

Xanadel's heart was heavier than the gold of the ancient, irilium clock. It ticked quietly, in the elfin dormitories of the queen's tower. Unheard, it chimed the hour as Xanadel, true to his promise, removed the sparkling red gem from his neck.

The turquoise flame within was now brilliant, glowing so bright the entire beach was illuminated. As Móran's hand crept over the jewel, the flame died. Ruby turned to amber once more, and the flicker, the dancing light, extinguished entirely.

Septimus rubbed his eyes, released, in that moment, from the torment that had kept him in Móran's thrall.

The wizard ignored him as he fingered the jewel. 'Ugly thing, isn't it?' he remarked, as he placed the amulet about his neck. He winced, slightly, as he did so. Septimus—and most of the audience—hoped it hurt.

But this was no time for hoping.

The darkness was closing in about them and it was a darkness deeper than the night and much, much more sinister. On the cliffs facing north, the dragons howled, causing Scorcher's spine to stiffen, and the wolves to bay their answer.

In the caves crossed by Wendleweed, Bickleberry, Garredung and Silvajar, bright eyes watched anew. The gemra, still weak, had fled here, to the very caves of the ground, and were not yet vanquished. The elves, now closer to the castle moat, crouched quietly and tried not to reveal their fright. There was magic abroad, and power. Even in these dark places, they could feel its presence. It was as if the world—the elfin world—was poised for battle.

Slowly, steadily, Garredung, accustomed to fear and thus more resilient, revealed the way. Silvajar, learned in the darker arts, flung charms of protection. It was fortunate, indeed, that he did.

Arikeet

'It is time.' Ramón stopped stirring his pot and looked beyond the towers to the beach below. No longer could he ward off the scents of danger and the poisons Móran had flung into the very air and earth of Elvenswolde.

No more could he hope that by the strength of his will and by his power alone, the state of unbalance could exist without disrupting the remaining elfin world and the six worlds beyond it.

He had conjured enough enchantment to ward off the inevitable, but the brew was evaporating as fast as his wishes strengthened it. No, the time was now. Now—the base magic was drumming in his ears, a dull, insistent beat that kept time to the tides and rhythms with the molten dark that flows hotly beneath the surface of each world.

'We must restore the balance. Your majesty, you must make ready. Arikeet, you shall be at my right hand. You have served me well at this hour of evil—I thank you.'

Arikeet bowed low, feeling both the solemnity and the honour of the moment. When he straightened, he blinked, for a shower of stars were streaming from his shoulder rank. They were forged in a furnace of magic and could only be bestowed by a Wish Maker.

A second stripe sat neatly next to the first, sewn in irrilium, with tidier stitches, by far, than the standard requisitions from the Department of Laundry and Uniforms.

'Well done, Wing Bearer of the Second Order of Merit!'

Arikeet was speechless. Simply speechless. Which was just as well, because Ramón had no further time to waste on niceties.

It had been typical of him though to take a moment in the unpleasant flurry of madness, to be kind.

Kind to a simple, insignificant wing bearer.

Kindness, he always said, was a mark of the kingdom. And the very Kingdom of Elves teetered hopelessly, helplessly, on the brink.

With one further look at the pot that was holding all the worlds together, brimming balance, burning malice, melding strength and hope and fear, the wizard waved his wand.

For a moment there was silence, then a tremendous whooshing noise that seemed to splinter the air like sharp fragments of crystal. To Arikeet's surprise they were gone from the gloomy towers and the smell of baked bread drifting from the kitchens. They were mercifully far from meticlaws oozing everywhere.

For an instant, the place they found themselves felt pleasant. Their toes, enfolded in soft, curling kid, touched gently upon the golden sands of the eastern shores.

Ramón bowed his head. Through the throng of ever gathering elves and fairies, Arikeet eyed the Wish Maker anxiously.

'You are tired, sir. You need rest.'

'Hush, Arikeet!'

Arikeet's words were private, meant for the Wish Maker, but several others were on the beach that day, and several others heard.

Septimus, the seventh son, silent in his disappointment, was roused by this familiar—and quite beloved—voice.

'Arikeet!'

The wing bearer—despite the awful circumstances—winked.

He'd longed to see Septimus again. But oh! In such strange circumstances! He could hardly have imagined worse, for the Wish Maker—so filled with energy and light—now seemed almost dull in comparison with the man who faced them.

Móran, who still twinkled, despite the state of his torn clothes.

The sands shifted as Scorcher banged his tail against the ground. He was impatient with all this business of power play. He wanted to see a good old duel in the fashion of dragons, where one was allowed to bite and snap and claw and scratch.

He regarded the ragged state of Móran's gown as a personal triumph. Indeed, despite the grim gloom of the moment, he felt a momentary twinge of intense satisfaction.

Scorcher was half inclined to enter the fray again, but a warning thought stopped him. Septimus, more than half mind-spent, did not think his nerves could tolerate another onslaught from Scorch—no matter how heroic.

He was, after all, a baby.

A little hatchling dragonette that the silver wizard could destroy, if he wished. Septimus could not bear to see Scorch's brave spirit dampened or his beautiful blue body lifeless on the shores of Elvenswolde.

'No!'

He implored Scorch to behave, but Scorch, indignant, could not resist a series of annoyed thumps with his tail.

It was curious, but as he crashed at the earth crossly, a glitter—the merest hint of glitter—caught Septimus's eye.

He wanted to believe that against all odds it was the amulet of Amberkine, but he knew such hope was too great, too profound, too coincidental to credit. Surely there were no coincidences in a world such as this—

He turned his thoughts away from the little mound Scorch had created, and watched in sadness as Ramón the Wish Maker faced his brother.

He seemed so old in comparison, and there was no twinkle in his eye, none at all. Septimus did not think that he had ever seen anyone look so solemn. He bore the weight of the world's worries on his wizardly back.

Ramón stood with Arikeet at his right hand and the king—the awakened king of Elvenswolde—at his left. His majesty denounced Móran in ringing tones, but the wizard only laughed. It was a piercing laugh, high pitched for a man, and most unpleasant.

'Tell your subjects, your majesty, how you—you *personally*—invited me back to this world, gave me the freedom of the land and the power of the planets aligned.'

The king, to his surprise, stepped forward, no longer the shell he had become, the broken vassal, the traitor enmeshed in the bonds of betrayal.

'The shackles are broken, Móran! I am your vassal no longer, but your king. I have confessed publicly to my folly, my vanity and my frailties. I openly acknowledge my betrayal of the forces of light now, as I did in the great chambers, this noon past.

'I do so now, again, openly, of my own free will and in the presence of these witnesses. I am humbled and grieved, and hope, in time, the people of this bright place will absolve me. But for now, I am strengthened in my resolve. I am your king. Go, leave this land, leave it now, lest by lingering you destroy yourself.'

There was a hush as the fairies and the elves, the mermen and the tree sprites, all bore witness to this message, all bowed, in reverence, to the king's return.

There had been whispers that the king was mad, driven so by the forces of dark, incarnated by Móran himself. To see him thus, even under the shadows, even here, on this beach, was to know that Elvenswolde was yet his own, was yet a beacon of the light.

There would have been a cheer, but for the hush that had fallen on Ramón and the sadness, so still, in his eyes.

Septimus glanced at the beach behind Scorch's tail. Yes, there was definitely a glitter, but if the exuberant little hatchling were to move, Móran would notice at once. Worse, Scorch being Scorch, he would bury it again forever.

It dawned then on Septimus that he'd been right—there was no such thing as coincidence in the great battles of light and dark, of balance and of chaos. If Lindaliss had fallen, then Amberkine begged to be found. It was the old way.

'Scorch!'

'Hey, Sep, I have an idea. I could fly back to the circle of dragons and implore them, by the thunder in the sky and the—'

'Scorch! Listen to me!'

The dragon stopped, mid-thought.

'You've a better idea?'

'It's not an idea. It's a command.'

'You have a command for me?'

Scorch's tail began to thump in surprise.

'Hey! Don't do that!'

Septimus had to stifle a groan and do his very best to look in another direction—anywhere except at the precious necklace, the fabled amulet of Amberkine that Scorch was rapidly uncovering with each thump of his little dragon tail. Sep could not actually see the jewel, but he definitely could make out the twine of dark rope. It appeared and disappeared, appeared and disappeared.

'Scorch!' You have to be still. Don't ask me why. If you don't know, you won't look and right now, I don't want you to look anywhere except straight ahead. If you have any liking for me at all, don't—don't thump your tail. Don't move, don't question—'

The dragon looked miserable.

'You have lost your mind, Sep.'

'I haven't. Trust me, Scorch. Can you—will you—trust me?'

Something in the tone of his mind-thought touched the little hatchling. He felt so full of love he was ready to burst. Only, he was not to do that. He was to stay as still as still—'

'Did you say I was not to breathe?'

'Pretty much. Breathe, Scorch, but for goodness sake don't sneeze or smoke or even gust a tiny trace of flame. Concentrate, will you?'

Scorcher nodded thoughtfully. Then, with the nobility of a martyr (for his tail wanted to twitch and he suddenly, very definitely, wanted to cough) he was as still and as silent as ever Septimus could have wished.

Septimus worried for the wizard—Ramón, of the light, the Wish Maker, and the bringer of bubbles. He worried more though for the amulet. It was only in listening to Móran that he'd fully realised its significance. The necklace had power, but only when united with the brother gem, the amulet of Lindaliss.

The dark wizard held Lindaliss, the amulet of the elf Xanadel, who was his brother, in spirit and in truth. If Amberkine should fall into his hands—

'Too dangerous to trust Scorch,' he thought.

He ignored the disgruntled reply in his head.

Could he translocate the jewel back into his hands? Too powerful a magic for a mere wish and he knew nothing of translocation. He was not confident enough of his powers to visualise such a thing.

If only Arikeet could help him! Arikeet knew so much more than he did about protocol and bottling—about transformation—Septimus's mind rushed back to the moment when the wing bearer had bumbled in his face, an irritating bee that had nearly been swatted.

Yes! That was it!

Septimus eyed Arikeet, hidden a little behind Ramón's sweeping gown. Their eyes met, and Arikeet smiled. For the fraction of an instant, there was complete harmony between them.

Something more elemental than mere recognition—brotherhood. Arikeet nodded with a perky gleam that confirmed Septimus's thoughts more than anything else—

Though he was not a mind reader, only, for heaven's sake, a lowly wing bearer (albeit now with a precious second stripe) something fundamental passed between them. He nodded imperceptibly, but the message he conveyed was more positive in its timbre than anything Septimus had ever felt before. Strange magic at work, this day.

Septimus thought quickly, crystallising his ideas even as the skies darkened and lightning forked in the far distance. He needed to wish Arikeet into the type of creature that would spot the amulet and grab it, unnoticed, from behind Scorcher's tail.

Not a bumblebee, of course. He needed to be able to visualise the creature perfectly and hope that its own nature would draw it to the stone. It was a pity that neither he nor Arikeet had the gift of mind talk. If they had, he could have explained what he wanted.

Now he had to rely on luck. For a moment, he doubted himself. Then, looking deep into Ramón's pain and Móran's sneering scorn, Septimus found his strength.

It was a feathered creature he visualised, one he had seen often enough in the trees of Rutherford East. Not a bee, but a bird. A rather handsome, perky creature, swift enough to fly, cunning enough to steal. In short, a rather common—but curiously delightful—garden pest.

He imagined, with fierce concentration, the ink black feathers, interwoven so handsomely, on its counterpoint, ice-white. A fitting juxtaposition of balance, if only he knew it.

Gymnorhina Tibicen. Septimus had learned the name off an aging Department of Conservation chart that was dangling from one pin in the corridor outside his classroom. (Mr Carlisle, deprived of the use of both cane and strap, delighted in sending him out of class, and he'd spent many a tiresome hour reading such junk.)

Gymnorhina Tibicen—he recalled all he had read—reflected on all he remembered: its quick little jumps, its black eyes, dark with intelligence—its curious attraction to all things shiny—yes, Gymnorhina Tibicen—the common magpie.

He had nothing against the creatures, and Sarah had once tamed one, seduced by its flute-like warbling and its amusing tendency to steal anything that was eye catching, or shimmered.

This was the tendency Septimus remembered. If Arikeet transformed to a magpie, he might—he just might—notice what the wizard had not.

Septimus hoped he would swoop from the sky and grab Amberkine with his beak.

He wished, so hard and so fiercely, that the lid blew off his wish bottle in the palace. The tooth fairies on the third floor were thrown across the room in surprise. The attentive wish fairies on the floor below rushed to catch the exploding bottle, streaming like starry pink champagne. There was very little in reserve now of the requisite purple bottling additive, but Ramón had taken the precaution of personally preparing for any incoming wish from Septimus.

To preserve the balance, he had also had to prepare a bottle for the dark wizard. This stood grim upon the countertop, bottle fairies waiting. As yet, they looked bored.

The weighing staff instantly approved the bottling price, mopped the mess, added extra sealing, a sprinkle of strength (to compensate for any liquid loss) and across the tides, the wish fluidly, magically, and potently, actuated.

Arikeet's transformation was so swift not even Scorcher noticed it, though Wendleweed (who had just emerged from the tunnels and melded into the crowd with the remainder of the messenger elves) was more observant.

He said nothing, however, not realising the importance until the magpie swooped quite close to the dragon and retrieved something shiny in its beak. In a fluid movement, he flew past Septimus and dropped his treasure, flying onward, ever on.

Wendleweed noticed, but hardly realised the significance, for his eyes were fixed on the wizards. The silver wizard was turning his smile—his mirthless smile—upon Ramón, his twin.

'Come, brother, anoint me or destroy me.'

There was a mocking gleam in Móran's eye, the type of gleam that was arrogant enough to ignore the danger.

The tattered robes that hung loosely about him gleamed. This was his moment.

He wished he could look finer, but hey, he was challenging his nemesis. Challenging to win. He could deal with tattered robes. Especially as he knew the very worlds were in the balance. His brother's flaw, his fatal, delicious flaw, was that he loved. He was born to create, not destroy.

In the tower of Castle Carne, the grim wish bottle ripened. The bored elves noticed, but were not enthused. There was no starry champagne, this time, only a very common, unworthy type of wish. No portents or omens, no invocations—The king's wizard apparently simply wished to look finer. The bottling elves spat out their gum (forbidden, but there was no one with a corrector wand anywhere in sight), shrugged and set to the very easy task.

A little tweaking here and there—the stopper—

Móran's beard trimmed quite cleverly, his gown restored (minus the runes, but with a much handsomer design of intertwining fleur de lis and asphodel, sewn elegantly in threads of red), his shoes acquired a bright layer of curling polish and he acquired a hat—very fine, with a phoenix feather flourishing in the wind.

The watching sprites gasped in the breezes, but the wizard did not so much as notice. His wasted wish bubble wafted to the sea and burst on gentle waves, far to Elvenswolde's east.

The challenge held. Lindaliss gleamed, for an instant, about the tall wizard's neck. In a mark of his arrogance, he used it to taunt Ramón. He hardly winced, now, as he wore it. Slowly, he held up his fingers—ten fingers—and traced an omen in the air.

Ramón, concentrating, did the same. The breeze shimmered with an unseen tension, a type of barrier that was reminiscent of the magnetic polarity Garredung had used earlier, to ward off the Gemra.

The bird swooped against the horizon, black and white, black and white, balanced—perfectly balanced—like the light and the dark. When it had dropped Amberkine into Septimus's upturned palm, all eyes had been upon the wizard and no one—not even Septimus himself—dared move or breathe.

No one, that is, except Scorcher, who could not help squealing— in dragonesque—because the magpie had pecked at his tail. A tiny touch of the beak—only necessary because it had been impossible to dig up Amberkine if Scorch was practically sitting on it!

The nip was enough to make a dragonette jump. He flapped his wings, checked his tail, quite forgot he was meant to be still, and caused both wizards to lose their concentration.

Amberkine no longer in its beak, the black winged, white winged, dark bird, light bird, flew swiftly to the silver wizard, unfazed by chants. He nipped at the brilliant, sun sparkled chain that hung about Móran's neck. The platinum that wound itself round a glorious, blazing prize. His beady eyes glowed bright. It was his nature, after all, to be drawn to all that glittered. Gymnorhina Tibicen, cheeky damned magpie!

Lindaliss glowed now in all her glory, a bright, turquoise fire that was deeper than the sea, brighter than the shores of Septimus's earth home.

The wizard screamed, a high-pitched wail that was nothing like his usual controlled irony. His hands grasped at his neck, but it was too late.

The bird, with a collective unconscious that forced it to steal, clamped onto a fire-forged link with his determined beak, and rose into the sky. Móran, half choked, hat displaced, frantically ungentle, grabbed at feathers, but he was not so swift as a bird on the wing.

The bird was drawn to Septimus. Drawn because of his mother, Sarah, who tended the wounded and the wild, who listened to the warbling of magpies, who helped when Gymnorhina Tibicen, in his distant past, had needed help.

He dropped the second jewel into the boy's trembling hand. Amberkine was already about his neck. Now Lindaliss, glittering more brightly than any jewel on earth, any diamond from the deeps of the worlds, flamed, positively flamed.

Septimus could hear the wind again, and the creatures of the sea, the dolphins calling from home and the sperm whales off the distant shores. He could hear the tiptoes of the kitchen fairies and the tapping of Madame Knorr's corrector wand. Distantly, he could hear Mr Carlisle cough and Sarah call out his name.

He exulted; his heart was bursting, he held, in his power, both Lindaliss and Amberkine.

He moved the one towards the other, Lindaliss, twisted on its chain, up to Amberkine—

'Wait!' The silver wizard's voice was hoarse and wolves began to circle. He concentrated his thoughts on the bird circling above Septimus. The bird, which he hated, at that moment, more than life itself. Arikeet danced with the breezes, half himself, half bird, half in transition, half wild.

Words poured from the wizard's mouth—words that sent nightmares to the dragons of Sarcalet, words that made Demetria's mouth dry and a few of Scorch's scales drop from his limbs like cracked dust. The fairies quivered and the tree sprites buried their ears in the very roots and trunks of trees, so poisonous was the sibilance, so deep was the dark. On the second floor, a wizard's bottle ripened with a deathly pop. Unfair, but then the wizard never played by the rules his brother so carefully set.

Arikeet, the handsome bird, the bravest of brave wing bearers, stopped flying. Suspended by the charm, his bright bird eyes regarded Móran intently. Then, as they clouded over to pearl, he fell to the ground in a flurry of feathers that signified nothing but death. Death the death knell, death, the dark, the anguished, the futile.

Ramón did not take his eyes off Móran, did not so much as pay tribute to the tiny creature that had died for light. That was the dark in him, the balance that permitted him this freedom.

The balance—the dark balance—that allowed him to keep his fingers erect, his spell in place. If he cried for Arikeet, his cries would displace his enchantment. He remained dry eyed, a fact that disturbed his twin more than anything else.

Móran thought he had Ramón's measure. He thought he could predict each action and reaction. In the silver wizard's calculations, he had overlooked the critical factor. He had forgotten about balance.

Elvenswolde: The Grave, the Merry and the Merrily In-Between.

Ramón had been careful not to permit his heart to become out of kilter with his mind. Both were one, anyway, one with the universe and the winds that break upon the shores, one with earth and one with the six worlds beyond.

Now, when he needed nerves of steel, he found them. Though his heart broke with the litany of lament, still he found it within himself to endure.

Arikeet, dear, fallen Arikeet, transformed from feather to his own, sweet self when he landed. His death pallor admitted of no succour, no relief. Septimus rushed towards him, stricken with grief despite the jewels that glittered about his person, still separate, but his to command.

If he could have wished for anything then, it would have been for the life of one whimsical wing bearer. Magic 101. But his wishes were spent and Arikeet could only smile—a single, breath-taking, beautiful smile of delight—before his eyes glazed. He knew, oh, he knew, what he had done! Magpie or wing bearer, he was the saving of Elvenswolde.

'Release me from this coil of magic! Your hands will tire and when they do, I will have my revenge. Release me now, lest my vengeance by visited on all the elves, on all the worlds, in each turret of Castle Carne and every cavern of the earth sprites.'

Ramón was still.

'Release me, I say!'

'I cannot trust you.'

'You cannot kill me either. You are a creature of light! So spine-less, so good! You cannot harm me! Do you think I did not play this end game over and over in my mind like one of those silly games of chess? I knew full well that if the odds turned against me, softness would be your undoing.

'Own it, creature of light! Own it! You cannot invoke the base magic because I, Móran, am your brother. Your love is your undoing and I laugh, I laugh in your face and over the dead body of Arikeet, son of Arikaan. Get this over with, Ramón, release me, as you know you shall. Your fingers shall tire quicker than your will, but your will itself is spent. Release me.'

Móran, bound by Ramón's counter-omen, drew quick breaths, unaware of the anger swelling in Septimus, or that Lindaliss and Am-berkine, the twin jewels of the base magic, were now joined as one. The gems, strung by Septimus with fumbling fingers as he listened to this speech, were now nestled together on the single rope. Lindaliss had a slight indentation, Amberkine the faintest extrusion. They fitted into one another, fire to fire, like yin and yang, like the interconnect-edness of our worlds, like magnetic peace.

They were blazing again: not red, or blue but a synchrony of the two vivid colours. Purple. Purple, in its purest form, reminiscent of the Wish Maker's robes.

Tears were streaming down Septimus's face. They were tears for Arikeet, tears for innocence lost.

Ramón, still concentrating, spoke with a slight quiver, though his will was strong. He spoke with love, but with sternness that knew no argument.

'Listen well, Móran. Know that to preserve the balance, the good within you, I embraced evil and the darker ways. To grant you light, I took in dark. Now, Móran, I shall use that dark against you. I shall kill you, as you have killed Arikeet.

'The deed will grant no pleasure, but neither shall it cause me pain. Not the pain I have endured before, nor the pain I feel now, with shadows over the land I love and the air sullied by your secrets. You shall die, Móran, and in dying undo the damage you have done.'

Ramón raised his hands. His fingers pointed in a curious position, one hand outstretched, the other twisted back in a manner that seemed impossible given his tendons and bones. He did not wince, but Móran paled when he saw it.

His pallor was more silvery than the garments which fluttered about his person. Very smart, they still shimmered, but palely, the enchantments stitched into their cloth loosened by Scorcher's onslaughts and hampered by the new red threads of fashionable fleur de lis and asphodel.

Ramón began chanting strange words, dark words that made the thunder roll in the distance and Princess Demetria again look up from her eggs. The waves began to crash against the cliffs and Móran, realising his brother's intention, screamed.

A high scream this time, a scream of pain that cut through the throng of onlookers on the sands and wafted through the castle turrets, through the fourth, the second, the first and the third until there was nowhere—not even the distant banks of Willowsham—unaffected by the lament.

'Wait!' Septimus whispered, but his whisper whistled in the wind, sending ripples through the world, causing Sarah the earth maiden to stop her stirring and Mr Carlisle to drop his chalk.

'Wait!' The words echoed on Ramón's magic, trembling on the force that quivered about Móran, holding him still.

Without removing his gaze from his brother's foul face—handsome yet marred, so marred by hate—jaunty feather blowing in the breeze—Ramón left off his chanting. The spell was not broken, but suspended, suspended by the only person capable of such suspension—he the seventh, he the son.

'Ramón the Wish Maker, I am Septimus, son of Septimus, brought to you by your wish from the world beyond. I wear about my neck Lindaliss and Amberkine, I hold in my hands the base magic.

'Do not sully the light by invoking the dark. You have spent all the darkness in your soul already and are now pure, pure light. Your brother Móran, the anagram of your namesake, the antithesis of your being, has committed to dark. Any goodness you perceived within him has been spent, spent with the slaying of Arikeet the wing bearer, Arikeet my friend.

'The balance is now in perfect harmony, for as you have no darkness, Móran harbours no light. If you do this thing, if you kill your brother, your namesake, you shall be setting the balances spinning again. Spinning, spinning, out of alignment, out of light. Let me invoke the base magic. Let me invoke the powers of Lindaliss and Amberkine.'

Ramón looked grave. This is what he had wanted, what he had set in motion, but now that it had happened, he felt it hard to let go of his grip. His fingers, still outstretched in that strange, contorted position, quivered. Then, slowly, he lowered them to his waist.

In that second, Móran broke free. He raised his own hand and spoke words that curled the blood, words that whirled through the sky and the air, the sea and the sands itself like poison. Silvajar, watching, remembered what it was to be a snake again. Ramón, listening, writhed in his own personal pain.

Septimus straightened his shoulders. He held out the amulets, sapphire blue, ruby red and burning, burning so brightly that they were hot—white hot—on his fingers.

The purple flashed from within, then from without, like lightning—huge streaks of purple—shooting from the stones.

'By the power of Lindaliss and Amberkine, Amberkine and Lindaliss, I invoke the base magic, the deep magic, the magic that is and always has been, beyond the treble, beyond the light, deeper than the dark. Base magic, calm this world, restore the balance, be, just be, be just be—Be, just be—'

Septimus did not know where the words came from. They just flowed from his lips like gentle summer rain.

Darkness fell upon Elvenswolde, the two wizards suspended in animation. Lightness returned, and slowly, slowly, the blanket of shadows lifted so that the four towers of Castle Carne were brightly visible once more and the fields of flowers changed their shades from sombre, muted aubergines and beige to the magical shades of spring. Slow things happened, subtle changes.

The wolves stopped baying and the gemra melted into the winds. The fairies breathed lightly, the elves felt released from bonds that had tightened, unnoticed, about their being.

Móran did not die. He stood, ashen upon the land, a sorry figure, and tired. Worn, worn, and spent. A wind—a twirling wind—enfolded his figure like a cold mist. He embraced it, invigorated by the cold, by the icy tentacles that crept over his being and proclaimed him a creature of the dark.

Not to die, but to live, to live on the edges of the sixth world as Ramón lived on the edges of Elvenswolde, the first. In this manner, the base magic found the balance, tilted the universe, cast shadows where shadows should be found, laced light with brightness, good with greatness.

It took but a second, but in that second, Móran was gone and the shadows lifted.

Birdsong filled the air, the sweetest tribute to Arikeet that the wing bearer could ever have wished. His still body, so lifeless upon the ground, vanished. In its place, a tree. A tree of light, sprinkled with magic, pruned with wishes, green with the first buds of spring.

A tree upon the sands, a fitting memorial to what was, what had been and what was to come. Aradight, son of Arikaan, blood twin of Arikeet, bowed low and cried. His tears mingled with Septimus's and gave that tree its first water, and the water was so fresh, so filled with the love of a brother, the marvels of Amberkine, the bliss of Lindaliss, that it was bound to grow as strong as its promise, as strong as the branches that were already, even now, beginning to bud.

Ramón, no longer suspended by the invocation of the base magic, smiled. He was still weak—it would take a long while before he regained any semblance of his strength—but his eyes held warmth and joy and love, the very marks of the wing bearer himself.

'Welcome,' he said, 'to Elvenswolde.'

* * *

The royal festivities lasted a week and a day, during which the king regained his health and Ramón was able to empty his turret of meticlaws, no longer oozing or smelling, but still a frightful mess. No magic could erase the stains, but several elves scrubbed diligently and the worst traces were now all but gone.

The weighing room did not escape—it had a spring clean such as it had never seen before, and thousand-year-old bottles of outrageous wishes were dutifully dusted and restored to their former sparkling glory.

The cleaning elves could not believe their eyes when Ramón walked in, and with a twinkle in his eye, threw them all into the rubbish.

'If they haven't ripened in a thousand years, then by criminey they never shall. Who wished this ridiculous stuff anyway? What is this?' He looked at a label. 'A villa in Troy? Please! This has long since expired! Just keep current wishes from now on. Say, the last century. No more than that. Oh, and throw out all the earth wishes. I'm heartily sick of them.'

Everything in Elvenswolde seemed to sparkle, the floors, the footpaths, the waters about the moats, the silver castles with their crystal turrets, even the messenger elves, who'd been thoroughly washed and put to bed after their strange adventures.

Garredung smelt particularly bad, but no one'd been unkind enough to point the matter out. It was much better, of course, when he, Xanadel, Wendleweed, Bickleberry and Silvajar were clean and clothed in robes of crimson.

Septimus was given multiple burn ointment and very soon his eyelashes and ninety percent of his eyebrows were restored. The remaining ten percent, still under regular siege from Scorcher, seemed to stubbornly refuse to make the effort. Still, he looked handsome enough, as many a young fire-fairy remarked.

Sep would blush to the roots of his scalp, for he had a distinct partiality for fairies, but was still kind of shy. (They were nothing like Tiffany Trewellyn, who he could manage much more easily!)

In a quite lengthy—and often boring—ceremony, Wendleweed, Garredung, Xanadel, Silvajar and Bickle were removed from their positions as messenger elves.

They were no longer to wear the livery of either the king or the queen. Instead, the elves were to be elevated to a new rank, created by Ramón and endorsed by the Council of Elvenswolde. Ever after, they were to be granted the Order and titles of Lindaliss, Keepers of the Amulet.

It was felt that the amulet was too significant to be borne or worn by one wearer.

Instead, the task would be shared by partnership and that partnership, whose very existence was forged by friendship, would serve as a beacon for all of Elvenswolde and the six worlds beyond it.

Xanadel was sentenced to another six months' swordsmanship, and was teased unmercifully by his friends, but he bore the ragging well. Garredung silently swore to watch his back in real combat, and Silvajar winked in agreement.

Septimus, garbed in the same red robes, was to be the sole bearer of Amberkine, as was foretold in the prophecies.

In an incredibly exciting ritual—not at all boring, this time—he was knighted 'Wishbinder.'

His skin still tingled as he thought on that moment, for magic weaved through his being as the King's sword touched his shoulder and he was asked to rise.

'Arise, Wishbinder.'

He felt himself, and more than himself. He felt, finally, actuated in the prophecies, for as the base magic once more returned to the deep, earth balanced elf, Lindaliss Amberkine.

As Wishbinder, Septimus was the blending, binding force that stabilised the worlds, held magic in its due position, and sustained the spinning of the earth on its axis. The very moons of Elvenswolde were part of the gravitational force thrumming in Amberkine, answered, separately, in Lindaliss.

Sep's robes were not as perfect as Xanadel's, for Scorcher had already burnt three holes through the fabric and was likely to do so again.

He could not keep still and kept breathing fire down even the kitchen elves' necks, so that he was sent out of the castle in disgrace—

but not before he was honoured with a citation for bravery, a casket of elfin rubies (not to be sneered at) and a hug from Septimus that had the little dragonette blushing from embarrassment. (He did not mind a private embrace, but for a dragon to be seen hugging in public—it was worse than being blue!)

As for being blue, he was fast becoming accustomed to the matter. The wood sprites—charming, utterly charming—seemed to think him cute.

Besides, he had only to look in the enchanted glass at Ramalo to see that he was really quite a handsome fellow.

He supposed that it must be the particular shade of blue he was born to. It was not as if he were navy, or the niggling type of blurry-blue which gave elves a headache. No, he was very smart indeed, very refined—he consulted the mirror again and breathed a tiny fire of satisfaction. One would not like to suggest Scorcher was vain, but a tiny bit puffed up in his consequence—well, Scorcher was Scorch, what can one say?

It took a while to convince the dragons of Sarcalet that his colour was not an incalculable calamity.

Princess Demetria, released from egg watching, huffed in excitement as she saw him soaring towards her, dragon wings outstretched, a mighty flier. (He was getting plenty of practice!)

The Myranderthuse and Argyll dragons were less welcoming, but forced to admit, after a thousand hours and three hundred minutes of council, that the shadows had, indeed, vanished.

Yes, yes, all concurred that this was entirely the little prince's doing. After all, elves were inconsequential creatures and could achieve nothing at all without some serious dragon intervention. The little prince... Yes, they had started to refer to him as the little prince—Scorcher would have preferred Bewarious Flesh-eatarius, but one couldn't have everything—the little prince had achieved what he promised.

They muttered over his citation—useless bit of parchment—but seemed more than pleased that he had a casket of elfin rubies to add to the treasure store of Mt. Zircon. For a young dragonette, that was considered a mighty achievement indeed.

The blue eggs were buried in the ground with a flourish. The spell was less powerful beneath the darkness of the earth and the coolness of the grass.

(Scorcher explained this patiently, but with a dragon twinkle in his eye. He was getting quite proficient at small fibs.)

He was granted a feast of wolf meat and willowblane sauce, a dinner he greatly enjoyed and was kind enough to share with all the other dragon hatchlings.

As for Septimus, well, the time came for a parting that was as sweet as it was painful. He had come to know and love his extended family, so different from Sarah of Earth, yet so similarly beloved.

There was Fairmeade the harp singer, Ganimede the water sprite, Raven the wing bearer, the twins Fillament and Scattadew (terribly naughty but impossible not to adore), Whistlethwaite the Starwatcher and Eros, apprentice wing bearer, were uncles. Then there were the cousins Lilly-light and Leandra (incredible braids, but as sharp tongued as they were pretty, and of course, Xanadel himself. Indeed, the entire order of Lindaliss—including Garredung and Silvajar—had crept into his heart.

He loved meeting the shy water sprites and thanking the earth sprites, who had helped Bickle and Wendleweed. He shook Master Hepple's hand gravely and pocketed an interesting vial of—he knew not what—but apparently it was invaluable in times of need.

It was hard to leave Elvenswolde, but he left knowing that it existed, and that knowledge gave him strength. He could return home Septimus, son of Septimus, Wishbinder. He was truly guardian of the Amulet of Amberkine. He need never doubt himself again.

The parting was swift. One moment he was staring into the kind, warm eyes of Ramón, the next he was home, running, breathless, past the ferns, past the Marlborough daisies, faster and faster until he was colliding with his mum, laughing and hugging.

Sarah, eyes shining, rushed to welcome him. Septimus smelt burning. For a second, he was confused. He thought it might be Scorcher—he'd become accustomed to the smell of smoke. Then he smiled. It was only mum's oven—something incinerating, he presumed.

Mr Carlisle wore a huge plaster across his bulbous-looking nose. He was grumpier than ever, and in a lot of pain. Apparently, he'd been stung by a wasp. (Giant!) Septimus smiled. It didn't take a genius to recognise the work of Aradight, bloody naughty twin of Arikeet, son of Arikaan.

The wing bearer's pledge had been fulfilled.

Book 2: of Earth

Of the Ancient Tapestries and Sooth Singers

Now, the sooth singers have sung their songs. The ancient myths have rendered their services and the world is alive, once more. The great tapestries in the highest towers of the enchanted chambers in Elvenswolde have twinkled their magic, as was foretold in the ancient myths. The songs of Ganymede and the whole line of sooth singers before him have been hummed in every grass and every sand across the spectrum of the seven worlds.

From the hills to the dales, the high places to the seas, the air has been tinged with the faint tripping of bells and basses, tremulous trumpets and harp strings, cymbals and song. The ancient soothsongs, spun in silk and woven in mystical stitching so fine the naked eye can see nothing of its potency, now lie dormant.

The prophecies of the seventh son of a seventh son, of the shadowing of elfin lands, of the powers of the intertwining of Lindaliss and Amberkine, of the invocation of the bass magic, the restoration of balance, the return of harmony, the death of Arikeet and the budding of a new life force have been stitched, then released, stitched, then released, until the stitches are set, their memories fading to vivid ink on silk, beautiful, humbling, but dormant and magic no more.

On a daily basis wanderers from far and wide pay a small tribute and are granted access to the official chambers of the Queen, on the lower levels of the high tower. They are permitted now to view what was hidden before, to gasp in awe at the wonder of the scenes depicted, to marvel at the colours and the exquisite craftsmanship of the huge, tasselled masterpieces that are now extraordinary art, stitched by the weaver elves, but no more than that. No more the carrier of secrets in threads of prophecy.

One tapestry, however, is not displayed in this manner. It remains in the antechamber of the queen, guarded by liveried elves, all the while twinkling, brilliantly twinkling, with the incredible secrets of the past and the future, the possibles and the *enchanted* possibles, the rivers of reason and the dappled dales of doubt.

> *May the raging of oceans call forth your name*
> *as thundering cumulus foreshadows your face.*
> *May ancient wild winds insane and insane,*
> *rip at the roots and the wild thorns—*
> *again,*
> *yes again.*
> *Take sand-soaked seas and lush lilacs blowing,*
> *take crushed camphor colours and bend us, allowing*
> *torment's sweet fingers its silence, its scents,*
> *the quivering quiet in the whispered,*
> *the meant.*
> *Bend us*
> *and bind us,*
> *bond us so much*
> *that shivering-soft sands*
> *shift restless to touch,*
> *and are warmed and are warmed*
> *with impossible heat,*
> *as senses awake,*
> *as melt-mind-mingled*
> *we meet.*
> *And all around, in echoes, in trees,*
> *in woodlands and forests,*
> *in lightning,*
> *in breeze*

the world is awaking,
alive and alive,
the grasses are singing,
brooks bubbling, banks brimming
wet wild birds are bringing
on wing and on whim,
intonations of poignance,
of passion,
of power—
intonations of perfect—
the perfect you are,
on glistening dew, on time shifting star,
such feelings, such fancies,
such pulses a-flight,
intonations of you,
intimations
so bright...

It foretells of many moments and it is trembling, even now, at the seams, tiny stitches unravelling, releasing small secrets of the immediate future, abuzz with what is soon to happen... yes, the left fringing on the far side, just beneath the rainbows of Dwellindon and the mountains of Sarcalet... yes, there, just there, the silks are twisting and secretly parting, little threads adjusting here and there... impossible to notice in the grand scale of the whole, impossibly huge, extraordinarily beautiful depiction.

Do you remember, readers, the day when it poured with rain in Elvenswolde? When the boots of the elves were wet, when no amount of curling polish could undo the damage of rain and mud, when Xanadel slipped from the kitchens, for once released from tasks, when the sculleries were ahum with the baking of bread and ollingstranga, where every floor was scrubbed, all wood waxed to high, industrious polish, when it was too wet to brave the woods or the beaches, and the shadows crept over the land in a cold drizzle of foretelling? The wolves of Astra began their roaming, the gemra crept through forests, their little hearts black as granite… the king lay in bitter stupor, wasted wish bubbles drifted aimlessly from windows, popping prematurely. Some oozed meticlaws and maggots, the bright nettles of nastiness. Wendleweed and Bickle flew across the stick-lethwaite…

Then, yes, then, the queen called for her finest stitcher elves and this huge, immense, impossibly magical fabric of the future had been woven, new prophecies intertwining and mingling with the old, mixing, blending, visualising, in animus and in rest, in the light of the pearly moons and in the bitter dark of that stormy afternoon.

Yes, then this elfin tapestry had been stitched by nimble hands, the silks chosen swiftly by the keen eyes of silk elves, in colours so subtle and true they activated magic with each tiny slip of a stitch. Magic and music—the treble, the high music of Elvenswolde—was invested and imbedded in this, the queen's custom-called piece, as her right, granted by the ethereal majesty of her cloak, and by her regency in this the kindom's most delicate hour.

In this way, the mythology of Elvenswolde has not ended, then: it is still weaving itself, the notes embedded and imbued. The details crystallise every day, are ever changing from rose to reds, poppy to cornflower. As new stitches loop and thread, old stitching leaks a little, runs—not due to poor craftsmanship but rather the opposite! Due to clever attention to time, and to the appropriate crystallisation of circumstances foretold. New chapters begin as old chapters end…

Even as we speak, the stitches are unseaming themselves, untwirling in twisted slivers of silk, here fading, here brightening, tiny fragmentary adjustments… there is a foretelling and the foretelling is beginning… tiny strands are enmeshing to the high music, can you hear, just faintly, the high trill that anchors Elvenswolde to its place as the highest arbiter of light?

It is beginning…

Tiffany Sees a Bee

Yes! Two nil!

Rutherham High had done it at last. A win—an actual win, not just a miserable draw. Septimus pushed the sweat from his face and thought the day was perfect. Absolutely perfect. Keith Luxton scowled off-field—good, he deserved to be beaten, stupid, bragging, stuck-up bully. Septimus could almost taste the coke waiting to be drunk. Lots of ice. Nope! No chance. There would be nothing but water in the chilly bins by now. So hot—a bee buzzed about his ears.

He blinked, then stood deliberately still. He squinted, because he could have sworn… no, he was imagining things. He had to be.

Septimus, Wishbinder, half earth, half elf, seemed a long, long way away. Here he was simply Sep, and Sep was about to be stung—not cool.

The world of Elvenswolde had been closed to him for nearly a year. The Guardian of the Amulet of Amberkine had nothing but a piece of glass about his neck to remind him that any of it had ever even been true.

Tiffany clutched his arm. He shook her off. Even in victory, Tiffany could be a bit annoying. For the millionth time, he wished she would stop 'liking' him, and move her crush on to someone else—anyone—but no, she persisted! She clung to him like one of those Pokémon. Which was it… not Pikachu… Squirtle? Damn, he wished he could shake her off without decimating her feelings. Maybe body odour—

He ignored her pouting lips, remaining as aloof as possible. Wisps of hair caught in his eyes. He pushed them aside.

The teams were milling about trays of club sandwiches. Marmite and cheese. Cokes being brought out of chilled bins…

The buzz echoed a smidgen louder. Septimus's vision blurred, and in that second he could see Aradight, son of Arikaan, blinking at him from the body of a bumbling bee.

Sep blinked. Tiffany's arm shifted, the smell of marmite drifted into the air, he could taste a blade of grass caught on his lip… the buzzing again, more focused this time. Yes. It was Aradight, he would swear it.

Eleven months of separation from Elvenswolde, and Septimus's memory was still acute. He had a certain fondness for elves. Especially elves like Aradight, who were not above stinging the likes of Mr Carlisle quite deliberately on the nose!

'Aradight?'

'Septimus, bearer of Amberkine!'

'I can't believe…'

Shhhh… people are staring at you. You look like you're talking to yourself.'

But before Aradight could say another word, Tiffany screamed. It was blood curling.

The type of scream that made any self-respecting person wince— or dial emergency services.

'Bee!' she yelled in Septimus's sensitive ear. 'Bee!'

Septimus just managed to dodge before a book came hurtling through the air. When he blinked, Aradight had disappeared.

The Multiple Problems Related to Dragon-Sitting and Other Minor Issues

In Elvenswolde, a dragon was groaning in pain. One might suppose, if one was at all acquainted with such a place, that this dragon was extremely cute, a curious shade of blue and particularly accident-prone. One might also suppose that his name was Scorcher. (Though naturally he would prefer to be known as Bewarious Flesh-eatarious.)

But one would be wrong!

The dragon in question was not blue, but a puke shade of green—and that was precisely what he was doing: puking. Beside him, another dragon—equally ugly—was coughing great gusts of smoke into the air. They looked like Indian ring signals, only much wider. The elves on the grassy banks of Willowsham below were terrified.

As if this was not enough, another more scaly kind of hatchling sat to the left of the puker and wailed in long, throbbing sentences.

She was singeing her nightgown with each bellow and very soon there would be nothing left of it. To a person of taste (like Scorcher, for instance) this might have seemed a good thing, for it was scattered with ridiculous frilly bows fashioned from the most hideous shade of Otris leather.

As a garment it was incurably offensive to the eyes. The hatchling seemed fond of it. As she burnt off yet another piece, her bellow grew loud enough to wake even the sleepiest of unhatched dragons in the hardest of uncracked shells.

Scorcher—ah, we have found him at last!

Scorcher shuddered, his delightful shade of blue paler than usual. He was much larger than when Septimus had last seen him, for dragons grow fast in Elvenswolde—none more so than a prince.

His wings had grown long and powerful, but they drooped now from sheer fatigue. He was bottle feeding a ravenous dragonette. When the creature finished, he helped it burp.

Not that it needed much helping—Scorcher winced at the disgusting sounds and tried very hard to ignore the smell.

He wished—oh how he wished—he had not got himself into such a pickle.

He longed to see his friend Sep again.

Septimus was the first living being he'd ever laid eyes on, after all, the person he'd bonded with from the very moment of hatching, the boy he'd hailed as 'mum' (much to his later embarrassment, when the difference between dragons and boys became more apparent!).

Yes, he longed for Septimus, with his expressive silver-blue eyes, and his intense grin. He longed to embark once more on the great adventures dragons were made for—protecting the realm of Elvenswolde, upholding the myths of Lindaliss and Amberkine… but no, he was dreaming again.

His tail drooped, a dragon tear threatened to drip from his enormous, dragon-lashed eyes. Those days were gone. The great quests, the vanquishing of Móran, the healing of the Elvin king… he sighed. He was left, quite literally, holding the baby. Or babies.

But nothing, a fierce inner voice of protest told him, nothing could really stop him looking out over the spires of Caste Carne and dreaming—lazy, hazy dragon—dreaming…

He closed his eyes and ignored the last wisp of nightgown that floated across his cheek then down, down into his nostrils until he could help it no more. He did what any dragon prince in his position would do. He sneezed.

Of Muffins and Elderflower Juice

Septimus waited till the last kid had straggled off home, but Aradight did not reappear. He closed his eyes and visualised, something he was out of practice doing, but was answered by nothing.

Elvenswolde was vanishing in his mind. He felt so frustrated and lonely.

Now, when it was all nearly very real again, Septimus felt that aching longing that only his mother, Sarah, knew how to put in to words.

Sarah, who had never herself entered Elvenswolde, but who sensed it like a mirror image. Sarah, who had married his father, a seventh son of Elvenswolde, making Septimus the seventh son of a seventh son. He was gifted with a heritage that hardly seemed possible.

Nothing much, after all, tended to happen on the South Island of New Zealand. It was as far from Elvenswolde as earth from Jupiter. Probably further.

He longed with a sudden passion, to be back in Elvenswolde, with the wind at his back and his amulet flashing bright with the hidden powers vested in it.

When the wind grew too cold to be standing out on the shores, looking across the Pacific at the ebbing tides, Septimus slowly dusted off the grass stains from his knees and began the long walk home.

Sarah was waiting for him. She seemed to know, even before he'd spoken.

'You have been called.'

Her voice was gentle, and her eyes seemed to pierce through Septimus, through his messy outer layers of tee and windbreaker, trailing shoe lace and cap, to his inner despair.

'I was too slow. I've missed the call. Mum, I think I'm like dad. I've forgotten how to visualise.'

Septimus kicked a clump of leaves on the deck, then slipped his pack from his shoulders.

Sarah laughed.

'*You* have forgotten, but *I,* it seems, have remembered.'

'Not funny, mum.'

She opened the door a little wider, allowing Septimus to duck under her arm as he always did, and enter through the sliding door that led from the deck.

There, drinking his mother's disgusting elderflower juice and scoffing down chocolate muffins, was Aradight.

He did not seem to notice that the muffins were burned, with little bits of chamomile flower (rather thorny) lodged in the icing. Sarah's combination of cooking and quackery was unappetizing bordering on dangerous, in Septimus's opinion.

Dressed in full wing bearer green, he was (between mouthfuls) grinning from ear to ear.

'Sep! *You* sure took a long way home!'

'Aradight! *Mum!*'

Septimus's astonishment was two-fold. Not only was he amazed to see Aradight of Elvenswolde in his home—the bridge between earth and Elvenswolde was very strictly enforced—but it was crazy that *Sarah* could actually perceive the delicate creature.

'How… how…' Septimus did not know how to formulate all the questions that were brimming in his brain like coloured popcorn, here a question… pop!… there a question… pop, pop!

Aradight grinned.

'Don't look so worried. Anthropology 202:

"One may mingle with earth folk and show one's true form provided it is in the strict performance of one's duties and one has the

necessary forget-me-dust to wipe away any associated memories."
Chapter eleven, pages 3-5 with a foreword by Ramón himself.'

He grinned. 'It so happens I have an entire bag of forget-me-
dust. When we have finished this conversation—and the delicious
muffins'—he eyed the last three longingly—

'Sarah will be dusted with the dust and her memory will dim,
though not, I think, completely. She is almost—almost but not quite—
of our world.'

His mum nodded. Her eyes misted up and she pretended to dust
crumbs from the table. (There weren't any—Aradight had seen to
that!)

This bit was always sad for her. Septimus wished it could be different, wished that he could take her by the hand, show her the places
he'd been, climb the rocks he'd climbed—

His mind flashed to the gemra and the darker things he had seen.
He shuddered a little and thought, perhaps, that it was as well she
hadn't.

'Don't worry, Sep... the forget-me-dust is fine. I understand
about it. At least it allows me to see Aradight now, in all clarity.'

Septimus nodded. His amulet had begun to glow softly about
his neck.

Unconsciously, he touched it. Móran? He grew anxious.

'Why have you come? Is Ramón ok? The bearers of Lindaliss?
They're all fine, aren't they?'

Aradight laughed. 'They're all good, as right as rain, box of
fluffy ducks, as you kiwis always say: Wendleweed has indigestion—
only to be expected, if you saw what he ate at the Feast of Ickledown.
Ramón has taken a holiday. Disappeared without a by your leave and
has not been seen since the rising of the second moon.'

'How do you know it was not... you know—'

Septimus felt anxious. Again, he glanced at the jewel about his
neck. It felt warm, but was not glowing as brilliantly as it could.

'Oh, he left a note for us, scribbled on a diamond. It hangs suspended above his cauldron and bothers all the poor cleaner elves who
want to wash out his pots. He's left a bottling spell that suspends all

wishes till he gets back, though some of the lesser ones are on auto pilot. It's great news for us wing bearers. Not nearly so much work, you know.'

'Where's he gone?'

Aradight shook his head. 'All very mysterious.'

'Funny to think of Ramón as having fun!'

'Yes, but not poor Scorcher.'

'Why, what's with him?' Septimus felt sudden alarm. He was very fond of Scorcher!

Aradight's eyes twinkled. 'I will tell you, as it was recounted to me by the great dragon Socon. He is an ancient creature and rather wise for one of his kind. I shall try to remember Socon's exact words—they were very, very amusing—and you will see why I have come and why Scorcher has such need of you.

'Apparently the little prince's wish bottle popped a few days ago and the price was paid with some of the elfin rubies he earned from the king.'

Septimus looked anxious. It must be very bad if Scorcher had paid the price of a wish bottle.

The Council of Sarcalet

The council of Sarcalet was gathered high above Mt. Zircon. In the dark sky its members circled, their great bodies quivering with strength and collective power. They were invoking the ancient runes, committed to the dragon ritual of choosing a new leader, as their ancient one faltered before them.

'We must set off into the wilderness beyond Elvenswolde to make our choice. We'll challenge and fight to the death, or fight until we have no breath left to spare, no flame to spark our nostrils. He who challenges, must prepare to leave the ring powerless, or else as the great leader among us.'

There was a murmur and several deep groans and growls. Dragons were appointed witnesses, challengers, the fierce judges of etiquette and form.

Princess Demetria was a challenger, though her son, much further down the slopes, rather fancied *himself*.

He was lost in pleasant daydreams as each elder of the circle intoned some boring chant or other, and the dragons collectively bowed and hummed (more like the most petrifying roars), puffing out steam at appropriate moments that somehow escaped him.

They escaped him because he was not really listening. He was watching instead his reflection in the crystal stream that ran off from Mt. Zircon and formed a waterfall pond at the base of the precious hill. He was almost mesmerised by his beauty, for indeed, he had grown into such a marvellously handsome fellow he could hardly recognise himself.

His wings were large, his talons had developed nicely, his eyes were a rather glorious gold. Here and there, bits of ruby scales gleamed brightly, offsetting his extremely dynamic shade of blue.

As a matter of fact, these were several shades—all very pleasant—ranging from royal blue on his tail, body and upper wings, to aqua on his limbs and a delicate shade of cornflower on his long neck extensions and lower wing tips.

His nose was silver (something of a disappointment because he would have preferred gold to match his eyes but still, the curve was quite distinguished and several girl dragons seemed to like its glowing colour.)

Most important though, he had grown the unmistakable curved, twisting horns of an adult dragon even though he was still merely a teenager. Scorcher, understandably, was particularly proud of those horns.

In the short space of the year or so when he'd been no more than a hatchling, he'd also developed a rather lovely roar. Deep and throaty and surprisingly loud for a Dargonville dragon.

He longed to try it out, now, in front of the elders, but he didn't quite dare.

Instead, he waited impatiently for the moment when volunteers would be called, row by row, dragon by dragon, to join the candidates for leader.

Yes, he was being bold, but a leader needed, after all, to be bold. He did not like the idea of battling Demetria, his mother, but he rather thought she would back down if it ever came to mortal combat between the two of them.

After all, she might be remarkably ugly, but she undoubtedly had a kind heart beneath all those hideous scales.

If she had not, she would have murdered him long ago, as nature had intended. He would have been crushed against the rocks or thrown from a cavernous height when the dragon princess first noticed the awful fact that his egg was blue.

Scorcher smiled—it was easy to smile about it now, but a year ago the matter had been far more serious, a humiliation he'd still not yet shaken off, and all the more reason for him to be eager to volunteer.

'Volunteers, please? Any volunteers? '

There was a sudden silence on the hill. Even the whooshing of wings had ceased, as if the circle dragons were suspended in mid-air, awaiting the moment of solemn truth.

Scorcher's heart lurched. This was it! This was his moment! No one else moved, not even Demetria, his mother, who he knew perfectly well was grooming for this role.

Apparently everyone was too shy, or not eager to be the first one to stake a claim.

Scorcher cleared his throat. Then into the silence he roared, filling his lungs with air, as he had practiced time and time before in front of the mirror pools near Castle Carne.

'I, Scorcher of the great line of Dargonville, shall be the first to declare myself on this mountain of jewels.'

There was an astonished silence all about the hills of Sarcalet. The air itself seemed still with anticipation.

Then, to Scorcher's surprise, everyone was laughing and clapping and congratulating him on being such a very brave and kind fellow, a dragon worthy of respect, a dragon who put others before himself in the true manner of princes.

Demetria was smiling proudly, holding a little tissue to her enormous nostrils, marvelling at his sacrifice. It was so kind of him, she announced, to offer to look after the hatchlings. Not *one* other dragon had volunteered for such a task!

A huge, speckled dragon the colour of pea soup muttered that this was hardly surprising, as looking after baby hatchlings—especially sick ones—could be hell.

It was then that the terrible truth dawned on Scorcher. He had not been listening properly. It was not time to volunteer for leadership, but rather for dragon babysitter!

Now, everyone was congratulating him and thinking him wonderful for making such a supreme sacrifice. How could he tell them it was all a huge mistake?

He spluttered, trying to find the correct words, but the whole of Mt. Zircon would know he'd not been listening to one word of the elders. Moreover, they would also know that he had *not* been kind or considerate!

Well, what could he do? Before he knew it, every hatchling in Sarcalet was being placed tenderly into his care. He was given several dragon bibs (the size of tablecloths, for everything dragons do are on a large scale) some nappies and an enormous bottle of dragon talc. It smelled good, but Scorcher was not in the mood for feeling comforted.

After many instructions (both to him and to the contenders), much delivering of dragonettes and their baby accoutrements, two disqualifications, six petitions for clemency and a lot of snarling and flame, the dragons of Mt. Zircon disappeared into the darkening skies, vanishing almost without trace.

If Scorcher had looked carefully though, he would still have been able to see the ripples of their tails etched upon darkening clouds.

Well! He was left alone upon the glittering hilltop. Alone, that is, but for a dozen or so screaming infants and the leftover remains of some wolf pie.

He was not very happy, and felt distinctly sorry for himself, especially when a patchy grey creature with a running nose managed to dribble over the crust he was saving till last.

He shooed the creature away, but then it, too, began to howl, so Scorcher just handed over the last piece (he'd lost his appetite for it anyway) beginning his slow descent down Mt. Zircon, nappy bags and all.

Luckily, the creatures all seemed to know to follow, but it was a slow business and Scorcher (who is still rather clumsy) managed to cause an avalanche of diamonds, opal and some type of gleaming rock known as alluvial gold.

It was a nightmare for him, for two of the babies had emeralds chip their tails and one (already a nasty bully at just two months) seemed to think the loosened gems were for throwing.

Scorcher breathed a huge gust of smoke at him, but did not dare do anything more than scold: the hatchling was half Myranderthuse and therefore probably already better at fire-breathing than himself.

He sighed as he comforted the cry babies and flapped his wings to hurry the remaining stragglers. One of them had nasty red spots on his face. He was using his milk claws (like milk teeth in humans, only dragons lose two sets of claws as well) to scratch.

Scorcher sighed, then offered to give him a ride on his back. For the first time that day, the hatchling smiled. The blue on Scorcher's back began to deepen: he'd looked quite sickly in the paler shade his fright had caused.

His heart softened instantly—he was very kind beneath his dragonesque bluster. Several hours later though, he was *still* giving rides to what seemed like a thousand sick dragonettes. His eyes were seeing double, triple, quadruple, and his nose had begun to run.

In the far distance, he could hear a series of terrible roars. Dragon smoke—fierce oranges—seemed to waft through the evening sky. He wished he knew what was happening, he wished he did not feel so sick, and most of all, he wished for his good friend Septimus.

* * *

Aradight stopped for breath and another two of Sarah's muffins. Nothing, he assured Sarah, tasted like these in Elvenswolde.

Septimus thought it just as well—he loved his mother, but baking was simply not her most major talent. He refrained, however from being sarcastic. Just grinned as his mother fluffed out happily.

'How did he make his wish come true?'

'He didn't. He *still* doesn't know what's happening on Mt. Zircon.' (As a matter of fact, *I* do—Demetria has just dehorned Gustaseous, so with him out of the field, it's just Slashstaceous to the quarter final. I'm pretty sure it is just a matter of time before she's crowned grand leader, but that's only *my* humble opinion.)

'Go on.'

Aradight took a quick sip. 'Well, just before Scorch sank into an ultimate sulk, Ramón appeared—complete coincidence! Apparently, his fish needed skinning and a little flame grilling. He was just north of Sarcalet and thought Scorcher might help.'

'And did he?'

'No, he managed to burn the meal to a cinder. Which meant that even though Ramón was on vacation, he had to magic up something more acceptable to eat. Enough, of course, for the entire nursery of dragons who were all salivating, and let me tell you, it took him hours!

'I think Ramón was more than a little sorry for Scorch by this time, but he sternly demanded at least ten of the elfin gems before fixing the price of Septimus's wish bottle. (You know how Ramón can be, such a stickler for process!)

Anyway, Scorcher did not hesitate. Rubies seemed a small price to pay under the circumstances!'

'And not a moment too soon, by the sound of it!'

Septimus felt that bubbling excitement within him. The amulet of Amberkine was growing warm about his neck and he was certain that deep within, the blue fires were beginning to flash as his past now seemed to meld with his future.

That familiar sense of interconnectedness was rising within him. Elvenswolde no longer seemed distant. He felt its presence beckoning, and could hardly wait to be off.

'Wait! One thing I was told to check.'

'What is that?'

'Have you had chicken pox?'

'Chicken pox? What are you talking about?'

Sarah interjected. 'Yes, a terrible dose when he was ten!'

'Ah, that's good, then. Poor Scorcher, after tending to all those dragonettes, it is hardly surprising that he he's sick. Dragon ipsicoccal D and G—very similar to chicken pox but attacks the scales, you know—it's a nasty thing. Nasty indeed. Wouldn't want you catching it and transferring it from one world to the other. Come, we shall make haste. Sarah, we thank you.'

Then Aradight, with a quaint elven bow, took Septimus's hand and began his visualisations. Septimus felt himself swept up in it, and very soon his mind was blank, but for some strange and heavy clouds, the clouds of sleep, no, they were clearing and he could see, far in front of him some mountain peaks... they were drawing closer... it was dark, but one of the mountains was gleaming... he felt it at last, that sense of strange recognition.

He was visualising Mt. Zircon... Aradight tugged at him and the picture faded a little, crossed a bit lower, a bit deeper... he was in a cave... gracious, he was in a dragon's cave beneath the shadow of Mount Sarcalet!

It was freezing and dark... he felt a little dizzy and he needed to duck his head—the entrance was quite low and narrow.

A moment later, he opened his eyes and waited for them to adjust to the dark. He was undoubtedly in Elvenswolde, he could feel it in his bones and in the tingling of his toes, still snug in his soccer boots. As he waited for the darkness to clear, he could hear moans and sniffles and snores and coughs.

Very soon, he began to see shapes.

In the Caves Below Mt. Zircon

As Septimus's eyes adjusted he saw grey blobs, silhouetted here and there in the cavern. He could not make out any particular shape other than the stalactites and stalagmites that glowed every now and them.

Then, as a dragonette sneezed and blew out a spark of dragon flame here, a puff of golden spark there, he could make out a few shapes and colours—mostly a ghostly green.

In the centre of this pile of dragonettes lay Scorcher, fast asleep with his great talons over his paws.

He looked exhausted, poor thing, and itchy, for he was very spotty—Septimus could hardly tell the difference between his handsome ruby scales and the enormous dragon ipsicoccal D and G spots that covered his entire body, from head to toe.

Now and again, he sneezed, and scratched in his sleep, but he looked altogether a very sorry sight. Septimus wondered, at first, whether this was really his good friend, for he'd grown so much he was hardly recognisable.

He did not wonder long.

Scorcher, suddenly alert to a new presence in his cave (as dragons are prone to be) opened one of his large, golden eyes. The triangular pupil dilated for a moment, then both lids opened, then Septimus found himself crashing to the floor in a great crunch of bones and boots.

The dragon, in his excitement, had stretched out and grabbed him, tripping over two of the hatchling's tails in the exhilaration of the moment.

Pandemonium naturally broke out as the dragonettes wailed, Septimus groaned and the enormous blue creature breathed puffs of huge, excited smoke in his face.

Nothing could have convinced Septimus more that this was, indeed, Scorcher, for the unfortunate aspect of having such a clumsy friend was that parts of him always seemed to ache.

Now, his back ached from being pushed backwards onto the cave floor, his leg ached from being squashed by one enormous, half-opened dragon wing, and his jaw ached from having hot breath dribbled all over it: this is not to mention the odd flame singeing an eyebrow or two.

'Get off, get off, you great oaf!'

Septimus could not shout this, for he'd had the breath knocked out of him during his fall, but he *thought* it. Strange how one slipped so easily into old habits.

The answer came back as a muffled roar in his head. 'Did I hurt you?'

'No, you just crushed my bones to pulp and burnt my face to a cinder. Nothing to worry about!'

The dragon giggled and scratched and tried to lick Septimus with his pink tongue. It was very long now, and warm and sticky.

'Sorry!'

Again, Septimus had to think his answer, for if he opened his mouth he would've had a giant tongue pressed against his teeth. He shuddered. He loved Scorcher, but really! The creature seemed just as horribly clumsy as ever.

'Yeah, right!'

The Wishbinder grinned and recovered from his squashed position.

The huge dragon seemed relieved and excited, so excited, that he began scratching at an enormous pace: so fast Septimus could only see the vibration of his claws against his scales.

'You need calamine lotion. Or Anthisan. Both are excellent for itches.'

'Do you have some? I am going mad with this damn pox... oh, hi, Aradight!'

But Aradight was too nimble for Scorcher. He transformed himself into a bee just in time to avoid being crushed by the dragon's friendly paw.

'Hi, Scorch!' Aradight said, after transforming back to his usual elven form. 'Just completing my final round for the day. Your wish was endorsed by Ramón himself.'

'Such a lovely wizard. I am so glad he has recovered his health. It was touch and go for a while…'

The dragon looked solemn as both he and Septimus remembered the darker days, when the very fate of Elvenswolde hung in the balance.

Aradight's tears blinked in the gloomy cave light, for he'd paid dearly for Elvenswolde's freedom. He'd lost Arikeet, his twin, and missed him fiercely.

Scorcher broke the sudden sadness.

'I wonder when Ramón will be back with some more fish? I could develop an appetite for it if it came in more than a snack sized package!'

'Ramón's fish is enough to serve a banquet hall at Castle Carne, you greedy creature! Besides, you burnt it all, so how would you know? Listen, I must go, now that my task is complete.'

'Very well! No chance of that… that… calamine, was it calamine?… stuff?'

'Calamine lotion. No, I am afraid not. It is only used on earth, though I don't see why it shouldn't work for dragons… have you seen Master Hepple?'

'No, I have not left this cave ever since I managed to crawl down Mt. Zircon with these whippersnappers on my back! Hey, remember when Ramón said we could have a reward more precious than rubies?'

'Yes, but I note you still received several flawless gems!'

'Yes, I was always a lucky dragon… but do you remember, Sep?'

'Of course I do! It was a very moving moment.'

'Did you ever dream we would spend our wish on babysitting duties and anthi… what's it?'

'Anthisan. No, I thought I'd spend it on self-healing—you know, from all your fire breathing.'

'Ha ha!'

'Hey, it's quiet! And the dragonettes are sleeping!'

That's because I am such a soothing person. And *you* have stopped stomping on their tails, tripping over their wings and sneezing on their pillows!'

'Ah choo!'

'See?'

The dragon grinned. 'Sep?'

'Yes?'

'Thanks.'

'No problem.'

'I guess friendship—true friendship—crosses all the boundaries.'

'I guess it does.'

'Wolfblane pie?'

'Are you mad? Friendship crosses boundaries, but digestion certainly does not! Wolfblane indeed! Want a chocolate?'

The dragon giggled. Behind him, half a dozen hatchlings opened their eyes.

And yelled.

Sep could see a whisper of smoke curling through several pairs of infant nostrils.

The wing bearer grinned.

'Guys, I hate to disturb this moving moment, but I better be off.'

'Sure. Thanks, Aradight.'

The dragon nodded vigorously. 'Yes, thanks, Aradight... Hey, what's in that sack?'

'What sack? Oh, this! It's just forget-me-dust... Oh, holly hocks!'

Aradight looked pale.

'What?'

'I'm in *so* much trouble!'

'Hey, calm down! What's the problem?'

'Oh, bloody, bloody hell! I'll probably be doomed to the kitchens with Madame Knorr! The corrector wand... I'll probably be hop-

ping in pain! I'll have a stupid purple blob on my backside for the
entire wing bearer presentation on Thursday!'

'What, what are you going on about?'

'Tell us, we're your friends! Perhaps we can help!'

But Scorcher sneezed at that point, which in no way made Aradight feel he was in any position to help.

'Tell us!' Septimus coaxed. He was greatly astonished to see a
competent wing bearer like Aradight looking so miserable.

'There's nothing you can do. I forgot to sprinkle Sarah with the
forget-me-dust and now, when I return, I will probably lose my wing
bearer's stripes. It is the worst kind offence, you know.'

Septimus did not know this, but he was not surprised. The base
magic kept the worlds separate and ignorant of each other. That was
part of how the balance worked, and he, he knew, was one of the few
exceptions.

'Mum will not use her knowledge. She will never betray my
father or, indeed, me, by revealing secrets.'

'That may be so, but only a great wizard or king can permit her
such knowledge. If every little wing bearer made judgments of human
character, it would not be long before our mysteries were uncovered
and the balance changed forever.'

'Yes, but in mum's case…'

'I agree. In your mother's case it's different, but I doubt the
Committee of Wing Bearer Ethics will see it that way! Ramón is on
holiday. He'd probably have been more lenient… oh jiminy jockle-
berries, unless I can rush back and sprinkle Sarah with forget-me-dust
I'll have to bloody well wave goodbye to my wing bearer stripes!'

'Go back, then!'

'It's too late! I don't know earth well enough to visualise in the
dark. Besides, there is roll call tonight. I have to be back.'

'Let us do it for you! I can visualise myself home, I am sure of
it!'

'Then how do you get back? Your entrance to Elvenswolde depends on Scorcher's wish. The bottling fairies won't be pleased to
do the same job twice. They'll become suspicious: very likely write

a report. I will be in even *more* trouble when the whole truth comes tumbling out!'

'What if Scorcher comes *with* me? Then I'm still attached to him, part of his first wish. He wanted to get better—mum has calamine lotion in her bathroom cupboard—wouldn't that simply be part of the first wish he made?'

Scorcher's excitement reverberated in Septimus's head.

'Quiet, Scorch! You're giving me a headache! Just give Aradight time to think this through!'

Aradight's panic subsided.

'It might... your visualisations would have to be *perfect* though, for Scorch does not know how to visualise yet... not in and out of Elvenswolde... that's surely a task for the seventh son of a seventh son...'

'I can do it!' Septimus hardly dared to breathe. Even Scorch seemed to be holding his breath, containing his dragon excitement.

The Forget-Me-Dust Calamity

'It won't work.'

Aradight's shoulders slumped. 'The elders are still fighting—they are on the ridge further than Mersham, towards the east. A day's flight back and most of them will be battered and bruised, too sore to fly. They will take the long way round, past Launsetton.

If they are anything like the last set of challengers, they will take a break, I suspect, by the slipstream of light. It flows east, upstream of the river of troubles. You will not see the dragons for days. For ten days they will feast upon wolfblane before making their return.'

'What, and leave me with those troublesome brats all that time?' Scorch gusted triple flames of indignation.

'Indeed! But you are proving a worthy nursemaid, Scorcher!'

'Hmph!'

'Can't we leave the little beasts to fend for themselves?'

'You know your heart is too soft to do that!'

'Please? Please Aradight? I will be so good… I will cause no trouble…'

'Famous last words, but *I* am in no position to lecture! I have to get back tonight. If I leave my sack here, no one will notice it's still full. I dare not just tip out the powder and pretend nothing has happened. It is dangerous for Sarah to have the knowledge she has. I'll not jeopardise Elvenswolde just to save my skin.'

'Very right! But if we can help?'

'If you can help, I suppose it might be ok! I'll ask the Order of Lindaliss if it has a moment to befriend a poor wing bearer elf!

Perhaps Xanadel might be inclined to mind a dozen or more dragon hatchlings—we'll never know unless we ask.'

Scorcher nodded in satisfaction.

'Xanadel and Wendleweed and ask Bickleberry too, mind! Preferably the whole order if we don't want chaos around here! The dragons are very tiring! Achoo!'

With an enormous sneeze (that woke Belgradious, one of the meaner dragonettes) Scorcher took the bag of forget-me-dust from Aradight.

'Hey! Give that back! No offence, Scorcher, but you are so clumsy you are likely to tear a hole in the bag and waste all of this stuff on Belcher, or whatever his name is! Get down, get *down*!'

For Belgradious was nipping at Septimus's ankles and trying to yank at the bag.

Septimus felt in his pockets and found a piece of chewing gum, which he flung as hard as he could into the dimness.

The dragon, sensing something interesting, immediately released his ankles—now distinctly sore and sporting several milk teeth holes like an Aztec anklet of some sort—and slunk into the gloom.

The last thing Septimus could hear before Aradight visualised himself back to the East Gate of Castle Carne was the frantic scratching of Scorcher, and a slow but rhythmic chew.

Belgradius, it seems, had found the gum.

* * *

Bickleberry and Xanadel were thrilled to seize the opportunity of being unofficial nursemaids to a series of naughty dragonettes.

Of course, Aradight might have glossed over a few of the more minor disadvantages, like their tendency to snarl, smoke, bite and chew, but there is no denying the principal keepers of the Order of Lindaliss were happy to oblige.

When they heard that Septimus was back in Elvenswolde, their delight was overwhelming. They would've set off for Sarcalet at once, were it not for the fact that it was dark, and the drawbridge round Castle Carne had long since closed.

There was no longer any danger from Móran (or none that they knew of) but wandering giants were known to wreak havoc in the Castle gardens if the moat was left unguarded at night.

As a consequence, the messenger elves had to wait for morning before setting off on their unusual mission.

They had to be utterly sensible about everything, for if word of the matter reached either the king or queen, poor Aradight would've been in terrible trouble.

Even now, he shivered and shook and hardly looked himself at all. He kept changing, at odd moments, into a bumblebee, which made Silvajar laugh, but not unkindly.

To settle him down, Wendleweed made a cup of toffee tea and Garredung, usually rather a sombre fellow, actually told a joke. It was not very funny, but it cheered Aradight.

All of the order wanted to go, of course, but in the end, it was decided by a serious game of paper, scissors, rock.

In Elvenswolde, real paper, scissors and rocks appear. The paper is made of ultra-fine, ice white parchment, the scissors are gold with very sharp points and the rocks are precious and semi-precious stones, usually topaz and emerald, but quite often rose quartz and diamond.

The winner gets to keep their object, so very few elves ever choose the paper, with the result that it is usually quite safe to choose rock. Only thing is, most elves want the jewels, so the game can turn out to be a very long one of rock, rock, rock, until someone, at last, has the brilliant idea of choosing the parchment.

Just one of the strange peculiarities of Elvenswolde and not one we will deal with any further here, though it is recounted quite eloquently in Elvenswolde: A compendium of games and their history.

It was decided—by this method—that Xanadel and Bickle would set out first, but Wendleweed and Garredung would follow a little later with a picnic lunch and several fresh tablecloths to serve as dragon nappies and wash cloths.

The evening shift would be Silvajar's responsibility, with a volunteer—either Bickle or Xanadel—staying on for an additional shift in the evening. That way, there would always be two elves on duty to deal with the hatchlings.

If Scorcher and Septimus did not return from their mission immediately, it would be up to the entire Order of Lindaliss to explain to the returning dragons what had happened to their hatchlings and why.

No one particularly looked forward to this task, but everyone was so excited that the bridge between earth and Elvenswolde had opened, once more, that they did not complain.

The elves had never before been in a dragon's cave. They did not like the smell much, but were surprised by the spaciousness and the opulent marble flooring that was reflected in the mirror pools and the crystal waters that flowed in fresh streams at the centre of the cavern.

Scorcher tripped over about seven dragon tails in his excitement to see Bickleberry and Xanadel again—dragons and elves do not frequently meet. (There have been some unfortunate instances of elves being gobbled by mistake, and, on the odd, excessively unfortunate occasion—on purpose.)

The hatchlings all cried in unison, and two were scratched by Scorcher's claws which made them snivel even more loudly. Luckily, Xanadel thought to bring a jar of honey-comfort-dragon-delight, a soothing cream that he applied liberally to the little creatures as he begged Scorcher to settle down and not set the entire cave alight with his dragon breathing.

Scorcher grinned. 'Not possible! Can't you see I have no furniture? No trinkets, no paper jets, no wooden chests for my jewels? No, I have kept my cave fire proof to avoid all disasters!'

At which moment he breathed an enormously large gust of fire and set all the dragon nappies and nappy bags alight.

The elves rushed to the crystal stream and with a hurried wave of the only magic wand they'd brought between them, managed to magic up some wooden buckets. In a flash, the fires were out, but the hatchlings all got soaked and Scorcher started coughing again.

'Oh, for heaven's sake, get him out of this cave before his racket wakes the last of the dragonettes!'

Xanadel, at his most sensible, sounded exasperated.

Scorcher looked hurt. His face itched and he generally began to look all miserable again. He decided to slink off and sulk while Septimus chatted to the former messenger elves.

'This should not take long. We just need to sprinkle the dust over my mum—she is quite prepared for it, you know—and hurry back. The biggest problem will be with my visualisations—I am out of practice, but I think I can do it. I will have to—Aradight's happiness depends on it and I owe Aradight a lot.'

'But Scorcher? Can you manage Scorcher?'

Septimus grinned. 'When have I ever managed Scorcher? But he and I are good mates. He won't let me down in his own mad, muddled way!'

'Where is he?'

'Oh, he has slunk into the bowels of the cavern. It seems to go on and on forever. I wouldn't be surprised if its trail leads right under Mt. Zircon itself!'

'Very likely. Dragons never like to be too far from Mt. Zircon, and Scorcher is apparently a prince of sorts. Seems he managed to organise palatial accommodations for himself.'

'Yes, but we'd better find him before he loses himself in his own home! Besides, I want to apply some of the honey-comfort-dragon-delight to his pocks. Apart from how it must feel, the poor creature looks utterly hideous!'

Septimus grinned. He could not help agreeing, but would not have dared say as much to Scorcher, for fear of offending him.

'I *hear* you!' came back the indignant mind thought from the back of the cavern. Septimus felt guilty. He had forgotten Scorcher could read his thoughts, just as he—most times—could read Scorcher's.

He was just about to apologise and tell his friend to stop skulking and sulking and generally being silly, when he felt, with certain shock, the dragon tremble from the very depths of the cave.

This was not a sick tremble, or even a clumsy tremble. It was a tremble of fear, or at least of the greatest concentration Septimus had ever felt.

'Scorch?'

There was no answer, only a mad buzzing in his head, almost as though Scorcher was trying to scramble his thoughts.

But that was impossible! Scorcher and he were friends! The dragon wouldn't shut him out, prevent him from understanding what was in his mind?

The buzzing grew so loud Septimus almost had a headache.

'Scorcher, *stop* that!'

Septimus had a sudden flash of blue, but then it melted away into the nothingness of a dragon-induced haze.

Sep hurried into the depths of the cavern, determined to see what Scorch was up to. He found him, at last, in a little twist to the left, bending under some stalactites. They were extremely gnarled and glinted in the shadows with hints of gold and an Elvenswolde metal called Quillion—very rare, and known for its magical properties.

Septimus ignored the stalactites and trod hard on his friend's tail. His soccer boots had spikes and even Scorcher could feel them through his scales.

'Ouch! What the heck are you doing?'

'What the heck are *you* doing, hiding your thoughts from me?'

'I'm not...' but Scorcher was blushing and Septimus knew him well enough to tell that he was lying.

'If you don't trust me, I'll just return to earth where I have friends that do!'

The guardian of Amberkine's words were hurtful, but he felt cross—very cross—with his dragon friend.

First he woke up all the hatchlings, then he sulked, then he hid his thoughts as if Septimus was his enemy rather than his very best, his very first friend in all the world, earth or Elvenswolde.

'I'm sorry, Sep. I don't want to involve you in this. Go away, will you?'

'Go away? Go away? Scorcher, are you crazy? What do you suddenly mean "go away" when Aradight is counting on us and when I've been away for nearly a year—three hundred and thirty-three long days to be precise?'

The blue dragon moaned softly to himself. Septimus was silenced when he saw very real tears roll down his itchy face and land in a giant dragon puddle at his feet. There is no sadder sight than a dragon tear, especially one of Scorcher's.

Septimus's tone became much gentler.

'Scorch? Scorch? What is it? You can talk to me, you can trust me. You know that you can. Something is bothering you. Maybe I can help. Come, talk to me.' He'd reverted to mind talk and the buzzing, at last, had stopped.

'Scorch?'

Scorcher stepped back and said nothing. But in that moment, that single, speechless moment, Septimus understood.

Sarah

Sarah was awash with memories. It seemed, now that the floodgates had opened, that she could remember more than just seeing Aradight.

No, it seemed that she remembered much, much more than her limited experience. She remembered the water sprites she had never seen, the wood nymphs, the dragons. She trembled as she remembered Móran, banished from Elvenswolde but still very much alive in another, darker world.

It seemed that her senses, once alert, were keener even than her son's. She could feel the tremors of all seven worlds, the growth, the music, the magic, the balance.

In her feet she felt the majesty of the base magic, in her head the delicious notes of the treble, all in total harmony, all trilling with a certain quiver of symphonic excitement, like some instrument not yet tuned to her world, but vibrant nonetheless.

She walked outside, into the pine forests, past the poplars and the ferns, past the Marlborough daisies and her grass-green cycads, lushly blowing in the Southern breeze.

She hugged secrets to herself. She forgot about shopping in town, or her work (someone else would have to open the library tearooms and switch on the heating), she forgot about worrying whether Septimus had a jersey or not.

Indeed, as she stepped deeper and deeper into the forest near her home, it seemed that her world was changing from earth to Elvenswolde, from ordinary to extraordinary.

In some ways—though she knew it was not true—it seemed that magic itself had crept into her and she was its very own, very special guardian.

She felt honoured, but also very vulnerable. It was too much knowledge for one of earth to bear.

She felt, for an instant, that the base magic held her in its thrall, that Móran, in one of the other worlds, was watching her, that earth had stopped turning on its axis and that the planet was in some kind of silent waiting

She wondered, as she bathed her face at the stream that was once so familiar now suddenly strange, why the forget-me-dust had not been sprinkled upon her as she'd expected.

Had that been accident or chance? Had that been with some kind of purpose? Impossible to tell, but she felt the waiting, and marvelled that at last, with clear vision, she knew. The boundaries were blurring for her, between earth and that other world. In a moment, she would be able to fly.

Of course, that was just a feeling, nothing true about it.

Sarah laughed at herself for even trying, but it was true that her feet felt lighter and her head felt almost like a balloon on her shoulders, daring her to just let go.

She was smiling to herself, reflecting on what Tom Watts or Ilene Reynolds (two very proper individuals) would do in her position.

What if they—and people like them—discovered that the lives they led with such monotonous regularity were not the only possibilities for themselves—that there was more out there than science or physics or pure mathematics?

That dragons were real, and wizards too, that there was a deep magic that formed the basis of all the worlds, more powerful than nature itself, or at least the nature of the world as it is taught.

What would they say then? Would they have the courage to believe, or would they shut their doors quickly, make up a gin and tonic on the rocks and ignore the facts as they presented themselves?

She would never know, of course, for Ilene and Tom would never be granted the glimpses she had been granted.

She treasured every moment, harbouring each one in her heart. She wondered whether Septimus could feel the connection she felt, and whether he was having any success with Scorcher (she'd heard many a tale of him!) and the other dragons.

Then, as she was in this quiet, contemplative state, she heard it.

Not the cooing of an earth baby, or the baaa of a lamb or the cheep-cheeping of a new born chick. No, it was a peculiar, throaty sound, gusty but strangely haunting, like a Celtic lyric caught on the wind. She needed no telling, somehow, that this was the cry of a baby dragon.

The gustiness ended on notes of sweetness a, tentative cry that melted her heartstrings and made all her motherly instincts come alive, as if born and reborn, shaped to sharpen the instincts, to transcend the delicate borders of earth and elf.

She thought she heard it, faintly in the wind, but the sound was replaced by turmoil and a strange anguish she could not understand, but which her heart leaned towards.

It seemed to her that the sky darkened and a sudden fear crept into her being.

The forest looked more closed than it had, and the air had a fresh crispness about it—the crispness of waiting.

In another world, far beyond her vision, a wizard stopped stirring his pot. His cloak was of silver, his nose long and distinguished. He was waiting, and somehow, his senses told him that this strange maiden of earth was his key.

A Dragon's Secret

Septimus leaned towards the stalagmites and touched his friend's long, bony scales. In normal circumstances he would not have contemplated such a thing, for Scorcher was clearly no longer a hatchling, and his adult armoury was too prickly and harsh to in any way be described as cuddly.

Septimus did not care.

He only thought about Scorcher and how he might be feeling. The enormous creature looked so, so sad.

'Scorch?'

The dragon turned about. For once his great dragon tail did not knock off ten ancient stalactites in his clumsiness. Instead, his movements were slow and he was very, very careful.

'What is it?'

'If I tell you, will you keep my secret?'

'Scorch, we're friends! You should not have to ask such a question. It is insulting.'

'Look.'

Scorcher opened his hands. His talons were long and black, but Septimus did not think he had ever seen the creature look so gentle before, or so besotted.

'I found it in the crack where the two caverns meet. See, there is a join over there. If you follow the darkness there is a cave system that branches both to north, north west and to the south. There is a small strand that links Mt. Zircon to this humble structure, but the path is all but closed and besides, I have grown too big now, to squeeze through.

'The point is that someone—anyone—could have crept in here unnoticed at some time. As a matter of fact, if one wished to abandon or destroy something without actually doing so, this is a perfect spot.

'It is cold from the crystal pools, there is no light for warmth or even accidental light (like when I might sneeze) for no one—not even me—ever comes down here.

'There is a path from Mt. Zircon which is unseen from the sky but can be used by a slenderer dragon than myself, maybe a woman. Or perhaps a huge dragon from north, northeast could have stolen in here, unseen. Alternatively, it is possible that destruction was intended all along.

'It's possible… coincidence alone might have caused it to bounce off some elderberry moss (very soft, you know) then find a chink in the passage system which would have caused it to roll—must have been gently because of the gradient—downwards. It is a marvel, in that case, that it was not pierced by a granite rock, but rather by this quillion stalactite. It is probably the magical properties of the quillion that ensured its survival.'

'Thanks for the geology lesson, Scorch, but if you don't want to die by instant throttling, you had better tell me at once what you mean by '*it*' *Wha*t it? *What* might have been destroyed? Step into the light, will you? It looks like you're holding a pebble of some sort, but I can't quite see. Come, tell me at once.'

Then Scorcher gently—infinitely gently—opened up his hand.

Even though it was very dark, and Septimus could just see the shadow of the creature's talons, his guess was confirmed. And though he could not, in the gloom, make out colour, he could work that out too. This was no pebble balanced delicately in Scorcher's hand.

No, it was an egg. Even without seeing it in the daylight, without the help of a wizard's flash of lightning to carve the sky in dramatic curves of brilliant brightness, Septimus knew.

It took quick wits and calm understanding to know that this egg—this particular sad, abandoned egg, must be a certain strange, shade of luminous blue.

The Dark Shall Sense and Creep

Móran could see nothing of Elvenswolde. Though he peered, night and day, in curious kaleidoscopes of earthen shades, though he struck tinder candles at the waxing and waning of their twin moons, though he called up incantations and howled at his creature Lennox, who resembled a wolf though his cunning was wilier than a fox, he could yet see nothing.

He was weakened by his last encounter with Elvenswolde, and by the joining of Lindaliss and Amberkine in that last, great challenge of the base magic.

Now he skulked in the lesser domain of the seventh world, a ruler, but not of that which he yearned to rule, a wizard but not yet over the realm of his desires.

Everything was dark to him. Everything of Elvenswolde, that is. His power was undiminished in the third world, where he dabbled from time to time. He'd never had any dealings with earth, either—no need to, chaos just seemed to sprout there of its own volition—but now he was drawn.

He wondered why, and why, of all places, to the tiny town of Rutherham, where Mt. Arthur meets the sea, and where it is a long, long way from more obvious cities of the earth world.

A cloud, long and thin, crept over the earth and caused a shadow to arch over the blue oceans surrounding the twin islands. Aotearoa, as it was known, in the Maori tongue. Not so different from ancient dragonesque of the fifth era.

He scanned the horizon searching for clues, his brewing pot overflowing and steaming with raw ideas.

Then he saw her, alone amidst the rata and the pine, the kauri and the silver birches that waved gently in the cool breezes of spring.

He saw her, and understood. Not love, but passion. Something of Elvenswolde was in her eyes. Her lips, though lazy with a longing he could hardly describe, were also beautifully sweet.

He felt a strong possessiveness of her. He wondered whether it was her beauty or her elven nature that made him feel that way. Yet she was of earth! She had nothing—could have nothing—to do with the world from which he had been expelled with such ignominy.

If he could have revenge, he would have, yet what could this earth child, slightly past her prime, more a mother than a maiden, have to do with the more ethereal other world?

He did not know, but as he watched her drink from the stream, crystal clear, so different from his cloudy visions of the elf world, he wondered.

* * *

The others were growing curious. Septimus could hear them advancing cautiously in the shadows.

'Leave the egg where you found it, Scorch! When we get back we will figure out what to do.'

'No! If it does not receive warmth, it is doomed. It will never hatch. Maybe it's already too late!'

Looking at it, Septimus thought that very likely it was. He did not say so, however—he was far too kind to make Scorcher more miserable than he already was. The abandoned egg seemed to be churning up all his old memories and first resentments. He, of all dragons, knew what it was like to suffer the tribulations of a shell that was blue.

'If it's too late, there's nothing we can do. If it's not, let us leave it here, where no one can find it or disturb it. It has shelter from the rain and has very likely rested here snugly for months. A few more hours will make no difference at all, but Aradight, think of Aradight! In a few hours he will be ruined if we don't help him. Come, Scorch!'

Septimus turned to go and watched as his friend dejectedly moved a small stone to wedge the egg back into place. He did not actually see Scorcher putting the distinctive blue item back in position, but he felt the change, for the dragon seemed suddenly cheerful again, a bit like his usual chatty self.

If Septimus had been at all suspicious, he might have wondered how it was that the dragon was suddenly so careful. For all the long, lumbering way back to the main entrance dome, he did not trip once, though he stumbled a bit on a tree root.

Thereafter, he was careful to walk only on the marble and to shuffle each giant claw off the ground so that he did not land up sliding, or gliding or plain falling flat on his handsome, silver (pity it was not gold) dragon nose.

As it was, Septimus was *not* suspicious. Why should he be? His head was filled with the urgency of getting back to Sarah and sprinkling the dust across her well-loved cheeks. He wished he did not have to, but he was wise enough not to try meddle with the age-old wisdoms of Elvenswolde. Sarah would understand—she always did. His heart filled with love for her.

Then, before they knew it, they were being hugged by Xanadel (a one-handed hug, for he was struggling with a giant dragonette who seemed to think the entire order of Lindaliss was a series of new baby rattles) and a handshake from Bickleberry, who looked most officious with a bib tucked in to a dragon with a nasty looking dose of Dragon Ipsiccocal D and G and—even possibly Z and C—spots.

Either way, there was a lot of firewalling—so much so that the sack of forget-me-dust was almost forgotten. Septimus wanted to give it to Scorcher, but Scorch was strangely reluctant and seemed to be holding his muscular dragon paw in a closed fist, something Septimus (who knew little about teenage dragons) did not understand.

In the end, it was he who clutched the powder bag. It was white in colour—a pure white that shimmered almost with silver. No, not silver—something more sparkly than that. It looked like it shimmered with stars, but if you gazed at it properly it was just white, after all.

A strange sack, and sewn all from one piece, ribboned in red with curling tassels that required only a simple adjustment of the hand to part open.

Apparently, elfin dust applied itself without too much shaking from the administering wing bearer. So long as the red tassels were correctly opened, sprinkling Sarah would be as easy as calling her name.

Septimus closed his eyes and visualised carefully. He hardly moved, at first, and was very disappointed to hear two dragonettes squabbling from behind him. If he could hear them still, then his concentration was not good enough. He tried not to hear Wendleweed scolding, or the arrival of the relief team from Castle Carne.

It would have been good to catch up with the other elves, but there was time enough for that later. He cleared his mind—told Scorcher to stop blocking his thoughts, the matter was tricky enough as it was—and took a deep breath inward.

Blood

Sara walked slowly back to her home. She had a peculiar feeling in the pit of her stomach, as though someone was watching her. The sensation was not comforting, but rather cold and cruel.

She was never usually fearful, but today she walked back across the small bridge and through the pines quickly, as though she were being followed, though she knew this was untrue.

She almost locked the doors of her home, but then scolded herself for being ridiculous. Instead, she put on the jug and prepared for herself a strange herbal concoction of chamomile root, ginseng and blackberry infusion.

Septimus hated this particular drink, much preferring 'normal' tea, as he made a point of saying, and milk with heaps of sugar.

Sarah stirred carefully and sipped slowly. Her head was filled with Elvenswolde. So full that she did not notice the sudden presence in her room, the stirring cold, the very hand of Móran stretching out towards her.

When she turned, it was too late. He was there beside her, smiling a silky smile, his cloak glowing a curious silver and spirals of some unknown language spilling letters above her head and curling in great coils across her kitchen floor.

'Who are you?' Sarah managed to whisper. She felt that she should be overjoyed at this sudden sign that that other world, whose presence she had so fiercely believed in but only been dimly aware of for so long, was now revealing itself to her.

She wasn't. She felt afraid, despite the handsomeness of the wizard's face and the strange smile that lurked upon his lips.

'I should ask the same of you. Who are you, earth maiden, to disturb my consciousness so? '

Sarah did not answer. She could not help noticing that the strange letters were coiling a little, and now again looked very much like silver snakes with little ruby eyes that became full stops and commas whenever she focused more closely.

She picked up her mug and drank deeply from its contents. It was better, she thought, to be drinking. That way she wouldn't be trapped into a hasty answer.

The wizard's eyes narrowed.

'What potion is that? I am unfamiliar with the smell and I am an expert in such matters.'

Sarah believed him and her heart sank. What chance did she have against a wizard—for there was no doubt in her mind that she was staring into the sly, slightly sarcastic face of one of the best.

Not Ramón—Septimus had had much to say about Ramón, and his face held none of the warmth and the wisdom she would have expected.

Móran? Her heart sank. She had to think it might be he, for his cloak was silver and he did not look kind. But Móran had been vanquished, was no longer a part of Elvenswolde... but then, anything might have happened in the year that Septimus had become Wishbinder, Guardian of Amberkine.

She knew the story well, though of course she'd had to be satisfied with imagining everything—the bridge to Elvenswolde was closed to her. And yet... and yet today she did not feel it was closed.

Besides, she could hardly ignore the truth of her eyes. Here, in her modest kitchen, leaning against her fridge magnets (she collected flowers, fairies and turtles) was proof positive that she was not dreaming, that that strange other-world was colliding, somehow, with her own.

A snake hissed and she jumped. The wizard laughed. 'Afraid of my curling 'g's?'

'Only if they bite. But I suspect they're just an illusion. Your magic will not be strong enough on this earth. If it was, the balance would be overset.'

'Ah, you know about balance, do you? You are no ignorant earth maiden. I ask again, who are you? Or shall I take you back to my world—the seventh world, whose very name I dare not utter lest it shatter your sweet little earth to pieces?'

Sarah trembled, for she did not know the wizard's powers, whether such a thing were possible, or where, even, in the great celestial scheme, the seventh world lay.

It was a place of shadows, she knew that well enough, for it counterbalanced Elvenswolde of light.

It was where, she remembered, Móran, the silver one had been banished.

No, she could not allow herself to be kidnapped. What of Septimus? What of her home, here on earth?

'Are you Móran?'

The wizard lost his smile. It was not often his name was spoken. It disturbed him that this insignificant woman of earth knew anything about him at all; it unsettled him and disrupted his powers.

He reached for his staff, but in earth it was a stick, a common stick, mildewed a little, but firm nonetheless. It was made of a bark that was hard, hard enough to stand the ravages of time, but brittle enough to break. He gripped it in the ancient way and for a moment it sparked, and the letters became lakes, and the seraphs, the curling commas, became the dreadful hiss of serpents.

Then it broke with the weight of the magic bearing it down, broke with the enormity of the wizard's wishes colliding with ground's gravity—the world of science and the world of magic balanced in unequal terms.

Science won, for the influence of earth is large. Móran suppressed his rage and threw down his staff, rendered useless. He lunged for Sarah, but she was too swift, and dodged his clawing touch even as she poured scalding jug water on his toes.

Móran roared, seizing her dress, long and flowing, pulling her towards him, pulling the earth maiden towards the shadows of the seventh world. He would drag her there, he would bind her, he would make her his slave… he was so enraged that his very anger gave him strength. His feet hissed with steam but he ignored them, ignored Sarah's earth scream, her chanted incantations…

He stopped. He felt the strength draining from his system. A witch, this creature of earth, for she was resisting him, resisting with her powers. He could not understand it. He shifted position and entered her thoughts. Ah! It was love, a mother's love, a woman's love… she was reflecting them back at him, using them as a shield… he sneered.

A woman's trick, but a wily woman… he looked about for a defence. He had the antidote for love, he needed only another staff. He would have to settle for one that was hewn of earth, now that his own was rendered useless.

His eyes flitted to the fireplace. That one would do! That one would do very nicely, thank you! He stretched out his hand and the ancient piece of wood, gnarled and sanded by Sarah herself, rose from the mantel and glided softly into his waiting hand.

In that split second, Sarah froze. The serpents flickered back, and this time they no longer seemed like an illusion, they seemed lifelike, their tongues flickering as if to taunt her.

It was a second where the world became an opening to some other world, a darker place that no man had ever tread. Sarah felt the pulling, the tug on her hair and her heart. She felt it and resisted it, though it seemed almost too big for her, too overwhelming.

She swallowed her fear and lunged for the staff, willing it to become the stick again, the tired, lowly earth stick she knew so well.

He'd taken it from her hearth, the very centrepiece of her home. He had stolen it from where it nestled among the brushes and pans, he had robbed it of its happy memories.

Memories of a better, brighter time, when she had taken Septimus on a bushwalk and found its rough shape lying sprawled in a pond full of rushes. They'd taken it and sanded it, she and Septimus, and treated it with love. It was dark swamp kauri, thousands of years old, dry from a hundred summers above ground but, burled and mottled with age. She and Sep had gingerly sanded off the splinters and weaker, rotten pieces. Like buried treasure, it had revealed ancient hues of rose amid the ebony, marvels in striations and planes, but geologically quite definitely of earth. It represented many, many evenings, tens of hours, incalculable company and the deep warmth of shared effort and home.

Now it was being used against her.

She felt the vacuum that Móran created, rushing her senses. She was being sucked towards an invisible hole, a hole that had no time, no dimensions, no boundaries she could understand. It was only now that earthly physics was beginning to make the discoveries of the deeper things, the vacuums, the untrammelled energies…

She forced herself to resist, to think of Septimus, to think of his father before him, of Elvenswolde, of all the little things she cherished, of happiness itself… she clung to earth as a creature of light clings to the sun. She closed her eyes to the shimmering serpents regarding her with ruby eyes.

Móran was startled at this show of strength, this unexpected resistance from a small creature. For Sarah was small to him, a creature void of magic—undoubtedly beautiful and startling to the senses, but insignificant in the great battles of the worlds.

He set down the stick and cajoled, coaxing Sarah through the vortex he had created. He offered her magic, freedom, the chance to live as queen… his queen… mistress of the seventh world, a world larger and more powerful than earth, a place for witchcraft…

Sarah remained unmoved. He whistled, and called up his hound Lennox…

Lennox from the darker world, Lennox, his creature in hatred, wilier than a fox, with teeth as sharp as burnished knives.

He came, as he always did when called, and at the sight, the very serpents quivered and turned, once more, to letters, strange letters, written in a language Sarah could not understand, a language which defied the base magic even as it invoked its powers.

Lennox the wolf eyed Sarah hungrily.

He had not had a meal in three days—Móran kept him lean and ravenous for just such occasions as these. He was clever enough to know the difference between off limits and prey. The woman smelled, to him, very much like prey. His mouth watered.

'Down, Lennox, down! She is to be frightened, not eaten. You can have her when I am finished with her.'

Lennox whined. He would rather have her now. He took a step forward but the wizard's whistle stopped him like a lash. His ears burned and his tail felt singed.

'Later, I said! Now bite her, just a little, just enough to convince her to cross my thresholds.'

Thirsting for blood, the creature needed no further telling. His padded feet crossed the space between wizard and woman in no time at all. Sarah did not know, at that moment, which was the greater horror: wolf or smiling warlock.

'Bite, Lennox, but don't disturb her beauty. An arm, maybe, or a little, teeny, taste of leg. Tear at the flesh but leave her fair face intact. It will be awash with tears and tears have always had their uses.'

The words were so calm, so hauntingly evil that Sarah thought she might faint. But fainting is no option for the brave.

'Eat, then. Eat, creature of the dark, but you will never know my name, nor the contents of my heart. If I have powers, they shall never be yours. If I have dreams, I hold them dear. Whatever you ask me, whatever you do, you shall know nothing of my thoughts. These are my own.'

Lennox howled and lunged towards her, piercing her skin with teeth that looked like rods of sparkling crystal. They would have sunk deeper, oh, so much deeper, but for the sneer of Móran. Lennox was held back with a steely smile—the glance was as sinister as it was keen.

Pain and shock shook Sarah. The graze on her skin brightened to blood and the very sight made her heart stammer and her legs stumble.

'A taste, I said, not a feast!'

Sarah watched the blood trickle slowly from elbow to fingers. It seemed that her ears became more finely tuned to the wind and that there was a sudden, rushing noise from the east. She closed her eyes and shivered.

Journey to Rutherham

Somewhere across time, Septimus was also shivering. He was freezing cold, the hair on his arms sticking straight out, like porcupine quills.

'Where are we?'

Scorcher had interrupted the visualisation and now they were lost, hopelessly lost.

Septimus groaned. Things looked different from a height, especially from the back of a giant blue dragon. Scorch's shadow was cast lazily across buildings and sea, elongating him, making him look thinner.

No one looked up, save an old lady in a camel coloured hat. She never saw the underbelly of a dragon, only that the sky was remarkably dark. Her spotted umbrella opened in an instant.

'Scorcher, you crazy lunatic, we are way off course! Stop distracting me!'

But Scorcher did not look nearly alarmed enough. His claw was still closed, but the anguished expression had vanished. In fact, he looked almost as happy as the night he'd been granted a casket of rubies!

To emphasize this sudden elation, he felt it necessary to swoop and dive. Septimus felt it necessary to scream, swear and clutch on for dear life. He was so sick he almost dropped the precious bag of forget-me-dust. It would have landed, for sure, on the spotted umbrella.

'Scorch!'

But the son of Demetria, the great Dargonville princeling, refused to listen. One more swoop and oops! He'd accidentally knocked out all of the power south of the Bombay Hills.

Was he electrocuted? No, only slightly blackened about his wing tips. Also, his talons tickled.

'Scorch! Slow down, you're wreaking havoc!'

'Ah, be nice, Sep! Tell you what, I'll write a poem in your honour. I'm quite good, you know!'

Septimus did *not* know. He was clinging on for all he was worth, and frankly Scorcher's back had prickles. He was really not amused.

Scorcher flashed a little fire. He was clearly showing off.

'Don't believe me? It must be my colour. Green dragons are all hopelessly illiterate. I, however, am...'

'... a pain in the neck!'

The dragon laughed.

The amulet about Septimus's neck glowed with its hidden fires. The bottle blue suddenly looked brighter than a Ceylonese sapphire. The deep fires within flamed to a brilliant orange. Danger.

Septimus hardly noticed, his head was spinning so much.

Then, of course, the tiresome dragon had to notice Rainbow's End far below. Very soon, he was offering flights to poor, unsuspecting children. He was apparently far more attractive than the swinging pirate ship, or even the rollercoaster. Septimus was furious and forced to open his little sack here and there, sprinkling forget-me-dust liberally onto the faces of astonished adults.

'Scorcher! We are wasting time! Have you forgotten Aradight? Hurry, hurry!'

So reluctantly, Scorcher melted three toffee apples and gobbled some pink candy floss down, stick and all.

He rose higher and higher, stopping only to roll in boiling mud at the geothermal pools in Rotorua. Then he spiralled past Whakawerrawerra, with its hissing geysers spewing heat and water from the depths of earth itself—very effective for a case of dragon Ipsicoccal D and G's, so they say.

The rising steam obscured his dragon shape. Lucky.

Septimus stretched his legs and tried to control his impatience. He was a kindly kid, and could see that the mud was soothing, the steam astonishingly pure and cleansing.

He was not so pleased, though, to find himself seated next to Scorcher's treasure. The object nestled next to him was clearly no ostrich egg (too big) and no earth egg. Its colour was suspiciously blue.

From the safety of twenty meters of mud, the dragon smiled. His teeth were large and uneven, and Septimus detected a developing cavity. (Too much Sticklethwaite, as it happened.)

'Scorcher!' Septimus called crossly.

'Get out of that mud this instant! You are a bad dragon!'

The bad dragon grinned and breathed fire, but only sparks emerged. Thermal mud was clogging up his nostrils.

'It will be safe, now. That is all I care about. Safe from braggarts and bigots like Cruncherton and Merchison! What if they win the contest? You *know* what dragons of the old school are like... they'll order all the blue eggs crushed. They will hunt them out, maybe even still put me or the princess on trial. Dragons have long memories. Thousands of years! It is unfair, Sep! Why should a perfectly wonderful hatchling be left for dead?'

'But you can't transport it to another world! New Zealand's MPI, in charge of biosecurity, will have a fit!'

'Who?'

'Ministry for Primary Industries. It is against the law! It will upset the balance!'

Even to Septimus this seemed like a weak argument. Scorcher did not deign to answer it other than with a muttered mumble.

'Oh, all right then!'

The dragon rid his nostrils of mud. Then he gave the most almighty of flamed roars and grinned.

'Isn't she just beautiful? Isn't she? Huh, huh?'

'Guess so. Lovely egg! How do you know it's a girl?'

'Oh, paternation of the shell, stuff like that. Lazy little thing! See, if I tap her she just rolls to the other side. But a warm and feisty heart! No doubt about that! See, she breathes faster as I speak.'

It was true, the blue seemed to shimmer a little, as Scorcher growled in his new adult voice. Septimus marvelled at this curious insight and at the tenderness of his great, clumsy friend.

He could wreak havoc with a thousand power lines, tumble over toes, but not once, on this long, strange journey, had he made a single crack in this pretty blue egg.

'Very well. We shall take it to mum. She's great with animals.'

Scorcher nodded and turned his back. He sniffed.

He did not want Sep to see his sudden tears. Besides, dragon tears could flood the region, clogging up the waterways, causing sudden tides, tsunamis in rare cases...

So he sniffed again. He'd grown very attached to his egg. It would be hard to leave it and return to Sarcalet, but he knew this was the safest thing to do.

He turned back to his friend, but unfortunately impaled the seventh son with his tail, so that Sep had to scramble to his feet almost in a daze.

A laughing daze, 'cos Scorcher was still Scorch, no matter how big he'd grown. The dragon felt more cheerful.

'Sorry!'

They flew, then, with no further mishaps (other than a slight playful splash into Lake Taupo, an enormous crater lake in the centre of the north island, and a quick circle over Huka falls.) When Sep complained, the dragon only smiled. It was not every day a Dargonville prince went sightseeing! Certainly not on earth, that is!

Scorcher accelerated, and Septimus concentrated on his visualisation... Wellington, the Cook Strait, the incredible Marlborough Sounds... horror flooded Septimus's bones.

A glance at the amulet showed it blazing. Scorch felt the danger too, for he scooped up the egg, threw Septimus up on the broadest expanse of his back and began his wing flap before the wishbinder had mouthed a single word.

'Visualise, Sep. Show me, just show me the way.'

Trembling, Septimus concentrated on the washing hanging on his line, on his bicycle propped up against the fence post, of the door to the kitchen, slightly peeling, the freesias in the drinking glass… almost, almost, he was there.

Then in one concentrated visualisation, he actually was, and the darkness was upon him.

The Wink

Dragon snacks were over, and the elves were exhausted.

Left-over dishes of minced newt brain and wolfblane softened in lard seemed to be scattered everywhere.

Xanadel, Bickleberry and Wendleweed were singing soothing songs. Xanadel sung the loudest, on account of the fact that his grandmother was a sooth singer. Unfortunately, the family gift had not been passed down, and even Silvajar, whose voice was not exactly melodious, winced.

Still, the dragonettes seemed to like it, for they stopped nipping each other and snarling whenever one of them was squashed. (This was frequently, because what with the hatchlings, the elves, the food, the nappy bags, the itching powder, the dragon rattles and the Garredung family potion bottle, the main hall of Scorcher's cavern was now messy and cramped.)

Bickleberry was not being very sensible. He was frolicking with the hatchlings and inciting them to play tag. Two ugly creatures had already broken off three stalactites and one centimetre of stalagmite in their excitement.

The quillion was oozing from both ceiling and floor, causing little wisps of magic to pop here and there, transforming this and that, until Xanadel had to stop his singing in annoyance.

Very soon, however, the hatchlings all yawned and after some encouraging head pats, burping, bed time stories and one (only one) threatened dragon spanking, the cavern was echoing with sleepy snores.

In the distance, the battle raged on. Occasionally, one could hear the fearsome sound of a dragon horn snapping, or a howl that made the entire order of Lindaliss shiver a little, and thank their lucky stars they were safe in Scorcher's uncomfortable cave.

They did not know many of the dragons, but they knew enough to hope that it was Demetria, not one of the older, bolder creatures, who won the contest. The King of Elvenswolde had always had a treaty with the dragons.

He granted them the fiefdom of Sarcalet to rule as their own in return for allegiance. It was a good arrangement, but if one of the fiercer dragons were to take the leadership… it would be a sad day if dragons and elves were no longer at peace.

The elves whispered quietly to themselves. Garredung was wearing the Amulet of Lindaliss, twin of Amberkine. He stiffened, as the blue fires deepened.

'Trouble, but far away.'

'Could it be the dragons?'

'It might, but their fight is not enough to invoke the base magic, or upset the balances.'

'What, then? Septimus?'

'I fear so.' Silvajar looked grim, for though there'd been a time when he and Sep were mortal enemies, those days were long gone, rendered void by friendship, trust and growth. Septimus was now the guardian of the amulet of Amberkine, and so they were bound by the jewels as much as by friendship.

Bickle, tired from patting scaly heads, looked up in alarm.

'Let's sit in a circle and invoke our elfin strength. Let's call to Lindaliss and fling the magic far. Perhaps, unlike our humble selves, it will know where it is needed.'

'Bickle, I do believe you are being sensible!' Xanadel smiled, though he was as worried as the others.

'There is nothing more we can do while we have the responsibility of the hatchlings. Let us unite our thoughts intensely, our love passionately, our truth utterly. Perhaps the quillion will help too. It hovers like mist, seeking direction.'

So it was agreed. The order of Lindaliss formed a circle and sat quietly, hand in hand, as their magic grew upon them like a cloak. Ramón, so far afield, would have been proud.

At the precise moment that the circle of elves was gathering force, Scorcher felt his wings rip against the glass sliding doors of Sep's earth home.

He bled from the sudden slicing of his scales. The blood distracted that other menace within, Lennox.

Lennox, circling Sarah and the silver wizard circling Lennox.

What a strange, dreadful sight. Septimus had only a flash to take it in, or understand that against nature, against all he knew of the magical order, Móran was back. Not in Elvenswolde, but almost worse, in his own home.

Móran and an Astran wolf. A wolf whose eyes were both bleak and very, very cold.

Those eyes had been on Sarah, drops of blood trickling down her arm. He wanted so much to eat her, but the wizard—his wizard—was unkind.

His hunger was growing stronger with her scent, so strong that he thought, any minute, he could rip at the leash of magic that restrained him. Ooh, so cruel that restraint!

How hungry the wizard kept him! Drops of wretched saliva touched the floor.

He knew it not, but it was the magic of Lindaliss, so far away in Elvenswolde, that kept him at bay. Now, the presence of Amberkine blinded him so that he could just smell blood. The difference between dragon and maid seemed not so very great, after all.

'Oops, sorry!'

Scorcher, not fully perceiving the danger, was worried about wrecking the earth maiden's door.

He grinned at Sarah—for he was partial to wood nymphs—then roared as Lennox lunged for his chest. At first, it was the roar of pain and sharp surprise.

Then the roar became something more. It was the roar of a full-fledged dragon on the hunt. Hungry, hungry for wolf meat and pride at the kill.

Lennox had no chance. The roar chilled him to the marrow as he turned tail, desperate to flee to the nether regions of the seventh world.

The wizard's charm held its force, binding him to earth and to the dragon's roar about his ears.

Scorcher's jaw snapped, smoke billowed from his nostrils and flames from his very breath. There was the strange, slightly pleasant sizzle of charred meat (rather like a barbeque, only faster), then Lennox was gone.

For an instant, the world was still.

Septimus—who'd scrambled off Scorcher's back—Sarah, the wizard… all looked transfixed at the enormous, powder-blue dragon. There was no longer a sign of Lennox.

Scorcher burped. 'Aah, excuse me!' he said. He dragon blinked.

No one understood a word. It sounded like *GGGrrr PPPPlew Rroarareerwwee*.

'Hey, aren't you…'

Móran did not stop to listen. The staff had only a faltering degree of magic—the interference of earth was too great. In this environment, he had a mere shadow of his power.

Worse, he felt the presence of love and friendship all about him. Then there was Amberkine… Amberkine that should have been his!

Fear suppressed his fury.

The dragon—silly creature—was staring at him curiously through the sliding door. In a moment or two his great, snaking talons would be inside… Móran found the opening to his world and fled.

Sarah, released from her fear, laughed a little shakily. She touched her arm and wiped the blood from her sleeve. Her nightmare was over. She hated dwelling on awful things she couldn't change.

So, brave woman, she smiled instead.

'Come in, Scorcher, dear! I assume by your beautiful colour—she didn't mention his clumsiness!—that you are he?'

The dragon blushed. Yes, the silver crest of his nose actually turned pink.

'Of course you are, though much handsomer than I expected!'

Septimus grinned. 'Yes, mum! And did you notice his appetite? An entire wolf and all before tea!'

'Talking about tea, dear, put the jug on, will you? That man has given me a nasty thirst. I will see if I can find a plaster for my arm and perhaps a bed sheet for Scorch—to bind his wing, you know?'

This Sarah did, and very soon they were sipping chamomile tea (Scorch's from a bucket) and discussing the pressing matter of the blue egg.

Sarah regarded it closely, then murmured it looked very much like accitarnia ori, a rare form of ostrich found on the islands of Malagasy. She was positive she could tend it for hatching, then feed it a protein diet of sorts, not wolfblane in lard, but possibly lashings of pork with a butter sauce.

She looked happy, happier than Septimus had ever seen her before. The wild yearning was gone from her eyes and he could almost imagine what she must have been like, on that fateful day when Septimus, his father, first missed the alignment of Ventrimuse.

No wonder he'd given up his world for her! She was beautiful and kind and everything a boy could wish for in a mum.

Septimus grinned, but his smile faltered as he remembered what had to be.

'Mum, you'll forget. You'll forget about Elvenswolde and Scorcher and all that you have seen. It will all seem a dream to you, the stories I tell will be stories only—ones you wish to believe, but are not part of.'

'I know that, Sep.' Sarah sounded suddenly sad, sadder even than in the face of evil, when she'd defied Móran himself.

'Let me keep the egg. I will tend it with care and if a dragon is born—well, I'll doubtless mistake it for accitarnta ori until it grows too large!'

'When it does,' Scorcher thought (and Sarah heard him too, which just goes to show something about genetics and her strange affinity for the other worlds, most curious in a human), 'I will come for it. I will span the worlds again even if I have to use every wish in the world and the last of my elfin rubies!'

So, it was decided. The egg, suddenly so warm with life, sparkled brighter than ever. It was placed in Sarah's sewing basket—empty—and tucked with a pillowcase of down-stitched feathers.

When Scorch politely mentioned dinner—for dragons get very hungry when they are having fun—he was taken far, far past the horizon to a place just off the shores of Kaikoura (eat crayfish in the Maori language), where he could catch crayfish, paua and rock lobster to his heart's delight. Kaikoura, he was told, had recently suffered a dreadful earthquake, but sea life was now regenerating beautifully. The Marlborough Sounds had incredible salmon farms, but this was strictly off limits to a greedy dragon. No matter, he was perfectly happy with lobster. He was remarkably good at diving, given his teeny tiny tendency to clumsiness and general calamity.

In fact, it was a regular picnic, for when they returned to the house, he obligingly cracked open the shells, barbecued them on his breath and refrained from eating all but a hundred and three of them. Cooked crayfish, he felt, were exactly like perfect dragon nibbles.

(He very politely did not mention that they were kind of tasteless compared with wolfblane.)

Septimus teased him mercilessly about his boasts about poetry.

Even Sarah teasingly referred to him as 'dragon laureate' until Scorcher got cross and determined to prove himself.

He took a deep breath, then was struck dumb by a sudden dose of shyness (not to mention an itchy recurrence of the ipsiccocal D and Gs).

Sarah soon soothed him, by dint of deft persuasion, the application of a mud pack, the provision of soothing lozenges, a large dollop of Anthisan, and of course, a kiss.

Septimus, who hated fuss, would have thought this treatment hideous. Scorcher, craving maternal love as all blue dragons do, lapped it up in bliss. Very shortly, he was able to speak, and soon thereafter, his nose silvered up in glory.

He puffed out his wings, knocked over the freesias (no one minded) and cleared his throat (which really wasn't necessary since he was using thought speech):

If I could at a banquet be,
seated right upon your knee,
The foods I'd really wish to see
Are the types we'd share, just you and me.

Let us take one plate—beware,
leave some crays: we must be fair,
Serve me wolfblane, one whole share,
for caviar I cannot bear.

If I could at a concert be,
Dragon-dreaming harmony,
I'd puff
out smoke in synchrony.
then hum with you in symphony

Let us choose viol and flute,
Eschew the cymbals and the lute,
Seventh son and Scorch still cute,
With soothing songs—
and roars on mute,

But oh, indeed,
I'm dragon dreaming,
Sarcalet is all its seeming
Septimus and me we're teaming
Magic, myth
and elves well meaning.

Then Scorcher looked at Sarah:

And though I seem to have a mum
it really is a lot more fun
to not restrict, in song and sum,

to only huge and only one…
So Sarah dear, pretty please,
on wings and paws and on my knees
When on earth, 'cross elvin seas
kiss my nose and make decrees,
Be my mum…
Oops oops oops
I'm going to sneeze!
Atchoo! Atchoo! Atchoo!

At which all the raked leaves, in pretty piles, flew into the air and scattered like petals over the lawn.

There was a moment's silence. Then Sarah clapped so loud her hands hurt.

'Well done, Scorch! You can be Sep's brother and my own, personal dragon Laureate!'

She tiptoed up and kissed his silver nose.

'Very distinguished,' she whispered.

'Much better than a gold nose. You shall have a prize.'

A prize? Scorcher was beside himself. He forgot to keep his head down and caught his long neck on the ceiling beam.

'Oops, sorry!'

'Never mind, dear, we can paint over the crack. Wait there, will you? No, not another step into this house!'

Scorch wondered whether Sarah would return with jewels. Septimus laughed and said it was unlikely.

In the end, it turned out to be better than jewels: better, that is, for a dragon struck by a severe case of the ipsicoccals.

Sarah handed him an enormous bottle of Calamine Lotion. The contents were pink and looked very, very soothing.

As large, loving flames billowed from his nostrils, Sarah ducked. Scorcher's kiss lit three birthday candles instead.

All too soon, it was time to leave.

Aradight was waiting and no one—not even the meanest elf—would wish him to be punished by Madame Knorr and her hideously correct (not to mention vigorous and mean-spirited) corrector wand.

Septimus hesitated over the forget-me-dust. He could not bear to sprinkle it over his mother, and almost believed he wouldn't.

Then a gentle wind, born of magic and peace and kindness, helped him in his task. The dust seemed to flow out the bag, out his hands and over Sarah.

Her eyes, when she gazed at them, were still bright, but that was the brightness of love. Of Elvenswolde and understanding, there was no recognition.

'Goodbye, mum.'

Septimus kissed her gently and her heart was just as devoted, though she moved in a dream. Soon her knowledge lessened, the dust spilled over her hair and the entrance to the seventh world snapped shut.

There would be no more openings between earth and that other, darker world.

Móran had gained access only through Sarah's heightened awareness of the forces, and the pull of Elvenswolde. She'd challenged the balances a little, but now that door was sealed.

Septimus breathed easier for it, though he was sad, so sad, for Sarah's sake. It was not only the seventh world. Elvenswolde was closed to her too.

Then it was time—high time—to leave.

Scorcher knew his own cave like the back of his talonned paw. He used his mind thoughts to guide Sep in his visualisation, so they ended up precisely—no fun detours!—where they had started: under Mt. Zircon.

Crunch!

Scorcher stubbed his toe on landing.

Three stalagmites dislodged as the echo of crunch runch unch unch unch seemed to echo like some orchestral chaos.

'We're back!'

Scorcher grinned, his spots now pink with calamine but fading fast.

Silvajar sat up first. 'The forget-me-dust? It's done?'

'It's done. Aradight shall not be punished for his kindness. I've hardly had a moment to thank him for bringing me back to Elvenswolde.'

Septimus helped Wendleweed to his feet.

'You shall, tonight. At the feast of the dragons, when the new leader is to be robed. It's also, of course, the traditional treaty signing ceremony so we had better find good seats!'

Scorcher had forgotten all about dragon politics with his excitements.

'Is it a very fierce dragon?'

'Of course. The fiercest.' Xanadel looked grave, but his eyes twinkled.

Scorcher growled.

'If I have to swear allegiance to that great brute Cruncherton I shall personally belch!'

'Hush! Learn to hold your tongue!' Septimus frowned.

'Oh, stop worrying! Shall we tell them?'

Xanadel giggled a little.

'Tell us what?'

The elves could hardly contain themselves.

'Scorcher is now a high prince!

'Demetria tricked Cruncherton into a corner and rammed so hard his horns cracked. She lost a tooth and suffered a severe case of Dargonzoalia concussion, but would you know it? The great oaf was so embarrassed he slunk away to Willowsham.

'After that, the remaining dragons lost heart.'

Well! It was no wonder the hatchlings all woke up.

Such a noise!

Such rejoicing as caused several stout stalactites to tumble to the floor. The cave shook for a moment, but no one seemed to mind. The force of nature must, after all, gain expression.

The elfin cakes were gobbled by all except Scorcher, who was feeling a trifle queasy. (Lennox was proving hard to digest.)

'Hurry, hurry. We have an audience with His Majesty at three. Ramón will be there and yes, Septimus, all the old friends. Your brothers too. Ganimeade, Fairmeade… you shall greet them before your return.'

And speaking of returns, at Sep's place, a little hatchling was plotting one as she cracked open just the teeniest, tiniest corner of her shell.

She caught sight of Sarah, staring at her, staring so intensely she could almost understand her thoughts.

Come to think of it, she *did* understand her thoughts!

The dragonette smiled.

She was adorable and knew it: perfectly pretty with lashes that curled across elongated eyes. She was also very, very snug in her feather down.

There was no better place for a shell—and she should know—she'd been squashed in a nasty crack under smelly Mt. Zircon for months.

She peeked out again.

Yes, she was still there, that earth maiden. She smelt of the wilds, of promises.

Through the crack, the cutest (and naughtiest) dragonette ever to consider hatching, decided to wink.

And Sarah, Sarah of earth?

She most solemnly winked back!

Acknowledgements

Thank you, dragons, wing bearers and messenger elves, for so diligently whispering this story in my ear. Since you have now progressed to quarrelling, interrupting and shouting out in turns, I suspect a sequel is standing by!

Thank you to the wonderful editorial team at Calumet, especially Steve McEllistrem, for both accepting this manuscript and editing with such skill and insight.

Thank you to Raoul, my incredibly gifted son, who will doubtless be cringing when he reads this, but I think everyone will agree his cover design is AWESOME!

Thanks to Rhaz, Raphael and Raoul, the inspiration for this entire tale. Without you guys, I would never have ventured into fantasy. (I can't remember which of you decided Bickleberry, Garredung and Silvajar were great names, but hey, thanks!!!)

Finally, to Clive, my best friend and, coincidentally, husband—life with you has been magical. Thanks for being my greatest admirer. You have given me the gift of self-belief.

Hayley

About the Author

Hayley Ann Solomon (MA) is an award-winning author and poet. She is published in multiple genres, including poetry through Proverse, Hong Kong, and historical romance through Kensington, New York. She features in several literary journals, including the annual Momaya best short story collections. Three of her novels have had second printings and nearly all have been released in digital format. *Wishbinder*, published by Calumet Editions, marks her debut as a fantasy writer. She resides in New Zealand.